ELIZABETH J. LOGAN

By Tom Rachman

*The Rise & Fall of Great Powers*
*The Imperfectionists*

# THE RISE & FALL
## OF GREAT POWERS

# The RISE & FALL OF GREAT POWERS

A NOVEL

# Tom RACHMAN

 DOUBLEDAY CANADA

Library and Archives Canada Cataloguing in Publication

Rachman, Tom, author
    The rise & fall of great powers / Tom Rachman.

Issued in print and electronic formats.
ISBN 978-0-385-67695-3 (bound) ISBN 978-0-385-67696-0 (epub)

    I. Title.  II. Title: Rise & fall of great powers.

PS8635.A333R58 2014          C813'.6          C2013-903092-1
                                              C2013-903093-X

This book is a work of fiction. Names, characters, places and incidents are products of the author's imagination or are used fictitiously. Any resemblance to actual events or locales or persons, living or dead, is entirely coincidental.

Printed and bound in the USA
Book design by Simon M. Sullivan

Published in Canada by Doubleday Canada,
a division of Random House of Canada Limited,
A Penguin Random House Company

www.randomhouse.ca

10 9 8 7 6 5 4 3 2 1

For my sister Emily

# THE RISE & FALL
## OF GREAT POWERS

# 2011

His PENCIL WAVERED above the sales ledger, dipping toward the page as his statements increased in vigor, the pencil tip skimming the pad, then pulling up like a stunt plane, only to plunge at moments of emphasis, producing a constellation of increasingly blunt dots around the lone entry for that morning, the sale of one used copy of *Land Snails of Britain* by A. G. Brunt-Coppell (price: £3.50).

"Take the Revolution," he called out from the front of the bookshop. "The French see it completely differently than we do. They aren't taught it was all chaos and Reign of Terror. For them, it was a good thing. And you can't blame them. Knocking down the Bastille? The Declaration of Rights?"

The thrust of his argument was that, when considering the French people and their rebellious spirit—well, it wasn't clear *what* Fogg intended to say. He was a man who formed opinions as he spoke them, or perhaps afterward, requiring him to ramble at length to grasp what he believed. This made speech an act of discovery for him; others did not necessarily share this view.

His voice resounded between bookcases, down the three steps at the rear of the shop, where his employer, Tooly Zylberberg—in tweed blazer, muddy jeans, rubber boots—was trying to read.

"Hmm," she responded, a battered biography of Anne Boleyn open on her lap. She could have asked Fogg to shush, and he would have obliged. But he reveled in pronouncing on grand issues, like the man of consequence he most certainly was not. It endeared Fogg to her, especially since his oration masked considerable self-doubt—whenever she challenged him, he folded immediately. Poor Fogg. Her sympathy for the man qualified him to chatter, but it made reading impossible.

"Because, after all, the fellow who invented the guillotine was a man of medicine," he continued, restoring books to the shelves, riffling their pages to kick forth the old-paper aroma, which he inhaled before pushing each volume flush into its slot.

Down the three creaking steps he came, passing under the sign HISTORY—NATURE—POETRY—MILITARY—BALLET to a sunken den known as the snug. The bookshop had been a pub before, and the snug was where rain-drenched drinkers once hung their socks by the hearth, now bricked up but still flanked with tongs and bellows, festooned with little green-and-red Welsh flags and Toby jugs on hooks. An oak table contained photographic volumes on the region, while the walls were lined with shelves of poetry and a disintegrating hardcover series of Shakespeare whose red spines had so faded that to distinguish *King Lear* from *Macbeth* required much scrutiny. Either of these venerable characters, dormant on the overburdened shelves, could at any moment have crashed down into the rocking chair where Tooly sat upon a tartan blanket, which came in handy during winters, when the radiators trembled at the task ahead and switched off.

She tucked back her short black hair, points curling around unpierced lobes, a gray pencil tip poking up behind her ear. The paperback she held before her aimed to discourage his interruptions, but behind its cover her cheeks twitched with amusement at the circling Fogg and his palpable exertion at remaining quiet. He strode around the table, hands in his trouser pockets, jingling change. (Coins were always plummeting through holes in those pockets, down his leg and into his shoe. Toward the end of the day, he removed it—sock coming half off—and emptied a small fortune into his palm.) "It behooves them to act decisively in Afghanistan," he said. "It behooves them to."

She lowered the book and looked at him, which caused Fogg to turn away. At twenty-eight, he was her junior by only a few years, but the gulf could have been twenty-eight again. He remained a youth in their exchanges, deferential yet soon carried away with fanciful talk. When pontificating, he toyed with a brass magnifying glass, pressed it to his eye socket like a monocle, which produced a monstrous blue eye until he lost courage, lowered the lens, and the eye became small and blinky once more. Whatever the time of day, he appeared as if recently awakened by a fire drill, the hair at the back of his head splayed flat from the pillow, buttons missing midway down his shirt and others off by an eyelet, so that customers endeavored not to spy the patch of bare chest inadvertently peeping through. His cargo pants were torn at the hip pockets, where he hooked his thumbs while declaiming; the white laces on his leather shoes had grayed; his untucked pin-striped shirt was frayed at the cuffs; and he had the tubular collarbones and articulated ribs of a man who scarfs down a bacon sandwich for lunch, then forgets to eat again until 3 A.M. His careless fashions were not entirely careless, however, but a marker in Caergenog that he was distinct in the village of his birth—an urban sophisticate, no matter how his location, how his entire life, militated against such a role.

"It behooves them?" Tooly asked, smiling.

"What they have to realize," he proceeded, "is that we don't know even what the opposition is. My friend's enemy is not my—" He leaned down to glimpse the cover of her paperback. "She had thirteen fingers."

"What?"

"Anne Boleyn did. Henry VIII's wife. Had thirteen fingers."

"I haven't got to that part yet. She's still only at ten." Tooly stood, the empty chair rocking, and made for the front of the shop.

It was late spring, but the clouds over Wales bothered little with seasons. Rain had pelted down all morning, preventing her daily walk into the hills, though she had driven out to the priory nonetheless and sat in her car, enjoying the patter on the roof. Was it drizzling still?

"We took in the Honesty Barrel, didn't we?" This was a cask of overstock that passersby could take (suggested contribution, £1 per book). The problem was not the honesty—encouragingly, most people did drop coins into the lockbox—but the downpours, which ruined the volumes. So they had become seasoned sky-watchers, appraising the clouds, dragging the barrel out and in.

"Never put it out in the first place."

"Didn't we? Forgetfulness pays off." She stood at the counter, gazing out the front window. The awning dribbled brown raindrops. Looked a bit like. "Coffee," she said.

"You want one?" Fogg was constantly seeking pretexts to fetch cappuccino from the Monna Lisa Café, part of his attempt to court an Estonian barista there. Since Tooly preferred to brew her own tea, Fogg was obliged to consume cup after cup himself. Indeed, Tooly had first discerned his crush on the barista by the frequency with which he needed the toilet, leading her to remark that his cappuccino conspiracy was affecting the correct organ but in the incorrect manner.

"Back in a minute," he said, meaning thirty, and shouldered open the door, its bell tinkling as he plodded up Roberts Road.

She stepped outside herself, standing before the shop and contemplating the church parking lot across the street, her old Fiat 500 alone among the spaces. She stretched noisily, arms out like a waking cat, and gave a little squeak. Two birds fluttered off the church roof, talons out, battling over a nest. What species were those? But the birds wheeled away.

Caergenog—just across the Welsh side of the border with England—was populated by a few hundred souls, a village demarcated for centuries by two pubs, one at the top of Roberts Road and the other at its foot. The high ground belonged to the Butcher's Hook, named in recognition of the weekly livestock market across the street, while the low ground, opposite the church and roundabout, was occupied by World's End, a reference to that pub's location at the outer boundary of the village. World's End had always been the less popular option (who wanted to carouse with a view of iron crosses in the church graveyard?) and the pub closed for good in the late 1970s. The building stood empty for years, boarded up and vandalized, until a married couple—retired academics from the University of Bristol—bought the property and converted it into a used bookshop.

Their business plan had been to subsist on spillover custom from the annual literary festival in nearby Hay-on-Wye, and the eleven-day event did funnel trade to World's End. Unfortunately, it had a negligible effect during the remaining three hundred and fifty-four days in the calendar. After a decade, the Mintons sought a buyer for the business, while retaining ownership of the seventeenth-century timber-and-stone property they had restored, including frosted pub windows, wrought-iron servery, plus inn rooms upstairs. An ad on the village bulletin board—crowded out by the notice of a performance by the Harlech Youth Brass Band—received no responses. Nor did a subsequent insertion in *The Abergavenny Chronicle*. Nor the distracted efforts of a gum-chewing real-estate agent named Ron. Their final attempt involved classifieds in a small-circulation literary publication, one crumpled copy of which found its way onto a train platform in Lisbon in 2009, where Tooly had picked it up. The ad said, "Bookshop for Sale."

On Tooly's visit to the place, the Mintons admitted that theirs was a money-losing business and that revenue had declined each year since their arrival. The best that Mr. Minton could say was "Perhaps it'd be interesting for someone who wants to read a lot. With a bit of youthful energy and such, you might do better than we have, financially speaking. But you won't get rich." Tooly paid their asking price for the business, £25,000, which included the stock of ten thousand volumes. They were moving back to Bristol, and agreed that the low monthly rent for the shop would include her accommodations upstairs, along with the use of the sputtering purple Fiat.

For Tooly, to suddenly become the owner of thousands of books had been overwhelming. Tall shelves ran down the shop from front to back, the highest-altitude stock unsold, dusty, resentful. On the walls were framed prints: a nineteenth-century map of the world; a cityscape of Constantinople; an Edward Gorey illustration of a villain clutching a sumptuous volume, having shoved its owner off a cliff. The caption was a quote from John Locke:

> Books seem to me to be pestilent things, and infect all that trade in them . . . with something very perverse and brutal. Printers, binders, sellers, and others that make a trade and gain out of them have universally so odd a turn and corruption of mind that they have a way of dealing peculiar to themselves, and not conformed to the good of society and that general fairness which cements mankind.

Against the stacks rested a stepladder that Tooly was always moving to Mountaineering and that Fogg—not recognizing her joke— kept returning to French History. Hidden behind every row was another of as many copies again, a shadow bookshop. On the floor were unsorted boxes, so that one clambered rather than walked through the place. And the damask carpeting was matted with molted cat hairs, once attached to a long-departed pet named Cleopatra.

To indicate sections, the Mintons had attached cardboard signs to the shelves, the subject in tiny cursive if written by Mr. Minton or in looping print with indicative sketches if by Mrs. Minton. Most sections were ordinary: Trees, Plants, Fungi; Recipes & Eating. Others were peculiar (always in Mr. Minton's tiny print), including Artists Who Were Unpleasant to their Spouses; History, the Dull Bits; and Books You Pretend to Have Read but Haven't.

Tooly had neither read most of her stock nor pretended to. But gradually she settled among all these books, aided by the amiable presence of Fogg, who'd assisted at the shop since his school days. The Mintons had encouraged him to leave the village and study European literature at university. Instead, he kept coming back with cappuccinos.

On this occasion, he had one for Tooly as well, since he'd forgotten her answer. Settling on his barstool behind the servery, he mouse-clicked the computer to life, streaming a BBC Radio 4 broadcast whose host strove to panic his audience about the modern world, citing Moore's law and cloud computing and the Turing test and the decline of the brain. "On any smartphone today," the broadcaster declared, "one has access to the entirety of human knowledge."

"They need a gadget," Fogg commented, muting the show, "that records everything that ever happens to you."

"What do you mean?"

"My point is that . . . what is my point? Yes, here: if these computers are getting so much the better, then soon—it's not beyond thinking of it, to be brutally honest—someone will invent a gadget to store everything that happens in your life. When you're little, you'd get implanted with it, a chip or something. Never have to worry about remembering passwords or arguing over what took place. In a legal dispute, you just pop out your memory chip and show it to the court."

"And when you get old," Tooly added, "you could watch the best bits again."

"They'll do it in our lifetime. It's a matter of time, to be brutally honest." Whenever Fogg stated something obvious, such as "it's a matter of time" (and what wasn't?), he spruced it up with "to be brutally honest."

"What happens to the memory chip after you die?" Tooly asked.

"They save it," he said. "Future generations could go back and see their great-great-grandparents doing things, and find out what they were like."

"Except for anyone who'd existed before the invention—people like us. We'd seem the equivalent of prehistoric humans. Don't you think? We'd be wiped away, 'swept into the same oblivion with the generations of ants and beavers,'" Tooly said, quoting a line whose author escaped her.

Fogg scratched his blondish stubble and looked up at the pressed-tin ceiling, as if generations of ants and beavers were gazing down, awaiting his rejoinder. "But our future ancestors could retrieve our memories somehow," he said. "People in the future could, sort of, come back and save bits that already happened."

"You're getting silly now. I need to file you under Sci-Fi. Anyway, if every second of your life was stored, there'd be too much to deal with. Nobody would have time to go over a memory chip containing everything that happened—you'd waste your life checking the past. You'd have to give up and trust your brain to keep the bits worth saving. And we'd be where we are now." She disappeared down an aisle, wending past boxes of stock. Tooly had such a particular gait, toes touching down first, balls of her feet slowly cushioning the heel to ground. When she stopped, her feet splayed, back straightened, chin down, a surveying gaze that warmed when she smiled at him, eyes igniting first, lips not quite parting. She descended the creaking stairs to the snug, sat in her rocking chair, resumed the Anne Boleyn paperback.

"The thing I wonder," Fogg said, having trailed after, ledger pencil flicking in his hand, "is whether horse is an acquired taste or if there's something genetic in liking it."

She laughed, enjoying this typically Foggian swerve of subject.

"Though I reckon," he continued, "that the French only started eating their mares and their colts and their other horse varieties during the Napoleonic Wars, when the Russian campaign fell to pieces, when they were retreating, and it was awful cold, and they had no proper food left. All they had was horses, so they made supper of them. Which is where the French habit of nibbling horses got its start."

"It was also at that moment that the French began eating frogs, which some of the smaller troops had ridden into battle," she said. "How much better life would've been if they'd arrived at the Russian front on marbled beef!"

"You can't actually ride cows," Fogg said earnestly. "Can't be done. This boy at my school, Aled, tried it once and it can't be done. As for a battle situation, a cow would be out of the question. What's important to realize about the French is that . . ."

The background Fogg calmed her. She had no desire to read more about the unfortunate Anne Boleyn. She knew how that story ended.

# 1999

TOOLY TOOK THE MAP from her duffle coat and let it expand like an accordion, then compressed it back to sense, folding the island of Manhattan into a manageable square at which she squinted, then glanced up, finding no relation between the printed grid before her and the concrete city around. Maps were so flat and places so round—how to reconcile them? Especially here, where manholes billowed, crosswalks pulsated stop-red, and the sidewalk shuddered from subway trains clattering underground.

Up Fifth Avenue she tramped, through tides of foot traffic, glimpsing strangers as they brushed past, their faces near for an instant, then gone forever. At the fringe of Rockefeller Center, she stood apart from the crowd and bit off the lid of her blue felt-tip pen, wind icing her teeth. She removed her mittens, let them dangle from the string through her sleeves, and drew another wobbly line up the map.

Tooly intended to walk the entirety of New York, every passable street in the five boroughs. After several weeks, she had pen lines radiating like blue veins from her home in the separatist republic of Brooklyn into the breakaway nations of Manhattan, Queens, and the Bronx, although their surly neighbor, Staten Island, remained unmarked. Initially, she had chosen neighborhoods to explore by their alluring names: Vinegar Hill and Plum Beach, Breezy Point and Utopia, Throggs Neck and Spuyten Duyvil, Alphabet City and Turtle Bay. But the more enticing a place sounded the more ordinary it proved—not as a rule, but as a distinct tendency. A few rambles had frightened her, past bombed-out buildings and dead-eyed boys. In

Mott Haven, a pit bull darted into the road in front of an oncoming truck, was struck, and died on the sidewalk before her.

She turned down Fifty-first Street—the buildings pronged with sleepy American flags, neon glaring from the Radio City Music Hall marquee—and stopped there, balling her fists till they'd warmed. Suddenly she burst into a sprint, dodging office workers, leaping around a blind corner, nearly colliding with a tourist couple. After two blocks, she halted, breathless and grinning because of her secret: that she had nowhere to run, no place to hasten toward, not in this city or in the world. All these people strode past with intent. Citizens had locations and they had motives, families, meetings. Tooly had none.

She resumed her urban hike up Broadway on its northwesterly diagonal past Central Park and through the Upper West Side, gravitating to the tables of used books for sale—fusty old volumes of the sort Humphrey loved. She checked the prices, but could afford nothing. She explored side streets, adding each to her map, admiring the fancy residences. Zabar's deli exuded the scent of cheese and the tinkle of classical music. "Yeah, I'll take a quarter pound of . . ." someone said. Tooly's meal was already decided—in her coat pocket, a squashed peanut-butter sandwich, wrapped in a newspaper page whose ink had imprinted the white bread, thereby offering the possibility of reading one's lunch.

A few students wandered past: the runoff from Columbia University dribbling south to these parts. They were around her age—twenty—talking loud and teasing each other. She looked at one, then a second, hoping they'd say something to her. Instead, they passed, banter growing faint behind her. So, uptown she went, investigating where they'd come from. Above 100th Street, the pizza parlors began in earnest, selling cut-rate slices to the college crowd. Beggars sat on the pavement, watching urgent sophomores, their cheeks still chubby and their foreheads spotty, rushing to exams, chattering about starting salaries.

Tooly meandered through the iron gates of the Columbia campus and ambled down the red-brick path of College Walk, as kids arrowed off in all directions. Might they take her for one of them? A doctoral student in zoology, perhaps, or a master's candidate in criminology, or a postgrad in organic chemistry—though she had no idea what such occupations entailed. She drifted out of the main campus, wandering toward a desolate sidewalk that overlooked Morningside Park, the public space down there abandoned to crack addicts and the heedless. Birds tweeted from tree canopies. Beyond the foliage, a strip of Harlem rooftops was visible; occasional distant honking.

A pig waddled up the stone stairs from the park, walked toward her, and barged into her ankle—it was an intentional jostle, not a misjudgment. She laughed, astonished at its effrontery, and stepped aside. The creature was black and potbellied, its gut dragging against the pavement, wiry hairs and a snub nose, not unlike the middle-aged human trailing afterward, holding a leash that led to a studded collar around the pig's neck. The two crossed Morningside Drive and turned onto 115th. Tooly followed.

Whenever she encountered creatures, Tooly yearned to stoop and pat. She'd never owned an animal herself, the disorder of her life having prevented it. The owner of the pig stopped before a six-story residential building, took a final puff of his cigarette, flicked it into the gutter, and turned for the entrance, which was framed with converted gaslights and wrought-iron curlicues. The snorty pig strutted in first, then the man. Tooly hurried after, sidestepping inside the building before the door swung shut.

The elegant façade belied an interior of dirty marble walls, dreary metal mailboxes, and a convex mirror by the elevator, ensuring that no one hid around the corner with a pistol. A sign demanded NO MOVING ON SUNDAY. She pictured residents going rigid—no moving!—every Sunday. The pig glanced at her, tracking her with suspicion. Its owner reached his apartment door, then turned aggressively. "You live here?"

"Hi," she answered. "I used to. A bunch of years ago. I was just taking a look around. Hope it's okay. Won't bother anyone, I promise."

"Where'd you live?"

"The fourth floor. Can't remember our number, but right near the end. I was here as a kid."

Tooly took the stairs, each landing tiled in checkerboard, each apartment numbered with a brass badge above a peephole. On the fourth floor, she chose a door and stood before it, envisaging what lay on the other side. This was her favorite part, like shaking a wrapped present and guessing its contents. She knocked, pressed the bell. No answer.

All right, then—this was not to be her long-lost childhood home. She'd pick another. She scanned the hallway, and noticed keys hanging from a scratched Yale lock. The door was ajar. She called out softly, in case the occupant had merely stepped away. No response.

With the rubber nose of her Converse sneaker, Tooly prodded the base of the door, which opened tremblingly upon a long parquet corridor. A young man lay there on his back, surrounded by shopping bags. He stared upward, eyelashes batting as he studied the corridor ceiling, utterly unaware of her in his doorway.

"Your pajamas are inside out," Paul remarked.

"Whatside who?"

"Late to be roaming, Tooly."

She checked the wall clock. "It's only sparrow past gull."

"You're sleeping in your socks."

"I wasn't sleeping."

"Need to take your socks off before bed, Tooly."

"Why?"

"Well." He contemplated this at length. "Well, no good reason—leave them on."

"I was thinking before."

"Hmm?"

"Was feeling worried."

"About?"

"Not really *worried*."

"You're the one who said worried."

"I got stuck thinking about—" She pointed to the empty cabinet, walked over to it as if drawn along by her forefinger, pressed the tip hard into the varnished wood surface, just above her sight line, yanked away her finger and scrutinized it, dead white from pressure, then regaining its blood flush. She did this again, pressing harder, and—

"What, though?" he interrupted.

"What what?"

"What were you worried about?"

"That I was going to die, and turn ten."

"Die? Why would you die?"

"In the end, I will."

"Not for a long time."

"And turn ten."

"Can't do both, Tooly," he said. "Well, you can. But there'll be a long gap in between."

As if to illustrate the notion of a long gap, she went quiet, her cheeks swollen till a breath puffed from her. "When I die, I'll be dead for infinity."

"When you're dead, there is no infinity. When you're dead, there's no such thing as anything."

"Nothing happening forever?"

"You could say that."

"Oh, but one thing else I was wondering," she said, unperturbed by this talk of eternal nothingness and buoyed by her ability to engage him in conversation and thereby delay bedtime, that nightly trip to infinity. "Mr. Mihelcic was saying how when—"

"Who's Mr. Mihelcic?"

"My science teacher. Who I said the hippopotamus looked like."

"Not to his face?"

"I said it to you. But I like hippopotamuses."

"Hippopotami."

She shivered at her mistake. "Hippopotami." Then, resuming, "Mr. Mihelcic said when you fall into a black hole you get stuck and it's impossible to get out. Like quicksand."

"Black holes are to be avoided, Tooly. As is quicksand."

She pressed her finger white against the cabinet, watching it slowly regain life, pressing it bloodless again.

He opened his mouth to speak, then frowned at a software manual in his lap, to which his full attention now returned.

She made three laps around the coffee table, stepping over his legs each time, and wandered down the dark hallway to her bedroom.

Hippos had yellow teeth that zookeepers needed brooms to clean, using giant tubes of toothpaste. What was it like inside a hippo's mouth?

After less than a year in Australia, this was their final night. Every surface in her bedroom was bare, only dust silhouettes where her possessions had been. She dragged the suitcase from her room, wiping her forehead in mime, though no one was present to see. Taking a run-up, she slid back down the polished hardwood floor to the threshold of the living room.

"You'll get splinters." He put down his work and folded his arms awkwardly. "Can you go to sleep now?"

She flopped into a pile, as if finger-snapped into slumber. Her closed eyelids flickered.

"Go to bed, please."

Tooly slouched away, stumbling on a suitcase strap in the hallway, banging her shin against the doorframe to her room. She leaped onto the bed, rolled to her back. Reaching under the covers, she drew out a book but left the bedside light off for a minute, pausing at the sound of Paul speaking from the hall.

"The next place," he said, "the next place is going to be better."

# 1988: The End

TOOLY PRESSED HER NOSE against the airplane window and breathed, steam on the glass expanding, receding. With the back of her hand, she wiped off the fog, then peered downward as far as possible into the night, finding no splashing seas below or colored countries as on wall maps, just darkness. Following takeoff, they'd flown over the Sydney Opera House and the Harbour Bridge, above endless Outback emptiness, over the twinkling lights of Bali and Sumatra. There was nothing beneath them now, as if this weren't a flying machine but a metal tube fitted with seats, windows shrouded, stagehands on the other side replacing backdrops, ushering in a new cast, prepped to yank away the cover.

An orange curtain dividing economy from business class danced, jostled by stewardesses on the exclusive side. A glassy laugh pierced the burr of jet engines. The dinner trays had been removed; the movie screen had retracted; the cabin crew had dimmed the lights. Most passengers slept, but the occupants of this bank of three seats—Tooly, Paul, and an unknown young woman on the aisle—remained alert. At any engine noise, the woman flinched. Meanwhile, Paul stared fixedly at his tattered hardcover, *The Charm of Birds*, illuminated by the overhead light, though he hadn't turned a page in twenty minutes. Tooly spread her long, tangled hair over her face, blowing strands, then chewing them, all the while observing the woman.

She wasn't alone in spying: a wolfish man across the aisle watched the pretty young lady, too. When he lit a cigarette, its toasty smell caught her attention and he offered one, springing open his Zippo lighter, swaying its flame at her.

Due to his asthma, Paul normally requested seating far from the smoking section. But the flight had been overbooked and the only two seats together were these. As smoke billowed closer, he leaned away. Tooly burrowed into the seat-back pocket for his throat lozenges. He sucked one desperately, lips puckered, cheeks lean.

"Why is it," Tooly asked to distract him, glancing at the dark window and finding a reflection of the two of them, "that when you look at the horizon it just stops? Why don't you keep seeing?"

"Because the world is round."

"So why doesn't it look bendy at the edges?"

He couldn't find an answer, so just frowned, and blew his nose into one of the many tissues clutched in a knot within his palm.

Paul was a pair of red spectacles with a man behind, arms tucked close to his body, as if to occupy as small a portion of the planet as possible. He'd resembled a youth for too long—till nearly thirty—and this had marked his confidence. As a young man, he used to wish for wrinkles, clenching and unclenching his face before the mirror. Years later, lines had materialized, but without the desired effect: a furrow creased his brow even when he slept, and a bracketed wrinkle sat between his eyebrows, like a parenthesis containing worrisome thought. His hair had gone entirely white, though he wasn't yet forty.

"When you see the blue part above the horizon," Tooly continued, "is that space?"

"The blue bit is sky," he answered. "The blue bit is the atmosphere."

"What comes after the atmosphere?"

"Outer space."

"When a bird goes into outer space, what happens?"

"It can't."

"But if it did?"

"It can't."

"But if one did once?"

The young woman in their row disentangled herself from the wolf across the aisle and stubbed her cigarette, thumbing the lipstick-smeared filter into the armrest ashtray shared with Paul. He held his tube of lozenges obliquely in her direction. With thanks, she accepted, assuming the gift to be flirtation, though it was merely a plot to divert her from another cigarette. As a conspiracy it failed, since the young woman took a second smoke from the wolf, lighting up while toying nervously with a Polaroid camera, asking Paul if flying was always like this.

He leaned toward her as if slightly deaf, interjecting "Uh-huh" or "Okay" to signal attention, though this interrupted her and gave the false impression that he wanted the floor. When this was surrendered to him, he realized it with alarm, removed his glasses, and shut his eyes tightly to locate an answer. Tooly, using her bare fingers, wiped his thumb smudges off the spectacles. He slid them back on, lenses tilting forward, which caused him to tilt back, as if aghast at the world. "What was your question?" he asked, sniffing.

"Can I try out my camera on you two?" She stood and focused it on them, much to his unease. When the print issued from the Polaroid, the young woman flapped it till the image appeared, holding it out for them to see. Paul took the photo, thanking her for the gift, which it hadn't been, and slid the snapshot into his book.

To block sight of such embarrassing scenes, Tooly shook out her hair and reached into the seat-back pocket, pulling out her novel and sketchpad. Each of her drawings began with a curl intended to resemble a nose. However, other facial features were beyond her, so noses accumulated page after page. She contemplated adding a few more, then opted to read instead, opening *The Life and Adventures of Nicholas Nickleby*, one of many volumes Paul had picked up during this never-ending voyage of theirs. He himself had no interest in novels, but bought them for Tooly whenever he found English-language sections in airport bookshops. He purchased indiscriminately, therefore she read that way: *Treasure Island* by Robert Louis Stevenson, *Cujo* by Stephen King, *I'll Take Manhattan* by Judith Krantz, *The Moonstone* by Wilkie Collins, *Fear of Flying* by Erica Jong, *White Fang* by Jack London, *Shōgun* by James Clavell, plus many works by Dickens, including this volume, which told of a dignified nineteenth-century Englishman compelled to teach at a brutish school for outcasts. Tooly had read the book already but, as with all her favorites, she'd stopped before its ending. It was dispiriting to witness her printed companions concluding their lives with a blank space at the bottom of the final page, so she halted earlier, returning months thereafter, flipping back several hundred pages to find them as they had been, deep in conversation, conceiving dastardly plans and sharp retorts.

She slipped from her seat, crouching in the floor space. Between strands of her hair, she contemplated these lowered surroundings: the carpet, filthy seat frames, carry-on luggage, castaway shoes. An old Indian lady behind her, who earlier had fought to open the tray table and shuddered Tooly's seat, extended her bare feet, rings on two toes. Impulsively, Tooly patted one. The toe twitched, shifted grumpily, then went back to sleep on a crumpled newspaper that was headlined with talks between Reagan and Gorbachev, alongside a photo of monkeys in South Korea employed to pick pine nuts and, the caption claimed, "working the equivalent of 100 men."

"What are you doing down there?"

She looked up, eyes dry with fatigue. "What?"

"I'm going to use the facilities," Paul said. "Stay put."

Tooly obeyed just long enough to watch his knees excuse themselves into the aisle. With him gone, she took a proper look at the woman in their row: blond hair in a ponytail on the side of her head, acid-washed jeans with ankle zips. The mysteries of the adult female— all sophistication and bewildering toiletries—intrigued Tooly. She'd had scant exposure to women besides teachers, maids, other children's mothers. The story of her own mother—that is, the account they told outsiders—was that she remained behind in the United States dealing with personal matters but would join them soon. Such a woman never did arrive. Another year passed, Tooly and Paul moved again, and repeated the tale anew.

"A bird!" Tooly fibbed, to draw the stranger's attention to the window. "Look, it's keeping up with us."

The woman leaned over, shading her eyes, finding only blackness out there.

"It's cold up this high," Tooly said, more softly now, since they were close.

The woman rolled a pink scrunchie off her wrist, gathering Tooly's chaotic hair and producing a side ponytail that matched her own. "Don't birds freeze outside?"

"That's why they wear trench coats."

The woman smiled. "Won't the belt straps hang down and get in the way of their wings?"

"They tie the straps."

"Imagine if they're flying this high and they get tired all of a sudden!"

"They probably glide to the ground. Paul would know."

"You call him by his first name?" the woman asked, amused, though her expression shifted. "Or, wait—is that not your dad?"

A sniffle alerted them to Paul's return. He stepped back to the middle seat and frowned at Tooly's ponytail. He viewed fashion with bemusement. The purpose of clothing, as best he could tell, was to keep one unembarrassed and at the right temperature. If an outfit served that purpose for a respectable period—twenty years, say—and at the lowest price available, then it was successful. He dressed identically every day: a polo shirt tucked into khakis, Velcro-fastened black shoes. "Your hair looks like a pineapple that fell over," he told Tooly. The woman in the aisle, with the identical style, blushed and turned away, ignoring them for the rest of the flight.

Only upon landing did Tooly close her eyes and drift off, longing for three more minutes. But time was up. Passengers crushed up the aisles, laden with bags, squinting at the queue ahead, sighing at each delay. Leaving the cabin finally, they stepped in a single stride from icy airplane chill into the sweltering tropics.

"Slightly humid," Paul commented, wheezing.

Despite the late hour, it didn't seem night in the airport, the dazzling overhead lights whitening all, with barefoot workers squatting on the floor, eating. Policemen watched the new arrivals: briefcase businessmen rushing for taxis; a backpacking couple chewing gum, jaws flexing in unison; fish-faced old men in Bermuda shorts, waddling down the hall, mouth-breathing.

"Landing cards," Paul said, thinking aloud, and grabbed two as they waited in line at the border control. "When were you born?"

"You know that."

"I know that," he acknowledged, filling it in. He looked around, startled at the slightest noise—he was rigidly tense in public with Tooly. A Velcro strap on his shoe had come unstuck, so she knelt to attach it. "What are you doing?" he asked irritably. "It's nearly our turn."

The immigration officer summoned them. Paul was a man who followed rules—indeed, their absence unnerved him. Yet whenever he addressed authorities his mouth became audibly dry. "Good morning. Evening," he said, sweat budding on his upper lip.

The officer looked down at the girl, at Paul again—then drove vicious stamps onto their passports, dismissing them. Paul hurried Tooly along, scanning left and right as they quit the terminal, his knuckle jabbing her forward, as if they might otherwise be dragged back.

In the taxi, she rolled down her window, reading illuminated highway billboards that rushed past, ads for Sanyo with curly foreign script, White Lion toothpaste, Johnnie Walker.

"Who's Johnnie Walker?"

"It's a drink. For grown-ups."

"Is it nice?"

"Makes you drunk."

"What's it like being drunk?"

"Like being awake and asleep at the same time."

"Sounds nice."

"It was meant to sound terrible," he said, looking down his glasses

at her. "You get sick and stagger around. People actually vomit sometimes."

The expressway fed into a multilane city street, clogged with traffic
until the vanishing point. The sidewalks teemed with locals eating at
stalls, cooks shaking iron pans, noodles hissing. Generator lights
burned above a night market that sold watches, videocassettes, Vietnam War paraphernalia. Neon signs advertised go-go dancers and
Ping-Pong shows, a blinking phantasmagoria past which foreign men
lumbered, draped over tittering bargirls.

Tooly had no memory of falling asleep, of being carried from
the cab or placed in bed. Paul woke her the following morning by
parting the bedroom curtains a smidgen, producing a column of sun
across the foot of the bed where she lay, still dressed from the flight.
Only her deck shoes had he plucked off, while the pink scrunchie had
been lost in the bed, her hair now a black octopus splayed across the
white pillow. She pretended to sleep still, peeping through a half-
opened eye. Every five minutes, he tiptoed back into her room, opening the curtains a fraction more, sunlight expanding in increments up
her covers. When it reached her eyes, she draped her hair over them,
nibbling a strand that fell into her mouth.

"Morning, Tooly." He shook her hand, as was his morning custom.
These daily handshakes were the only occasions that he touched her.
Even passing the salt, Paul avoided her fingers, placing the shaker
close to, rather than in, Tooly's hands.

"Where are we?"

"Your new bedroom. Our new apartment."

"But where?"

He parted the curtains, revealing floor-to-ceiling windows, the city
spread out beyond. "This is Bangkok."

# 1999: *The Middle*

AT THE SQUEAK of Tooly's sneaker, the man on the floor sat upright and torqued around, staring at her.

"You okay?" she asked.

He leaped to his feet, stumbling over bags of groceries on the parquet around him. He was in his early twenties, brilliant black hair, paper-white skin, blood-flushed cheeks. "I'm fine," he replied. "Fine. Please, could you close my front door, please?"

She did so, reverting to the solitude of the building hallway, twirling away. She passed other closed apartment doors, considering each— then glanced back. His keys still dangled in the lock. She returned and silently removed them.

Could take these to use another time. But better to be invited in right now. She knocked.

He opened immediately—must've been at the peephole—and scanned her. Tooly's wardrobe was striking for its mismatches: a red duffle coat over an oatmeal cable knit and lime bell-bottom corduroys, all smelling of mothballs (their previous lodgings having been racks at a Salvation Army thrift store in Long Island City, Queens). Beneath these layers was a figure consisting of bony sections and soft sections, not necessarily ordered according to the preferences of fashion. Her shoes were Converse low-tops—one red, one black—and, hidden under her corduroys, she wore men's thermal socks up to her knees. Her face was bright, as if just splashed with water, freckles on the bridge of her nose, and she wore no makeup, never having learned its correct application. Indeed, she forgot to consult a mirror most mornings, encountering the world in a state of discomposition until she glimpsed her reflection somewhere, shivering with amusement, then catching the tips of the brambly bob cut between her lips and chewing. A damp strand adhered to her cheek now.

She flicked it away and smiled. "You left your keys in the door."

He took them, nodding in thanks. "I'm an idiot."

She made no move to leave.

"Thanks," he said hesitantly, beginning to close the door.

"One second," she said. "Just that—sorry if I intruded. Just—this is a bit weird. But I used to live here, actually."

"How do you mean?"

"I grew up in this apartment. Haven't been back to New York in years, but I was walking by the building and . . . Is it insane if I ask to peek in? Tell me if it's insane. I'm getting a flood of memories just standing here."

"Place is a bit of a mess right now."

"In that case, I'll feel right at home."

He began to object but gave in, and took a step back, nearly losing his footing on the abundance of Chinese delivery menus scattered on the floor. They exchanged names, shook hands awkwardly.

The building belonged to Columbia University, which rented out apartment shares like this to its students. Yet, of the three men residing here, only one actually attended Columbia. Duncan himself studied law—"But not here," he said confusingly, leading her past the first bedroom, rented out by an MBA student named Xavi (pronounced "Savvy"), who was currently at class. The other roommate, Emerson, was also away, attending a literary-theory seminar.

Duncan nodded dismissively toward the bathroom, but she went right in for a look. Its filth affirmed this as the domain of young heterosexual males: a dirty basin surrounded by empty gel jars and cardboard toilet rolls; pubic hairs and dried urine on the rim of the open toilet; a mildewed shower curtain concealing a grimy tub. "I did clean that once," Duncan noted, almost with surprise.

"How come?"

"I needed to use it. The doctor told me to."

"The doctor told you to take a bath?"

"For my nose."

"Couldn't you wash your nose in the basin?"

"I . . ." He looked over, laughed shyly.

Each roommate had chores, but to clean was to surrender. "Emerson volunteered to do the floor once, which was pretty interesting. We didn't see that one coming at all."

Duncan led her to his room: dirty laundry bursting from the closet, glasses of bubbly old water, a laptop and modem beside legal casebooks. On a rickety stand was a Yamaha electric piano. The walls bore just one poster, depicting the countryside in Japan, where he'd taught English for a year.

She looked around the room. "Really brings back memories."

"Sorry everything's so chaotic."

"Not at all," she said. "I like squalid boy places."

"In that case . . ." He led her to the kitchen, the sink heaped with dirty dishes and pans, oven clock blinking an eternal 12:00. One cupboard was filled with scrunched plastic bags, while another contained sinister jars of pickle juice and a packaged stew that had expired in 1998. "Normally, when girls come over they never come back."

"Fools." She drifted onward.

"Guess you know your way around," he mumbled, following her into the living room, the dining table piled with junk mail for kids who'd long since graduated but had yet to inform the mass-mailing departments at Victoria's Secret, Macy's, and L.L.Bean. She raised the window—"I loved going out here"—and stepped onto the rickety fire escape, inadvertently flipping an ashtray there. Below were bare trees and parked cars, the potholed tarmac painted with XING SCHOOL.

"My elementary school was right near here," she improvised, returning inside. "Went there from eight till eleven."

"How was it?"

"Heaven."

"Not a word I normally associate with elementary school."

"Oh, yeah? You didn't like yours?" She took this opening and burrowed in, inquiring into his schooling, his plans, and those of his roommates. Emerson, an unpopular member of the household, was doing a doctorate in comparative literature. Xavi, who came from Uganda originally, was Duncan's best friend and had been since high school in Connecticut.

"That's where you come from, Connecticut? From one of those posh old families there?"

"No, no. First generation." His dad, Keith, hailed from Glasgow, an architect who'd transferred to New York three decades earlier to build skyscrapers or die trying. Today, he was the director of design at a partnership in Stamford, Connecticut, specializing in atriums at shopping malls. As for Duncan's mother, Naoko, she'd reached New York from Kobe, Japan, in 1973 to study art at Parsons. She and Keith met as foreigners in the big city, their accents bemusing locals, though they understood each other perfectly—that is, they misunderstood each other sufficiently. As a child, Duncan read of kilts and haggis and the treachery of the Campbells, played snare in a fife band, kept a Scottish flag in his room, and effaced his Japanese half. This reversed in junior high, once ethnicity had become chic. By college, he described himself as Japanese. After graduation, he moved to Yokohama, intending to teach English and become fluent in his mother's tongue. It proved a disaster. "I don't normally get into this."

"Come on," she said. "You'll never see me again."

He'd had no friends in Japan, and learned little of the language, except how impossible it was, with honorifics and respectful forms and humble forms—and myriad ways to get it all wrong. After years of claiming to be Japanese, he learned how un-Japanese he was. Wasn't anything anymore. "This suddenly required me to have a personality. I hadn't planned for that."

"Oh, don't be silly," she said.

It was Xavi, then starting business school at NYU, who'd encouraged Duncan to apply to law school there, and even found them a sublet near "the university." Unfortunately, it proved to be the wrong

university, Columbia, at the opposite end of Manhattan. The official
tenants here were two Columbia students who had fallen in love while
falling in hate with their assigned third roommate, Emerson. The lovers' plan was to claim that they still lived at Columbia, so their con-
servative families would keep paying rent while they secretly took a
place together in Chelsea. In subletting, Xavi and Duncan got an
amazing deal—with the downside of having to schlep downtown for
school.

"So," he said, "tell me something about you."

"Here's something: I saw a pig downstairs."

"Not running wild, I hope."

"Some guy was taking it back from a walk. A huge fat potbelly."

"The guy?"

"The pig."

"He lives on the first floor," Duncan said. "He's a composer."

"The pig?"

"Yes, the pig."

She laughed.

"Sorry—you probably need to go," he said. "I don't normally talk
so much. Hope it was cool seeing your old place." He took a step
toward the door.

"Duncan, how come you were lying on the floor before, with the
shopping bags everywhere?"

"I hoped you'd forgotten that."

"Did you fall?"

"It's this weird thing. You're going to think I'm insane."

"I don't mind insanity, as long as it's reasonable."

He sighed, then confessed. Often, when crossing the Columbia
campus with groceries, he had this fantasy of lying down on College
Walk, all the kids stepping over him, nobody stopping for days and
then weeks, rodents nibbling at his groceries, he getting thinner, looking up through the tree branches, during the rain, the nights, until he
just disappeared. Captivated by his strange thoughts, he had returned

home, called out to ensure that he was alone, then lain down right there.

"If you're doing nutty stuff at home," she said, "you need to think about closing the front door properly."

"That was an error in retrospect."

"Lie down now," she said.

"How do you mean?"

"I want to show you something from when I used to live here. But you have to lie down a second, right where you were."

"On the floor?"

"Exactly as you were."

Haltingly, uncertainly, he obliged.

She hooked the chain lock on the front door and returned to Duncan, knelt, opened her duffle coat, and lay atop him.

"What are you doing?" he asked softly.

"Human blanket."

They remained still for a minute, his heart thudding, palpable through her sweater.

A key entered the lock. The front door hit the chain and shook.

She rose calmly, while Duncan scrambled up with such haste that he nearly keeled over from dizziness. He unhooked the chain lock. "Hey," he said.

It was Xavi, who proved to be quite a dresser: smoking jacket, violet scarf, tortoiseshell glasses. Rather than shaking her hand, he held it. A grin spread across his face. His glinting eyes closed languorously and, when they opened, looked to Duncan.

"She used to live here," Duncan explained.

Tooly remarked again on how many memories it had stirred up.

Duncan nodded stiffly, opened the front door. "When was it you lived here, exactly?"

"I'm so glad to meet you," she said, and took the stairwell down.

As Tooly strolled back downtown, she glanced at other buildings. No matter how she imagined their insides—parties veering out of control, kitchens with faucets running, angry couples playing cards for real money—the truth was always more peculiar. In a vertical city, cramped dwellings were the only territory unreservedly reserved, each home an intimate fortress. Yet they were so easy to penetrate. ("Don't want to intrude, but I used to live here. Might it be possible to take a quick look? I happened to be passing and—wow, even just standing here, so many memories!") Mostly, one needed only to knock, say a few lines, enter. Why limit yourself to the outside when you could walk right in, peek at their lives—maybe even leave with a useful nugget.

She took out her pen and the newsprint that had wrapped her peanut-butter sandwich and jotted down all she'd gathered in this encounter, dredging her memory for every detail worth recounting to Venn.

Duncan had been awkward, clumsy, alone. So easy to capture a boy like that. She grew melancholy thinking this, and it took a moment to recognize why: something in him had reminded her of Paul.

Tooly turned sharply from the notion and tried to keep writing. But she gained little cooperation either from her hand—she shook out icy fingers—or from her will, which resisted parsing the boy's candor for something to exploit. She scrunched the newsprint, discarded it in her pocket. His life and hers had intersected for a few minutes; that would be all.

She kept perfectly still on the sidewalk, studying the faces of pedestrians, her cold hands balled, her pulse increasing. She had the urge to run from here, and did.

# 2011: The Beginning

AFTER THE MONKS had abandoned Llanthony Priory hundreds of years before, the Norman-Gothic complex crumbled gradually, the cathedral walls left without a roof, the stonework patched with mustard lichen, naked to centuries of drizzle, raindrops striking where once an altar had been.

Behind the ruins rose the Black Mountains and, this morning, a thick mist. She hiked as if into clouds, over grassland spiked with thistles, past grazing sheep, straight up the hillside. The mist dissipated as she ascended, her green rubber boots squelching, the muscles in her feet gauging rocks under her slippery treads, the ache in her thighs a pleasure, strength flagging but pace increasing.

At the top, a wild wind pulled and pushed her, fluttering the cable knit tied around her waist. The plateau widened, its edges lost to sight, a chalky path banked by heather and bracken for miles, the spine dividing two nations. To the right lay England: quilted countryside seamed by hedgerows and trees, every field fenced in and farmed. To the left was Wales: a tangle of rambling green, flinty farmhouses, forbidding woods.

The sunlight shifted and mottled the land. She paused under its rays, closed her eyes, absorbing the warmth. When the sun shone—and days passed without a glimpse of it—she hurried beneath. But it was rain that exhilarated her, watching through the bookshop window, the world hushing, sidewalks vacant. It wasn't feeble drips that thrilled her but torrents—when raindrops exploded off leaves, choked drainpipes, drummed the attic roof at World's End. Once, a thunderclap sounded in the afternoon and Fogg gasped, though he masked it by noisily turning the page of a book on Mongol hordes.

"Storms are beautiful," she'd said.

"Storms are wet."

"Come on, you softie. When nature does something strong, dramatic like that, it's exciting. Don't you think?"

"Would you consider an earthquake exciting?"

"Well, if you could just watch it—imagine—if no one got hurt and nothing of value was destroyed, then yes, it'd be incredible. Like when you see pictures of molten lava."

"Nothing nice about molten lava when it's shooting at you."

"It never has shot at me."

"Nor me, to be brutally honest."

From behind her closed eyelids, she perceived a darkening. The sunlight had migrated along the moorland. A speck of rain hit her cheek. The drizzle fell noiselessly, the wind shouldering thin raindrops into diagonals that darted one way then another, like shoals of fish in a nervous mass. She watched wet dots multiply on her blouse; the cotton clung to her small breasts and belly. Back in her twenties, she had considered her body parts irrelevant to the whole of herself, as if she lived in a container unrelated to the contained. When she caught sight of herself today, thinner than once, she thought less of shape than of time, which had arrived, its incursions marked by the coarsening of her. She gazed at her rubber boots on wet stalks of grass, vision blurred by beads of rain that hung from her eyebrows, shivering at each step.

A crow flew overhead. Needs a trench coat, that crow. Do they mind the rain, birds? Paul would've known. But only thoughts of *this* place and *this* time were allowed: her legs marching beneath her. She inhaled. The joy of empty thoughts, occupied by senses alone. If she were ever to write a book (and she'd never consider it), it would be on the satisfaction of thinking nothing. What a dullard I've become! And what a book that would make! It would cure insomniacs, at least.

The trail descended through woods, across farmers' fields, over a stile, past the ruins. Back in the Fiat, she flung her wet cable knit into the backseat and adjusted the rearview mirror, amused at the sidelong image of her bedraggled self. The drive home was twenty minutes down a one-lane road, her toes curling as onrushing lorries appeared around each corner, she swerving into hedges to let them pass. Her car was a spine-jarring contraption lacking shocks, seatbelts, or a passenger-side window, the missing pane covered with plastic sheeting that flapped furiously as she drove. Through holes in the rusted floor, she glimpsed asphalt rushing beneath.

Tooly pulled in at the church parking lot, and sparrows—battling over scattered rice from a weekend marriage—took flight. For nearly two years she had lived in the village, yet she had no friends here. Reserve was the norm in these parts, which suited her. The place let her be, and she'd grown fond of it. The newsagent, the village doctor, the solicitor, the police constable, the butcher's apprentice in red-striped apron smoking on his delivery bike. The pie-and-chip shop on Unicorn Street, the village clock, the monument to "those sons of Caergenog who fell in the Great War 1914–1918," with a wreath of plastic poppies.

To the locals, she was known as the bookshop lady, seen hiking on public paths, a little foreign—she was "from away," as they put it. In her defense, she wasn't English. The Welsh were much concerned with "the English," a term uttered curtly, as of neighbors who barge into one's living room on a Sunday, monopolizing the cakes and conversation. Worse still, the English language had supplanted their own, whose wondrous native words were still extant on traffic signs— CERDDWYR EDRYCHWCH I'R CHWITH—but unpronounceable to many of the Welsh themselves. At least their lilting accent held fast in English, words articulated as if there were spaces bet ween ev e ry syl la ble.

She entered the shop and took the staircase up past the inn rooms, each furnished with a four-poster bed and a hay-stuffed mattress, every chest of drawers smelling of lavender. In the kitchen, the floor-boards bore the impression of a now departed range, its border outlined in caramel stains. The bathroom contained a clawfoot tub, while the water closet had a wooden-seat toilet, which flushed with a cold chain, the tank trickling.

Rather than lodging in one of the inn rooms, Tooly had settled in the attic. She'd evicted the spiders, disposed of the broken furniture and the gramophone, then scrubbed the splintery floor and wiped the porthole windows to transparency. Up the attic ladder, she had shoved a double mattress, leaving it on the floor. She slept under the rafters, her nose cold by morning.

Clothes still damp from her walk, she undressed and stood nude at the window, only her head visible from the street. She preferred not to hang curtains, and it was too high for anyone to spy. On the floor were piles of her clothing, plus a canvas bag large enough to contain everything. This was all she owned. Over the past decade, she had discarded anything of value.

Once dressed, she went down to the shop, counted out the float, entered yesterday's sales into the computer (this never took long), reversed the OPEN/CLOSED sign, and unlocked the front door. Opening time was 10 A.M., but she was always early. By contrast, Fogg was always late.

"Caught in traffic," he explained, dropping a folded newspaper from under his chin, placing his cappuccino on the bar counter. His house was a four-minute walk from World's End, so "traffic" was understood to mean a queue at the Monna Lisa Café. It was his habit to arrive every morning with a hot beverage and a cold periodical. He bought a different publication each day, and they took turns reading it, holding a discussion in the afternoon. Till then, or at least noon, he tried to limit his jabbering, disappearing behind shelves, his location perceptible by coffee slurps emanating from Geography or Political Thought.

When the morning was quiet like this, she read up on her latest hobbies, tried books that customers had recommended, and dusted.

Formerly, she'd played music from a cassette player on the servery, the same few tapes she'd been addicted to for years. But those cassettes were gone. Weeks earlier, a crotchety old couple had entered, both in identical anoraks and looking so alike that it was nearly impossible to say which had once been groom and which bride. They walked around single file, then returned to the servery, where one of them gathered a handful of Tooly's mixtapes. "We need something to play in the camper van."

"Those aren't for sale," Fogg said.

"They can be," Tooly interposed. Any income was worth accepting at this point. "Don't you want to see what they are first?"

"Prefer music. Doesn't matter what kind."

"You prefer music? To audiobooks, you mean?"

"Prefer music to conversation."

They agreed on fifty pence per tape, and the couple counted out the coins while Tooly stared at the stack of cassettes, with titles like "Year 2000 Mix by D-Mac." They'd been produced years before by her then boyfriend, Duncan McGrory, and included extensive liner notes about the musicians (Fiona Apple, Lynyrd Skynyrd, Tori Amos, Bob Dylan, Creedence Clearwater Revival, Tom Waits), written in lettering that shrank as space ran short, asterisks added to asterisks. Tooly regretted the sale before it had concluded, but refused to reverse herself. That had been weeks earlier. No point dwelling on it. "Shall we put on the radio?" she asked Fogg, handing back a novel he'd lent her.

He went behind the computer and live-streamed Radio 4. "Did you enjoy that book?" he asked. "Utter rubbish, I thought."

"Terrible. Why did you recommend it?"

"It was so awful, I thought: Tooly has to read this."

"You're the only person, Fogg, who recommends a book because you hate it."

"Hang on." He scurried away, voice drifting back through the stacks, overlaid by radio chatter. "If you didn't like that book," he called back, "you have to try this one."

"Does it involve an alien playing the saxophone?" she asked. "If there are aliens playing the saxophone, or any other instruments, or even just being their alien selves without any musical inclination—if there are aliens, Fogg, I'm banning you."

"That's a bit rough," he said, returning with a paperback.

"Okay, I won't ban you. But I ask one final time—aliens?"

"No aliens," he promised, adding, "There may be an orc."

"Is there or is there not an orc?"

"There's an orc."

Fogg's most salient quality as an employee was his ability to be present while she fetched a sandwich. Beyond this, he contributed little that could be quantified. But she would not have wanted to continue without him. World's End earned nothing, meaning she paid him from her personal savings, a small and diminishing sum. Within a couple of years, she'd be insolvent. Yet she observed her bank balance nearly with impatience for bankruptcy. This was the most fixed abode she'd known, and she couldn't shake an urge to lose it.

A person like Fogg was so different from her, formed in considerable part by his location. He was inextricably *from* here, this village, a place findable on Google Earth (how he loved spinning the digital globe from Paris to Caergenog, zooming down to the roof of the shop). His continued residence in the village, he said, was because staying here was "*la pièce de* least *résistance.*" That was ungenerous. He remained partly out of decency, because his family had a devastating summer when he was fifteen, his elder brother paralyzed from the waist down in a car accident, his father's affair uncovered through credit-card charges at a hotel, his mother suffering a breakdown. The father left, and the family had not recovered, Fogg holding them together since. Four years ago, he'd nearly married. But his girlfriend went to do theater in London and met a new man there. They'd stayed friends, till she sent photos of her newborn. "When you open the baby-photo email," Fogg said, "it's like your friends waving goodbye."

He and his ex exchanged messages once in a while, she inviting him to visit, he responding, "Would love to—when?," and she taking months to reply. He didn't even know what she looked like anymore: on her Facebook profile was a picture of the baby.

Stuck in Caergenog, he had developed an imaginary parallel life, one in which he'd done an undergraduate degree in French literature at Durham University, a master's at Cambridge, two years' research in Paris, living in a garret on the Left Bank, or, as he called it, "the West Bank." Central to his persona was the conviction that Caergenog was wrong for him, that he and his friends were a class above their context, that any setbacks or rejections were due to the backwardness of this place. One day in a month, he arrived at work in a black mood. Otherwise, he was touchingly buoyant.

"Do you feel more English or more Welsh?" she asked him.

"French," he answered. "How about you? Do you feel French?"

"Why would I? I'm not remotely French."

"You feel English, then?"

"I'm not English."

"How about Welsh?"

"I'm not Welsh. You know that, Fogg."

"We're like a lost tribe, people like us," he mused. "No traditions, no birthright, to be brutally honest. All of us have an acorn of sadness," he continued, pressing the magnifying glass to his eye. "You notice our tristesse only in passing, like a door to a small room in a house where outsiders may not enter."

"You're very poetic today, Fogg."

"Into which you get but a passing view," he went on, mistaking her irony for encouragement. "An acorn of sadness," he said, proud of the phrase, which he muttered on his way to organize Pirates, Smugglers & Mutiny.

Around noon, their first visitor arrived, a regular who couldn't be termed a customer, for she used World's End Books only as a showroom for online purchases. This was increasingly common, the practitioners identifiable by their note-taking on prices and ISBNs, and their failure to ever buy anything. Some openly consulted Web prices on smartphones and, hand on the doorknob, lamented how few good bookshops remained. Tooly wasn't indignant: you couldn't stop a tidal wave by wagging your finger at it. She considered bookselling to be a terminal vocation. More discouraging to her was that the heavy-weights on these shelves held such puny sway. No matter their ideas and worth, they lived as did the elderly—in a world with little patience to hear them out.

If few people came to buy books, many came to sell. Everyone was clearing their shelves these days. The question was no longer what she could pay (a pittance) but whether she had space. Her areas of personal interest included vintage cookbooks, especially outmoded advice for the young lass, such as *Mrs Beeton's Book of Household Management* (1861) or *Saucepans & the Single Girl* (1965) by Jinx Morgan and Judy Perry. She had also built up the Zoology section, adding tragic histories of the bison, rare volumes on rare birds, oversized editions of nature photography. As with all coffee-table books, she bought first, then wondered where to put them.

Mr. Thomas made the first purchase of the day. A man in his late fifties possessed of multitudes of Welsh-speaking grandchildren, he visited World's End once a month. Back when he attended school, education was viewed as an irksome delay before farm employment—an attitude that produced two varieties of citizen: those who scorned book learning and those who revered it. Huw Thomas—scar on the tip of his nose, head like an upright loaf, always in homespun cardigans—was among the reverential autodidacts. But he'd sooner not talk about it, and deflected her conversational gambits, standing at the servery counter with a volume in each hand, like a child before the librarian's desk. (She never found a pattern in his selections. Today, it was a history of the Boer War and *Alice in Wonderland*.)

"Get all you wanted, Mr. Thomas?"

"No, thank you."

"Can I help you find something else?"

"No, thank you."

"See you again, Mr. Thomas."

"Very well, then. Best be off."

The bell on the door tinkled after him, a false calm before a dozen schoolkids swarmed in. Hardly a feral pack of readers, these were junior shoplifters testing their skills, glancing around furtively as if they'd invented the art. Impressive how much a schoolbag swallowed. Sometimes she let them get away with it, unless a previous haul had been discovered in the rubbish bins on Roberts Road, in which case she stopped the culprits on their next foray, speaking discreetly at the door and sending them away. The rude ones—there were a few—she crushed with choice words. One brazen boy had kicked the door when he left, giving her the finger as he ran backward until, most pleasingly, he fell flat into a puddle.

She checked the time—had a lesson this evening. "Mind if I . . . ?"

"Say no more, say no more," Fogg responded. "Off you go."

Since her arrival in Caergenog, she had engaged in an adult-education frenzy, taking classes in sewing, home repairs (unexpectedly gripping), music. For a spell, she'd driven every Tuesday night to Cardiff for an art course, where she did life drawing in charcoal, acrylic, and oil. Each medium confirmed her lack of talent: every arm came out longer than its leg; ears were tea saucers; fruit resembled basketballs. Lousy though she was, Tooly adored it, and even improved in a plodding way.

"Will we be doing a class on noses?" she'd asked the instructor, an irritably failed sculptor.

"What?"

"Can you help me with drawing noses?"

"What?"

When the course ended, she sorted through her work and couldn't justify conserving a single piece. Nevertheless, she drove home with a still life, called "Apples—I Think That's What They Were," and nailed it up in her attic quarters. The sight of that canvas, its comical terribleness, still made her happy.

Now and then, a classmate invited her for a friendly drink and a gossip. Prue, a recent divorcée taking the home-repairs course in Hereford, asked what Tooly did besides work at a bookshop, and heard of her daily hikes. "Should get a bit of a walkabout myself," Prue said. "Lazy since the kids."

She arrived at World's End one morning, buying a romance novel to be polite. Tooly drove them to the priory and marched upward, her acquaintance keeping up only till the foothills, then battling bravely in the middle distance. Tooly waited at the top, admiring the countryside, as a human dot clomped closer, expanding into a woman. "Brought the." Wheeze. "Brought the wrong." Wheeze. "Brought the wrong shoes."

"It's flat from here on," Tooly said, continuing down the ridge.

"You walk!" Wheeze. "So!" Wheeze. "Fast!"

"Not that fast. Do I?"

Afterward, Prue thanked her. She never asked to come again.

Partly, Tooly had engineered it this way. Friends required a life story. Your past mattered only if others sought to know it—it was they who demanded that one possessed a history. Alone, you could do without.

That was why she and Fogg got along so well. He accepted her evasions, never pried.

"What are you mastering tonight, then?" he inquired.

She held up her ukulele.

"To be brutally honest, I'm not familiar with a large oeuvre of ukulele compositions," he said. "What led you to pick up the instrument?"

"Just decided one day," she replied. "When you lock up, bring in the barrel, I think."

Already on the drive to Monmouth, rain poured down. At the home of her teacher, she rushed from the car, ukulele and sheet music under her shirt. On her request, they practiced "The William Tell Overture." She played one part, her teacher accompanied, then they switched. What delight, this synchrony, the development, leaning into the phrases, a melody emerging from black dots on the staves, marks inked there in 1828, communicating across all this time! It was such excitement that, at times, she could barely strum.

She drove home jerkily fast, foot tapping the rhythm on the gas pedal, singing at full voice—"Dada-dum, dada-dum, dada-dum-dum-*dum*!"—accompanied by the flapping plastic sheet over the passenger window. At the parking lot across from World's End, she nosed the car around for a free spot—at night, the place filled with patrons headed to the Hook.

What about dropping in there for a glass of something to amplify her good cheer? She took a wander up Roberts Road, the rowdy banter growing as she approached the pub. A group of laborers—faces worn by sun, dirt, and cigarettes—sat at the picnic tables outside, gripping sloppy pints, eyeing ladies out on a hen night, heavy gals in stilettos, ankles tattooed, thighs goosebumped, floppy bosoms held up with underwire scaffolding. On the opposite side of the road was the legion bar, reserved for veterans of foreign wars. Now and then, a boy who'd fought in Iraq or Afghanistan took a break from darts and glowered at the pub across the way, at the wobbly girls giggling over spilled cider.

As Tooly passed between these two drinking holes, hawkish men on each side registered only her short haircut, pale lips, and sexless fashion, which rendered her invisible to them. If ever a man fancied her these days, she suspected him of low standards, of being a goat in heat. Were she to enter the Hook, she'd find many such goats. A tipsy one might make for brief amusement. But in a village you couldn't avoid your mistakes. Best to return home. She wanted only a glass of mild intoxication tonight. A bottle of Pinot Noir was already open in the kitchen.

She filled her glass too high and, lips to the brim, slurped it to a more seemly height, then nibbled crackers and cheese, humming "The William Tell Overture" with wine-purple lips. What a marvel, this drink! Past a certain age—about twenty-six, was it?—after the last flickers of the younger self, a pressure grew inside her during the course of each day, butting against the limits of her existence. Until, at her first nightly sip, she dilated, the tightness eased, and she floated in thoughts, outside time. She cupped a hand over her brow and gazed out the latched window at the farmland beyond Caergenog, all blackness at this hour. She took a pace back, watching a reflection of the kitchen and of herself, wine level decreasing over the minutes.

Down the stairs she went, treading tipsily through the darkened shop. Within arm's reach were so many sublime minds—she could awaken them off the shelf (no matter the hour, they were more alert than she), bid them start, and encounter a soul fitted with perception like hers, only sharper. But tonight it was the computer that lured her. She cradled the keyboard in her lap, giving a little shiver as the machine blinked and whirred, icons populating the desktop, her face lit by the screen.

Tooly had long shied away from computers, associating them so strongly with Paul. And she'd managed to avoid them better than most, living as she had, disconnected from wires, traveling city to city, job to job, taking positions that required minimal technological skills. The longer she'd gone without a computer of her own, the more mystifying all the digital hubbub became.

But World's End, for all its bound paper, came with a few microchips, too, in the form of this clunky old desktop, a senior citizen at age four. Fogg had taught her how to enter sales on it, and had insisted on showing her around the Internet, too, extolling its marvels and scope by searching for her name—though he was rather crestfallen to discover no results whatsoever.

For more than a year, Tooly had remained aloof from that computer. At most, she tried simple Web searches like "ukulele," nearly scared at the landslide of hits. Then, gradually, she explored a little further. Eventually, hours vanished there. Like a black hole, the Internet generated its own gravity, neither light nor time escaping. Cats playing the piano, breasts and genitals popping out, strangers slandering strangers. The lack of eye contact explained so much of what happened online. Including her own new habit: prowling through the past.

In recent weeks, she had started searching for names, old ones, of lost friends, former schoolteachers, fellow pupils, acquaintances from cities she'd left years before. Through the online murk, she spied their lives, piecing together what had happened: colleges, employers, married to, activities, interests. An employment history on LinkedIn might suggest a glittering start—Trainee to District Manager to Vice President—followed by an unexplained Self-Employed. The "Lives In . . ." on Facebook provided unexpected locales: Oslo or Hanoi or Lima. If she and they had maintained contact, the progressions from school to career to family would have passed so gradually as to be unremarkable. But online profiles converted the increments of life into leaps, transforming schoolchildren into graying parents in an instant.

How odd to have quit so many places and people, yet be preoccupied with them now, as they were surely not concerned with her. Still, Tooly never contacted those she peeped at, conducting her compulsive searches under the pseudonym Matilda Ostropoler, which combined her proper first name with the last name of a former friend.

All this nostalgic prowling—invariably after a few drinks—promised gratification yet left unease. It was as if a long spoon had been dipped inside her and stirred. Unlike in books, there was no concluding page on the Internet, just a limitless chain that left her tired, tense, up too late.

Time to switch off. Time to go to bed, look at the rafters, restore the memory of her music lesson. If she closed her eyes thinking of the fingerboard, would her brain practice while she slept?

She half stood—then roused the computer, testing its promise of satisfaction behind each next click. At the top left of the screen appeared a flag, a Facebook friend request. Because of her pseudonym, such requests came only from lurking weirdos. She clicked it, intending to decline.

Except she recognized this name: Duncan McGrory.

Tooly walked away from the computer, down the closest aisle, tapping nervously on books as she went. It had been years since her last contact with Duncan. How had he found her? Mouth dry, she stood with her finger over the mouse button. Read his name again. She clicked yes.

Within moments, he had messaged her: "Desperately trying to reach you. Can we talk about your father???"

She clenched her clammy hands, wiped them on her shirt. Her father? Whom could he mean?

# 1988

"Don't."

"Don't what?"

Before Paul had walked in, Tooly was jumping on her bed, watching the view of Bangkok fly up and down through the window. Upon hearing him, she bent her knees and grasped the covers in a breathless crouch, feet flexing on the quivering mattress. "I'm not wearing any shoes," she said in her defense.

"Don't be argumentative about everything."

She took a ballet leap off the bed and crashed to the floor, tumbling across the cool tiles, landing on her belly, then rolling onto her back to show that she was unhurt.

"People live below us. Stop that."

Paul was particularly tense that morning, expected at the U.S. Embassy in less than an hour to start his latest contract. He was an information-technology specialist for Ritcomm, a private company hired by the State Department to upgrade diplomatic communications overseas. The larger American embassies, such as here in Bangkok, had mainframe computers with telecom links to Washington, allowing them to check the latest "bad-guy list" whenever a foreign national sought to visit America. But many smaller U.S. outposts had never been linked to the network, and were obliged to consult ancient documents on microfiche. Paul was overseeing upgrades around the world, traveling to each dinky consulate, where he conducted a site survey, installed the Wang VS able to open up a 3270 emulation, ran BNC cables to every desk terminal. Finally, the staffers could connect at 9.6 bps via the phone line, type in a name, date of birth, place of birth, and wait for a hit.

Each of his assignments lasted about a year, during which he based himself at a hub like Bangkok and·traveled throughout the region, doing his best to avoid time at the suffocating embassies. Diplomats there often styled themselves a ruling class, treating support staff like servants. Paul might be assigned to fix a faulty dot matrix, for instance, or told to exorcise gremlins from the ambassador's monitor. On embassy days, he tried to vanish among the swarms of staff and visitors—just another guy slouching out of the cafeteria with a Styrofoam box for lunch. He avoided others' company by choice, although this was not the only reason he made himself unknown.

Tooly watched him hobbling around in one black Velcro shoe, his polo shirt tucked into pleated khakis. He sniffed—air-conditioning congested his sinuses—then swallowed, Adam's apple rippling, neck dotted with razor-burn blossoms. "Where's my other shoe?" His anxiety pervaded the apartment, and her. The disquiet of others was an undiscovered force alongside gravity that, rather than pulling downward, emanated outward from its source. Unfortunately, she was excessively attuned to his nervous pulses. She joined the hunt and discovered his lost shoe under the couch. Disastrously late now, he grabbed for floppy disks and printouts. At the door, he stopped. "Oh, no."

"What?"

"Where are you today, Tooly?"

"What?"

"What are you supposed to be doing? I can't just leave you here."

"Isn't there a housekeeper coming?"

"Not till Thursday." Paul always endeavored to keep them prepared, yet the narrowness of his attention caused lapses. He was a man who could grind at a programming conundrum for thirty hours and resolve it elegantly, then look up to find all else in decay. "Goddamn!"

"I don't mind staying on my own."

"I mind," he said.

"Can I jump on the bed?"

He checked the time. No choice but to leave her there. He came near to an apology, then locked her inside.

This new apartment was large and modern, constructed in the late 1970s, ceilings low, furniture sparse. The windows hummed with AC units, which blew up the skirts of the curtains. In Paul's room, open suitcases lay on the bed. His computer, a high-performance DEC workstation, was always shipped ahead. She was forbidden to touch it alone, yet did so now, turning the dial on the cube monitor and flicking the I/O switch, floppy-drive light flickering. Within minutes, a green cursor fast-blinked on the black screen.

He had taught her a program once, and she typed it in now, then hit Return. The words "Hello world!" flashed onscreen. Tooly imagined that the machine was alive, and typed back "hello." But the cursor blinked dumbly. She was only talking to herself.

She left everything exactly as before and ventured into his en-suite bathroom, closed the toilet lid, and climbed up. Tooly parted her unbrushed hair as if it were curtains and peered between, voicing imagined dialogues with acquaintances from previous cities: stewardesses, travelers, and other forms of grown-up. In the mirror, she inspected herself, ears protruding, forefinger fish-hooked in her mouth. All her clothing was rolled up at the hems. She was supposed to grow into it, but remained little. In every class photo, Tooly was at the front—next to whichever resentful boy genetics had consigned to a similarly low altitude.

It didn't feel as if that reflection in the mirror was really her.

She slid open the mosquito-screen door to the back balcony. The morning sun glared through smog. Beyond the apartment complex stood rusty corrugated shacks and banana trees where birds chirped. She fetched Paul's binoculars, sneaking them off a high shelf, popped the eye caps, and wiped the lenses on her T-shirt, the glass squeak-squeak-squeaking. With a finger raised ("Careful!"), she returned to the balcony.

Tooly deplored birding, among the dullest activities ever conceived by adults. Animals were endearing when they were crude versions of people, but birds weren't human at all. Paul said birds had evolved from dinosaurs, which was hard to believe, given that dinosaurs were notably interesting. Nevertheless, she looked everywhere for birds. On the occasions that she spotted one, the sighting pleased Paul, and she wished for that rare effect. Generally, she seemed to irritate him.

"Which do you like best," she'd once asked him, "birds or people?"

"Oh, birds," he responded emphatically, adding softly, "Definitely birds."

Back inside, she clasped in each fist a corner of her T-shirt, stood under the ceiling fan, the propeller chopping air. She remained motionless, her heart rate increasing until she sprang forward, sprinting through the living room, leaping onto her bed, landing on her knees, then bounding off again—through the kitchen, into the empty maid's quarters, squealing till she remembered that she oughtn't. She jammed a handful of shirt into her mouth, fabric dampening as she galloped around, sucking breaths through her nose. On the front balcony, she halted, looking down onto their lane, where construction workers toiled, bicyclists queued before a food stall, a street tailor hunched over his pedal-operated sewing machine. All those people down there and she up here—how strange that there were different places, events happening at that moment, and she wasn't in them. There were people she'd once known doing things on the other side of the world at that instant.

She ran back inside, grabbed her book, and belly-flopped onto the couch. With the thick paperback of *Nicholas Nickleby* spread before her, Tooly went still. When reading, she appeared comatose and deaf. Yet inside she moved all the faster, hurrying along a tall wooden fence through whose knotholes she observed extraordinary scenes: a whip-bearing butcher cleaning his hands on a leather apron, say; or a pickpocket with a stump for an arm; or a crafty innkeeper eavesdropping on clients. Sometimes she found her view blocked by a mysterious word—what, for example, was an "epitome"? Nevertheless, she hastened forward, finding the next knothole, having missed only an instant. To disappear into pages was to be blissfully obliterated. For the duration, all that existed was her companions in print; her own life went still:

"May I—may I go with you?" asked Smike, timidly. "I will be your faithful hard-working servant, I will, indeed. I want no clothes," added the poor creature, drawing his rags together; "these will do very well. I only want to be near you."

"And you shall," cried Nicholas. "And the world shall deal by you as it does by me, till one or both of us shall quit it for a better. Come!"

She considered the word "shall," wishing to utter words like that to stammering friends who inquired, "May I—may I go with you, Tooly?" To which she'd reply, "You shall!"

Paul stood beside her, lips moving, words emerging but not sounding yet, her ears still switched off. A stick of dried spaghetti in her mouth, she finished the chapter, then closed the book. "I saw a tree babbler," she said.

"Where?"

"In a tree."

He lowered himself into an armchair, rubbed his face. "Don't eat raw spaghetti."

"I shall not."

"Why are your lips green? Were you tasting toothpaste again?"

"Maybe."

"Just have something normal from the fridge."

"There wasn't anything normal."

"What was there?"

"Nothing."

He frowned disbelievingly and rose to check. But why *would* there have been food? They'd only moved in the day before. Every cupboard was empty, the fridge unplugged. He had left her alone for ten hours. "Nothing since breakfast?" he asked.

"I didn't have breakfast."

He opened all the cupboards again, ashamed of his oversight and uncertain how to respond. He checked the clock. (In place of numbers, its display had birds; instead of chiming, it twittered on the hour. By now, they could tell time by birdsong.) "It's blackbird past owl," he said. "I have to feed you."

"You shall."

She described the tree babbler but fell silent when the elevator doors closed after them—he opposed talking in elevators, since outsiders could hear. They crossed the building's courtyard, which was lined with frangipani trees and flanked by twin fountains, spray misting the hot evening air. "Nothing at all?"

"That spaghetti," she replied. "When I was on the balcony, I saw places down the road where they have food."

"We're not eating things from the street, Tooly."

"Can I try?"

"There'll be proper restaurants," he said. "They probably have Italian in Bangkok. You like spaghetti."

"Can I see down our street first?"

"You saw from the window."

"Only from high up."

"Well . . . okay. But follow me and stick close." He stepped from the complex and onto the *soi*, directly into the path of a motorcycle, which swerved around him, its whoosh fluttering her T-shirt. Walls ran along both sides of the lane, hiding the expat apartment buildings, while electricity cables hung from utility poles like vines. They walked single file toward the main road, Sukhumvit, passing a cart of tropical fruit on ice: papaya spears in plastic bags, skinned pineapples, hairy rambutans. The shopkeeper attacked a mango with a butcher knife, severing it on a tree-stump cutting board.

Gray blotches spattered the dry pavement. It was rain—from specks to a gushing torrent within seconds. They speed-walked for

Sukhumvit, where tuk-tuk taxis awaited. "Can we take one?" she asked.

"They're not safe," he replied, the downpour plastering white hair over his forehead, rain dribbling down his spectacles. "It's like a cart—you can just fly out. We need a proper taxi."

They continued into the deluge, rain overwhelming the grates, water rising out of the gutter.

"Look!" she said. "Rats! They're swimming."

"Don't look at them, Tooly! They're diseased. Tooly—keep up!" Glancing left and right for a taxi, he hurried onward, inadvertently leading them down Soi Cowboy, a strip of winking-neon bars, with hookers sitting cross-legged on stools, smoothing down miniskirts, gabbing in Thai above tinny pop music. They spotted the *farang* man and cooed. One waved innocently at Tooly, who waved back. "Don't!" Paul told her. "Really, don't."

She spotted a taxi and flapped her arms at it, then tugged Paul's shirt so that he might turn and believe he'd discovered it himself.

"Here's one!" he exclaimed, pushing past, nearly treading on her. "Hurry, I've got us a cab!"

Communicating to the driver that they wanted lasagna was beyond Paul, so he allowed the man to drop them outside a place in Chinatown.

A waitress ushered them into No. 2 Heaven Restaurant, past a tank of underbite fish, which glared at each new customer, and with good reason. Framed photos of suckling pig, roast lobster, and shark's fin soup hung on the red-gold walls. Paul took a metal water carafe and slopped a wave into her glass, which filled with a fast glug and overflowed onto the maroon tablecloth, a dark patch that expanded.

"Do animals get haircuts?" she asked.

"Which animals?"

"Rats."

"They don't need them. Their hair doesn't grow long."

"It just stops growing?"

"Yes."

"So why doesn't people's?"

"People's what?"

"People's hair."

"Tooly, please. We're about to eat." He raised his menu.

She consulted hers. "You don't like sweet-and-sour, do you."

"No," he confirmed. "I want food that can make up its mind."

"What is 'cheeking breast'?"

"It should say 'chicken breast.'"

"They have something called Unique Leg of Camel. What's 'unique' mean again?"

"One of a kind."

"Isn't every camel leg one of a kind?"

He pushed his glasses up the bridge of his nose. "Please, Tooly, let's not talk of animals at the table."

This made discussing the menu difficult. Eventually, she defied him, speaking so fast that he didn't have time to object: "They have something called 'lamb without odor' and 'slice pigeon.'"

"We'll get the chef's special noodles," he informed her, closing his menu. "Plus crab meat with asparagus." Paul always picked for her. It never occurred to him that this was bossy.

"I shall tell them our order," Tooly said, swiveling around for a waiter. "Excuse me!"

"Tooly, quiet."

"Then how do we get them to come over?"

"We wait. That's why they're called waiters."

The staff confirmed his interpretation, chatting at length by the fish tank, then vanishing through the swinging kitchen doors for dishes that sailed past their table. Tooly swallowed hard, suddenly famished.

She folded and refolded her napkin. Paul did the same. Now and then, he refilled their water glasses. Something to say! She wished for a sentence. When they were on flights or at home, there were distractions. But dining, seated opposite like this, there was nothing. Silence sat between them as if upon its haunches on the table. She watched the uniformed doorman, who watched the fish, which watched Tooly. "Is that man a soldier?" Tooly asked, knowing he was nothing of the sort.

"He's a guard."

"Why do they have a guard at a restaurant? In case the cheeking escapes?"

He looked at her, uncomprehending, then at his water glass from several angles.

A waitress arrived and food came soon after—a huge bowl of soup they hadn't ordered. Tooly launched herself at it before Paul could protest. She spooned it in ravenously, while he held her hair out of the way. Plates seemed to emerge from the kitchen at random, dishes served whenever it suited the cook. Presently, another arrived. "Oh, no!" Tooly said. "Fish!"

"It's not one from the tank," Paul said unconvincingly. "Anyway, we have to eat it or it'll be perceived as an insult."

"By the fish?"

Paul chewed on one side of his mouth, gazing off as if there were something untoward about dining, a necessary embarrassment like toileting.

"Was your job okay today?"

"Was it okay?" he said, the wrinkle tightening between his eyebrows. "I heard that my father is sick."

"Shall we venture to America to see him?"

"Why are you talking like that?" he said. "I just told you my father's sick."

"Sorry."

"We can't go back. And that's that."

When Tooly was younger, she had met Paul's father, but had no memories of him, only images from two photographs: one of a cheerful bald man with a mustache and a butterfly collar clowning around; the other of a youth in an army uniform. Burt Zylberberg, a basketball player in college and later an insurance salesman, had converted from Judaism to Catholicism as a young man, and served as a chaplain in World War II. During the Anzio invasion, an explosion shredded his legs. He and his wife, Dorrie, had intended to start a family after the war, but the extent of his wounds precluded that. They adopted a boy, Paul, and settled in Northern California. They were jovial parents, particularly Burt, an indefatigable optimist despite his infirmity. But they were so different from their adopted child, an earnest boy without any spiritual inclination. Yet he was intensely loyal to them. Whenever people asked if he thought of finding his real parents, he grew annoyed—he had no curiosity about those people, and never developed any. Paul went on to study computer science at UC Berkeley, which gave him access to high-end mainframes. In the wee hours, he haunted the computer lab, partly because all the interesting hardware was available then, but also to escape his peers' cavorting. The hum of mainframes produced in him a conditioned response of tranquillity. During his final year of college, a surprise came: his parents informed him that he had an elder brother. When World War II was breaking out, they'd given up a baby, and that child had grown up and found them. This biological son—having just met Burt and Dorrie—already interacted with them with an ease and warmth that were alien to Paul. Rather than spurring him to seek his own biological kin, the development instilled the sense that he had no origins at all.

Paul placed his credit card on the bill, and went to the toilets. Tooly waited and waited, then wandered toward the front door, which a waitress opened for her. Outside, the air was hair-dryer hot and smelled of exhaust. Pedestrians gushed down the sidewalk, a human river coursing past the Chinese-Thai shopfronts displaying vases, gongs, ceramic lions, meat grinders. She found herself swept away, bundled along among strangers until the end of the block. On her return to the restaurant, Paul had still not come back from the bathroom. She approached it, heard his inhaler hissing in there, and she whispered his name.

Sheepishly, he edged out, a water stain down his trousers. "The sink area was all flooded but I didn't see," he said. "I leaned against the counter and got soaked. It looks . . ." As if he'd urinated down his khakis.

"I'll ask for a napkin," she suggested.

"Don't say anything, Tooly!"

"Can we just run out?"

"I haven't got my credit card back."

"I could knock over the water. Then everything will be wet and they won't see the difference."

"That's a terrible idea."

"I can run through the restaurant and you chase after me, shouting that I poured water on you."

"We can't do that."

But they did, to the bewilderment of the waiters and diners. Paul hunched forward in humiliation, mumbling his lines. "Why did you do that?" he said, rushing after her.

"I poured water all over you!"

"You're a bad person! Where's my credit card? Look what you did!"

"I threw water all over!"

Outside, he crossed his hands over his crotch as she searched for taxis, waving wildly at the passing traffic. "Don't make a scene," he pleaded.

In the cab, Paul said, "I wasn't really angry in there."

"I know you weren't."

They arrived back at Gupta Mansions, took the elevator up, unlocked the front door. "Good to be home," he said.

As they looked at this latest apartment, it felt like home to neither of them.

# 1999

BLINKING TO WAKEFULNESS, she glanced at her few possessions with estrangement: corduroys splayed across the floor, sweater and coat heaped on sneakers, bra twisted over a low-rise of books. She pushed open her bedroom door and clomped across the main room toward the toilet.

"Good mornink," Humphrey said in his thick Russian accent. Seated on the couch holding a book, the old man nearly said more, but thought better of it, knowing Tooly to be grumpy at this hour, barely 11:30 A.M.

She lapped water from the bathroom faucet, then returned to her bedroom, pulled on her oatmeal cable knit and a dressing gown, its belt dragging along the cold concrete floor. At her window, she raised the blinds, contemplating their little-trafficked street under the shadow of the Gowanus Expressway in Brooklyn. The sidewalks were icy that November day. Shoes hung from the power lines, tossed up there years earlier by kids who'd long since grown into adults.

Much as Tooly wanted to impose her mood on the morning, she couldn't resist Humphrey in the other room. He'd probably been waiting hours for her company. When she joined him, he had a steaming cup of coffee for her on the Ping-Pong table. She collected it, sat at the other end of the couch, and frowned in order to win a few minutes' silence. He turned a page, pretending to read, though he peeked at her from under his overflowing eyebrows, raccoon shadows below his eyes, creases around his mouth, which kept tightening, ready to pounce on a conversation, then relenting. Humphrey, who was seventy-two, wore baby-blue slacks high around his gut, a polyester dress shirt of the small size he'd once been, and a loosened paisley tie, all from the thrift shop. Bits of stubble, like toast crumbs, adhered around his thin lips and prickled the cords of his throat; one ashen sideburn was longer than the other, giving the impression that he might tip over. "I'm so tired," he sighed, "of being loved for my beautiful body."

She smiled, took a sip of coffee, and plucked the book from his hands: *The Maxims of La Rochefoucauld*.

"I also have maxim in life," Humphrey informed her. "My maxim is never let Tooly Zylberberg take book, because it goes and never comes back."

"If I borrow a book and like it," she contended, "it becomes mine by law."

"I overrule this law."

"I appeal to a higher court where I'm the judge, and I uphold the law."

"System is flawed," he observed.

"I have my own maxim in life: Why is it so freezing here?" She reached behind the couch frame to where he dumped his bedcovers each morning and dragged up his comforter, wrapping herself in it. (He slept on the couch and made efforts to move from it minimally. His seat was at the far end, amid a swamp of newspaper pages that he'd flung into the air in contempt. Under the cushion, he stuffed clippings and crosswords that over time had elevated him; each time he sat, newsprint crunched.)

Considering her swaddled in his bedcovers, Humphrey remarked, "You look like bear hyperbating for winter."

"A bear doing what?"

"Hyperbating."

"What is 'hyperbating'? Sounds like a bear that can't stop masturbating."

"Don't be disgusting pervert!"

"It's a reasonable conclusion, Humph. There aren't that many other words that end in '-bating.'"

"Plenty words end in '-bating.'"

"Like what?"

"Like . . . Like 'riverbating.'"

"What is 'riverbating'?"

"'Riverbating': when there is echo, you say it is riverbating."

"'Reverberating,'" she corrected him, "isn't a word that ends in '-bating.'"

"Okay, I give you other." He paused. "Here, I have it: 'verbating.'"

"'Verbating'?"

"When you speak something and I repeat it back same, then I am saying it verbating."

"'Verbatim.'"

"Yes, sure."

Their current home was on the upper floor of a two-story storage space, with lightbulbs hanging from bare wires, the furniture damp. This main room served as kitchen, dining room, sitting room, and his sleeping quarters. She worried that he did this as gallantry, to ensure that she had the lone bedroom. Anyway, he was unmovable. Intermittently, she made efforts to clean the apartment. As for Humphrey, he was never renowned for tidiness. "My nature abhors the vacuum," he said. In explaining his inertia, he cited a principle of physics that had yet to appear among the standard Newtonian laws: Slob Gravity. A slob such as himself, he claimed, struggles under a greater burden than others, being subject to a higher force of gravity. "More you are slob, more heavy gravity is."

Over the years, he had amassed a huge library that was notable chiefly for its wretched condition. These were great works but pitiful volumes: disintegrating paperbacks of Kafka, Yeats, Goethe, Cicero, Rousseau. There were oddities, too, such as the user's guide to Betamax, travel memoirs about countries that no longer existed, histories with half the pages and half the centuries missing, causing the Ming

Dynasty to contest the Wars of German Unification with one swish of the page. Many volumes had come from garbage cans or boxes left on the sidewalk. This was less a library than an orphanage. His stated plan was to read everything ever printed. He claimed to be nearly there. Were it possible, he'd have read in the shower. But Humphrey's books had little to fear from onrushing water, he and soap being on terms of only passing familiarity.

When they moved to this city several weeks earlier, Humphrey had gone immediately to explore the New York Public Library, awed by the ceiling fresco of heaven in the Rose Reading Room, at whose front bench he sat, watching readers submit chits for books. As in previous cities (their most recent being Barcelona), Humphrey's next priority after books was finding the chess. This he located in Washington Square Park, where he watched ex-con hustlers facing off against nerdy grandmasters. He'd also discovered a Carmine Street store, Unoppressive Non-Imperialist Bargain Books, where he could indulge another hobby, debating politics. He was still unconvinced about the Cold War. According to the world, capitalism had won that contest, but Humphrey called it a tie at best. He couldn't see capitalism lasting. What was the point of any system, he asked, if it only encouraged the worst in humanity, elevating self-interest to a virtue? He described himself as a "Marxist, non-practicing," and certainly seemed a Marxist in the sense of being broke.

His sole source of income was consulting for wealthy book collectors who sought to expand their hoards. He surveyed their shelves and identified which editions were lacking and where they might be found, marshaling his impressive recall of antiquarian bookshops around the world. The collectors (it was almost exclusively men who suffered this acquisitive hunger) viewed him as an idiot savant, a novelty act notorious for smelly clothing, thick accent, and gruff manner, along with rumors of an ancient stint in jail. Humphrey's consultations were free, but the custom was to give him a volume of moderate value, which he immediately sold to Bauman Rare Books for spending money.

"Hungry?" He fetched a paper bag from the kitchen containing two stale croissants and one bruised avocado. Humphrey rejected the idea of meals, eating whenever he felt it appropriate, not because it was the ordained hour. His sleep followed the same principle: he remained up all night if reading, or slept till dark if the day offered nothing of note. To allow a clock to dictate one's life was mere conformism. He emptied the bag onto the Ping-Pong table and invited Tooly to join him.

She dipped a croissant into her coffee, losing half the pastry in the mug, flakes floating, as he rhapsodized about his mushy avocado. Humphrey prided himself on the purchase of expired produce, which he talked supermarket stockers into saving for him. Despite moderate indigestion, he kept Tooly and himself going this way on almost no money. And Humphrey wanted nothing more than this existence: nibbles and books, gesticulating and pontificating, with Tooly there to answer back. "Movement is overrated," he said.

She herself was subject to the laws of Slob Gravity, able to remain inside for days, her nose in books, consuming whatever vittles materialized on the Ping-Pong table. At other times, though, she marched outside, walking tirelessly around the city, marking her map, scanning for building doors left ajar and talking her way inside. Whichever condition—activity or indolence—held sway, Tooly struggled to break its spell. When slobbing around the apartment, she could barely propel herself farther than the bathroom and back. When striding block after block, she required a force of will to return home at all.

"Do you think," she asked, following an hour of reading on the couch, "that I should get dressed at some point?"

"It's nearly one P.M.—throw caution out of window."

"If I threw caution out the window, I'd have to open the window. It's too cold," she said. "But I should get ready."

He knew this meant a meeting with Venn. "Why you should go? Stay here. Is more comfy. You wait and I find you nice job." Another of his pastimes was writing on her behalf to grand organizations, informing them of a young lady they must employ. She wished he'd stop this, but few of his correspondents answered anyway. When they did, Humphrey claimed it as the nearest miss. Yes, perhaps the U.N. secretary-general hadn't hired her, but he had answered on proper letterhead.

"It wasn't Kofi Annan who wrote back," Tooly noted. "Some person in his office. An intern, probably."

"Small details," he said. "I beat you in chess?"

"I really have to go." She sneezed, and his face lit up. Humphrey kept pharmaceuticals under his cushion, and prescribed to anyone who as much as cleared his throat. He especially loved treating her—he had done so often when she'd been sick in childhood. But Tooly couldn't oblige with an illness today. "It was only dust."

"Fine, fine—you must go to meeting? Go," he said. "Just because I can at any moment fall, and my heart stops, and nobody here to call help? No problem. I wait on floor trying to breathe till you come home."

"I ban you from falling over and dying while I'm out."

"I die very quietly. I try not to bother you."

"I know you're joking, Humph, but I'm actually starting to feel bad."

"Do what you like." He leaned on her, rising unsteadily to his feet. "But *I* am going out. Cannot sit around all day. I have items and activities."

"You idiot," she said, grabbing him for a cuddle.

"Leave me, crazy girl!" He squirmed away, sweeping the mussed gray-black hair off his forehead. "You don't go to see him. You come with me on book consult. No?"

"Sorry, Humph. And I'm walking there, so I should leave."

"At least you take subway with me. It's very colding outside."

"For a Russian, you're so whiny about the weather."

"I am low-quality Russian."

"I'll accompany you to the station. But that's it."

When they stepped outside, she inhaled deeply and the cold air seemed to awaken her a second time. A burning smell was in the air—

welding at the ironworks across the street. Their corner was dotted with industrial workshops, many in red-brick garages inside padlocked chain link fences crowned with razor wire. They cut down Hamilton Avenue, walking against the flow of passing vehicles. A few bereft brownstones gave onto the rusted expressway undercarriage, with the Red Hook projects on the other side.

Outside the station, Tooly stopped. "I have my own things to do, Humph."

"How you can walk all way to Manhattan?"

"Stop trying to keep me here!" she said, laughing.

"I make law that it is illegal for you to walk today."

"I veto your law."

"Who gives you veto power?"

"You did."

"I un-give."

"I launch a coup d'état and write a new constitution that says I can go. There, done." She kissed his wrinkly cheek; he wiped it away.

Striding off, she marched hard up the block, speeding to outpace her guilt. But it caught up, dragged her to a halt. Tooly drummed her lower lip. Couldn't just leave him. She spun around and went back, fed her token into the turnstile. She found him seated on the platform, leafing through Hume's *Essays, Moral and Political*.

"My darlink," he said. They sat in silence. The low ceilings and joists down here, paint peeling—it was like stepping inside a mechanical object. "You are so capable and clever, darlink," he told her. "You will do wonderful things in your life."

"We'll see."

"You come back for me—very nice. But you go now," he said. "You walk. I survive. Muggers don't dare fight me."

"You'd hit them with David Hume."

"Worse: I read it to them." His old brown eyes reflected her momentarily, then gazed up the tracks. A train rushed into the station, its scratched-up windows etched with gang signs and initials. She watched as he boarded alone.

She resumed her hike, dodging pedestrians and overruling traffic lights all the way up Smith Street, through downtown Brooklyn, across the Manhattan Bridge, her mismatched sneakers moving fast—red, then black, cold air gusting up her corduroys—pace increasing almost to a run, as she tried not to beam too stupidly at the thought of who awaited. On arrival at the Bowery, she looked for him; not here yet. Sweat budded across her upper lip, glittered on her forehead.

To occupy herself, she took out her felt-tip pen—a few new streets to add from this latest hike—and fumbled in her overcoat pocket for the map. But it was missing. Had it slipped out somewhere on the road? Damn! Weeks of effort wasted. Never get attached to objects, Venn always said. Aargh—where was he? She stood at the corner of Hester Street, shivering.

Minutes passed, and she promised herself to leave after just one more. That one passed; another began. She looked to the left, the right, behind her, back again.

"Well, well," Venn said, cheeks broadening as he swept her alongside him in a one-armed hug. "Why'd you keep me waiting, duck? Come on."

Whenever they met, his voice resonated in this way—it was as if he spoke directly inside her. His wild beard was shorn these days, though reddish-brown stubble still bristled on his cheeks when he smiled, fan lines crinkling around his eyes. Despite the cold, he wore no overcoat, just a navy turtleneck that smelled of cedar.

She intended to be furious, but he'd made her laugh already. Anyway, indignation fizzled when directed at Venn. "Can we go indoors immediately," she asked with mock annoyance, "or walk very fast, preferably huddling together? I'm seconds from hypothermia here."

"Hypothermia is good for you—everything goes warm. You moaner! Come on." He took her hand and threaded it into the crook of his arm, his body dwarfing hers. Venn was like a devilish older sibling, offering that brotherly combination of wholly unreliable and utterly trustworthy. As they walked, she glanced obliquely at him, grinning. She allowed herself to be led along, paying no mind to her route for a change, the city shrinking away.

She'd seen so little of Venn since their arrival here from Barcelona. He'd come a couple of weeks earlier to set up the basics of whatever business had lured him to New York. So far, they'd had only one other meet-up in this city: a walk around Central Park, followed by drinks and talk and laughter at a bar under the Empire State Building. Cities changed; never their friendship.

But after that she'd not seen Venn for weeks, and realized that New York might be one of those places where he'd prove a rare presence. Patiently or not, she'd have to wait. He never had a fixed telephone number or a permanent address where she could find him, instead residing in the bed of his latest girlfriend, which changed frequently. Tooly had met many of them over the years, always variations on the same towering floozy. As an adolescent, she had viewed these perfumed ladies as womanhood personified, a state she'd one day achieve. Tooly was grown now and still hadn't reached it, but she retained a sense that *those* were proper women, not she.

Venn led her along Canal Street, past a bakery selling *cha siu bao*, and pushed open the next glass door, entering the foyer of a six-story building. He pressed the call button for the freight elevator, whose sliding door opened upward with a clatter, revealing a wizened black man in calfskin jacket and woolen suit pants. Warmly, he greeted Venn, ushering them in, and turning the half-wheel that operated the elevator, dry cogs grinding, the rickety cage hoisting them toward the top floor.

"How are you, my friend?" Venn asked, hand resting on the elevator operator's shoulder, his other surreptitiously slipping a ten-dollar bill into the man's pocket.

"It's all good," he replied shyly, loving the attention from Venn.

"You don't go crashing this elevator with my girl here, all right? We want a nice soft landing."

"Nothing but the best, my man."

They stepped out into a large industrial space, once a nineteenth-century factory, converted to a sweatshop at the start of the twentieth, and lately transformed into cubicles. A smutty skylight provided scant illumination, while the windows were blacked out to prevent reflections on the computer screens, producing a permanent dusk, just the flicker of TVs on the walls, broadcasting financial news. The space was divided into steel-and-glass units, each containing desks, telephones, beanbags, dartboards, and chattery young professionals kneading stress balls and procrastinating. The centerpiece, however, was a yellow school bus, whose interior had been stripped to turn it into the conference room.

Tooly wondered about the purpose of all this, but a gathering crowd required Venn's immediate attention. He led them into the school bus, adults tripping on kid-size steps, banging their heads inside the darkened interior. For several minutes, Tooly waited by the goods elevator, hands clasped behind her back, tapping a rhythm on her behind.

An emaciated bike courier for a dot-com grocer appeared, shouting, "Some dude called Rob ordered a box of sour keys?" A dozen people barged from the bus and a feeding frenzy ensued around the candy, leaving Venn to deal with the stragglers.

A short guy with a long goatee drifted to his cubicle near Tooly. He stared at her. "And you are . . . ?"

"Nobody," she answered.

"Okay, let me tell you something. You're standing right by my box, okay? I pay for it, right? And you're, like, distracting me right now. If you don't work here, then—with utmost respect—could you get lost?"

Hearing this, Venn squinted across the room at her, shook his head, then approached. "Dear, dear, dear," he said, causing the man with the goatee to turn hastily. "You don't talk to her like that. When you deal with Tooly," he warned, "you're dealing with me."

The man swallowed hard. "Sorry, brother. Totally didn't realize this was your friend." Blushing, he turned to her. "Apologies. That was out of line. Just, you were—"

Venn interrupted, addressing her. "Ready to move on, duck?"

"Ready!"

With that, he led Tooly gently away, winking at her.

"What the hell?" she whispered. Venn had certainly landed on his feet here—she'd never seen him in an office like this. In Barcelona, he'd spent most of his time at a grim factory on the outskirts, where an associate produced metal hooks to hang *jamón*. The man employed illegal immigrants from Romania, which had inadvertently involved him with some serious criminals. He was just a small-business man, and Venn was the only person he'd ever met who dealt with tough guys like that, so he'd asked for help. Venn obliged, yet ended up sympathizing more with the factory laborers than with his own associate, so he'd moved on. Next stop, New York.

Glancing around demonstratively, Tooly asked, "But this place isn't yours, is it?"

"Mine? I never own anything, duck."

"Well, you seem to be running it."

"Don't I always?" He winked.

The property, Venn explained, belonged to a venture capitalist named Marco "Mawky" Di Scugliano, an ex-Bear Stearns guy, brought up in a family-run restaurant in Hammonton, New Jersey, called Spaghett'About It, where he had been shot in the stomach at age eleven for resisting an armed robbery. The bullet, Mawky claimed, had introduced him to Jesus. Also perhaps to the use of profanity, given his motto (printed on the back of every business card): "This is the fucking time." The school bus had been his idea, a lifelong fantasy that required movers to bust open the roof and lower the vehicle in by crane, costing forty-five thousand dollars, though Mawky told people "almost a hundred grand." This was to have been his headquarters, but the plan flopped owing to the impossibility of lighting a room with such high ceilings; plus, people were always banging their heads inside the bus, and it proved impossible to get ISDN up here, the only option being dial-up. So he'd dumped the place for a new one on Twenty-sixth Street, overlooking the East River, a space so massive that employees were issued Razor scooter boards just to reach the bathrooms. He had asked Venn to make something of this junker, and that led to the Brain Trust, a cooperative that cost members five thousand dollars to join, plus two thousand a month to rent "a box," as the cubicles were known.

"Okay," she said, "but what are they actually doing?"

"It's a lab. Anything these guys come up with—any idea that turns into something—the creator gets a controlling stake in the resulting company. At the same time, all members of the Brain Trust own a piece, too. If a person is wealthy but unoriginal, they benefit—they just ante up for more shares. If they're rich in ideas and poor in cash, they can sell their Brain Trust shares to someone else. They bet on themselves, but on the group, too. Unlike in a normal office, everyone here wants their colleagues to succeed. Anyway, that's the theory."

He led her to a nearby box of two young women, former junior ad execs who'd quit to apply their wits to personal enrichment. One explained click-through ads to Tooly, rambling about "being first in the space," "bricks-and-clicks," and "online play." Tooly responded with what must have been an absurd question, since the woman asked with dismay, "Wait, are you even on email yet?" (Tooly had tried it a couple of years earlier, but she avoided computers.) The ad women droned on ·about how a million clicks at six cents each would equal six million dollars in profit. Venn suggested that they check their calculations, and led Tooly to another box.

"This guy is interesting," he said, tapping on the glass.

A programmer in a T-shirt depicting a Rasta mouse smoking ganja rotated in his desk chair. "Big guy! Wassup?" he said to Venn, indifferent that the monitor behind him was on an AltaVista search for "Maria Bartiromo" and "naked." His idea was a website called www.totally-annoyed.com, on which anyone could post complaints about companies and receive real-time apologies. Presented as a service for customers, the site was secretly funded by corporations, offering them a way to hive off clients who pestered help lines and drown them in a never-ending blah of automated apology, all generated by an algorithm called A.S. (Artificial Stupidity) that varied the regrets automatically, leading customers down an unctuous road to nowhere.

The next box contained four chubby guys in button-downs, their workstations piled with ravaged pizza slices, Big Gulps, and Mentos wrappers. Theirs was a spot-the-celebrity start-up, in which members of the public would phone in with tips about the location of famous people around New York (and later, Hollywood, London, so on). The info would be fed to subscribers on their pagers or to cellphone update services. The guys had already spoken with an angel investor who'd bandied around the figure of two million dollars. The site, www.spotcha.com, was to go live by year's end, and was guaranteed to become "*the* kick-ass brand of the twenty-first century," they promised, slapping high fives.

Venn led her onward.

"They're not seriously getting money for that, are they?" she asked him.

"Nearly anyone is getting money who's not an absolute clown."

"And they don't qualify?"

"These VCs sit around plotting how to earn off all the nerds they used to beat up," he said. "They move these guys into offices, give them free Handsprings, Nerf guns—one geek could equal their yacht."

"And the cooperative thing? That works well?"

"Not really," he said, amused. "They're all at each other's throats. That's what they were talking to me about before. This place is a comedy. But it has a view from the roof." He led her up a narrow staircase.

It was windy up there, with glimpses of City Hall, the distant antennae of the World Trade Center, and water tanks on surrounding high-rises. The roof was covered with tar paper, its low wall overlooking Canal Street six stories down. Venn was a man of a thousand acquaintances and hundreds of lovers, yet she was his only friend. If Tooly had an area of expertise in the world, it was Venn; she had studied him for years.

He was brought up on a small island off the coast of British Columbia, a speck of rocky brushland eight hours from Vancouver via three ferries and an interminable drive through the forest. A hundred people lived on this island year-round, castaways by choice, many on a commune called the Happening, founded by American draft dodgers and a changing cast of artists and loafers. Traditional relationships were forbidden in the Happening—nobody "possessed" anyone in matrimony or otherwise, and parents didn't exist, just brothers and sisters. Nevertheless, certain women favored certain children, and from this one deduced bloodlines. The boys were banned from owning toy guns and girls were allowed no dolls, though a jolly Swede produced marvelous little vehicles from wood, until a drug dispute forced him off the island. Around the nightly bonfire, the adults held forth about the world with a mixture of logic and lunacy, being at once highly educated and highly stoned. As the kids roasted marshmallows, the adults toked, recited poetry, danced badly, sang full-throatedly to the wilderness. Soon the children were sampling their parents' stashes and sneaking into the cabins of seasonal residents. The preteens swam to the adjacent island, hopped the ferry to Vancouver Island, hitchhiked down the coast and slept on beaches, rolling tree leaves to see if they might be smoked to any effect.

In time, the Happening happened less: its founders were short on supplies; the kids got cranky. The adults could have sought employment on the mainland, but society was exploitative. So they pilfered from it, applying to the Columbia Record Club under false names, reselling the albums to a store in Campbell River. One mother and son specialized in defrauding chain restaurants in Victoria, while others burglarized island retirees whose homes they cased under the guise of neighborly visits. When someone heard that provincial law gave children under eleven immunity from prosecution, the parents had their youngsters shoplift to order in Vancouver. Unfortunately, most of them bungled and were caught, prompting two RCMP officers to visit the Happening for a stern chat. This petrified the other kids but not Venn. By his teens, he'd become the commune's chief provider, a hero by dint of his gumption. A few of the grown-up women even made advances to him. But by age fifteen he'd wearied of this narrow life, surrounded by adults with unfinished college degrees, working as incompetent handymen and pseudosculptors, somewhere at the edge of the Pacific Ocean.

With a fake ID and genuine manners, he trekked across Canada, sojourning in Calgary, Winnipeg, Toronto, and Montreal, where he befriended a group of traveling Australians. After obtaining a passport that falsely stated his age as eighteen, he accompanied them home. It was his first time on an airplane and his first time out of Canada. Venn worked odd jobs on the Queensland coast for a spell, then did a summer at a mobile abattoir in the bush, butchering livestock for farms too remote to get their beasts to a slaughterhouse. At seventeen, he followed the backpacker trail through Indonesia, then Vietnam, a country whose war he'd heard about since childhood. He worked in bars across Southeast Asia. At twenty-two—just a little older than Tooly was now—he arrived in Thailand, managed a bar in Pattaya, then moved to Bangkok, where he encountered an aging Russian exile, Humphrey, over a chessboard. At which point began their long association.

Venn's childhood at the periphery of the world had implanted a craving for its center, and he moved incessantly in search of vibrant locales. Over the past decade he'd tried Jakarta, Amsterdam, Malta, Cyprus, Athens, Istanbul, Milan, Budapest, Prague, Hamburg, Marseille, Barcelona, and now New York. His occupation changed as often as his location, from construction worker to supermarket butcher to club manager. He'd been the driver for a pawnbroker, the confidant of an aging mandarin, an independent contractor, an entrepreneur. He had no snobbery and worked lowly jobs, if needed. Yet the trajectory of his occupations charted a steady climb upward, as did the company he kept.

When Tooly first met Venn, his confederates were charlatans and crooks, drawn to him like worms from damp ground. They had intrigued her once. But criminals only enchant those who haven't known many. Soon she found most of them repellent. But these days

Venn's cohorts were young Wall Street professionals, mini-masters of the universe playacting like mobsters, pulling up in hired limos outside the Old Homestead, each ordering a porterhouse for two, huge serrated knives spurting medium-rare blood across the tablecloth, wads of cash smacked onto the check, nobody asking for change. They were bullies in their sphere, naïfs beyond. So they idolized Venn, a man who'd seen the truly unsavory, who'd met those with really dirty money. He knew how to reach the bad guys, what to do if caught in a bind, how to procure documents, how one moved assets and boomeranged them back to place of origin. He represented access to an underworld. At least, that was the illusion he sold.

What rankled Tooly was how much time Venn had to spend in the company of creeps. "It's the worst part about how we live," he affirmed. "Always dealing with this awful outer circle of people. Hardly get to see my inner circle."

"Your inner circle? Who's that?"

"Well . . ." he said, pondering this, then smiling. "Actually, just you, duck."

It didn't matter that others had status and rank; he cared nothing about that. How else to explain his years of kindness to her and Humphrey. Indeed, Venn was fondest of outcasts who, like himself, recognized the pretense everywhere. He was a man who took no part in society, never voted. He was a being wrought of his own will, belonging to nothing. He'd not known or cared which of those bearded men wandering through his childhood had been his father. As for his mother, he'd kissed her goodbye. Family meant nothing more than did random names in a telephone directory. The relations that counted were those of choice, which made friendship the supreme bond, one that either party could sever, and all the more valuable for its precariousness.

He had no delusions about ending the long reign of fools in the world, yet he insisted on decency within the small realm that he could affect. She had seen him rent hotel rooms for addicts to whom he owed nothing, give loans to bums who would never pay him back.

Once, he covered a flight home for a Filipina trafficked into prostitution in Cyprus. He intervened with great physical courage to protect the frail, such as whenever thugs bullied Humphrey, or the time a lustful drunkard in Prague tore off Tooly's shirt. If Venn delivered violence, he did so without a shout or shove beforehand. He just struck. Aggression terrified Tooly. Yet she found herself *wanting* him to apply his violence sometimes, he alone imposing the justice that was everywhere absent.

The wind on the roof swept Tooly's hair across her face. "Is there something I could do at this place?"

"There aren't really jobs," he answered. "It's not that kind of situation."

"What about a project for the two of us?"

"Our friendship is the project, as far as I'm concerned." He looked down at the street. "What you need to do," he said, "is go into advertising, like those girls downstairs."

"Shut up," she said, laughing.

In recent years, in recent countries, Venn had alluded to a project—that they'd soon work together, as she had longed to do since childhood. In fact, they *had* done small jobs when she was little, though it had taken her a while to realize it. He'd have her knock on strangers' doors in new cities and ask to use the toilet. A minute later, he'd knock himself, claiming breathlessly to be the father of a lost little girl—had she come this way? He entered, touchingly relieved to find his girl, accepting a glass of water with thanks and making his targets' acquaintance. By the time these strangers offered him something—say, a place to stay or a job—they practically forced it upon him. People loved his company, just wanted his presence.

For her help, Venn used to treat her at the best hotel restaurant in whichever city they found themselves. On the way, he stopped at a junk shop and bought them elegant used overcoats, then led her into the opulent eatery, waitstaff gliding before them to a table—it was his lovely daughter's birthday, Venn declared, so treat her like royalty! He spun further yarns, captivating the management and drawing Tooly into his fibs. They consumed oysters and champagne (she sipping from his glass), pheasant and roast potatoes, cheese plates, and as many sweets as she pointed to on the dessert trolley. Once coffee and brandy had been ordered, Venn chaperoned her toward the washrooms. In hotel restaurants, these were typically outside the dining area through the lobby. Only after a few such banquets did Tooly grasp why they always went straight through the rotating lobby door, onto the sidewalk, and away. A steaming coffee and a glinting brandy snifter arrived at their table, along with the vast bill folded discreetly on a silver tray. That charming man and his adorable daughter must be in the washrooms still, the waitstaff reasoned. Nothing to worry about—they'd return. After all, those overcoats still hung from their chairs.

As Tooly grew older, she witnessed other shortcuts: how one might vacation for nothing by befriending a shy local of the opposite sex, earning free room and board, even a tour guide for a few days. Another game involved posting reward signs for a lost key inside a tourist-jammed train station. She put on a hiker's backpack (stuffed with Humphrey's laundry) and sought out the smokers—always easiest to start a conversation with. Any mean-faced jerk was her preference, the more unpleasant the better. She borrowed his lighter, sparked a cigarette, and complained that she had to fly home early because her grandma had fallen ill in Florida. While stepping away to the vending machines, she entrusted her backpack to the guy, then returned with a look of astonishment and something in her palm: Hey, is this that key on the reward posters? At a phone booth, they called the posted number. Frantic with excitement, the key's owner promised to drive over immediately with the generous cash reward; he'd arrive in an hour. Alas, Tooly couldn't wait—she had her flight to catch. However, the man on the phone (Venn) demanded that she wait. Appearing befuddled, she thrust the phone at her new acquaintance. Venn told him that this girl had just agreed on five hundred dollars for the key—give her the money now and I'll refund you as soon as I arrive. Hell, I'll quadruple it, if you stay put: two thousand in cash, *plus* the five hundred you gave the girl. Her unpleasant new companion sprinted to the closest ATM (Tooly helpfully pointing it out), and withdrew as close to five hundred dollars as possible. She gave him the key and hastened to the cab stand—no time for the airport train now! When, after an hour or two, the guy was still waiting, he irritably tried the number on the reward posters. It rang and rang.

But such high jinks had dwindled away—Venn came to see them as cheap, as did she. And he was occupied with more legitimate endeavors now. Yet he looked after her all the same, arranging her travel to each new city, finding lodgings for her and Humphrey. Weeks might pass without word from Venn. Then he'd phone. His voice—grin audible—immediately erased her disappointment that he'd not been in touch.

He was maddening, he was unpredictable, he was late. But he always arrived in the end. So, she waited.

"Any brilliant new ideas?" she asked.

"Lots, duck. But what are yours?" He gazed across at the rooftops. "I brought you here to see these kids downstairs—your age, more or less—coming up with things. You don't want to end up like Humph. Need to make your own propulsion."

Humphrey sent those ridiculous letters on her behalf ("Attention New York Times: I have young lady you must be interest in . . . .") because he was certain of her quality. Venn was more measured, and that wounded Tooly. But he was correct: she *had* produced nothing. Humphrey always claimed that the tumult of the twentieth century had ruined his prospects, that he'd been "cornered by history." But Tooly had grown up in an era of relative calm, after all the proper history had ended. She'd been too young to understand the hoopla of the Berlin Wall falling or the protests in Tiananmen Square, her awareness dawning around Operation Desert Storm and the L.A. riots, countries splitting up and ruining all the maps, then the O. J. Simpson trial, a computer that beat humankind at chess, the cloned sheep named Dolly, an English princess dying in a car crash, the most powerful man in the world fornicating with an intern. They were scatter-shot events, none relating to any other, and certainly not to her.

What, she wondered, would it have been like to live in an impor-tant era? How would she have acted during world wars? Humphrey had raised her with World War II and Soviet totalitarianism as the signal events—*that* history was her place and time, far from the ba-nality of this peace. These days, it was as if the whole world, even New York City, aspired only to be Seattle. She wished the present would impose itself on her and determine her course.

"Come," Venn said, leading her back downstairs.

As they strode along Canal Street, he said nothing. She wanted him to speak, so that she might learn his mood—Tooly hated this quiet (though traffic blared beside them). Hated being useless to him, offering nothing. She *had* achieved things in this city, slipping into a few homes. But to what end? For a few minutes' company? To peek at how college kids lived? Quizzing that student on 115th Street had pro-duced nothing. He'd been harmless, which was the problem: you meddled with bastards, not with some shy kid.

Venn scanned for a free taxi, his attention shifting to the next ap-pointment. This encounter was about to end. A long wait till the next.

She'd hoped this would be a full day together, the beginning of a fresh adventure with him—at the very least, a long meal or a long walk. But it was over already. With a presentiment of her coming solitude, she watched him.

But hang on. Don't disappear.

"I did do one thing," she blurted.

Before intending to, Tooly found herself describing Duncan and mentioning Xavi and Emerson—even the guy downstairs with the pig. To make herself sound industrious, she inflated everything, sketching a setting that was fat with potential. "I realize they're only in college," she said, "but they must have parents."

"Most people do, you'll find."

"I got tons of stuff on them." She searched her coat pockets for the crumpled ball of newsprint where she'd jotted notes upon leaving that apartment. She read aloud her scribbled fragments, watching Venn for the detail that would snag him, sharpen his gaze.

None did.

"Sorry," she said.

"Don't apologize to me, duck. Never any need for that," he said. "Look, if you want, keep digging around up there. Or give the boy lawyer a call sometime, see what comes of it."

"I'm so stupid—I don't even have his number."

"How'd you manage that?" he asked, chuckling.

"You say I'm not supposed to write numbers down anymore!" Contrary to his preferences, Tooly had long kept a little phone book. She crossed out every number after they left a city, but he still preferred that they only memorize information—after all, the people they encountered were not necessarily types one wished to be connected to in writing.

"So you did get his number," he asked, "but can't recall it?"

"I didn't even ask," she admitted. "I hate getting numbers. They want mine back, and I never know what to say."

"Say you're moving and don't have a new phone line installed yet."

"Hey," she exclaimed, nostrils flaring, "that's what *you* always tell *me!*"

Grinning, he shut his eyes, lids flickering. Tooly frowned, meaning for him to see when he looked up. Instead, he walked on. She couldn't stop herself hurrying after. "You idiot," she said, threading her arm under his, inhaling the wet-wood scent of his sweater.

Venn was busy reviewing the scrap of scribbled notes about the students—how had he even taken that from her? "This paper smells like peanut butter."

"My sandwich was in there," she said, grabbing it back. "See— never worry about me writing stuff down; I can always eat the evidence."

He burst into laughter, which caused such a surge of joy in her.

"It's decided," she announced. "I'm going back up there. And I'm getting something useful for us from these college kids. Okay? Just tell me what you'd like."

"Little duck, you know what works."

Venn touched her cheek, causing her to fall silent. He entered a taxi, leaving her alone on the caterwauling street.

# 2011

SHE PASSED JUST ONE HIKER in the Black Mountains that morning, a small boy with a large rucksack who mumbled a greeting that Tooly cheerfully returned. It didn't seem like the world up here. The villages below remained attached to modern life. But the hares and sheep darted away whichever the century, whatever excitation swept the valleys, whether menfolk were conscripted, if decades later they reminisced of war, if long after that their widows sat alone for supper.

In the distance down the ridge, something caught her attention. A group of walkers, maybe. But they were approaching too fast. Dirt bikes? She squinted. Those weren't people but ponies, the wild ones that roamed these hills. They were a mile away but galloping—in two minutes, they'd be on her. The path was only as broad as a car, with thick brush on either side and sharp slopes beyond. The ponies grew distinct now, about twenty of them. She waded into knee-high bracken. Could the animals veer off the path and trample her even there?

But upon arrival they had slowed to an amble, scarcely glancing at this strange human observing them from the brush. They grazed before her, foals between mares, a chestnut youngster on twig legs, a heavy-gutted gray stallion with tail swishing. Tooly held still— a thrilling arm's length from wild animals. She tried to memorize this instant, all the more urgently because there was nobody to share it. Once, she had read a story in which a man, dying in an asylum, sees "a herd of deer, extraordinarily beautiful and graceful," run across his imagination. If this moment returned to her years hence, what would she recall? A memory of having wanted to remember?

Abruptly, she turned from the ponies, striding down the steep hillside, tripping through bracken, speeding to the point of danger. It was futile, she knew, to ruminate.

"Desperately trying to reach you," Duncan had written. "Can we talk about your father???" What gave a boyfriend from a decade before the right to bludgeon her with punctuation? Her father had been beaten and robbed in New York, Duncan explained via Facebook messages. Whatever falling-out she'd had with the man, she needed to fly out immediately and help. Well, yes—that sounded reasonable. Except that Tooly had no idea who this father could be.

She had never mentioned *any* relative when she and Duncan were together. But after he lost touch with her in New York, it transpired, Duncan had gone looking for her, only to find her father living at a storage space near the Gowanus Expressway. The old man conveyed nothing about Tooly's whereabouts—instead, he had made Duncan play chess.

And, with that, she knew this "father" could only be Humphrey.

Little stirred her as did thoughts of the past. Starting with—well, how to describe what had happened? She didn't consider it a kidnapping. What, then? Taken from home, left in the care of a stranger, moved around the world. Those events had seemed to be heading toward some purpose, only for everything to collapse in New York.

The lack of a proper ending gnawed at her still, no matter how she had tried to forget. For years, she had awaited Venn's return. She had moved from one country to another, taken on lovers, changed jobs, yet retained the expectation of another life—a wormhole through which she'd one day slip, rescued by his company. Only upon buying the shop had she suspended this. It had been crushing, then almost a relief: no longer wandering, no longer believing herself distinct from those she walked among. Instead, she came to consider herself rather less worthwhile than average. As Venn had done, she razored away the unnecessary: companions, conversation, affection. She understood now all that he'd once said to her, and longed to tell him so.

But it was Humphrey who had now popped back into her life. Was it crazy to think Venn might be involved? If she went out there, might he be waiting?

Tooly gazed up the hillside, straining for a last glimpse of the ponies. But she absorbed little of her surroundings. None of this mattered. Her bookshop. Nothing. The past simply outranked the present, and it awaited her in New York.

THE PLANE DESCENDED toward the city, its winged shadow gliding over the ocean surface. Tooly, who'd flown so often in her life, had become nervous about planes in recent years. She clenched at each wobble now—when the engines roared into action, when they fell silent.

In the terminal, a Homeland Security officer with elephantine legs and a crackling walkie-talkie watched the hordes plod by, bleary JFK arrivals dragging bags and babies and time zones behind them, their shoulders and hopes sinking at the monumental immigration lines— fault of the terrorists or fault of the response, depending on one's politics. She recalled how nervous Paul had been whenever they crossed a border. At the counter, a thick-shouldered agent with a dapper little mustache took her American passport, flipped the pages slowly. "Welcome home, ma'am."

The outer boroughs of New York rushed past the window of the yellow cab, with Tooly crammed behind a bulletproof divider implanted with a blaring television that she couldn't shut off. The driver chatted on a hands-free, and Tooly kept looking up, thinking she was being addressed, only to realize that he was speaking Punjabi.

In her two-star midtown hotel, she awoke in the dark—that under-the-soil blackness of a hotel room with the curtains drawn. Syncopated police sirens blooped faintly from the street below, as if a kid were in there pressing buttons. Demonic red digits glowed beside her: 4:31 A.M.

Cupping basin water to her mouth, she roused herself, parted the curtains, and discovered an Orion's belt of office lights. On the television, she read descriptions of pay-per-view movies: "A former marine falls in love with a native of a lush alien world"; "Two NYPD detectives must retrieve a valuable baseball card." Every commercial seemed to be for pharmaceuticals. Possible side effects included unpleasant taste in mouth, dizziness, abnormal thoughts and behavior, swelling of the tongue, memory loss, anxiety, getting out of bed while not being fully awake and doing an activity you do not know you are doing.

Would she disturb those in the next rooms if she practiced her ukulele? To be among people again, in close quarters, required an adjustment. When she left Caergenog, placing Fogg in charge, he had insisted there was no such place as "away" these days, because of technology. But *this* seemed "away."

In about twelve hours, she'd see Duncan. How would he be? Angry? He had never been that way when they were together. But in their online exchange he was curt, mentioning coldly his wife, kids, job. When she requested a phone number for Humphrey, he told her to just come out there. Your father needs you. Not just a phone call.

Hours later, she awoke again, a different self on second rising, parting the hotel curtains on a different city, too: sunlight gleaming off skyscrapers, geometric patches of sky. It was Saturday, but in the offices across the street a few human shapes approached their desks, rubbing their faces as Windows started. In the hotel lobby, a brass revolving door swallowed Tooly, spat her into the metropolis, her entrance punctuated by doormen whistling for cabs and the bap-bap-bap of horns. She navigated without a map, knowing her way without knowing how, the topography within her still, though latent for more than a decade.

In her absence, New York had been invaded by cupcakes. Joggers ran barefoot now. Hipsters wore nerd glasses and beards. And walking had become an obstacle course, pedestrians inebriated on handheld devices, jostling one another as they passed, glancing up dimly at the shared world, then back into the bottomless depths projected from shining glass.

When she lived here, people were always lamenting how New York had changed, how Mayor Giuliani had cleansed Times Square of its gritty charm, turned it into a bland Disneyland. But the city had gentrified further since. Maybe it was just the experience of knowing New York over time, that it kept tidying up. Or perhaps it was the experience of living generally, that you hitched yourself to a particular period but places refused to remain anchored, jarring you at each reacquaintance.

She arrived at Grand Central for her 4 P.M. train, people fast-walking in all directions, an explosion of humanity with rolling bags. In Caergenog, the church parking lot would be full right now, Saturday-night drinkers at the Hook, ponies wandering the windy ridge. It would be dark up there, lights dotting the valley.

Upon her arrival in Stamford, she hesitated before the station exit, surprised at her nerves on seeing Duncan again. A silver BMW pulled up; the passenger door clicked open. He nodded at her. "Welcome to sunny Connecticut."

He'd become rather middle-aged: a hunch and a paunch, skin dull, eyes fatigued. She saw already the elderly man he would become, while the youth she'd known grew faint. "Jet-lagged?" he asked, glancing from Tooly to his lap, where he balanced an iPhone on one thigh, a blinking BlackBerry on the other. A notepad lay on the dashboard. She hadn't seen his handwriting in years. Architectural block letters on graph paper evoked him so powerfully—even more than the man himself, somehow.

Driving toward his home in Darien, he pointed out the sights: a pond where he'd ice-skated as a boy, plus the old Post Road, a stagecoach-mail route in the early years of the republic that now of-

fered SmartLipo, laser hair removal, and Bob's Unpainted Furniture
Gun Exchange.

Duncan was a partner at a Manhattan law firm now, head of a
household, and self-possessed as he'd endearingly not been when
younger. She perceived irony in the way he spoke to her, as if he'd
discussed her earlier, perhaps with his wife—had said that Tooly was
just so, and now before him she was proving exactly that. What had
Duncan said she was? A little false? A little untrustworthy?

He turned sharply into a driveway. "Home."

Before exiting, she said, "About tomorrow?"

"There'll be time to discuss that later," he said, getting out. "Meet
my family now."

"Sure. Of course." She took out four cellophane bags of wrapped
Swiss chocolates. "I brought presents for the youngsters. They each
get a bag, I thought, to avoid civil war."

"They'll explode if we let them eat all that," he said, struggling to
unlock the house door with a mobile phone in each hand. "May have
to take control myself."

"Will not, you thief. I'm handing them out now, and you're not
interfering."

"Three of them over there," he said, back-kicking the door shut and
nodding toward his seven-year-old identical triplets, who lay on an
Oriental rug in the living room, one bopping to huge white headphones, her genetic double playing a game on a smartphone, the third
goggling at an iPad. All three were dressed as fairies, in leotards with
gossamer wings.

"Abigail?" Tooly said. "Which is Abigail? Stand and identify
yourself—this is for you. Actually, doesn't matter who gets which.
Are you Chloë? And you're Madlen? Eat them fast, before your father
confiscates."

Each girl snatched a package and ran to the couch.

"Four candies each and save the rest for later," he said. "All right,
girls?"

The triplets settled cross-legged, picking through their respective hauls, wings quivering as they dug forearm-deep into crinkly cello-phane.

"And your boy?" Tooly asked, raising the final gift bag.

But Duncan was shouting upstairs for his wife. "Hail to the chief! Bridget!" No response. "Girls," he asked, "where's Mommy?"

They ignored him, gorging themselves.

"Bridget!" he shrieked, calling down to the basement now. "Bridge!"

"Mommy!" one of the triplets cried.

Another added, "Mom-my! You got uh vis-i-tuhhhh!"

Soon all were yelling. Houses with children—Tooly had forgotten about the shouting.

Chloë started dialing her phone.

"Honey," Duncan told her, "don't call Mommy. She's probably just studying upstairs."

That's where they found her, earbuds in, which explained her fright when Duncan tapped her shoulder. "Oh jeez, hi," she said, clasping her necklace. "Why didn't you tell me your guest got here?" She clipped back her dirty-blond hair, nudged up black-rimmed glasses, and offered a handshake. Tooly would never have put her with Dun-can. She was considerably taller, for a start. Not that this precluded a match, but it wasn't what you expected.

They found the eldest child, Keith (known as Mac), playing Kinec-timals on his Xbox 360 in the den. Whenever he moved, it controlled a cutesy puppy onscreen. Though, when you saw the eight-year-old falling on his back, then on his hind legs, it looked rather like the machine was doing the controlling.

"Seriously, Mac, isn't that kind of a baby game?" Duncan asked.

Chastened, the boy turned it off. Whereas the triplets had traces of Asia in their slender features, with long black hair swishing like pride-ful little ponies, Mac was a plump boy who shared his mother's pale Irish-German coloring.

"You didn't hear us calling?" Duncan said. "We were all calling."

Mac accepted his bag of chocolates and thanked Tooly, standing barefoot before her, his big toes crossed over each other.

"We're about to eat dinner," Duncan said. "You can try them after. Just be patient."

"Oh, let him have some," Bridget said.

Duncan counted out just two, then placed them on the table.

Dinner proved raucous, not just owing to the cross-purpose conversations but because of the laptops. Checking email was discouraged at mealtimes but—fortunately for Abigail, Chloë, and Madlen—there was no rule against playing Justin Bieber videos on YouTube. The triplets kept jumping from their seats and setting off new clips.

"Aren't there *nine* planets?" Duncan said. "Can someone Google that? Not with your knife and fork, Mac. You're getting sauce in the frickin' keyboard, man!"

"I'm not Googling. It's Wikipedia."

"How on earth," Bridget said, "did people find out stuff before Google?"

"The library?" her husband suggested.

"Like on iTunes," one of the triplets said.

"Not an iTunes library, Maddy," Duncan told her. "Like an *actual* library."

"Whatever, dork ass," she responded.

The family exploded into laughter, Duncan above all, and Madlen beamed, staring in red-faced delight at each adult in turn.

"Keyboard's filthy, you guys," Duncan said. "Let's try and not total that computer in, like, its first six months of life."

"How do you spell 'planets'?" Mac asked.

Bridget answered, "Like it sounds, honey: plan-ets."

Mac whispered those sounds to himself, typing each letter as if depressing a key might explode something. He read it back, looking to his mother: "P-L-A-N-I-T-S?"

"With an *e*," Duncan said. "She told you: plan-*ets*."

"An *e* where?"

"An *e* . . . aargh!" He dropped his spaghetti-spun fork and leaned over to type it himself. Aloud, Duncan skimmed the Wikipedia entry. "Only eight planets now? What the hell? When did that happen?"

Mac wandered away from the table.

"We're still eating, Mac."

Tooly helped clear the dishes and, on her second return trip to the kitchen, bumped into the triplets, who were taking turns licking the pasta scoop. "Can I try one of those chocolates I brought you?"

They stood before the fridge door, guarding their bags from her.

"Not even one?" Tooly remembered girls like this from school days—nasty little things in pretty little costumes. To be outfoxed by seven-year-olds again!

Bridget insisted on finishing the cleanup and dispatched Tooly and Duncan to the den, where he flipped among cable news channels.

She could have raised the matter of Humphrey again, but Duncan seemed intent on first asserting his current station in life, as if to efface how he'd been when she knew him. "So tell me more about what you do now," she said. "I know law, but what, exactly?"

"Transactional-slash-corporate."

"You slash corporations?"

"The corporations do the slashing. I'm their humble servant. Lots of preparing contracts, setting up stacks of paper for the business folks when they come in for their big meeting. When I'm in the middle of a major deal, I'll do like a hundred-hour week."

"You enjoy it?"

"I do, weirdly. Anything is interesting if you look at it long enough. The worst part is the people I'm hired to work for. Not unusual to get a call Friday afternoon from some jerk of twenty-three at a private equity fund going, 'Sorry, guy, but I need you to spend every minute of your weekend doing this. Need it on my desk nine A.M. Monday.'"

Bridget entered. "Is he moaning about making partner?" She patted his thigh, inadvertently knocking the BlackBerry between his legs.

He collected it, reading emails as he spoke: "So, I made partner on schedule in January, right? It's supposed to be the brass ring after eight years, okay? But now I'm getting shit on just as hard as I ever was.

Senior partners still telling me what to do. Haven't gotten a significant raise."

"What you're witnessing," Bridget said, "is the first time Duncan has been present on a weekend in four months."

"Oh dear," Tooly said. "Just as you guys get a break, I turn up and force you to host me."

"No, no. It's cool to have guests," she said. Bridget had also studied law at NYU, but hadn't worked as an attorney because of the kids. To her delight, she was about to start part-time at a firm on Wall Street, which explained her studying. "It's piecemeal to start—paid by the hour to sit in a room with a bunch of other contract attorneys, scrolling through a database of millions of emails. But they could order me to do photocopies and I'd be, like, 'How many?' Actual conversations with actual grown-up human beings again. Yay!"

Duncan switched to a different news channel. "Yes, yes," he muttered at the pundits. "Unsatisfied with ruining the economy, you dickweeds are now going to fix the world."

"He's not allowed to say things like that around people at work," Bridget explained. "Hence the ranting at home."

"Tragically accurate," Duncan said.

As they sat there, sipping Shiraz, bathed in the light of cable news, Tooly contemplated him. It seemed so improbable that their two bodies had ever had sex. How did people get to that stage, the clothes-pulling part? The whole endeavor struck her as absurd for a moment.

"What's the smile for?" he asked.

"Just thinking about your old place. With Xavi and Emerson."

"Right."

"And Ham the pig downstairs."

"Hmm." He returned his attention to the TV, evidently not wanting to discuss the old days.

They insisted that she stay overnight—it was late, and both McGrorys had drunk a bit much to drive her to the station. Duncan showed her to the basement suite, passing a workbench piled with dusty luggage and compact discs.

"Still big on music?" she asked.

"Oh, yeah," he said sarcastically, "I'm so cutting-edge that I learn about bands from my daughters."

Mac, who had followed them down to the basement, stared up at his father.

"How much do I have to pay you to get a repeat performance of 'Free Bird'?" Tooly asked Duncan, smiling.

"Not happening."

She clasped her hands pleadingly. "Just a bit? You have to! Your son needs to see this!"

Duncan shook his head gruffly, as if she'd done something offensive.

"What's 'Free Bird'?" Mac asked.

"Nothing, nothing."

The boy looked to Tooly, then back at his father.

"Seriously, Mac. Time for bed. No discussion."

The boy trudged upstairs.

"Now," Duncan said uneasily at the door to the suite, "before *you* go to bed, I should hear what you've been up to these years. You just vanished."

She had ample practice derailing such inquiries. But Duncan, having known a younger Tooly, retained access to that version of her. Plus, she'd eaten his food, drunk his wine, was staying in his basement. So she found herself summarizing the past eleven years. How, in her early twenties, she'd worked her way across America, taking all manner of short-term jobs: waitress, clerical, shop clerk. She spent a year in Chicago, three more on the West Coast, then traveled around Latin America, falling for each new place, poring over property sections in the local newspapers. Until, weeks later, she yearned to escape that place, and did. At one stage, she participated in a one-month expedition down the Amazon, but left when the man who'd invited her proclaimed one morning, "The sight of you making your tea, getting it just right, makes me want to pull my hair out. I'm sorry. I had to say it finally." She tried Europe, working briefly at an expat listings magazine in Paris, then went to Brussels, where she took a job at a souvenir shop and dated a Congolese musician. Next, she toured Spain alone, developing an ache she couldn't explain. At a flamenco hall in Seville, she met an Argentine woman and they spoke all night about books and travel. Afterward, as Tooly walked back to her hotel, tears came into her eyes. So, so lonely. In defiance, she hadn't met with the woman as planned, instead traveling onward to Portugal. She stood on a train platform in Lisbon one evening without any reading material, so picked up a scrunched literary journal whose articles were so dull that she perused the classifieds, happening upon one that stated, "Bookshop for Sale." She had been nearly thirty then—perhaps time to try something rooted.

"I get to read all day long," she said.

"Cool."

"You wouldn't say that if you saw my life—very *un*cool."

From professional habit, she ran her finger down a stack of glossy hardcovers on the workbench, each volume a recent doomsaying bestseller about the profligacy of a culture whose capitalist soul Duncan himself serviced. This was his "apocalypse porn," Duncan said. Nonfiction titles like *Age of Greed: The Triumph of Finance and the Decline of America; Collapse: How Societies Choose to Fail or Succeed; That Used to Be Us: How America Fell Behind in the World It Invented and How We Can Come Back.*

"They look unread," she noted.

"Delirium amazonus," he said. "I buy off Amazon in the middle of the night. Stuff turns up two days later and I'm, like, 'I'm not reading this!' Help yourself." He paused. "What's your number here, by the way?"

"How do you mean?"

"Your cellphone."

"I don't have one; I'm the last person on earth without."

"This must be rectified." He fetched an old mobile and charger they kept as a spare. "If you have a problem in the night, phone us upstairs."

"Thank you, Duncan, but I've been making it through the night without help since approximately age thirty."

"Feel free to call home or whatever. It's just a Nokia dumbphone, but it's got credit on it."

"Thank you. Very kind."

"The bed down here is squeaky, we were told by the last occupants."

"I'll get in and remain motionless."

"So," he said, standing taller, "before I go back upstairs, we need to touch on the big issue."

"Yes, absolutely, please. This mugging," she said. "What happened, exactly?"

"He doesn't even remember it, so we'll never know. To give you the background, I'd been dropping over to your dad's once in a while, just checking in on him. Sheepshead Bay is way the hell out there, and I was—"

"But wait. I still haven't heard the whole story of how you two know each other. You said you found him after I left New York?"

It was Xavi who had figured out where Tooly lived, from a marked-up map she had misplaced at their apartment. They'd trekked out to this street in Brooklyn near the Gowanus Expressway and found some old guy looking out the window. They waved for his attention, pressed the buzzer. Did he know where Tooly was? Was he a relative? Her father?

Yes, maybe he was her father, but who were they? They explained themselves, and Humphrey buzzed them in.

"So weird to think of you, him, and Xavi playing chess there," she said.

After that first meeting, Duncan went back alone, hoping to interrogate Humphrey. But he had no more success—the old man truly didn't know where she'd gone. When law school got crazy, Duncan quit looking. He met Bridget, and that helped. He graduated, passed the bar, joined Perella Transom Fife LLP, started a family, moved back to Connecticut, and never thought of this guy, the father of an ex-girlfriend. Until, one afternoon, they bumped into each other at a hospital. Duncan had been visiting someone there, while Humphrey had minor surgery scheduled. They spoke briefly, then the old man— mortified—asked a favor. The hospital required an emergency contact number. Could he use Duncan's?

"I was the only person he knew in the whole city to put down," Duncan said. "He honestly did not have one other number. A few days later, I'm at the hospital again. He's recovering from surgery, so I drop in. He promised that, once he got better, he'd take me for dinner. I said, 'Sure,' in the way that you do, not expecting people to follow through. After the operation, he actually calls me. Since he's too sore to travel, I drive down to where he'd moved in Sheepshead Bay. That's when I saw how he was living. You'll get a look tomorrow. After that, we kept in touch here and there."

"Incredibly nice of you. I know how busy you are."

"It was either me or nobody," he said pointedly. "Anyhow, I hardly ever went down there. But flash-forward to last year. I happened to be in Brooklyn one Saturday morning, so decided to drop in. I get there, and find your dad sitting in the stairwell of his building. He goes, 'They've taken everything!' He doesn't have his hearing aids in, so he can't hear me. I have no way of asking anything. He's got these marks on his throat like someone choked him. I get a piece of paper and pen, and write in big letters, 'What happened?' He looks up and goes, 'Your writing is terrible. You'll never get a job as a secretary.'"

She smiled sadly. That was Humphrey, all right.

Since the attack, he had declined. "I'm not saying he's lost it," Duncan specified. "Part of the problem is his hearing and his sight. That cuts him off. When a place is noisy, he can't hear properly, which he finds upsetting. He stays mostly at his apartment. Goes deep into himself. I need a fishing line to reel him back to the world."

"This is sounding way worse than you described in your messages. How is he even managing on his own?"

"There's a Russian woman I pay a few bucks to clean up, get his groceries, hang out with him most mornings."

"That's really generous of you."

"Basic decency," he said.

"And I guess they can talk Russian together."

"Didn't know your dad spoke Russian," he said. "I apologize, by the way, if I downplayed the situation. Just, this thing has consumed way too much time these last few months. My wife is upset, my kids are upset. I'll be honest: I was getting desperate. Tried everything to find you."

"How did you?"

"He mentioned how your actual first name is Matilda. I typed that in."

"With his last name."

"With Ostropoler, yeah," Duncan confirmed. "Sorry if you were trying to get away from him, but you need to be involved."

"Wasn't trying to get away."

"Well, sort of unusual not to talk to your dad for years, or even know where he was. Or him you."

This made her sound so callous. She wanted to justify herself. But that required saying too much about their own past. Neither wanted to get into that.

"Sometimes I used to tell Bridget—I'm not even kidding—I told her I was working late on a case and actually snuck to Sheepshead to check on him," he said. "It's like I was having an affair. I'm the only guy in the tristate area who cheats on his wife by visiting a man of eighty-three!"

"But he knows I'm here, right?" she said. "And he wants to see me?"

"Of course. And it should be fine." Duncan paused on the stairs, uncertain whether to say more. "But still," he warned her, "you might want to brace yourself."

# 1988

LUXURY CARS BLOCKED the entrance to King Chulalongkorn International School, engines snarling as a pair of sweat-soaked Thai guards checked credentials and pointed families toward the parking lots. The vast complex—elementary school, middle, and secondary, over acres of southeastern Bangkok—was on display for International Day, an annual celebration of the diversity of bankers, diplomats, journalists, shady expats, and spies rich enough to send their children here.

Once inside, the kids ran wild, unleashed by parents and yet to be harnessed by teachers, with classes not starting till the following week. Some had arrived in school uniform; others wore street clothing, with Izod Lacoste and Polo Ralph Lauren in abundance. Childhood hierarchies reasserted themselves, abandoned during summer and tweaked now according to the growth spurts, the arrival of new dweebs, the repatriation of schoolyard idols.

"Tooly?" Paul asked, as they waited outside the administrative offices for a tour. "Were you in those same clothes yesterday?"

She wore shorts from which her little legs jutted, one sport sock pulled high, the other at her ankle, deck shoes squashed at the back to allow entry without lacing, T-shirt specked with soup stains from the Chinese restaurant.

"You didn't wear that to bed, did you?"

"I don't think so."

He glanced around, assaulted by high-pitched shrieks everywhere. The children segregated themselves according to gender but, since this was elementary school, the boys' voices were just as shrill as the girls'.

"You don't smell, do you?"

Before she could answer, a young teacher with ginger hair approached across the open-air courtyard.

"Let me do the talking," Paul told Tooly, thrusting his left hand into his pocket, thinking better of it, wriggling it free, then pocketing it again, lip curling upward to catch a sweat droplet. "Don't draw attention. All right?"

Mr. Priddles smiled at each of them in turn, sandy eyelashes fluttering. He had been assigned to sell them on enrollment here, and led Paul and Tooly through the impressive facilities—playgrounds, band rooms, canteens, an aquatic center—describing the plethora of pursuits available.

They passed a pond with rainbow carp bulleting through the water, and Tooly paused. A tortoise stood at the pond's edge, looking at her. "Is he alive?"

"That's our new school pet, basically," Mr. Priddles told Paul, ignoring her. "We're running a competition to name it. Oh—excuse me, one sec." He hustled off to chasten a rowdy trio of second graders for running near the pond.

Entry forms were stacked by a ballot box, with a pencil hanging from a string. "What's a good name for a tortoise?" she asked Paul, picking up the pencil and chewing the end.

"Don't. That's not clean."

"What?"

He took the pencil. "Tim?"

"Who?"

"Tooly, pay attention. Naming the turtle: Tim."

She hesitated, disliking his suggestion but not wanting to reject it.

Two small boys bumped up against Paul, like a couple of waist-high mobsters. "What's the difference between a tortoise and a turtle?" one demanded.

Paul blinked. "Hmm, is it like the difference between a crocodile and an alligator?"

"Nooooooo!" the boy howled. "Tortoise has round shell and turtle has flat. Turtle has web feet and tortoise has normal. Bet you don't know how old tortoises get."

"Hmm, twenty?"

"Nooooooo! Tortoises live to, like, a hundred and fifty-five years old. Bet you don't know the difference between a typhoon and a hurricane."                .

"One is a strong wind and . . ." Paul speculated, plucking at pit stains forming on his shirt. "Or is that a hurricane? I didn't mean that. Is it . . . ?" He shut his eyes, rummaging for facts untouched in years.

The boys ran off.

"Is a typhoon where . . . ?" Paul opened his eyes, finding his interrogators gone, only Tooly before him, filling out her entry slip. He fumbled for his inhaler. "Children," he remarked, "they know facts about things. How do they *know* these things?"

"I don't know the difference between a hurricane and a thingy." She dropped her entry into the ballot box, having written "Jasper," which suited a tortoise. "Can I pick him up?"

"Who up?"

"The tortoise that doesn't have a name."

"We're not allowed, Tooly."

"Why not?"

"The teacher said." He'd said no such thing, but Paul often concocted regulations to bolster his authority.

When Mr. Priddles returned, he asked if Tooly wished to touch the animal. She did, and stroked its shell, tortoise limbs paddling slowly in air.

"Just one remaining issue, basically," Mr. Priddles said. "We received a dossier from her previous school in Australia, but it seems to be about a girl in ninth grade."

"Tooly's nine years old," Paul noted, "not in ninth grade."

"Yes, I realized when we spoke by phone. Alas, their error caused us to reserve her a place in ninth grade. We *do* welcome your daughter. Just not sure where to put her. Strict limit on class size and—"

"I'm starting fifth grade," Tooly interjected, fearful that someone's mistake might consign her to a class of teenagers doing algebra exams and cross-country running.

Mr. Priddles flashed her an artificial smile, then resumed his exchange with Paul. As the men spoke, she ventured in ever-larger circles around them, drifting farther from their orbit until she was able to spin through a doorway and out onto a playground, where she watched older girls playing volleyball. A teacher ordered them to the main field for the International Day festivities, and Tooly trailed a distance behind.

At each new school, in each new country, she presented a new personality. It crystallized during the first weeks of school, after which there was no changing—people wouldn't let you. In the end, you became what they expected you to be. At previous schools, she'd been diabolical, girly, a tomboy. But this time she had little urge to invent a new self, knowing it would be wiped away once they left. Even close friendships at her previous schools never lasted more than a few pen-pal letters after her departure, each note shorter than the last, until the responses stopped. It was just her and Paul; all else passed.

Among new children, she always spotted the outcasts first, and had read enough novels to prefer them. Sometimes this let her down— certain kids deserved social banishment. But hidden among the losers, she suspected, were her kind. What she longed for was a person who'd say, as none ever had, "This is all so fake, isn't it? Wink at me sometimes and it'll be our sign."

The main field lacked cover from the scorching sun, so parasols were out, hats were on, and hands shaded brows. Parents occupied the plastic seats before the temporary stage, while hundreds of children sat on the grass around them. Tooly scanned the crowd. She found Paul nowhere.

The principal, Mr. Cutter, tapped the microphone, exhorting the kids to simmer down and take a seat. Tooly knelt on the grass, layering hair over her face to block the sunlight. After a tedious welcome, the principal inaugurated the International Day parade, in which kids from the fifty-two countries represented at the school tromped across the stage in traditional outfits from their homelands, sweating under headdresses, tripping in curl-toed boots, stating into the malfunctioning microphone "Welcome!" in different mother tongues. The procession—every nation in alphabetical order to avoid charges of political favoritism—concluded with the lanky daughter of Zaire's ambassador, who whispered her greeting and scurried away.

Principal Cutter retook the microphone to announce the winner of the pet-naming contest. "After much discussion, we decided *not* to allow names of Teenage Mutant Ninja Turtles. Sorry, boys," he said. "Drum roll: our school pet for the year 1988-89 is henceforth known as . . ." He drew out the suspense. "Her name is . . . Myrtle the Turtle!"

"Myrtle?" snorted the parent of a losing entrant. "Are you kidding me?"

"A turtle?" another grumbled. "Isn't it a tortoise?"

"What's the difference?"

While this perplexing question rustled through the crowd, hundreds of kids scrambled for the picnic tables, aware that a potluck lunch was soon to materialize.

"Not all at once, you guys!" Principal Cutter said, to no avail.

Thai support staff distributed plastic plates and forks, paper napkins, bottled water. Many mothers and the occasional father opened Tupperware containers of homemade (maid-made) food across the tables. Tooly entered a queue at random and exited holding a plateful of parsley-flecked meatballs with spicy sauce for hats, the native dish of a country she never identified.

She weaved through the crowd, attempting to appear headed somewhere, then sneaked into a building, past an Olympic pool, through the girls' changing room, down a long hallway of lockers, passing a Thai janitor to whom she said hello, though he only looked down. The cafeteria was empty except for six boys younger than she, all boasting of disgusting food they'd eaten, including (they said) elephant and live snakes. One claimed to have eaten human being, though this turned out to be only his own toenails. At the presence of a girl, they fled.

Alone at the long refectory table, Tooly chased a slippery meatball around her plate, then parted her hair curtains and consulted the wall clock. A teacher had once told her that, viewed in the timespan of the universe, a human life lasts just a fraction of a fraction of a fraction of a second. Her life didn't feel like a fraction of a second; things took ages. Time may pass quickly for the universe, but she had never been a universe.

When she returned to the administrative offices, Paul had still not materialized. The secretaries paged him with no result, finally dispatching a search party of sixth graders. A Malaysian girl found him locked in one of the basketball courts. "Like a labyrinth in there," he muttered in the taxi home.

"I'm not in ninth grade now, am I?" Tooly asked.

"No, no—they'll find space in fourth or fifth."

"Fourth?" she exclaimed, looking at him. "Didn't I do most of that already?"

"Let's not make a fuss. There's not a huge difference."

But how could grades be compared? Each person you fought or befriended would be different, every teacher changed, your life unfolded in another way. Instead of escaping school after eight more years, she'd be sentenced to nine. An extra year of life wasted.

Being young was so unfair, and you couldn't leave. That was the difference between childhood and adulthood: children couldn't go; grown-ups could. Paul made them leave every year. Just packed up— another city. Whatever you hated disappeared.

She looked out the taxi window. "I only . . ."

He waited. "Finish your sentence, Tooly."

"They named the tortoise."

"What?"

"Tim," she lied.

"That was your suggestion," he said. "Good, Tooly."

"You thought of it."

"Well, it was our idea." He reached over to shake her hand. "Let's take it as a sign—this is the school for you."

CLASSES DIDN'T START till the following Monday, so Tooly found herself confined to the apartment again, though the live-in maid had now arrived. Previous housekeepers had been beloved friends to Tooly, so she greeted this woman with much optimism. Shelly was a Lao speaker from the northeast with a slight hunchback, possessing every skill required to endear herself to a Western household: she ironed flawlessly, kept purified water in the fridge, knew how to make spaghetti bolognese and to fry eggs, kept the floors sparkling, the surfaces dustless. Yet she proved a less-than-calming presence. When Paul or Tooly entered a room, Shelly bowed her head, pressed her palms together in the *wai* praying gesture, and hurried away as if someone had stamped at her.

To avoid provoking this distressing reaction, Tooly hid in her bedroom much of that first week, bounced on her bed, and read. When she needed food, she listened until the sounds of Shelly—the slop and slurp of rags squeezed into the water bucket, the scuff of flip-flops, her surprisingly sweet singing—had passed before darting into the kitchen to eat pomelo segments. When Tooly returned, her bed had been made, dirty clothes removed from the floor, pencils lined up on the dresser table beside her sketchbook of noses.

Minutes after Paul returned from work each evening, Shelly tinkled a brass bell in the living room, calling "sir and madam" to dinner. Tooly bounded from her room, and the maid ran away into the kitchen. During the meal, Paul studied software manuals or lists of birds. Tooly tried to think of something to say.

He looked up. "A man from the embassy invited himself over. He's considering a move around here and wants to see the building. I couldn't get out of it. He's here for dinner Wednesday."

"I can't come, can I?"

He shook his head.

But on the day of the dinner Paul tried to compensate by returning home early with a special treat for her, a videotape of *WrestleMania III*. Owing to a misapprehension, Paul believed her to be a pro-wrestling enthusiast. She was not. But Tooly couldn't find a way to say otherwise without disappointing him. So they spent hours watching the TV spectacles together, always with the sound off, since he considered the commentary biased.

"Can you remind me," he asked, slotting the tape into the VCR, "is George 'the Animal' Steele on André the Giant's side?"

"He isn't on anybody's side," she answered. "He's part animal and helps whoever he wants."

"Where's he from, Tooly?"

"Parts unknown."

They watched in silence, Paul wincing whenever a wrestler slammed a folding chair into the forehead of a rival. "It's said to be fake," he remarked. "What do you make of that whole controversy?"

"The whole what?"

"Do you think it's fake?"

She shook her head, watching the screen.

After a few bouts, Paul consulted his watch, rose, and strode to the television, depressing the knob with his kneecap, a scene of walloping pandemonium sucked into the center of the screen, leaving a white mark for a second, then glassy gray. "Nice?"

She nodded, thanked him, went to her room. Tooly was supposed to stay out of sight if ever he had visitors, but she left her door slightly ajar to eavesdrop.

The guest was a sun-leathered former U.S. marine with a blond mustache. Bob Burdett had fallen for Thailand eighteen years earlier when sent from the Vietnamese battlefront for seven days of R & R (rest and recreation) or, as the troops called it, I & I (intoxication and intercourse). After the war, he'd stuck around rather than return to Arkansas, and sought work at the U.S. Embassy. But foreign-service postings were above his pay grade, and, anyhow, lasted only two to three years; if they went longer, the theory went, American personnel risked identifying with the natives, an ailment known as clientitis. Anyone determined to remain long-term could always apply for a local-hire gig, which was what Bob Burdett had done, ending up as head of the car pool, a position with low status and low pay that reinforced his distaste for the Ivy League diplomats who sailed in and out every few years. "Don't suppose you got a beer for me?" he asked.

"Oh," Paul responded, glancing at Shelly—when it came to drinks, they kept only Fanta, milk, and water in the house. She dashed downstairs, returning breathlessly with six bottles of Singha as Paul concluded his abbreviated tour of the apartment, bypassing Tooly's room altogether.

Bob Burdett inquired into the building and its services, commented on the city and the characters at the embassy, mused on expatriate life in Bangkok. Most expats, he explained, fall prey to the three-year itch. "By which I mean hating the locals and bitching about the help—how you can't find a good mechanic, how everything's better back home, how people actually *work* stateside. Don't matter how good-intentioned folks are on arrival, they turn mean within three years. In my opinion? People are the same all over God's earth. Just the food is different."

As if on cue, Shelly entered with dinner. Conversation stopped, only scratches of cutlery on plates, Bob Burdett's beer bottle clunking on the table. "Might I ask that pretty maid of yours to kindly bring me another of them beers?" By dessert, he'd downed five, and either alcohol or tedium had turned his talk to politics. "Quite a situation back home, wouldn't you say?"

Paul murmured agreement.

"My concern is that we backslide," Bob Burdett continued. "We're a strong, prideful nation under Reagan. Like he told Mr. Gorbachev, the most important revolution in the history of mankind began with three words: 'We the people.' Don't need another Jimmy Carter apologizing for who we are. Without the United States of America, this world falls on dark times. The Europeans? They'd be talking German now, weren't for what our daddies done. Am I right? Same for the Koreans."

"The Koreans would be speaking German?"

"You drunk on Fanta, son? I'm saying that, without us, Korea would be nothing but a bad neighborhood of Red China today. That's what I'm saying."

"Okay, I see."

"I'm a student of history, and I can tell you one thing about these Soviets. You look at the great powers in history, you find there's only one way to defeat an evil empire: on the battlefield. The Spaniards and their empire? Brits knocked out the Armada, and that was it. Napoleon? Overextended in the Russia campaign. Ottomans? Beaten down in the Crimean War, finished off in the Balkans. Austro-Hungarians? Kaput because of the First World War. You eliminate evil through war, not peace. Trust me. I'm a marine, and nobody hates war more than a man who's seen it. But it's a fact. We overcome these Soviets with force. I'm telling you now, you'll hear all manner of hooey at the embassy about perestroika and glasnost. By God, I hear a lot of it. But now is the time to act. You strike when your adversary is weakened. That's right now. Can't sit around and wait for the Communists to build back up. Goddamn term limits—what we need is Reagan for four more years. You with me?"

"I don't know that much about—"

"Don't say you're voting Dukakis. Do not tell me that."

"Uhm, actually, I probably won't vote."

"Not for nobody?"

"Just, I haven't lived in America for so long now," Paul said, sniffing. "Seems wrong for me to pick who's in charge."

"Ain't you alone doing the picking, son—rest of us get a say, too! It don't matter how long you been overseas. We're always Americans, wherever we end up. And you'll move back sooner or later. Plus, I bet you go stateside pretty regular on home leaves."

"I don't really take home leave. I have too much work."

"Don't take it *ever*? Your momma and daddy back home, they don't mind?" he asked, adding hastily, "Excuse me—I'm assuming your folks are living. That's impertinent of me."

"No, they are."

"And they're good with that?"

Paul said nothing for a moment. "Actually," he said, "I heard some troubling news about my father's health a few days ago. Something serious. I . . ." He cleared his throat.

Tooly held her breath to hear better.

"He'll be in my prayers," Bob Burdett said. "That'll take you home quick, I guess."

"I've got things here. It's not possible right now."

They ate in silence.

"I never asked if you served," Bob Burdett remarked.

"Served?"

"The armed forces."

"I didn't really consider it, to be truthful."

"Where'd you go to college?"

"Berkeley."

"Hell's bells. You mixed up in them protests?"

"I was just studying computers."

"Guys studying computers can't be subversives?"

"I never really knew those people."

Bob Burdett slurped his beer. "Your housekeeper's a little cutey."

"Maybe don't say that so loud, please."

"Don't matter if she hears—probably likes it. You stay out here a while, son, you'll find everything's for sale in that department."

"I don't think that's true," Paul stated softly.

The conversation stalled; rain pattered outside.

"I was going to ask you," Paul resumed, as if working up to something crucial, "about the rainy season." He cleared his throat. "Do you know when it formally ends?"

"Formally?" Bob Burdett chuckled. "Not sure they got no official ceremony."

"Humidity's bad for my asthma."

"You picked the wrong city, son. All we got out here is humid. Maybe you ought to turn right round and go back to the U.S. of A.— except, kind of seems you don't like the place."

"What do you mean?"

"Heck, if my daddy was ailing and—"

"I have things I'm trying to deal with here," Paul said. "Doesn't matter what I'd *like* to do. This is what I *have* to do." He took a breath from his inhaler.

"Guess you got a real important job," the guest conceded. "That's top priority for people these days. I'm from another era. If my people were in need, I wouldn't be out here doing no car pool, I promise you that."

"It's . . . it's . . . it's not like I'm out here for fun," Paul said. "Okay?"

Tooly—hearing his unsteady voice, his dry mouth—clutched the hem of her T-shirt.

Bob Burdett persisted. "Maybe that's what they teach you in college: put yourself first. You can wait out here till your daddy's funeral, I guess. Or you not going home for that, even?"

"I have a *duty* to be here right now, and if I—"

"You don't know the first thing about duty. You don't care about your own blood. Don't care about your country. Don't know how you're going to vote. Don't know *if* you'll vote. Thank you kindly for supper. But, Lord above, what is wrong with you, son?"

"Nothing's the matter," Paul snapped. "Okay?" Tooly recognized from his tone that he'd lost his temper. He repeated himself shakily— "Nothing's the matter"—saying that he couldn't care *less* about voting, about politics, about empires, about who ran what, who succeeded Reagan, who led the Communists.

Bob Burdett reminded Paul to act like a representative of the United States out here, then recalled that his host wasn't an embassy officer, just a contractor. "Another mercenary," as he put it. "Going around for a paycheck and a piece of tail."

"Can you leave my home," Paul said, voice trembling, knocking over his chair as he stood. "Get out of my home. Okay? Scolding me like I'm an idiot! Like I'm here for a good time! This is my home. Not for you to come in and lecture. Any duties I have, I'm aware of. Fully aware of. Okay? I don't need you to tell me. What I do concerns nobody."

"Don't concern nobody?"

"Can you go, please?"

Bob Burdett's chair squeaked as he rose. "Sometimes," he said slowly, "there's things that are bigger than you in the world."

"Are you being threatening now?"

"Sometimes," the guest repeated, voice hardening, "there's things in life that's *bigger* than you."

There were smaller things, too, and one emerged from her bedroom.

"I can make my eyeballs vibrate," she said.

Bob Burdett—looming over Paul—turned at the sight of the little girl and stepped back, cocking his head. "Well," he said, "hello there, little lady. And who might you be?"

Paul, voice choked, answered hastily, "My daughter. She's my daughter."

"Well, howdy, little girl. Nobody told me we had young folk on the premises. Do excuse my profane words. I enjoy firing off the occasional political firecracker—keeps things lively out here in the tropics. No harm intended. None taken, I trust." He nodded at Paul, then smiled at Tooly. "Didn't hear me say no cuss words, did you, sweetheart?"

She looked at each man in turn, unsure if she was in big trouble. "I can make my eyes vibrate."

"I'd be most appreciative, young lady, if you'd provide a demonstration."

She opened them wide and performed her trick, eyeballs moving fast from side to side, to the approval of Bob Burdett. "I seen it all now," he exclaimed. "Yes, I have."

"And I can count a minute exactly," she said. "You can time me."

Bob Burdett readied the stopwatch function on his watch. "Go right ahead."

All fell quiet, but for the fizz of Fanta. Finally, she raised her finger.

"Fifty-eight seconds," Bob Burdett said.

"Sometimes I get it exactly."

"Darn good." He ruffled her hair, which made Paul wince. "You all should come around to my place sometime, meet my dog. This young lady's got a momma? Bring her, too."

"My wife's in America," Paul said. "She's busy at the moment."

Bob Burdett looked at Tooly. "You don't prefer staying there, with Momma?"

She glanced at Paul, then at the guest, then back at Paul.

"All righty, then," Bob Burdett said. "Thank you both for the hospitality. And your momma gets here, you all come over and meet Pluto."

"What kind is he?" Tooly asked.

"Good old mutt, like his daddy." He smiled thinly at Paul, broadly at Tooly, and left.

As soon as Paul and Tooly were alone, she asked, "Am I in trouble?"

He shushed her, hastening to the window to watch until the

guest had departed Gupta Mansions and could be seen walking up the *soi*. Paul closed his eyes, shook his head. "Damn," he said. "Damn."

"If your father's feeling sick," she ventured, "*should* we go there?"

"Yes," he shot back. "I should be there helping. Right now." He pinched his thigh. "But we can't go. And you know that."

TOOLY LOITERED OUTSIDE the building, seeking a pretext to return. She figured it out.

"I have a question," Tooly said, when Duncan opened his front door. "Can you introduce me to the pig?"

"Hey. You again."

"The one that lives here."

"Despite appearances, no pig lives in my actual apartment." Though studying, Duncan welcomed any distraction from case law. Plus, he rarely had female company, and tended to do whatever it commanded.

He also happened to know the animal's owner, Gilbert Lerallu, having provided advice in his dispute with city authorities over whether the Vietnamese potbellied pig, Ham, should be defined as "livestock" and thus banned from residential premises. Gilbert was a composer of harpsichord music, his latest self-released album, *Moon-harps*, having sold eight copies worldwide, including those purchased by his aunts. They tried his door.

Taking a walk was entirely Ham's decision, according to Gilbert. Since the pig failed to communicate opposition, they borrowed a leash and led the porker outside. It was near freezing. Duncan wore only a hooded Eddie Bauer sweatshirt, but insisted he was fine. Ham's bristly back steamed. When Tooly touched the pig's nose, he snorted—and prompted her to hop back in fright and pleasure.

They crossed the Columbia campus, the snuffly pig waddling between them, his snout beaded with condensation. The neighborhood had never acclimatized to this swine in its midst, so students stared as

Ham promenaded past Low Library. Duncan seemed at a loss for what to say, their only common reference being her previous visit. They'd talked for a while then, and with seeming freedom, yet she had revealed nearly nothing. "Is walking a pig different from walking a dog?" he said finally. "Do you think?"

"I have the impression Ham wouldn't fetch like a dog."

"Would he sit?"

"Sit!" she commanded.

Duncan looked at her—indeed, he appeared the more likely to obey. They tried other commands and, upon reaching Riverside Park, toyed with taking Ham off his leash to let him run free, as were several dogs, a couple of which sniffed the air near the swine, then bolted.

"Maybe let's keep him on the leash for now."

They resumed their walk. He asked what had brought her to these parts again. "I thought you were passing through town."

"I'm passing through again."

Before he could pursue this, Tooly had questions of her own. As a method of self-concealment, hers was powerful: few people, when presented with the possibility of discussing themselves, preferred to hear of another. From sincere curiosity, she asked him about law school. "I imagine everyone doing mock court cases where you stand up and cross-examine hostile witnesses, and they deny being there on the night of the murder."

"That has not been part of the curriculum," he said, shivering, hood up, the cords yanked tight, leaving a pale oval of face peeping out. Law school, as he told it, was largely a matter of poring over judicial opinions. "Basically, you read these things without any understanding of what the topic is, or why it's relevant. Then it all boils down to one exam. And those grades determine a hundred percent of what you do for the rest of your life."

"Sounds highly stressy."

"It is highly stressy."

"Are the teachers horrible?"

"Depends. A lot never practiced law—law schools don't like to sully themselves with professors who've done stuff. It's like most of these professional schools—a matter of paying your fees and surviving. We're not learning how to practice law," he concluded. "We're learning how to be lawyers."

As for which legal discipline to pursue, he was leaning toward something noble, because the NYU do-gooder ethic pushed students that way. Public defender was a possibility. Still, he wasn't sure. If you had brains, they said, you did international corporate law.

He shuddered so intensely that she undid her duffle coat and draped it over his shoulders, forcing her residual warmth onto him. Duncan objected weakly while trying not to look directly at her figure, now more evident without the coat. He fastened his attention elsewhere—tree bark, the pig, a fence—then found her, head cocked, looking directly at him, smiling. "Nice and bracing," she said. They remained there for a minute, breath clouds alternating, his gradually synchronizing with hers.

He tried further questions, asking where she was from, noting her odd way of talking, inquiring about her age. Tooly gave her birth date, which surprised him—he'd taken her for older. His other queries she dodged, which punctured the exchange and left them in silence till they reached his building. This time, Tooly wasn't talking her way in; to do so twice would look suspicious.

"Well, I should go," she said, touching his hand, which was cold and fettered with the leash. She took back her coat, stooped to pat Ham, and strolled off. At the corner of Amsterdam Avenue, she glanced back, catching sight of him struggling to push the pig toward the building. Ham remained doggedly, or perhaps piggedly, in place. Amused, she turned away.

But Tooly did not complete her pivot on that icy sidewalk.

Her legs kicked up, her arms flailed, her behind slammed into the concrete. Rather than springing gracefully to her feet, she waited, her breaths dissolving upward, backgrounded by the nimbus of a streetlamp.

A pig snout entered this tableau.

"You okay?" Duncan asked breathlessly, having run over.

"I'm broken for life."

"Seriously?"

"Not seriously. I'll just have a purple bruise that, when I try to admire it in the mirror later, will be too far around to see."

The pig sat on her.

"Argh!" she said, laughing. "Crushing me!"

Minutes later, Tooly was inside his room, just as she'd planned.

Duncan dropped a compact disc onto the tray of his stereo, which swallowed the album and sighed to life. "I'm obsessed with this song right now," he said.

She closed her eyes to appear appreciative, but had a long-standing aversion to music, dating back to school days. When she looked up, Tooly found herself being observed and turned away—shyness still caught her out sometimes. "Can't figure what he's saying," she said, sipping a beer Duncan had pilfered from the shared fridge. "Is it 'Comma—please arrest that girl'? Seems a bit extreme to imprison her for using a comma."

"It's 'Karma police/Arrest this man.'"

"No way. And even if, in the most crazy of situations, you were right—"

"We can check the liner notes."

"Don't. I hate ruining my opinions with facts. Even if your version is right, what's it mean? It's madness!"

He smiled, began to say something, then went for another disc, stacking CDs on the stereo, finger hovering above the Play button. She let him beaver away there with his cueing and reviewing, and kicked off her Converse, sitting cross-legged on his unmade single bed. The space looked so different. Perhaps it was the effect of sitting here, viewing everything from the inside, rather than as she'd met this place, peering in.

He kept starting tracks, promising they'd be amazing, then losing confidence and switching discs. To her, some songs sounded pointy and others round. When Duncan discussed music it was by reeling off band names, singers, guitarists—legends to him, nobody to her.

What occupied Tooly was not the sounds but the sight of his animation. He wobbled his head, mouthing lyrics that he lacked the courage to sing aloud, telling her, "You need to hear it a bunch of times before you get into this. It's this bit here—listen. Where the drums kick in? Whenever I hear that, it's . . ." Anticipation thrilled him: to know what neared, the chorus approaching, almost there, and then—yes! He spun to look at her, eyes warm.

How did this boy see her? For that matter, how was she this time? With any new man, Tooly exhibited a self slightly different from that presented to the previous guy (not that there had been so many). She found herself inhabiting a new character, uncertain whether this edition was more or less true, and whether there was a pure state of Tooly-ness at all. Even when alone, she wasn't sure what she was like.

Given her lack of musical knowledge, Duncan wanted to burn her a mix CD. However, she had no compact-disc player at home. There was a radio at her apartment, but with a tape recorder?

"I'll do you a cassette. But you have to tell me what you're into."

The only music she knew was from parties, jukeboxes at bars, muzak in stores. She never remembered the name of anything. "I used to like the *Ghostbusters* song." He took this as a joke, though it hadn't been.

Tooly gave a little shiver. "Now *I'm* getting a bit cold." She lifted his hooded sweatshirt from the floor. "Would it be okay?"

"No prob. Go for it," he answered, bashful at the implied intimacy, looking hard at his stereo.

She slipped it on, excused herself to the bathroom, and drew his wallet from the kangaroo pocket—she'd noticed him stowing it there when they were outside. Tooly read his college ID, the Connecticut driver's license, his credit cards. She wasn't taking them. Stolen goods were shabby, like walking around with evidence against yourself. But information had worth, held invisibly in your head—provided you could memorize long numbers. To Venn's chagrin, she wrote things down. "Hey," she said on her return to Duncan's room. "You have a pen I could borrow?"

"Got tons." He opened a box, inadvertently spewing ballpoint pens everywhere. He scrambled around on all fours, collecting them off the floor. "I'm an idiot. Sorry."

His shame punctured her. She watched a moment, then took off his hoodie and folded it in his closet, the wallet inside.

"Why'd you need a pen?"

"Just to write down the song names."

"I can do that. If you're into it, I can put down notes on each band."

"Actually, I should go." No point sticking around. Yes, anyone could be mined, but not everyone should be.

He looked up, spurned. "You don't want your tape?"

She sat on his bed, sipping his roommates' beers, while Duncan toiled. Making a mixtape took longer than expected, particularly when its creator believed that each track implied something and that the compilation as a whole contained greater meaning still, the entirety of himself distilled onto a ninety-minute Maxell XLII. Tooly grew tipsier and sleepier and chillier, dipping her feet under his duvet, then pulling it up to her knees, her waist, finally drawing the covers to her chin.

She awoke in darkness, a sheet over her nose quivering as she breathed. She recalled a song ending but none replacing it, lights turning off, covers shifting. The two of them remained fully dressed, chastely back-to-back, he compressed into a gentlemanly sliver of mattress against the nightstand. She blew the sheet away, swallowed dryly, and gazed at the ceiling. The room was boiling now, radiator pipe hissing snakishly.

She got out and stood in the apartment corridor. Voices came from the room of the student she hadn't met yet, Emerson, who was bickering with his girlfriend. All was dark save a thread of light under Xavi's door, a rustle of textbook pages, the squeak of highlighter pen. Was *he* worth looking into? Just kids here. Tooly looked through a window at the street—how forbidding her cold walk home. She touched her behind, bruised from the choreographed crash landing on the pavement, and sneaked back under the covers, pulling herself close to him.

The next morning, she found a cavernous hollow under the sheet where Duncan had been. He tiptoed back into the room, hair wet, patting his jean pockets, readying for class. "Time I got up," she said, pushing off the covers, only to pull them back. "When do you leave?"

"Well, my class is at Vanderbilt," he said, thinking aloud. "I'll need to take the one or the nine train down to Christopher Street, so . . . out of here in nineteen minutes."

"I'll be gone in eighteen."

"I dreamt someone arrested me," he said.

"It's about time someone arrested you. Hey, when's your class start?"

"Ten."

"You've got ages!"

"Do you even know what time it is?"

"No. But I think you're too late for it anyway—they're starting without you. You should come back under the covers. It's cozier than the subway."

"Can't."

"It's an emergency."

He hesitated, then pulled off his dress shoes and slipped in beside her, sticking to his side of the bed, one foot touching the floor. She sat up, leaning the point of her elbow into her pillow, and considered Duncan. She reached her hand toward him. He started, embarrassed by his own surprise when she flattened her palm across his cheek.

The strangeness of other people—so solid when near; alive, but objects, too. This close, his features lost detail, absorbed in fuzziness. A sensation rose in her, a surge outward and a crush in, a need to push him away, pull him back, to rush to the window and throw her clothes onto frosty 115th Street, leap naked back into the bed, goosebumped and shivering. Instead, she held still.

This time she left with plans to meet again, and with his number, too, which she'd add to her phone book.

"What's yours?"

"Don't know," she said. "I'm moving and don't have my new line yet."

"Moving where?"

"To be decided," she said, twitching her nose at him.

His lips parted, but he didn't ask more.


Back home in Brooklyn, she took a nap, weary after a night in that cramped single bed. When she awoke, a hush had fallen, the storage space trembling as an overloaded truck rumbled down the Gowanus Expressway. Humphrey entered her room with a cup of instant coffee, a trail of brown drops specking the concrete floor all the way back to the kitchen.

She sat up and took the mug with thanks. No need to explain her overnight absence—he covered his ears if she alluded to romances. Humphrey declined to acknowledge her transition from little girl to grown woman, still treating her as he had when she was young: like his comrade and intellectual equal. Anything else was private. Which was fine, since she preferred to keep sexuality to herself, persisting with the neutered fashions—mothball-scented men's clothing and boyish sneakers—that she'd adopted in early adolescence. By now, these outfits made her comfortable; a dress was unthinkable.

"What is your name again?" Humphrey asked, sitting at the foot of her mattress.

"Tooly."

"Who you are?"

"Shut up," she said, smiling.

"You remind me of Leibniz."

"Of who?"

"German philosopher from years 1700 and after. He has messy haircut like you also, and dies after foot stuck in avocado."

"How do you die from an avocado?"

"If you cannot understand, I'd rather don't explain. If you are not intellectual, is not my business."

She shut her eyes, entertained, then stood right there on the mattress, stretched her arms toward the ceiling, squeaked. "I walked a pig today," she said. "Or yesterday. When is it now?"

"Tomorrow. Now go wash," he told her. "I have items to discuss."

She knew this ruse well. He wanted company, had been lonely overnight without her, probably waiting up till after midnight, listening for the door. They had lodged together for years, sharing homes in a dozen cities. The cause of each move had been Venn. Abruptly, he'd be leaving town and invited Tooly to meet him a few weeks later in his next city (best not to travel all together). Humphrey liked to accompany her, no matter how this complicated matters—all his books to ship! In some cities, Tooly met up daily with Venn, and was his companion, confidant, ally. He even cooked for her sometimes, or took her out with his associates, guys who would otherwise have snubbed her but whom he silenced to let her speak. He and she might walk for miles, people-watching and kidding around—such vivid periods, those were, that days passed and she read not a word. At other times, it was just Humphrey for weeks.

She showered and, given the late hour, got right into her pajamas. Humphrey awaited her at the Ping-Pong table, the right pocket of his slacks stuffed with balls to save himself stooping when one bounced away—if any shot required rapid movement, he called it "out."

"It's not out just because you don't bother returning it, Humph."

"If not then," he asked, "when?"

But after just two points he put down his paddle and returned to the couch. "We need to go somewhere else."

"Go where?"

"We go somewhere civilized together. Why," he continued, "we must follow Venn always?"

"What would you and me do," she teased, "if we went our own way?"

"Like now: items and activities."

"Ping-Pong, reading, and chess?"

"What more there is in life?"

"And where, even if we had money?"

He looked at his shoes.

"Come on, Humph. Don't get mad at me."

"This is most stupid thing."

"What is?"

He found no cause for anger, so became low. "Don't be exasperate with me." Humphrey toed his way through heaps of reading material, picking up decrepit works and dumping them on the couch. He sat heavily, books leaping from his impact and landing open, as if waking with a start. Fingers laced over his belly, he turned to her. "Sit, sit."

She was on the verge of doing so when he raised his hand with alarm. "You nearly sit on John Stuart Mill!"

She removed the volume by this esteemed gentleman, then plopped herself on whosoever happened to have the misfortune to remain under the shadow of her bruised backside. "Don't care if it's Plato or Aristotle."

"Is not my fault you are not intellectual," he lamented, and handed her a copy of the closest book to hand, *The World of Yesterday* by Stefan Zweig.

Since they met more than a decade earlier, Humphrey had supplied her with books in this random fashion. Works on the Bronze Age, the cosmos, the First World War, the Renaissance, Greek myths, the race to build the atom bomb, Roman emperors, Voltaire and Locke, Muhammad Ali and David Niven, architecture, diaries of the infamous, gambling scams, economics, Groucho Marx. They passed thousands of hours pleasantly page-turning together, he determining which facts and mystifications were to constitute her education.

Only one form of book did Humphrey disdain: made-up stories. The world was far more fascinating than anyone could imagine. In made-up stories, he contended, life narrowed into a single tale with a single protagonist, which only encouraged self-regard. In real life, there was no protagonist. "Whose story? Is this my story, with my start and finish, and you are supporting character? Or this is your story, Tooly, and I am extra? Or does story belong to your grandmother? Or your great-grandson, maybe? And this is all just preface?"

"I'm not having kids."

"Sure you are. And then whose story? Your grandson's? Even what we say now, this is only background to his story, maybe. What about that? No, no, no—there is no hero. There is only consciousness and oblivion. Nothing means anything."

"Nothing?"

"Be afraid of people who say there is meaning from life. Meaning only comes when there is ending."

"I don't agree with that."

"Because you read too many tall stories when you are short girl. You believe things end in beauty. You think loose strings tie up."

"Not necessarily." She stretched out on the couch, stuffing her socked feet under him for warmth. "Did you talk to anyone yet today?"

"Many persons."

"Who?"

"John Stuart Mill, for example. Also Jean-Jacques Rousseau. Maybe you hear of them?"

"I don't count dead philosophers. And before you tell me those aren't philosophers but eighteenth-century thinkers, then—"

"John Stuart Mill not even born till nineteenth century, darlink."

"Did you talk *out loud* to anyone today?"

"I talk to you now. Are you not counting as twentieth-century thinker?"

"Not sure I qualify as a great thinker of the twentieth century, no."

"Whatever century you are not a thinker in, I talk to you. Satisfied?"

She grabbed him around the middle. He fought weakly to escape, Ping-Pong balls popping from his pockets, bouncing everywhere. "How long cuddling must last?"

"Torture, is it?" She knew herself to be the last person on earth who still embraced this musty old man. She gave him a peck on the cheek.

"Incredible what I put up with around here," he grumbled. "I wouldn't believe, if I did not see it with my own ears." He looked at her. "Tooly, I must tell you serious items."

"Items and activities?"

"Stop teasing. I have things to say."

"About?"

"About . . ." He stood unsteadily, turned as if caged, took his seat.

The history of Humphrey was a convoluted one. In certain accounts that she had heard, he'd escaped the Soviet Union as a young man and left his parents behind, never to see them again. But in another story he was playing poker with his father, mysteriously present in South Africa. Confusing the situation were myths that circulated: that he'd lived in China and worked for Mao (too industrious to be credible); that he'd been a croupier in Macao (surely not—his arithmetic was abysmal); that he'd dealt in stolen penicillin in postwar Vienna (he did seem to know a lot about pharmaceuticals); that he was privately rich (no evidence of this); that he was destitute (ample signs); that he was a Jewish aristocrat whose Mitteleuropa family had lost everything in the war (there was nothing aristocratic about the man).

According to Humphrey himself, he grew up in Leningrad in the 1930s, in a secular Russian-Jewish family. Like most Soviet citizens, they suffered appalling privation during World War II. However, wartime constituted something of a gap in his tale. One of his chess friends when they lived in Marseille, a rabbi who'd served two years in prison on a charge of money laundering for a Colombian drug cartel, once asked Tooly what sort of war Humphrey had had. "He's a Jewish person from Europe," the rabbi noted. "He's the right age. In my community, you often don't know what sort of a war they had till after they die. Then someone mentions something at the funeral."

But Humphrey had not suffered the worst horrors of that period, had certainly never been in a Nazi camp. He said dryly, "I did not have privilege of going through Hitler holocaust." Whatever *had* happened, he remained after the war in the Soviet Union, where he grew to adulthood with increasing disenchantment toward the government, his wisecracking ultimately leading to a stint in jail. Subsequently, he escaped the USSR, ending up in South Africa after a fool advised him to stow away on the wrong ship. This young intellectual of the Russian-Jewish tradition found himself at the southern tip of Africa, surrounded by the dim-witted cruelty of the apartheid regime. He couldn't stand it, so left, and traveled the world. Uprooted, transient, and with the wrong mother tongue, he never achieved much. As Humphrey put it, he'd been "cornered by history." That is, his youthful intent to consort with the Great Thinkers had been destroyed by the idiocy of his era.

"I must talk to you," he reiterated. He found a near-empty bottle of vodka in the freezer, emptied the last drops into a wineglass, inhaled its fumes. At the Ping-Pong table, he bounced a ball.

"Well, talk."

"You think I joking," he said, and downed his vodka. "But I am worry. Something can happen to you. Very soon."

"Yes, yes, I know—disaster if we don't run off together."

Humphrey fetched the empty vodka bottle, miming as if to wring it for another drop. He drank modestly—rarely more than a single shot—and disdained drunkenness, which he considered the domain of trivial beings. Today, however, he needed another slug, so ventured into the Brooklyn night for more vodka. "When I come back," he pledged, "I have important items to tell you."

"I'm on tenterhooks."

"You don't going anywhere."

"Won't."

Minutes later, the buzzer rang—he must have forgotten his keys.

But it was a woman whose voice crackled over the intercom. "Hel-loooo! Anybody there?"

Amazing: she just followed them, wherever in the world they went.

"Ahoy," Tooly answered, and held down the button to spring the building door.

Regally, Sarah Pastore entered, kissing Tooly on the head and embracing her with a rub of the back, after which she twirled her cherry-red dyed hair, piling it up, then letting it cascade down her back. She pointed to her right cheek, directing Tooly to plant a peck into the bull's-eye center, which she did. "Cute as ever," Sarah said, sizing up Tooly.

The same was not true of Sarah. She was a worn forty-two, her proportions out of proportion, bony nose almost manly, the fedora self-consciously eccentric now rather than sexy. For years, she'd been an eternal twentysomething. Now Tooly had reached that decade herself and inadvertently chased Sarah from it.

"How long's this stopover?" Tooly asked, and placed another kiss on Sarah's cheek, more firmly now, as if to impress there the affection she struggled to summon.

"Tra-la-LA-la, DEE-DUM. Tra-la-LA-la, DEE-DUM," Sarah sang, striding away to explore this latest abode. "Who can say?" Sarah was a recurrent feature of their lives, residing with Tooly and Humphrey for spells, even traveling with them. But months could pass without word of her. Then Venn took pity, apprised her of their latest whereabouts—and there she was.

"What brings you this time?"

Sarah sang, "Happy birthday to you/Squashed tomatoes and stew/You look like a monkey/And you smell like one, too." She took out a cigarette. "You're turning twenty-one soon."

"I'm aware."

"Where's Rumpledstiltskin?"

"Out buying supplies."

"And everyone else?" By this she meant Venn. "Don't know why, but the birthday song has been tra-la-LA-la-DEE-DUMing in my head ever since I was at this department store on Madison and Sixty-first. What's that place, the expensive one?"

"No idea," Tooly said. "My clothes originate from a slightly lower class of shop."

"You know what we'll do?" she said, taking Tooly by the wrists. "Go on a shopping spree. Your birthday present from me. Shall we?"

"But *paying* for things, please."

"Of course paying for things. What are you even talking about?" She considered Tooly's outfit: pajamas with a motif of racehorses, collar buttoned to the top, dressing gown. "It's a crime to leave you to your own devices. In pajamas at—what time is it?"

"Yes, what time *is* it?"

"But you're lucky," Sarah said, scrutinizing Tooly like a car tire. "With that shape, you could wear anything. Bitch."

Tooly twisted away. "So could you."

Sarah walked to the back window, surveying the unedifying view: vehicle lights inching along the expressway. "Beautiful winter's night," she said, running her finger along the windowsill, across the wall, across the kitchen cupboard. "Love your new place." She righted a toppled chess piece, pawed without interest at periodicals and books on the couch, organizing them into piles, then entered Tooly's bedroom, plucking a sweater off the floor. "Where do you *find* this stuff? The Salvation Army?"

"Yes."

Sarah gave a false smile, sustained by impatient muscles. "Was thinking the other day of the ice bar. And my Honda Dream. Remember that big cop?"

"You were cool as a cucumber."

"Oh, hooray! How nice to hear."

Sarah cited old times to affirm their bond, as if shared events united people, regardless of the content. Yet the occurrences Sarah cited were not exactly those that had taken place. Hers was a record of merriment and constancy, populated by heroes and villains, rather than the ambiguous blurs that others constituted. She erased scenes, especially disasters precipitated by her mistakes, attributing those to enemies, a growing army as years passed. If someone disputed these accounts, dark clouds formed in her eyes. Venn alone baldly refuted her claims and survived. But Sarah herself barely made it through such exchanges, taking his comments like so many stabs.

By now Tooly was less interested in the statements than in the person before her, who had once been so mesmerizing, a scintillating woman in a world composed largely of men. How often Tooly had wished for Sarah to swoop in like this and spirit her off for an adventure that—at the time—seemed the pinnacle of sophistication. Buzzing around some Mediterranean city on the back of a motor scooter, attending parties in Prague, learning Sarah's postural rules of attraction: you know a man is attracted if he turns his body *toward* you when passing in a narrow corridor; if he studies your face when you speak, though you are looking elsewhere; or if he stands straighter as you approach. The prospects for any affair, Sarah stated, were all in the degree to which the male slouched.

How captivating Sarah had been. Yet whenever Tooly had most longed for her company was when Sarah proved most elusive. She would turn up promising adventure, then be gone by nightfall. It happened in Jakarta, after Sarah traveled in on the same flight as Tooly and Humphrey, only to disappear at the airport. Then she'd joined them in Amsterdam, with the emotional pull-push that became the hallmark of her dealings with Tooly. In Malta and Cyprus that summer, she sought to transform the teenage girl into a mini-Sarah. But when she found them in Athens she gave Tooly the cold shoulder for two weeks. In Milan, Tooly witnessed Sarah snorting cocaine for the first time, and heard incessantly about her turbulent relations with a married millionaire. She and Sarah clashed in Budapest, made up in Prague. The woman had exploded in rage in Hamburg, smashed a window with her little hammer and stormed out, then located them months later in Marseille, as if nothing had happened.

For years, Tooly's opinion of Sarah had swung between adulation and contempt. But recently had Tooly recognized her mistake: all these comings and goings, of which she had long believed herself the principal object, concerned her only peripherally. Sarah returned for Venn, sought a pretext to be with him, even though he had rejected her years before. Each time Sarah failed anew, she shifted her attention to Tooly, meddling with the girl to bother Venn, knowing how close they were.

Today, she talked and talked. Tooly shut her eyes, concealing the thoughts behind them.

"What?" Sarah asked. "What's funny?"

"Nothing's funny," she answered, shaking her head. "Just thinking."

"See, you're the same—still laughing at life! That's what's extraordinary about people. Nobody changes! At heart, everyone's the same at eight as at eighty."

Tooly nodded as if this were surely true (though surely it was not). Abruptly, Sarah switched rails, careening into a convoluted account of misfortunes that, by no fault of her own, had led here. "And when I went in—this will stun you—they'd taken everything. Changed the locks even, pricks."

"So how did you get in at all?"

"I didn't. I told you—they changed the locks."

"So how'd you know they took everything?"

"You haven't met these people," she responded. "I'm telling you, the woman is psychotic. You don't realize how things are in that part of the world. People will take you into the forest, machete you, and sell you for bush meat. The police are corrupt. You have no recourse. I was told—you're not going to believe this—I was told they'd put me in prison (imagine a prison *there*!) for up to six years. I'd not even done anything. It's enough to make you . . . No?" A classic end to a Sarah story: she, unjustly cast out, mistreated, slandered. Amazingly, she believed what she said, which became truer by repetition. But to claim victimhood again and again without seeming a fool obliged her to depict humanity as increasingly malign. Needfully, her worldview darkened year after year.

Sarah's latest plan was to move to Rome and reconquer a city abandoned a half century earlier by her father, a former Fascist now long dead. There was a leather-goods store that belonged to an Italian friend, Valter, a married accountant whom she'd often mocked because he loved her. Sarah had an eye for fashion, she said, so would run the place. "Best part is you're coming with me! You'll be my assistant. Aren't you excited? You're almost twenty-one now. Time to move on. You'll fly back with me, agreed?"

"Sarah, I'm not luggage."

"What a thing to say! I'm trying to help you. Came all this way for you."

"I'm fine here."

"Well, never say I didn't have your best interests at heart. Okay? Anyway, I'm staying a few days."

"I need to check with Humph."

"Check what?"

"Just let him know you want to stay."

"You've got a huge mattress—there's not space for me for a couple of days? Remember when we used to share your tent? Seriously, I don't see why you're making a big deal of this. Are you trying to humiliate me?"

"No, Sarah. Last thing I want." Tooly reached for her, was pushed away, then placed her hand on Sarah's upper arm, stroked it, as if soothing an animal.

"You're so happy to see me!" Sarah said. "How cute!"

Tooly had spent so many years adjusting to the storms of Sarah that the habit of tranquilizing her overpowered the wish not to. To break the pattern, Tooly stepped away and rested her hand on the kitchen counter. Sarah placed hers atop, nails blood red.

"You all right?" Tooly asked.

"I'm fine." She cleared her throat. "God, I don't know." At times like this, verging on the confessional, she evoked an aging actor before the dressing-room mirror, regarding the sagging vacancy. There *was* vulnerability in Sarah.

"I hope," she said. "I hope that bitch gets her comeuppance. I really do."

Tooly had lost track of all the bitches, found no need to seek clarification on this one, another among the legions opposing Sarah. And it was partly true. The world did thwart her, but not because it conspired to that end. Obstacles materialized because they did for all. Her paranoia was a form of egoism, that merciful failure of the imagination. But the truth of her condition was worse: nobody plotted against her because nobody thought of her at all.

"How happy you were when I saved you!" Sarah said.

"How do you mean?"

"In Bangkok, when I saved you." Sarah perceived the flicker of irritation. "Oh, come on—don't act like you're still loyal to Paul."

"Anyway," Tooly said.

A bang came from the door downstairs.

"Probably Humph," Tooly said. "I'll go check." She hastened downstairs, frigid air rushing in from the open door.

"Hello, darlink," Humphrey said. "You come out in pajamas? I would not believe it, if I do not hear it with my own eyes."

She leaned in to whisper, "The empress is back."

His expression transformed to disappointment, then annoyance. "I have to talk to you about important things," he said. "Why empress is coming now? She is staying?"

"Seems so."

He stared miserably.

Sarah opened the apartment door. "Talking about me?"

"No, no," Tooly said.

"Liar."

In the following days, Sarah rarely left, reading fashion magazines purloined from nearby stores. She was short on money, until a wire transfer came from Valter in Italy. After this, she vanished into a bar on Hoyt Street, finding overnight lodgings with the younger men carousing there, followed by awkward scenes in the morning when they said versions of "Gotta run to work; mind leaving?" Sarah returned to the apartment, where Humphrey hid behind his books, and she chain-smoked at the window overlooking the expressway, waiting for Venn to call.

# 2011

THE BOOKSHOP WAS CLOSED on Sundays, so when Tooly phoned from Connecticut, intending only to test her borrowed cellphone on a familiar number, she expected no answer.

"World's End," Fogg said.

"Oh," she responded, "you're not supposed to pick up."

"Isn't that the custom when these things make noise?"

"Why are you at work today?"

"Not really working, to be fair. Just popped my head in to see everything's in order."

"Very conscientious of you. But, sorry, I should go. This isn't my cellphone and I was only—"

"You'll be chuffed to hear I did the Honesty Barrel this morning even though it's Sunday," he said. "I'm admiring it through the window as we speak—a thing of beauty. No rain this morning. There are miracles, yes, even in Wales. What's the time by you? Middle of the afternoon in America, is it?"

"It's six here."

"Is that tomorrow morning? Or yesterday evening?"

"It's six in the morning. And it's today."

"It may *feel* like today to you. But you're still in yesterday."

"Fogg—we're on the same day, you nut. It's Sunday in both places."

"Can't take a joke now you're in America. And what on earth are you doing awake at six o'clock on a Sunday morning, if you don't mind me asking?"

"That's when I get up."

"Don't believe a word of it. It'll be the jet lag. I'd like to try that one time—nice bit of jet lag on a holiday to America."

"I'd happily trade places," she said. "And this isn't a holiday. Actually, I miss the shop."

"Shop didn't say a word about you."

"I'm slightly surprised that you haven't burned it down yet."

"Burning's not scheduled till Thursday, I'm afraid."

"Fogg," she said, "aren't you at all impressed that I'm calling you with a mobile phone?"

"I can barely contain myself. Utterly jubilant. You'll be ringing on a daily basis now. I'll be a bag of nerves." He took down her number and provided his own in case of emergencies. In the background, the bell above the shop door tinkled.

"Customer?"

"Probably wanting directions. Yesterday was beyond busy—three people came in," he said. "Well, should be off and deal with this."

"You've become disconcertingly attentive."

Children's footsteps thundered above her—Duncan's triplets awake and running across the floor.

"I should go myself," she said.

Tooly took an early train into Manhattan to allow the McGrory family a little time together. She attempted to rest at the hotel but was too anxious, running through her questions for Humphrey, shaky to know that answers were hours away now. To expel tension, she set forth on the long hike to south Brooklyn.

Her walk took hours, yet she arrived in Sheepshead Bay early, so continued onward to the Russian enclave of Brighton Beach, wandering down its main avenue, shadowed by the elevated-train platform. Whenever subway carriages clattered overhead, sunlight strobed over the street-level nail parlors, clothing wholesalers, bankruptcy consultants. Side streets provided distant glimpses of sand—this was as far south as Brooklyn went before hitting ocean. Along the boardwalk, stubby seniors in wraparound shades gripped radios that crackled in Russian. The Atlantic sloshed now and then.

To prepare her, Duncan had insisted on meeting a few minutes beforehand. "We have to be punctual," he informed her, locking his BMW outside the Sheepshead Bay station. "Your dad gets agitated if people are late, thinks he's got the time wrong."

"This apartment he lives in—you said it's not great, right?"

"Well, the building got attention in the local press when a couple of Uzbek guys there were arrested for playing tennis with a mouse."

"That's horrendous."

"It's a weird place. You'll see."

Graffiti covered the glass entrance door, spray paint having run in long streaks under each tag. Duncan punched a code into the digital access pad and shouldered inside, finding a nervous Chinese man who'd just emerged from an apartment, key still in lock. The man said, "No, no," waving them away.

They climbed the winding staircase, passing grimy windows that overlooked the street from ever-higher aspects: cars, then electrical poles, then rooftops. The floor got dirtier as they went, litter every-where, an abandoned kiddie bike with training wheels, a broken um-brella, cigar ash.

The place she shared with Humphrey in Brooklyn a decade earlier had been run-down, as had Duncan's apartment share on 115th Street. But they'd all been passing through; the squalor was transitory. Here no one was going on to better things. They were staying and rotting. It was a flophouse, one person to a room, shared bathroom at the end of each floor, communal kitchen at the other. Most of the inhabitants were men, jobless, addicted, ill. "Your dad has been here a few years now. I thought you should see it," Duncan said, as if she deserved a little guilt for this.

Many of the gun-metal doors were dented, as if kicked repeatedly. A torn Tigres del Norte poster hung from one. Another was open, a fat shirtless man with a hair net seated in a deck chair, chewing his hand. From other rooms, conversation emerged in various languages along with the pungent scent of food. "This is him. Door's always open. I tell him to lock it, but you know what he's like."

"Should we knock?"

Duncan just pushed in. The door hit an obstacle but he squeezed past, disappearing from sight. Tooly, who hesitated in the hall, heard him asking, "Did I wake you?"

In response came, "Hmm?"

Tooly turned her back, closed her eyes, heart pounding.

Duncan called to her, "You coming in?"

The door was impeded by a white leather armchair. She turned sideways to edge in, and saw first the back of Humphrey's head, then his rheumy eyes. The room contained a bed piled with documents and books, a window with blinds down, a small television on a chest of drawers, a bar fridge, microwave, and sink, above which hung graph paper with Duncan's distinctive handwriting: TURN OFF TAP! Around the room, he had posted further exhortations: LOCK DOOR AT NIGHT!; TOILET PAPER IN DRAWER! A stench, like spoiled stew and floral air spray, filled the room.

"He just woke up," Duncan said.

Humphrey scowled, tangled white eyebrows overhanging his lids, face like a walnut shell. He wore a red sweatshirt and oversized bluejeans—she'd never seen him in leisurewear and it looked wrong, as if he'd been dressed by someone else. He had lost weight, too, his jeans cinched with a rope. Duncan raised the blinds. Humphrey gripped his chair, arms shaking from exertion as he pushed himself to his feet.

"Humphrey," she said. "Hello."

He blinked, the heavy sacks under his eyes quivering.

"I walked all the way here from Manhattan," she went on. "I know you disapprove of physical exercise, but I enjoyed it. Was thinking on the way down that I should've brought you some smashed potatoes."

He shuffled past her, arm outstretched to feel his route, overgrown yellowing fingernails ticking against the wall. He stumbled on a book, which made her and Duncan lurch forward. But he was fine. Lips pursing, slackening, he turned to Duncan, stating softly, "Go out."

"You want a moment alone with Tooly?"

"Have *her* go out. I want her to leave the room. Now, please."

Tooly went rigid, not just at his statement but at how he delivered it. The man she had known was Russian. This old man—it looked like the same person; surely, it was him—spoke as if English were his native tongue. She looked to Duncan, then to Humphrey.

She hastened around the armchair and into the hallway, closing his door behind her. From inside came muffled voices. What, what, what was going on here?

A neighbor burst from her room, shouting "Fuckin' *told* you!" and flung before her two little boys, then slammed the door, leaving them in the hall. Giggling maniacally, the brothers—the elder about eleven—pounded on the door for their mother, rattled the handle, screamed for a few minutes, ran at it with karate kicks, looking over at Tooly to see if she was impressed.

"We've all been thrown out," she told them. From inside their mother's apartment, music boomed. The older boy sprinted up the corridor, spat at the closed windowpane. The younger kid lay on the floor, finger up his nose, staring at Tooly.

Duncan opened the door. "You can come back now."

Humphrey had changed into a collared shirt, which was tucked into his roped jeans, and he'd put on a tie. His hearing aids were in now and he wore bifocals, whose lenses split his clouded old eyes across the middle.

"Is there somewhere I should sit?" she said, watching Humphrey. "I'm not sure where to go. It's a bit cramped."

He pointed to the armchair, but she declined—that seemed to be his seat, the white leather darkened in his smudged shadow. Duncan sat on the edge of the bed, so she did the same. Shaking, Humphrey lowered himself into his chair, curled forward, chin against tie, hands compressed between his thighs, as if bracing for a punch.

"We woke him. Waking is always difficult," Duncan told Tooly, who nodded brusquely, hating to discuss someone who sat across from them. "Yelena was here this morning," he said, of the Russian woman who was paid to help out.

"I don't recall."

"Did you enjoy your lunch?"

"Didn't have any."

"There's a pizza box in the sink."

Humphrey turned to consider the evidence. "Yes, some pizza. Wasn't good, which is why I didn't remember it."

Tooly tried to catch his eye, to inquire with a glance, What the hell is going on?

"I didn't offer you coffee yet," he said.

Tooly stood to make it, but the jar of Nescafé was empty.

"Was telling Tooly," Duncan said, "that waking can be difficult for you."

"Feels strange," Humphrey said. "Apprehension. But not about anything. If you fear something concrete, you can do something about it. But I don't know what I feel frightened of."

"His vascular system isn't working properly," Duncan continued. "That's what the memory-clinic guy told us. His brain doesn't get the blood it needs."

"I don't want to exaggerate the problem," Humphrey said. "It's uneven. It depends on what cells are attacked."

"You must be happy to see your daughter."

Humphrey grunted, laughed uncomfortably.

"I heard that someone robbed you," Tooly said, looking at him hard, though he failed to meet her gaze.

"I was told I was robbed. Don't remember any of it. Attempts were made to strangle me. This is where my problem stems from, I think."

"The attack seems to have affected his memory," Duncan said. "Short-term, particularly. But there are other problems. He forgets how to do stuff."

"I don't want to exaggerate," Humphrey said. "It depends on what cells are attacked. Blood doesn't flow in that direction."

"What sorts of things are you forgetting, Humphrey?"

"I can't remember to tell you."

"Sometimes you come up with ancient memories," Duncan remarked. "You told me about milking a cow when you were a boy, which must have been eighty years ago. You remember?"

Humphrey remained silent at length, sniffed irritably. "I find your questions odd, frankly."

"I have a feeling you gave those muggers a punch or two," Duncan said. "Didn't you. He's a tough one, is Humphrey."

"If only I could get the bastards on their own for a few minutes," Humphrey said, adding, "with someone holding them down, of course."

Duncan laughed. "The problem is that he's isolated here. Which doesn't help."

"I don't know these people around me. Don't know who they are. It's a lack of community."

"At least you have Yelena coming in," Duncan said.

"Yes, but we're like grandfather and granddaughter. Not friends," he said. "I haven't offered you coffee. I have a thing of it somewhere."

"We're fine," Tooly said.

Nevertheless, Humphrey rose agonizingly to his feet again, muttering about people moving things, and tossed aside piles of clothing and books. He found the empty Nescafé jar.

Duncan whispered to Tooly, "I need to go. But you stay."

"Let me walk you down," she said.

For the first time, Humphrey looked directly at her. "I put on my tie because you were coming."

"I know."

On the street, Duncan asked how it had felt seeing her dad, and hoped that their falling-out, whatever its cause—"None of my business," he added, not wanting to know—had been shelved.

"I found," she said, needing to smuggle this in before he went, "I found that harrowing."

"Yup. Well . . ." he responded, wanting to hand over this problem.

"But, Duncan, you shouldn't be the one paying for Yelena," she said. "You've been too generous already."

"Hey—I'm a lawyer," he said, unlocking the BMW.

"Being a lawyer means you pay? Doesn't being a lawyer mean everybody else pays?"

"Means I'm richer than book persons such as yourself." On his notepad, he wrote the door code to Humphrey's building and tore off the sheet. "Let him recharge a few minutes, then you can go back."

However, she kept walking, unable to return yet. All the time she'd known Humphrey, he'd scarcely spoken a correct sentence in English. Had he been tricking her for years? But what she'd seen upstairs clearly wasn't a trick. Hard to imagine that Venn could be involved. If only she'd remained unaware of all this, never witnessed that wretched room where at this moment he probably sat, slumped forward in that dirty white armchair.

The room was messier on her return—clothes dumped, books scattered. It was evening now, but the blinds remained up. He stared at the darkened window, house lights dotting the view.

"Me," she said, shutting the door. At the shudder of its closure, he turned, sloshing a glass of vodka in his hand.

"Don't need to shout." He failed to orient toward her voice.

"Why are you looking over there?"

He swiveled uncertainly.

"Humphrey? Can you see me? Point to where I am right now."

"I don't like tests," he said. "I keep my chair here behind the door. When people come in, they have to stand in front of me, and the outside light makes a shadow around them. But it's too dark now." He spoke to her midriff. "Some people were here before."

"Me and Duncan."

"Was that yesterday?"

"Today."

He harrumphed, unconvinced, and moved the vodka glass to his lips, puckering to meet the splash of liquid, which dribbled down his chin.

"You're enjoying that," she said.

"I intend to drink myself into oblivion."

"Don't say that."

"There's no point in staying. Nothing anybody can do."

"I didn't come here to help you." She sat on his bed, watching him. "In some ways, Humph, you *seem* like you used to. But you talk . . . Maybe it was a joke or something. I'm—were you pretending before? I mean, it was *years* that we knew each other. But this is you talking now, right?"

He sipped his drink.

"So," she asked, "where are you actually from?"

"Me?"

"Who else is in this room? Yes, you."

He shook his head.

"You're not going to say? Why not?" she asked. "How many times did you tell me how you'd been 'cornered by history,' that you would have been some great intellectual but your era had ruined everything? That was crap, I guess. Thanks."

"I'd tell you," he said. "But something blocks it out, blots it out. Things that I know very well. These blanks in my memory."

"How am I supposed to believe this?"

His attention roamed. "Can I offer you a coffee? I have a thing of it somewhere."

She held up a full container of Nescafé that she had bought while outside.

"Yes, that's the one," he said.

Tooly excused herself to the communal bathroom down the hall. A fluorescent beam flickered in there. A hole had been kicked in the wall under the hand dryer, baring dusty pipes and insulation. Residents had thrown trash in there: a used tampon, an empty bottle of white rum. She entered a toilet stall, its door hanging by one hinge, a bloated cigarette bobbing in the bowl.

When she got back, Humphrey was making instant coffee using water from the faucet.

"Wait, wait. Isn't there a kettle?"

He shook off the question, handing her a lukewarm mug.

She stepped toward the bed, inadvertently toppling a stack of books. "Reminds me of my shop in here. But you had way more books than this. What happened to your collection?"

He shrugged.

"You still read all day long?"

"My eyes don't work. Someone got me a magnifier with a light on it. Makes no difference. I can't hold things. Something wrong with my hands."

"You don't read *at all*?"

He frowned in disgrace.

"But, Humphrey," she asked urgently, "can you talk to me honestly?"

"How do you mean?"

"First, where's Venn? Do you know?"

"What are you talking about?"

"I haven't heard from him in eleven years now. It makes no sense," she said. "I'd assume he didn't want anything to do with me. But even after everything fell apart in New York he kept helping me. Remember the bank card?"

After parting from Venn, she had used that "magic bank card" only in emergencies, considering it his money. Each time she spent from that account, the balance jumped back up. When the card expired after five years, a replacement arrived at her then-address, an apartment in Caracas—even from afar, Venn was looking out for her. Thereafter, she spent token amounts in every city she visited, so he'd always know her location. Eventually, the balance stopped bouncing back. And when that second card was to expire no replacement came. To safeguard his money, she used the balance to buy an asset: her business. When he returned, she'd sell it and repay his loan. Except that the value of World's End had only diminished these past two years.

In any case, Venn never appeared. Had something befallen him? Was he in trouble somewhere and needed her? "Seriously," she said. "You have to explain. Starting from Bangkok. I was too young to understand it then. And I never wanted to discuss what happened with Paul. But I think about all of that now. A lot." She looked at him. "Humphrey?"

He shifted in his armchair, flustered. He ought to understand what she wanted—he recognized that much.

"Are you and Venn in contact still?" she asked.

He had no answers. She kept asking but he kept failing, growing increasingly distressed.

They sat in silence for a minute. No point humiliating him.

"I own a bookshop now," she said.

"Did I make you coffee yet?"

She prepared it this time, taking their mugs to the stinking communal kitchen, where she scrubbed an aluminum pot left by another resident and boiled water. When she delivered his steaming mug, he perked up, took it from her, splashing coffee on his hands, though not seeming to register pain. "Sometimes I get sugar from the kitchen," he said. With difficulty—how unsteady he'd become—Humphrey led her back, directing her to a box of sugar with a spoon sticking out. The sugar was crawling, ants marching up and down.

"That's infested, Humph."

"It's not mine," he replied, serving into his coffee a heaping spoonful of wriggling black-and-white sugar.

"Humph! Don't!"

He gulped a fast sip, beaming, by far the jolliest she'd seen him, and went for another scoop.

"Wait." Gritting herself, she flicked off ants, adding a clear spoonful to his coffee, stirring.

He sipped, compressed his rubbery lips, exhaled—"Marvelous! Absolutely delicious and delightful!"—then gulped the rest in two swallows. He plunked his mug on the kitchen counter, eagerly accepting her offer of another, which he drained while the coffee still scalded, his words emerging in steam: "Oh, I like you."

"You approve of my coffee-making?"

"I like you as a person, as a human being. I quite love and adore you."

"Don't say that."

"I've known you a long time."

"A long time *ago*," she corrected him.

"Was it?"

"Remember all the crazy stuff you taught me when I was small? Saying there was that explorer who got kidnapped in the jungle and the natives put ice cream on the soles of his feet, then brought in a goat to lick it off—the worst torture ever invented. I used to lie in my tent thinking of goats."

"No, no," he scoffed, though he appeared pleased to have concocted such bunkum. "If you like, you can tell me things I did. There are parts I don't recall. You can tell me what happened."

"What happened when?"

"What I did."

"In your life? Humphrey, I have almost no idea."

"But I thought we knew each other."

"I came here so *you* could tell me things. Not the other way around. And I'm not your daughter, and you know that, so stop telling Duncan that."

He bowed his head.

"Is this just a game, Humph? I can't tell if this is real now."

"Nothing, not even dictionaries, can tell you what anything means," he said. "The reality of things is just sad, for the most part."

"What do you mean?"

On he went, speaking as the snow-blind stumble downhill. She struggled to follow his course, her eyes tightening till she gave in, led him back to his room, her arm tensed behind him in case he stumbled.

"I'll fetch you dinner, get it ready, then take off. Okay?"

But he wanted no food, nor help getting into bed.

"Anything I have to do before leaving?"

Humphrey sat in his chair, staring at the dark window, as if he'd flipped the CLOSED sign over himself and there was no further business that day. She made her way around him, and glanced back. This was to be her last sight of this old friend: a tuft of cotton-wool hair above the back of the armchair. She closed the door, stood in the hallway, hand on the knob.

Tooly hastened down Voorhies Avenue, heading not for the subway but south toward the water. She yearned for one of her exhausting hill walks, without intersections or pedestrians. The best she could do was the Brighton Beach boardwalk.

It was dark at this hour, perhaps dangerous. Someone could rob or assault her. Neither scared her right then; neither seemed possible, distracted as she was. Anyway, she had nothing for anyone to take. Except, she recalled, Duncan's spare mobile phone. She held it by her side, ready to fling it into the sand if anyone menacing approached.

Tooly made it safely to the Coney Island end and back, striding fast to the edge of Manhattan Beach, where she stopped, listening to the lapping ocean in the dark. Had someone asked where on the planet she was, she'd have required a moment to respond. Wind flicked her hair. The tide pushed a lip of foam up the beach.

Her hand lit up and a voice came from it. She raised the phone to her ear.

"What's the whooshing?"

"Why are you on my cell?" she responded.

"You just called me," Fogg said.

"Did not."

"I promise you."

"Must've hit speed dial by mistake. Sorry."

"What's that whooshing?" he repeated.

"I'm at the beach."

"Living the high life," he said enviously. "On the beach, drinking margaritas."

"What time is it there, Fogg?"

"Where? Here?"

"Yes, there. I know what time it is where I am."

"To be brutally honest, Tooly, I don't even know."

"Thank you for being brutally honest about that."

"I'm a night owl," he informed her. "Still, can't say I'm accustomed to many calls at this hour. Makes me feel right important."

"Glad to hear it."

"Now," he said, "what can I do for you?"

"Nothing—this is a mistake call."

"Shall we end it, then?"

She said nothing for an instant. "I need to fly back."

"You only just got there."

"I know, but . . ." To explain required telling him more. She offered an abridged version of the truth. That the old man here was not her father. That, as a girl, she'd been taken from home. That she wasn't sure why. She cringed to say this—her past cohered so poorly. All she heard was inconsistencies, blank patches, and the questions surely occurring to Fogg now: What had become of her parents? And these people who'd brought her up—who were they?

"This old man is one of them that raised you?"

"To say Humphrey raised me is—well, he did a bit. But a strange sort of upbringing. I never asked him to. I don't owe him anything."

"You sound a bit upset about it."

"Not upset. I had just hoped he would help me. But he can't, so I should go. I feel sorry for Duncan. But if he wants to be rid of this situation he has to let Humphrey manage on his own," she concluded. "I don't know. What do you think?"

"Sounds a little harsh, in truth."

"I know. But I came here to figure stuff out. And I—"

"Who else could help?"

"Who else could explain this? Nobody I'm in touch with anymore."

"Have you searched online?"

"These aren't people you find on the Internet. And I've tried," she added. "We never registered for anything, never signed in anywhere. If you saw my phone book from back then, you'd get a sense. Page after page of scratched-out numbers—we never stayed anyplace, nor did anyone we knew."

"Why not try calling a few of the old numbers?"

"First, I didn't bring that phone book here. Second, I'm on a borrowed cellphone and can't do endless long-distance. Third, those numbers are ancient, Fogg. This was long before mobiles—back when there still was such a thing as 'away.' Speaking of which, I need to get off this line."

"Is your phone book at the shop?"

"No, it's in the attic."

"I could try a few numbers for you."

"I'm not having you cold-call random people from my past."

"I wouldn't mind."

"Fogg, it's pointless. The only person in there who's relevant is someone I'm *not* dealing with. If I trusted her to say anything useful, I'd have tried ages ago."

"Go on—give us a name."

"Even if you got her, she's never saying anything by phone. And I'm not taking a pilgrimage to wherever she is now. She'd make me, for sure. Keep in mind that whatever I spend on travel comes straight out of World's End—you know that, right? Its funds are mine. If I go broke, that's it for the shop. This isn't worth it."

But that was untrue. The mere prospect of meeting someone from that time had already brought her rushing out here. And this visit with Humphrey—even speaking aloud the name Venn again—had stirred up such disquiet, all the puzzles as upsetting as ever. And Sarah had been there for all of it.

"Let's find the lady," Fogg proposed. "Then you can decide what's to be done."

"You must be enjoying it alone," Tooly said. "Doing everything you can to keep me away."

"Not at all," he said. "Only, it's a bit of a mystery story now."

# 1988

PAUL PARTED HER bedroom curtains, then shook Tooly's hand to bid her good morning. At 6 A.M., she moved like a confused snail, but there was no time to dawdle. The school microbus arrived soon outside Gupta Mansions, trawling the expat warrens of Sukhumvit for students lacking chauffeured cars. Even at this hour, traffic was thick: sooty vans piled with rice sacks, green-and-orange taxis, motorbikes twisting through the gridlock. She rested against the bus window, contemplating the weird city inching past.

The teachers at King Chulalongkorn International School were much like her previous ones. There were the gentle and the spiteful; those who gazed out classroom windows muttering about years till retirement; those who believed themselves capable of transforming each child—of being the one whom every pupil would remember.

Her fourth-grade homeroom teacher was Mr. Priddles, who'd given Tooly and Paul their school tour and then had snapped her up for his class—at least until a spot opened up in fifth grade. She had completed this level of coursework before, he reasoned, which promised high marks, an elevated class average, and better prospects for his second consecutive Teacher of the Year award.

Mr. Priddles—a thirtyish Englishman with trendy denim shirts and gelled ginger hair—was adored by his pupils, which made Tooly's a lonely and secret loathing. Part of his popularity came from playing a ghetto blaster during class and having the kids transcribe pop lyrics. "It's about engaging with the written word," he said. "Two poems written a hundred years apart, yeah? Both are poetry. One is not better. To say that someone called W. B. Yeats is 'better' than someone called Sting is a construct, basically."

Each day, Tooly arrived praying that a fifth grader had left—that someone's dad had become president of somewhere, they'd flown home, and she could escape her horrible class. Yet inwardly she doubted her readiness even for fourth grade. Much of each class, she sat awed by the knowledge rattling around in other kids' heads and absent in hers. To conceal her incompetence, she rarely spoke, which led the other pupils to deem her stuck-up and perhaps smelly.

"Take out a piece of paper, everybody," Mr. Priddles said. "Time to kick butt, guys!"

The much anticipated writing test was today, producing the first marks of the term—critical to establishing Mr. Priddles's early lead in the Teacher of the Year race. The subject was "The Old Days," and the kids could write on any period—the objectives were legible handwriting, orthodox spelling, complete sentences. Tooly could provide none of these, for she had forgotten paper. She whispered to the boy behind her.

"You want to *borrow* some?" he responded. "Or you want to *keep* it? If you *borrow* it, you have to give it back. Or you want to *keep* it?"

"Can I have a piece?"

"*Can* you? Or *may* you?"

Tooly glanced around for someone else to ask.

Mr. Priddles intervened, asking the boy, "*May* she have a piece of paper, Roger?"

"She may," the little pedant replied, handing it to the teacher.

"Now, then," Mr. Priddles said, holding the sheet out of Tooly's reach. "Say, 'Pretty please.'"

"Please."

"Not to me. To him. Pretty please."

Softly, she did so.

Mr. Priddles lay down her reward, one sheet of paper. "Now what do you say?"

She hesitated, looked up. "Thank you?"

"Do you mean that?"

"Yes."

"Very good, then." He left her to work.

Tooly stared at the blank page. Each time she raised her pencil over it, her fingers trembled. Why was she even here? And why did everyone love Mr. Priddles when he was so obviously horrible? Was she the only one who noticed this? She looked at the others writing, then back at her sheet. Several times, she tried to imagine the old days, yet the present days kept intruding.

"Time's nearly up!" Mr. Priddles said eventually. "Finish up, cowboys and cowgirls. One minute, then hand them in."

She had written nothing. Everyone else was getting up. Panicking, Tooly joined the mob crushing toward the front, slipped her blank page among theirs, and escaped into the hall.

The next day, she stood before the principal, insisting that she *had* handed in her work. It must've gotten lost. They knew she was lying and told her so. Tooly reiterated her predicament: she wasn't even supposed to be in this grade. Please.

"Maybe that *is* the problem," Principal Cutter acknowledged. "Maybe you *have* been in the wrong grade."

Tooly's despondency switched to excitement. Someone was listening! He placed a few calls and, minutes later, she had a new homeroom teacher, the affable Miss Fowler. In third grade.

Tooly pinched her stomach, saying nothing as she left the office. She had to do *two years* of her life over now.

After a week in third grade, Tooly was offered the chance to repeat her writing test under the supervision of a parent. If she performed at a superior level, the principal would consider—just consider—fifth grade, where a space had opened up.

Paul set the allotted twenty minutes on his digital watch, found her a pencil and paper, and started the countdown. Although she had an uncanny ability to know the length of one minute, Tooly suffered an equal inability to estimate longer periods: they stretched infinitely, then ended all of a sudden. Paul called time and lifted away her sheet, though her work was unchecked, uncorrected, incomplete. She hadn't written one-third of what she'd planned to say about the old days.

"I didn't get to the end."

"We can't cheat."

"Just to put some small things in? Please?"

"They said only twenty minutes."

Tooly lay on her bed, listening to the computer in Paul's bedroom whirring and blipping as he began work for the evening. She crept back into the living room, drew her assignment from his briefcase, and resumed writing, continuing for nearly forty minutes, terrorized by the possibility of his return. One last time, she read over her essay. It was perfect:

# Intrduction

People led a very different life from us in the Old Days. They did not travel alot because of the bad conditions. They had no radios telephones or any other means of communication. They had no television so they saw plays or listened to music instead. The punishments were very hard and cruel. Their clothing was very different from ours. The rich ladies wore beatiful colorful dresses and lovely hats. The poor had less clothes.

People were tougher and noisier than we are now they were quick to lagh and sing but also quick to quarrel and fight.

They were fearful of wichcraft, but respectful of others of higher rank.

They were usually married at 14 yrs, or there about, middle aged at 30 yrs, and not many lived to an old age.

They made cheese. Alot of fruit ~~was grown~~ was grown especially apples and cherries. The rich and powerful land owners siezed the common land and fenced it in as their own.

People liked to have their houses decrated beautifuly with carvings. They also liked attrative chimneys. Not all houses were made of wood. Infact many of them were made of brick.

The sailors who manned ships in the Old Days lived a hard and often dangerous life. Their ships were small and cramped. The men lived in front of the ship which was damp and like the rest of the ship infested with rats.

A woman who nagged her husband was tied to a ducking-stool and ducked in a pond or river. She could also have a scold's bridle put on her head. In the bridle was a piece of iron which was fastened across her tounge and kept it still.

## THE END.

She counted the paragraphs—eight, the most she'd done in one go. She slipped the test back into Paul's briefcase. The following morning, he stuffed it into an envelope and signed his name over the sealed flap, sending it with her to school. Tooly handed it in, jittery with excitement.

That evening, Principal Cutter telephoned her home to give the result. She handed the receiver to Paul and ran into her room. After he'd hung up, Tooly rushed back, heart pounding, to learn the grown-ups' verdict on her life. "Did he say I can go in fifth?"

Paul collected his binoculars. As a special occasion, he said, they were going to look for birdlife at Lumpini Park.

In the early-evening heat, he gazed up at the trees, as she gazed up at him in agony. "Keep your eyes out for bulbuls and bee-eaters," he said. "You hear that? That was a coppersmith barbet." He directed Tooly to a leaking hose, at which a blue-winged pitta drank.

Paul pressed the binoculars to her eyes, his unsteady grip making for a dizzying view. "Your principal," he informed her, "says it's not believable that you wrote so much in twenty minutes."

"But you timed me! Did you tell them?"

"I can't cause a commotion. Can't draw attention over this. Do you like that bird?" he asked, by way of apology.

"I don't know."

"You can stay in third grade."

"No, please," she said, looking at him.

"Or you can go up a grade."

"To fifth?"

"Back to fourth, with your teacher from before, the one everyone says is so good."

"Mr. Priddles?"

The Thai national anthem burst from the loudspeakers, as it did each evening at 6 P.M. Everyone fell silent and stood at attention, even the joggers, chests heaving, sweat rolling down their faces. In hired boats on the lake, people stilled the wobbling vessels.

"But I—"

"Shush," Paul said.

"I wasn't supposed to be in that grade," she whispered. "It's—"

"Shh!"

The school gave her a failing mark for the writing test, which drove down Mr. Priddles's class average; he might not win Teacher of the Year now. Even more vexing, this girl—whom he'd generously taken into his class—turned out to be a defiant little thing. She never laughed at his witticisms, though others were in hysterics. She was a dud, and he was saddled with her.

Thereafter, whenever she asked a question Mr. Priddles pretended not to hear. When she handed in work, he rejected it on any pretext: "Wrong color pen!" He ridiculed her before the others and—to their delight—once tied Tooly to her desk with a scarf after she stood up without permission to look out the window. If she approached him after class, he spoke sweetly, while looking as if he might spit on her. "Mustn't moan all the time," he said. "It's all subjective anyway."

"What does 'subjective' mean?"

"It's when the person in charge decides."

His contempt transmitted to the kids, who treated her as if she were diseased. One day, a boy sneaked up behind her in the hall and choked her for no reason. She stopped trying after that, read novels under her desk, and did her best to lower the class average. Whenever

Mr. Priddles played pop songs, she exerted herself not to hear or to absorb the idiotic words. At lunch, she stole away to read her book, erasing an hour. Had it been possible to cut longer stretches from her life, she would have.

Later that week, during Mr. Priddles's class about poor people, he played "We Are the World," the lyrics printed on the blackboard:

> *It's true we'll make a better day*
> *Just you and me.*

The question was whether the final line, grammatically speaking, should read "Just you and *I*." As Mr. Priddles rewound the cassette, Tooly mumbled a mysterious word—"brimstone"—from the book secretly open under her desk, realizing too late that she'd said it rather loudly.

"Pardon us?" he said.

Everyone looked at her.

She chewed a strand of her hair. "Nothing."

"Share with the class."

"Uhm," Tooly began, "there's just a thing, 'brimstone,' that I don't know what it is."

"You mean 'grindstone,'" he corrected her. "It's what you put your nose to."

A boy asked, "Why do you put your *nose* to it, Mr. P?"

"It's a totally cool saying, isn't it?" he replied. "Basically, it means working hard."

Tooly consulted the page on her lap—the word was indeed "*brimstone*," with neither grind nor nose in sight. "Brimstone," she repeated.

"I. Don't. Think. So," Mr. Priddles said in a rising scale. "And what led you to this particular off-topic interruption?"

She didn't hear his query until the paragraph she was reading came to an end, at which point Mr. Priddles stood, arms folded, before her, saying, "The whole class will wait . . . . Earth to Matilda? . . . Paging Miss Zylberberg?"

When she looked up, a boy yawned at her, his mouth wide like a lion's. "Brimstone," she repeated.

Mr. Priddles snatched the book from under her desk. She watched it being led off by its front cover, which almost ripped under the weight of the hanging pages. He dumped the volume, *Dombey and Son*, in the trash can and—to his pupils' uproarious joy—spent the rest of class pouring drips of his Pepsi over it.

She boarded the microbus home, realizing only in traffic that she'd forgotten her book bag in the classroom, which meant that she'd fall even further behind, and—worse—that Mr. Priddles had her private things, including her sketchbook of noses. She'd have to beg for it. Tomorrow fused in her mind with its successors, a chain as infinite as a mirror reflecting a mirror. She dreaded days and wanted no more of them.

That evening, Paul brought out another wrestling video. She asked permission to watch a bit of the Seoul Olympics, which kids had been talking about at school. But he was boycotting the Games because of the opening ceremony, during which the South Korean organizers had released doves that settled on the Olympic cauldron. Instead of chasing away the birds, the organizers just lit the flames, roasting the doves on live TV. This, he believed, said all that needed saying about the Olympic spirit. Consequently, as the world witnessed Ben Johnson beating Carl Lewis in the hundred-meter dash, Paul and Tooly watched a videotape of the Iron Sheik throttling "Rowdy" Roddy Piper.

"How was school?" he asked.

School was a country and home was a country, and the two sent each other letters but never met, Tooly the emissary shuttling between.

"In art," she said, "we did paintings of a volcano. Everyone had to draw themselves on the side of it, having a picnic, and then we all died. But everyone had to die of something else, not from the volcano."

"Hard to believe: during a volcanic eruption, dying of something else. Incredible bad luck, at a minimum."

"It was just pretend."

"I realize. But still. Or-or-or, what's the point, really?"

"I got killed by a slingshot."

"That's not going to happen. If there's magma and toxic gases, no one would have the presence of mind to fire a slingshot." He cleared his throat. "It's a reminder of how dangerous they are."

"Volcanoes?"

"Slingshots. But, yes, volcanoes, too." He returned his attention to the muted wrestling on TV.

As the roast chickens in tights bounced each other off the ropes, Tooly wandered into her bedroom. When the door closed, she flopped forward onto the mattress, remaining facedown for a minute. She sat on the floor before the air-conditioning unit, chilled teardrops blown across her cheeks. In the bathroom mirror, she studied herself, curious to see her face, the crumpled expression, dull bright eyes, these features so arbitrarily affixed to her nature.

She heard the television click off; a hiss sounded from Paul's inhaler; he flipped noisily through a book on birds. "You coming to read with me?" He had so little to communicate, yet always wanted her beside him. She sat on her bed, resisting the force of his will. Air conditioners thrummed. Shelly's mop slopped. Paul blew his nose.

"You're really settling in at this school," he said when she returned. "Better than the last one."

On her way home the next day, the microbus idled under the sun, heating the metal chassis and broiling the children inside. They were two blocks from Gupta Mansions and, with this gridlock, it would have been quicker to walk. But they weren't allowed out before their home addresses. She reached her arm through the open window, hand swiping torpid air as the bus shuddered in place, exhaust coughing from its tailpipe.

On the sidewalk was a tall Western woman who took a small hop with each step of her leather sandals, straps wound around her ankles. She wore genie pants and a shirt with a mandarin collar, her slender arms clinking with bangles. She drew both hands behind her head, twisting and winding her chestnut hair into a chignon, stabbing the pile with a pencil plucked from her lips, then approached Tooly's window. "Hello, you."

Tooly stared, unsure whether to reply.

The woman added, "You're just the person I've been looking for." She placed her hand on Tooly's tanned forearm, ran her fingers down its length to the little hand, which she held.

Tooly knew she should pull back but did not, instead looking directly at the stranger, whose head was cocked with such fondness that Tooly could not look away. Neither could she hold the gaze, so glanced shyly down, then back up.

The microbus lurched forward, tires turning less than a rotation, leaving the woman a step behind in the road. A couple of other kids looked at Tooly for an explanation. She turned from them, searching for the woman, who approached again, her face softening in a smile. "So hot today," she said. "But I love it like this. It's our sort of weather." She winked. "Want to come out and walk for a bit?"

"We're not allowed."

"No? Ah, well." The bus pulled ahead again. "Goodbye," the woman called out, and walked away.

"Okay," Tooly replied softly. So empty that word sounded to her. A motorbike buzzed past. Pedestrians in flip-flops hurried through gaps in the traffic.

But the woman—her mother—was gone.

# 1999

TOOLY HAD PICTURED college life as wild and wanton. But Duncan and his roommates proved disappointingly straitlaced, notwithstanding the squalor of their apartment. They spent hours at classes and the library, toiling further once home. When darkness fell, they scarcely noticed, lit by the glow of their laptops, until someone walked into the room and flicked on a light.

Occasionally, Tooly passed a whole day alone there, perusing the bookshelves in their rooms, listening to music that Duncan had introduced her to. She ran the length of the parquet corridor in her socks and slid into the living room, where she browsed mail. In part, she lingered to avoid her home in Brooklyn, overwhelmed as it was by Sarah and her mercurial moods. In part, she lingered to find something of value. But there was another reason, of which she was a little ashamed: she liked this lifestyle—her version of college, which included neither examinations nor tuition fees, just people her age who had read books and had something to say about them. In the evenings, she lounged on Duncan's bed and helped him decipher the findings in, say, *Carlill v. Carbolic Smoke Ball*. Or she wandered into the common areas to watch TV with Xavi. She prepared meals for Duncan while he studied; sometimes she fed all of them.

But days passed before anything qualifying as "sexual relations" occurred between her and Duncan—not that it was entirely certain in these times of the Clinton-Lewinsky administration quite what constituted "sexual relations." Anyway, he attempted nothing, as if unsure what was permitted and that he might be accused of criminally misinterpreting her signals. He lamented that, even in this age of gender equality, men still had to make the first move—guys were the ones who risked catastrophe. She disputed this, pretending to be unaware of any subtext, though she lay nude under the covers. Finally, she got fed up and took action.

"You're quite good-looking," he responded, as if in warning, "and I'm really not. You are aware of this?"

"I have a thing for ugly boys."

"Wasn't expecting that answer."

"From now on, McGrory, I make it against the law for you to malign yourself. Only I get to."

"And you make the laws?"

"Yes," she said, kissing him. "I am the legislative body."

She had slept with young men like him before, and they tended to fall into two categories: boys who concealed their astonishment at being allowed to touch female parts; and boys who sought to demonstrate their virility, as if Olympic judges awaited in the closet with scorecards. Often, young men sought reviews, wanting (not wanting) to hear how they rated and ranked—though not how many others that ranking might include. "Tell me. No, wait—don't tell me. No, do . . . Why did you tell me?" Their self-absorption was not infrequently followed by professions of love. When quitting such types, she was surprised how they argued the matter, as if affections were up for negotiation. In Duncan's case, he had such a low opinion of himself that all he expected was for her to withdraw.

But he had ample cause to esteem himself. Aside from his growing legal expertise, he had an exhaustive knowledge of music, played the piano decently (though he loathed practicing), and could draw effortlessly, able to reproduce in two dimensions anything that confronted him in three. On a sheet of inkjet paper, she sketched a nose. Within seconds, he had elaborated it into the nuanced face of a man with a pencil between his lips. He placed the pencil between his own lips and looked at her, trying not to smile.

"I'm so envious," she said.

"It's a useless skill." Growing up, he had expected to apply this talent to becoming an architect like his father. But Keith McGrory had discouraged it, and Duncan conceded. "Anyway, architecture in New York is just for developers nowadays," he told Tooly. "There's almost an anti-design aesthetic—like they have to make buildings look cheap to demonstrate that they're being efficient. This city is built for the market, not for beauty." He began to gain momentum, then halted. "These aren't even really my views. Just stuff my dad says. But I do sort of believe it."

Even after a couple of weeks, he remained timid, preferring to have sex half clothed. She was struck by how many guys were ashamed of their bodies, when that was supposed to be an exclusively female preoccupation. Men were not only shy but shy about being shy. His self-consciousness had been exacerbated by the comments of his first girlfriend, who'd seen him in boxer shorts and remarked that a woman would kill for legs like his.

Tooly suspected a further cause for his awkwardness: he suffered from a conviction that women had for centuries lain miserably beneath hairy copulating oafs, with their liberation arriving sometime around 1968, after which every dignified man was obliged to compensate for the preceding millennia of orgasmic self-interest. This made sex a matter of due diligence. But she liked to giggle during—the act was so near silliness, in addition to being so near ecstasy. He remained powerfully embarrassed anytime he gained pleasure, as if he'd revealed himself as a shill for the patriarchy.

One time, it was different. He failed to put on a condom. Both noticed but neither interrupted the act. On the contrary, they continued more intensely, his self-consciousness gone for those minutes. The omission was ridiculous. For her to lose control of the situation—to risk tying herself to him—spooked Tooly. It aroused her, too.

Legs around him, both of them sitting up, she necked with him at length—not as a prelude to further activities but as an end in itself. No other animals did this, did they? Lips and tongues, eyelids fluttering, the disappearance from place and time. His eyes were swimming when she opened hers.

"Hello, you abomination," she said.

"Hello, you beast."

"You are a blotch on the soul of humanity."

"Thank you, cannibal."

"You're welcome, evolution-defying organism."

He hesitated, thinking up another endearment.

"Are you stuck, you botched cubist experiment?" she asked.

"I'm not stuck, you absurdist painting."

"You're copying me on the art front, you moral vacuum."

"I'm not, you monstrosity."

"You are, horrifying blobfish from the deepest depths of the abyss."

That won—he laughed, kissed her chin.

In the background of this new affair, a civil war raged in that apartment between Emerson and Xavi, centering around the refrigerator. Emerson—in Billabong shorts and Reef sandals, plucking his chin beard indignantly—claimed someone was stealing his food, and applied raging Post-its ("Theft Is Wrong") to his tofu burgers, Ben & Jerry's frozen yogurt ("Not Yours"), even the Brita jug ("EMERSON water"). This played into the hands of Xavi, who took giddy pleasure in needling his roommate. Emerson resented Xavi's and Duncan's very presence, considering them interlopers in Columbia housing. He believed this justified his treating the common areas as his own, riding his mountain bike into the apartment, dumping it in the living room, mud-caked wheels spinning.

Of the three roommates, Xavi studied hardest yet also managed to be the most sociable, constantly off to parties, always dressed astonishingly: purple ascot, red jeans, paisley pocket square. He had moved to the United States at age seventeen, sponsored to attend high school in Connecticut and in possession of one battered suitcase, two silver suits, three black-and-white photos of his fiancée, a favorite Parker pen, and a toothbrush. Duncan—hardly a social success at that high school—befriended the new African kid, ate lunch with him, drove him around on weekends. By graduation, Xavi had become cultishly popular. He won a scholarship to Rutgers, and persuaded Duncan to enroll, too. In the dorms, Xavi proved a further success and always told his fans what an awesome kid Duncan was, insisting there was way more to the guy than it seemed.

There was more to Xavi, too, though he hid it. His family belonged to the Tutsi tribe, a group mistrusted across the African Great Lakes region as an intellectual elite. In the summer of 1994, when he started at Rutgers, extremists from a rival tribe, the Hutu, were seeking to exterminate every Tutsi in Rwanda. Most of his boyhood friends joined a rebel force to fight the Hutu supremacists. Perhaps he should have gone back to fight. But he had not, submerging himself in American college debauchery instead, learning the rules of beer pong, promiscuity, and the backward baseball cap. After the genocide—eight hundred thousand of his people and their allies slaughtered within weeks—Xavi still failed to return. Indeed, he stopped writing letters to his fiancée, then to his family. Yet all his college cavorting ended. Five years later, any party he attended was for networking, a word he'd learned in B-school. Xavi willed himself to success, which alone could rationalize what he had and had not done.

Her other pal there was Emerson's girlfriend, Noeline, often found marking essays in the living room. A recently appointed assistant professor in the English department at Columbia, she was about thirty, with multiple earrings, a discreet nose stud, platform sandals, and toe rings. She and Tooly shared cigarettes on the fire escape, taking them from a soggy pack of Camel Lights, although Emerson—a health freak—made it known that the stench of smoke on Noeline disgusted him. Born to a Dutch mother and an American father, she'd grown up shutting between The Hague and Houston. Her parents were biologists who had conceived her while at Harvard, only to find university positions on opposite sides of the Atlantic. As an undergrad at Smith College, Noeline had engaged in a three-year affair with a female professor. For grad school, she attended Columbia for comparative literature, embarking on her first romances with men there, with a mixture of misgivings and enthusiasm. She'd met Emerson at a graduate seminar, and maintained that it was just a fling, their relationship a feminist irony: with all the clichés about the older male prof seducing the co-ed student, she had reversed roles. (Though, as her ex-lover at Smith observed, in that cliché the professor spirals into disgrace and ruination.)

As for Emerson, he believed he was certain to follow her path to a faculty position. But he was more cocksure than scholarly. To save time, he avoided reading books, preferring reviews, especially vicious ones, which filled him with relief, while raves made him sullen and sent him to Yonkers and back for a restorative bike ride. (He ran, biked, and swam unworldly distances.) In Emerson's view, every important thinker had one key work, and he sought to own a copy. However, his chief activity seemed to be arguing with Noeline. "Either address the issue or don't," he said. "But, please, spare me your drive-by bitching."

That such a bright and layered woman had fallen for Emerson—a mediocrity in search of an admiration society—was a cosmic vote for pessimism. So Tooly avoided talking to Noeline about him, dwelling instead on what linked them: books. They had read hundreds of the same works, yet in a completely different way. Tooly took a book as the creation of one particular brain, while Noeline viewed text as context, each work the fruit of its times, sown by manifestos, fertilized by historical events, harvested in orchards that petered out, burst forth again, producing a landscape known as the Culture. Such classification, Tooly argued, wrecked a work—akin to seeking the soul of a girl by dissecting her body.

Thankfully, Duncan had no objection to Tooly's extended sojourn there—if anything, it offered relief from his terror of the December exams. Casebooks rose on his desk, higher than his hairline. "I am, quite literally, over my head," he said, surfacing every few hours with an attempted witticism about *Wabash, St. Louis & Pacific Railway Company v. Illinois*, then returning to what he called "my pit of litigated despair."

Despite (or because of) his anxiety, Duncan wrote his exams without apparent disaster. Afterward, he swore that he wouldn't read another word of case law until the end of the millennium, by which he meant just over two weeks.

Soon everyone would be leaving for winter break, and Tooly suggested a year-end meal. All were invited, warring parties included. Duncan insisted on cooking, since she had fed him throughout his exam period. Xavi was responsible for bringing strawberry cheesecake. Emerson and Noeline provided the Merlot.

The apartment assumed an air of goodwill that had been absent in preceding weeks. With the worst of their stress gone, the students recalled their status: they belonged to the educated elite, damn it, and it was time someone cleaned the toilet! Gallantly, Emerson volunteered, yellow rubber gloves up to his elbows. Xavi did his part, too, scrubbing the kitchen, while Duncan swept the common areas, disposing of soda cans, take-out menus, month-old sections of *The New York Times*. They set up Emerson's boom box in the living room and played Prince's "1999," whose chorus prompted Duncan to request that they *not* party like it was 1999. "I didn't party at all this year."

"If you party like it's 1999," Xavi said, "we all leave, and you log on to a chatroom with people from Finland."

Noeline uncorked the wine and everyone gathered to inspect the label, playing at being grown-up. Perhaps that was all adults did anyway, only some of them convincingly.

Duncan banned everyone from the kitchen, his pasta sauce faintly bubbling. Tooly leaned in, offering assistance—but only if needed!

"Actually," he replied, pulling her in.

She tucked her hair behind her ears, clasped her hands behind her back, and looked over Duncan's shoulder into the pot, where his sauce had reduced into a tomato glue. She tapped her lower lip, turned to him, and, overwhelmed by affection, kissed his cheek.

He couldn't find her an apron but offered a dish towel, which she had him tuck into the top of her sweater. To preserve herself from

Humphrey's cooking, Tooly had taught herself dishes over the years, typically from cookbooks collected at charity shops. She set to work now, dicing and sautéing and simmering, he watching with elbows on the counter, chin cradled in his palms, thanking her repeatedly, muttering that he was an idiot, then falling silent and frowning like a little boy. So much did he convey this impression that she reached over and touched his nose with her fingertip.

"Sorry," he said.

"For?" She returned to the pot. "I'm not promising deliciousness, given the limited ingredients. But edible, I can predict." The meal was meatless spaghetti bolognese since Emerson had recently become a vegan.

She had Duncan deliver the serving bowl to the table, at which point there was a belated scramble for the vinyl chairs, with textbooks and mail-order catalogs flung to the floor.

The chatty bunch of them fell quiet while blunting the sharp edge of appetite. Tooly plunged her fork into a tangle of spaghetti, left it upright, throat clenching as she swallowed saliva. She watched them eating for a moment, relishing her role, the capable cook, really part of this place.

Xavi opened his full mouth to tell Duncan, "I love you, brother, but you did not have a hand in making this. It is highly good."

Only Emerson offered no praise, nose wrinkled as he picked out flakes of dried oregano. "I know this is vegan, supposedly. But were any animal products used at all?"

"Do you consider the onion an animal?" Xavi asked.

"I don't."

"You may be safe, then."

As their inebriation increased, Xavi pinged Emerson with provocative questions, urging him to tell the table about his upcoming seminar: "Originary and Beyond: The Gap in Alterity Discourse."

"And by 'The Gap,'" Xavi asked, deadpan, "you mean the clothing company?"

"Not the store, you cretin. The figurative gap: gaps on the page, gaps between words, the gap between the thing and the originary." With anyone outside the department, Emerson spoke slowly, as if English were their second language. "The gap in the Lacanian mirror."

"The gap in your teeth in the mirror?"

"I don't have a gap in my teeth, you dick. Look," he continued, "all gaps are essential, in the true sense of the word 'essence,' when we presuppose an overarching gap between the Self and the Other."

"The other what?"

"*The* Other. *L'autre*," he said. "You can go back to Hegel on this. Look at the master-slave dialectic; it's all right there. You need to sit down with Heidegger, Badiou, and the Marxist psychoanalytics for a few hours. Otherwise, what is there to talk about?" For him, opinion gained validity only if footnoted by one of the university-press pinups—Kristeva, Lyotard, Baudrillard, Saussure, Lacan, Derrida, and others whose careers offered hope to those seeking gainful employment without communicating a single clear thought. He yearned to be venerated for brilliance but lacked it, so found support among others with similar needs. Theirs was a religion of obfuscation, composed of several gods and many priests, but not a single ordinary believer.

As Emerson prattled on, Xavi clapped and laughed, his face hidden behind his long fingers. Impressively, Emerson persisted, moving on to his doctoral thesis, of which he had produced two hundred eighty-three pages, meaning that he was still miles from finishing. His work had something to do with the hermeneutics of roller-coasters in Continental literature.

"Do you spend a lot of time riding them?" Tooly asked.

"Why would I?"

At first, Emerson had toyed with writing his thesis without the letter *e*, in tribute to Georges Perec, the wild-eyed Frenchman known for composing a novel without that devilishly useful letter.

"You should write it without any vowels at all," Xavi suggested. "Without any letters even. Just numbers."

"You idiot. You're totally missing the point," Emerson said.

Noeline had the capacity to shut down this silliness within seconds. What she lacked was the floor: each time she spoke, Emerson talked over her. Only when the conversation drifted to politics did she sit up straighter, lean forward, make her voice heard. "You don't really believe that," she told Xavi.

"Of course I do," he confirmed, smiling. "I love this mayor."

"You're not allowed," Emerson said. "Giuliani is a fascist. Amadou Diallo could've been you, *mon frère*. I'm sorry, but a black man cannot be a Republican. You know what those guys stand for?" He pushed on, lecturing Xavi about right-wing isolationism and racist indifference to the developing world.

"So I should go crazy for your big buddy Bill Clinton?" Xavi responded.

"At least he believes in humane globalization," Noeline said. "Say what you like, but we're living under the most principled leader this country has known in ages."

"So principled," Duncan quipped, "that you can pay cash to sleep in the Lincoln bedroom."

"Once you put aside the right-wing smear campaigns, what is there?" Noeline continued. "This administration is presiding over the biggest boom in the postwar period. Clinton has evolved the United States from a fundamentally self-interested state to one that intervenes morally around the world. No one in history has promoted the human right to democracy like he has."

"President Clinton bombed countries to distract people from impeachment," Xavi rejoined. "If he is such a humanitarian, why do nothing to stop the genocide in Rwanda?"

"Hey," Emerson interjected, "Clinton apologized to Africa for that."

"He was honest enough to act in Kosovo *despite* impeachment," Noeline argued.

"Got so boring in the end," Duncan said. "Lewinsky and her beret—please don't make me watch that clip again."

"I'm on your side; that was insanely cruel," Noeline said, though this wasn't quite his point. "The Republicans obsess over tawdry bullshit because they've got nothing. They actually *want* stuff to get bad for the country. Seriously, you cannot support these people."

"What do you think?" Duncan asked Tooly.

Events of the present day felt so distant to her. She'd been taught (by Humphrey, though she never mentioned him here) that the truth about humanity had been revealed in the rise of the Nazis, in the Holocaust, Soviet totalitarianism, the mindlessness of groupthink. Only outsiders had a chance at decency. The nature of any group was to annihilate the integrity of its members. "I always wonder what it'd be like if we were in wartime," she said. "I mean, if we'd been living back then. Like you guys were students at a university and you were teaching at one, Noeline. Except that this was Nazi Germany, and I didn't tell you anything about who I was because—"

"You *already* don't tell us anything about who you are," Xavi said, causing the others to laugh, since she had a deserved reputation for secrecy, evading questions about where in Brooklyn she lived, whom she lived with, what she did beyond hanging around here.

But Noeline wanted to hear this out. "Let her finish. So the scenario is Nazi Germany?"

"Right. And imagine that I was secretly Jewish. But during the meal you found out. That's the sort of thing I wonder: Who would turn me in? I ask myself that about practically everyone I meet."

"So," Xavi asked, "would we?"

They all looked at her.

Tooly sat higher in her chair, flattered by the attention. "Okay, I'll tell you." She turned first to Emerson.

"I am one of the righteous Gentiles," he said.

"You, I think, would not save me. Actually, you'd turn people in."

"Fucking cow!"

Xavi clapped and laughed. "Me next. Come on."

"I think that . . . you would protect me if it wasn't too dangerous. If it was really risky, then no."

"That's fair. I can accept that."

Noeline said, "Afraid to hear what you think of me."

"Yes, you'd help me," Tooly said. "You'd stand up for me. I'm pretty sure."

"Hope so; I think so."

"Me?" Duncan asked.

Her mouth went dry. Tooly had been so vain about their interest that she'd failed to know her answers beforehand. She realized what the next would be, and couldn't stop it. "No," she told Duncan. "In honesty, I don't know that you would."

He gave a short fake laugh.

She added, "But I don't know."

It was too late. She had wounded him, and knew it by the smile he tried to raise.

The conversation continued. Emerson took the floor again, droning on about kairos and chronos, Nietzsche and Bergson's *fonction fabulatrice*. "Eschatological fictions of modernism require action. Just as—speaking of the Nazis again—Hitler's myths required the purging of the Jews."

"Required the purging?" Tooly said. "That's a casually unpleasant thing to say."

"You're not Jewish for real, are you?"

"That's not the point."

"Have I offended you?"

"You have."

"So," he concluded, "you *are* Jewish."

Noeline, avoiding eye contact, stood. "I'm doing the cleaning-up tonight." She carried their plates into the kitchen, failing to upbraid Emerson, which she could have done so effectively. It was true—when you joined a group, even a couple, you lost integrity.

The room altered before Tooly, its occupants assuming the forms they exhibited when first she'd encountered them: young, cocky, vulnerable. They were drunk tonight, capable of viewing only themselves in blurred magnification. Listening, nodding, laughing, she had two epiphanies, and couldn't decide if they were contradictory: that she could never belong to this milieu, which was beyond her understanding and experience; and that she could master all these people.

2011

Graffiti blotted out the train window, so she had to peer through scrawl to view the outskirts of Rome gliding past. The express to the coast picked up pace through the sun-bleached Lazio countryside, past thirsty vineyards, camper vans in empty fields, ragged horses in minuscule paddocks. Every few minutes, litter increased on the tracks, climaxing at the next station.

At Anzio, she lugged her bag off the train and crossed an empty boulevard, following a cobbled lane that descended toward the sea. The vacation apartments were shuttered, summer high season yet to arrive. She strode through a ghost town.

The building lobby was cool marble. A breeze wafted through open windows in the stairwell. In a week, there would be the cacophony of family chatter here, stairs gritty from beach sand, slapped with wet sandals. At a third-floor door, she knocked. From the other side, a voice responded in English—"Yes, yes, coming! Don't leave!"—as if Tooly might otherwise spin on her heels and run.

Merely opening the door, Sarah burst forth in a gush of personality, posing three questions and hearing none of the answers. Her warmth was evident, as were the physical changes since their last encounter, her features assuming an increasingly manly configuration as she neared her mid-fifties, despite evident attempts to cling to earlier decades, with dyed strawberry-blond hair down to her waist, a Mickey Mouse halter top, and pendulous earrings that stretched her lobes, like two hands waiting to drop their luggage.

"Let me give you a kiss," Sarah said.

"Let me come in first," Tooly replied.

"How are you? Make your cheek available—I'll give you a peck. Stuff all over my hands." She held up her fingers, sticky with dough. "I must warn you, the place is a disaster area." Yet the apartment—airy, with turquoise tiles and French windows—seemed perfectly neat. "Come," Sarah said, turning with difficulty toward the kitchen, her right leg treading awkwardly.

"You all right?"

"It's just my hip," Sarah said, leaning against the kitchen doorjamb. "Have I really not seen you since my car accident? That's ten years ago now. They can't seem to fix me. Did you notice right away?"

"Only because I've known you so long."

"Hmm," Sarah responded, staring a little too long. "Liar."

Tooly deposited her bag by the door, taking a moment to gather herself for more Sarah, who insisted on immediately giving a tour. Guest bedrooms radiated off the living room, everything furnished in a seaside theme—a glass vase filled with dried starfish and cockleshells, a menagerie of ships in bottles, the walls nautical blue, decorated with childish paintings of red yachts on green seas under pink skies.

Sarah flicked a switch that sent the terrace shutters grinding upward, midday dawning in the salon. "Damn this thing," she said of the slow-rising contraption, and wrenched apart the French doors—such a hungry, insatiable welcome. "Go out, look."

The view gave onto other holiday apartments much like this one, with gaps between the structures offering glimpses of the Mediterranean, waves cresting soundlessly.

"Come see what I've made. Or should I keep it a surprise? Why are you looking at me like that? Do I have something on my face? You're not happy to be here. I can tell."

"I flew halfway around the world to be here."

"I have been so so so so so so *so* looking forward to you coming," she said, grabbing Tooly's hand. "To show you where I live—the town, too. There's this restaurant we can try on the waterfront—I've been wanting to go for ages. The best in Anzio, and I never get to try it. Only thing is that we have to be gone from the apartment by next weekend."

"Sarah, I'm not staying." Coming here *was* worth it, Tooly reminded herself. Just be patient—you rushed Sarah at your peril. Survive a few hours, get what's needed, then get out. "I have a hotel in Rome booked for tonight."

"I don't charge for rooms here. Pick whichever you want. Which do you like? Are you hungry? How was the flight?" Sarah kept posing questions like this, never allowing for answers: where Tooly lived now, what she did, who that man was who had phoned. It was Fogg who had found her, having dialed various scratched-out numbers in Tooly's old phone book before achieving the desired combination of a working line and a respondent who didn't hang up. This led to another number, then a third. Several calls later, he reached Sarah.

"Had a lovely Welsh accent," she said. "And he's your guy?"

"No, no. Just works for me."

"Sounded yummy. I picture him as a rugged man of few words."

"Yes, Fogg is exactly like that."

Although Sarah passed to other questions, Tooly answered those that had been asked and forgotten, describing the bookshop and life in her village. Caergenog never felt as if it were *her* village when she was there, but very much so when she was away. She mentioned her classes: drawing badly and playing music worse. (Sarah laughed—people often responded that way when Tooly mentioned the ukulele.) She hurried her answers, since Sarah exuded such impatience, fidgeting, longing to speak again, only to ask something else.

"And you cut your hair short. Why?"

Tooly mussed it. "Easier to deal with."

"Bit severe, no? Is that the impression you want men to have?" Sarah nibbled orange polish off a chipped fingernail, her lashes lowered, baring violet eyelids like two little plums. She looked up. "You aren't at all interested in what I cooked?"

They entered the kitchen, which smelled of lemon zest, whipped cream, vanilla extract. "Can I see?" Tooly asked.

"No! Don't look in the oven!"

Tooly made as if to dodge around and peek.

"Don't!" Sarah said, giggling, unable to spin because of her bad hip, instead grabbing Tooly's shirt. "I've made tons of everything, so I want you to overeat. Promise you will. Time?"

"It's about noon."

"Been up since dawn."

"What for?"

"Well, you were coming." She opened the fridge, unloaded plate after plate. "And potato salad, too. You remember who absolutely adored potatoes?"

"I do." She wished Sarah hadn't alluded to Humphrey, which punctured the illusion of travel, that places you left just stopped in your absence.

Sarah continued, "I bought fish. *Sogliola*. What's that called in English? I never remember fish names. Anyway, it's the most expensive they had, so I got two. Look, each has both eyes on the same side of its head." She unfolded the waxed paper to display two soles.

"Four eyes, staring at us."

"Did I show you my new glasses yet?" Sarah disappeared into her bedroom and returned holding spectacles. "Unattractive, aren't they."

"Can't tell if you don't put them on."

Sarah did so.

"They look fine."

"The same as Sophia Loren wears," Sarah noted, gaining confidence. "The saleswoman told me that. Must admit, they do make everything clearer."

"That's often a benefit."

"Try them on."

Tooly obliged.

"I hate you—you look beautiful. I'll never be able to wear them now." Sarah valued looks above all other human traits, perhaps because she'd chanced into good ones, a corruption more dangerous than riches, given that the body's wealth always runs out. Her wearisome preoccupation had led Tooly to vow never to care about presentation. But it hadn't ended up quite so. She did have preferences: a distaste for tended beauty; a fondness for scruffiness, for the sort of men Sarah would have considered unkempt peons; and a strident neglect of her own, admittedly ordinary, endowments.

Tooly slid the glasses back onto Sarah's face, and the older woman hugged her, quite unexpectedly. "I need a cigarette to celebrate your arrival," she declared. "Keep me company." Her bedroom was the only area in the apartment where she was allowed to light up, so she lay on the bed propped up with pillows, kicked off her sandals, painted toenails stretching, crystal ashtray on her belly. She tossed over a loose cigarette, but Tooly didn't smoke anymore. Sarah tried to cajole her into resuming, to no avail. Once, Sarah's white-green packets of Kool Super Longs had seemed the paragon of elegance, but her draws were urgent and coarse now. "In the winter out here, you sleep late and watch a bit of TV, and, next thing you know, it's dark," she said. "Much better now, with the daylight back. Hey, let's go out. I can show you the town before lunch. I just need to change."

"Can't you go as you are?"

"Not with my glasses on!"

"Come on—wear them."

The background whisper of waves increased as they strode down Via Gramsci heading for the sea. A motor scooter droned past, two teenage boys in beetle helmets with unclipped straps fluttering, the portly driver shouting at his passenger above the engine buzz. Tooly looked toward Sarah but found only empty space, turning to discover her several steps behind, limping hurriedly to keep up. "You go so fast!"

"Sorry, sorry," Tooly said. "It's habit. Throw a coin at me if I do that."

"I absolutely will. Look, there's another," she said, stooping to collect more change off the ground. This was Sarah's pastime, developed in recent winters here: an urban treasure hunt for coins that people had dropped on the sidewalk. "If I don't reach fifty euros for the month, I become quite agitated," she joked. "Keep your eyes open around parking meters especially." She squinted at the pavement, having left her glasses at home.

At the dock, the jetties sat empty, the fishing trawlers out for the day. Waterside restaurants were prepped, awaiting fresh seafood. The footpath curled an upward course toward a cliff edge at which stood an ancient Roman villa, its crumbled rooms carpeted by grass.

"Nero and Caligula were born in Anzio," Sarah noted.

"Nice pedigree."

Sarah pointed across the cliff at the sea. "And that's where the Allied landing took place in World War Two—thousands of young men killed right here. In 1944, all that blue sea was gray with landing craft. Beautiful young men stuck in the holds. Lots of them with just minutes left to live."

Paul's father had been wounded at Anzio, Tooly remembered. "Do lots of tourists come pay tribute?"

"To be honest, there's not much to show that it even happened. Now and then, they find machine guns underwater. There's a couple of military cemeteries and a museum with dusty old uniforms and a few sad letters home. But the reason people come to Anzio these days is to swim and tan," she said. "Oh—do you feel that? It's going to rain. My hip feels funny, which means rain. *There's* a reason to crash your car!"

"A built-in barometer."

She gripped Tooly's forearm affectionately.

In the kitchen, Sarah fetched napkins and checked recipes, tapping her lower lip.

"I do that," Tooly said.

"Do what?"

"Tap my lip like you were doing."

"Do I? You're copying me," Sarah said, eyeglasses back on her nose, finger running down the cookbook page. "Now leave me to put on the finishing touches."

Tooly waited in the living room, hearing the clack of knife on cutting board, a pan sizzling, faucet running. She glanced into the kitchen, intending to offer help, but saw Sarah inadvertently knock loose an implant of upper teeth as she tasted sauce on a wooden spoon. Tooly pretended not to be there and waited on the terrace.

They ate blini canapés with salmon roe on sour cream to start, then *frittura di paranza* with lemon quarters, and pan-fried sole with potato salad. Approval produced such joy in Sarah that Tooly found herself offering it more heartily than merited. Sarah was on a high, swollen by Tooly's enthusiasm—until the dessert, a rum baba that failed to rise properly. This was a special visit, she said disconsolately, and now everything was ruined. She knew that to be irrational and admitted it. But the intractable lifelong argument between what Sarah knew and what Sarah felt drove her to the cigarette pack. Dejectedly, she lit up in the kitchen, mindless of house rules now.

"What do you do out here?" Tooly asked. "I mean, day to day."

"Whatever I want. Watch TV. Go grocery shopping. Keep the apartment clean. We get these rains, being near the water, and if I don't clear all the leaves they block the drain, and the terrace floods. So I take care of that. What else? I have my treasure hunt."

"The neighbors? Who are they?"

"No idea. I'm invisible. You pass a certain age as a woman, and nobody sees you anymore."

"Course they do."

"You'll find out; you'll become a ghost one day. Though it's not all bad. You get to watch things happening: men and women appraising each other. I can just look, and not have to deal with the sex anymore. Men are never that clean, are they, and they're hairy and sweaty. Sex isn't ever that pleasurable for women—really, it's just the pleasure of being wanted."

"Not sure I agree with any of that."

"Men *are* hairy."

"Yes, that part is true," Tooly conceded. "Not necessarily a bad thing. Within limits."

"The right amount in the right places."

"Well, yes. True of everything."

"What strikes me," Sarah continued, "is that men are such savages—they don't fold their clothes, they pee on the toilet seat, they barely wash—yet when it comes to their views on women they're suddenly so concerned about how everything looks. Each barbarian becomes an aesthete about the female body, all of a sudden expecting perfection."

"Lots of the men I've encountered seem pretty grateful to settle for what they get. Though maybe that's the ones who go for me—not, perhaps, the most discriminating category."

"Don't undersell yourself, Tooly. What you present is what the man buys."

"Honesty in advertising. That's what I offer."

"What's weirder still," Sarah continued, "is how women are the opposite: we're tidy and neat; we respect decoration; we groom; we use fabric softener, put rinse-aid in the dishwasher, feather our nests. Then we share those nests with some stinking bird who's the opposite."

"I don't use fabric softener, and I don't actually know what rinse-aid is. Then again, I also don't have a hairy man in my house."

"That's probably why."

"Because I don't use fabric softener? God, imagine if you're right. And men *can* be nice-looking," she added, voice fading as Sarah resumed.

"Around here, I could vanish and no one would notice. I *will* vanish next weekend. That's when the owners get back, and I run away like a dormouse." She was headed north next, to an out-of-season ski lodge in Alto Adige, near the Austrian border.

This was how Sarah survived nowadays, house-sitting empty vacation homes, residing in the right places at the wrong times: a ski resort when the slopes were muddy; a beach house when it rained on the sea.

"I feed cats sometimes and water plants. It's not bad. Sometimes they give me spending money." The owners were wealthy men for whom she had once been the other woman. They offered charity now, and she lived at the whims of pity. If their plans changed—a forecast turned splendid for the weekend, say—she had to go.

Sarah scooped grounds into the moka coffeemaker. "You know, I wondered about you," she said, back turned, reaching into the cupboard, clattering through crockery for espresso cups.

"Wondered?"

"I mean, what happened to you?" she said. "Where did you go? You cheap runaway—not even caring about those who brought you up with blood, sweat, and tears." Sarah was a person who got the tone all wrong, who stood at the threshold of a subject, pretending a lack of interest, then barged in. "I suppose you're *so* very angry at me."

"I'm not angry."

Sarah shooed away this denial. "And you're not well," she said. "You're clearly not."

"What do you mean? I'm fine."

"You look sickly. You look ill. Like you're starving away."

"You're starting to sound like you were my mother."

"Such a hurtful thing to say."

They stood there, gazing at the bubbling espresso pot.

"You asked how I spend my time here," Sarah resumed. "One thing I was embarrassed to say is church. Don't worry—I don't try to foist it on people. Just something for me. But I find it comforting. And interesting. A different way of seeing what happened. A way to forgive myself."

"You blame yourself for things?"

"Of course."

"Such as?"

Sarah poured the coffee. "Sugar?"

Tooly saw the sugar bowl in Sheepshead Bay, crawling with ants. "What do you regret?"

"But are you staying overnight? You didn't pick a room yet."

"I have that hotel booked in Rome," Tooly repeated, clearing dishes to hide her irritation.

"Don't bother with the plates. Just leave them, if you so desperately want to get away from me."

"I like doing dishes. It's a weirdness of me, one of many. Everywhere I go, I insist on doing the washing-up." Despite her outward cheer, Tooly bridled at the familiar rigmarole of Sarah. Years of being plunged into unease, years of trying to coax her out of moods. "I was thinking of those stories you used to tell me," Tooly said, and heard herself appeasing again. "About those animals when you were growing up in Kenya. Must've been quite a childhood, out there in the wild."

"Wasn't that wild."

"I imagine leopards leaping out whenever you left the house."

"We had a garden like everybody else. Could've been anywhere."

"People say if you're born in Africa you have the place in your veins forever."

"I don't say it."

"Italy's more like home now?"

"How could it be?"

"Would you ever go back to live in Kenya?"

"I left for a reason. It was small-minded and remote. White Africans talk interminably about how gorgeous it is—the land, the land, the land. Bores me to tears. Kenya *does* have proper countryside; all other landscapes look wrong when I see them—overgroomed and hacked up. But why would I go somewhere just to look at land?"

"You've not got relations left there?"

"None I'd want to know. And Mummy and Daddy are long dead."

"I don't remember you visiting them."

"Why would I? They were otherwise occupied."

"How so?"

"Sipping," she responded. "My mother drank to get unhappy. Daddy just soaked."

Tooly had heard these tales of woe before. Perhaps she should have sat through them all again. But she just couldn't. "Sarah, I came here to talk to you."

"Which is what we're doing."

"I need to ask you some questions."

"How dramatic."

"About Humphrey first."

"The old darling!"

"Sarah, where's he from? Somewhere in Russia, right?"

"Yes, of course."

"Well," Tooly responded, "I've seen him recently. You know his accent? It's gone. Can you explain that?"

"Don't know what you mean."

"He talks like an English speaker now. It's like hearing someone completely different. Not completely," she corrected herself. "The voice is the same. It still seems like him."

"I don't believe you."

"Why would I invent that, Sarah? What possible reason? I came here for help in figuring things out. Stuff that you know. Stuff that pertains to my life."

"What on earth could you mean?"

"Tell me about Venn, then. Where did he go?"

"What's that supposed to mean?"

"What else could it mean?" She looked up at the ceiling. "I find it disappointing—extremely, extremely—that you won't ever be direct with me."

"I'm the most direct person in the world," Sarah responded with astonishment.

"Then please try, right now."

Over the next two hours, Tooly peppered her with questions. Sarah had been there. Could she not just *explain*? Rather than doing so, she spun interminable yarns, depicting herself as innocent and kind while flinging blame on everyone else—above all Venn, whom she depicted as the improbable devil in her tale, with Humphrey as the saint.

"That's not what happened," Tooly interrupted. "Do you honestly believe what you're saying?"

Sarah lit a cigarette, flapping at the air to clear the smell. "You know what we should do after you go back to your shop?" she said brightly. "We should try Skype together. No one ever agrees to do it with me. I'll show you how tomorrow."

This visit had been folly. Another round of make-believe with Sarah.

"I'm not here tomorrow. I've made that clear."

"You're being silly—so much I can tell you still."

"Right now, then. Just one thing."

"Well," Sarah said, "you have to ask me a question. Or how else am I supposed to—"

"I've done nothing but ask questions for the past two hours!"

"You want to go over Bangkok again? Reminisce about the good times with Paul?" She mimicked him: " 'Careful now! Shush, or you'll scare away the birds!' "

"*Don't* do that. Don't. Okay?"

Sarah sighed, eyelashes fluttering. "Well, I suppose we were a bit rough on dear old Paulie. Both of us were," she said. "Still, a little hard to discuss Bangkok if I can't mention him."

"Fine. Tell me about New York, then."

"Well," Sarah answered, "quite devotedly of me, I traveled to that hovel you and Humph were sharing in Brooklyn, all just to see you. I came offering a job for you here in Italy, as you may recall. But you refused to hear me out. Sent me away in the most spiteful fashion."

"Be serious. You came to see Venn, not me."

"I was there to protect you," Sarah protested. "I knew things were going wrong."

"Not this again."

"If I was there purely for Venn, why did I never see him on that trip?"

"Because he wouldn't see you."

"Did you ever ask yourself why?"

"I know why—because you were unbearable to be with."

Surprisingly, Sarah failed to retaliate—no hissing fury, no venom. "Each time I turned up," she responded sadly, "wherever it was in the world, he always met with me. But not that time. I wasn't worth much anymore, I suppose."

"You're the only one who thinks in terms like that," Tooly said. "And don't claim you were so very concerned about my well-being. I shudder to imagine what would've happened if Venn hadn't been around when I was growing up. You, disappearing every other day for some personal freak-out, or whatever those were. You weren't looking after me. He was." That bank card, a reminder of their bond, in her pocket everywhere she'd traveled alone. "Has he not been in touch at all?"

"Let's get back to Humphrey. How *is* he?"

"I told you, he talks completely differently. There's clearly something I don't know here. And I think you do."

"All I know is that Humphrey was the great friend of your childhood. An utter darling!"

"Can you answer my question, please?"

"You should thank me for Humph. I always made sure he kept you company."

"Kept *me* company? Humphrey had nowhere else to go. I kept *him* company, if anything. He was a hanger-on." She thought of his reading material, little snacks on the Ping-Pong table. "Maybe that's not the right word, but I—"

"Very fond of you, Humphrey was," Sarah said. "He and I tried everything to help you. Even in New York, we tried. But you wouldn't come with me. You wanted things a certain way, and there was no shifting you. Just like always. Just like it was *you* who decided how things ended up with Paulie."

"We're not discussing him," Tooly reiterated. "Can we stick to the topic?"

"Oh, I'm sure Humphrey told you everything already."

"He told me nothing; that's why I came here."

"And how nice that you did! Having *such* a lovely time, Matilda."

"I'm not. You might be. I'm not."

"Give some thought to dinner. That restaurant is supposed to be fab."

"This is absurd." Tooly stood and fetched her bag. "I'm going back."

"I'll try not to look too gloomy," Sarah responded. "If I frown too much, I could get wrinkles one day. Keep your face in a state of permanent immobility—that's my advice. I try not to have any expression whatsoever. Which is easier when you're on your own."

Tooly boarded the next express for Rome. In the carriage, a group of ratty teenagers played music from a cellphone; a man clipped his fingernails. As the train prepared to depart, she glimpsed a fiftyish woman hobbling along the platform. It was Sarah, in fresh makeup, scrutinizing each window in turn, hoping to be spotted, and that her guest might rethink. She paused at Tooly's window. But without glasses she saw nothing, and continued past.

The train chugged into a pelting rainstorm, its hydraulic doors sighing open at each shabby station on the Roman periphery. Tooly repeated to herself that she'd been right to leave. Nothing to learn from Sarah, nothing owed to her. Yet the image remained: Sarah looking blindly at her. She'd be returning to the apartment now, probably soaked from the downpour, flicking on lights in the spare bedrooms, plumping the cushion on the kitchen chair, still indented from her departed guest.

Sarah had sculpted her own past so vigorously in the retelling that her memories had chipped loose from the events themselves, detaching her from others who'd also been there. It had never occurred to Tooly that dishonesty had the consequence of isolation.

Unfortunately, Sarah's isolation cut off Tooly, too: Who else was there to consult about that time? Was there any point in trying again with Humphrey? He might remember something. Even just a clue to what had happened. It was no surprise that he'd deteriorated this much, confined to that armchair, without conversation or reading. But she could rouse him—she'd always had that effect.

Tooly gazed out the rain-streaked window, drenched countryside rushing by. Returning to Wales was impossible now.

# 1988

PAUL STOOD, then sat, then stood, then went to his room, then returned, and told her. His father, Burt, had passed away. Paul knelt before the VCR, pressing buttons. "I should have been there."

Tooly was unsure what to say. "If you try hitting Play and Record at the same time, that's what I—"

"I know how to operate a video machine."

The next morning, she got up two hours late for the microbus—Paul hadn't woken her. Nor had he turned on the air-conditioning in the living room, which was sweltering. The apartment had a strange desolation. She crept into his room, found a long lump in his bed.

He turned to face her.

"It's late on the bird clock," she whispered.

He nodded.

In the kitchen, the housekeeper, Shelly, was in a frantic state. "Everybody sleeping!" She asked if they would be at home all day—they hadn't warned her! She didn't have lunch supplies! It wasn't fair to do that!

Tooly climbed for the cereal boxes, poured a bowl for Paul, overfilling it with milk. She delivered it to his bedside, but he had no interest. "Don't you have your job today?" she asked.

"Yes."

"Are you going?"

He stared at the ceiling.

"Can I pour cold water on you?"

"Why would you?"

"To wake you up."

He flipped over, giving her his back.

She opened his curtains, parting them in stages, as he did when waking her. Paul rose and went into the bathroom, stood before the medicine-cabinet mirror.

She clambered onto the closed toilet seat with a can of shaving cream and sprayed a white whoosh onto his face, then ran the safety razor down his cheek, as she'd seen in television commercials. But she did it too softly, drawing only a puff of foam, no stubble. She tried more firmly. A crimson dot of blood rose through the white. Terrified, she glimpsed his face in the mirror. "I didn't mean to," she said, and ran into her room.

He did not emerge that day. She tried reading in the living room, but couldn't finish a single page. She stood outside his door—she should do something, but didn't know what.

Mr. Priddles had once told her class that, whenever they encountered problems at home, they should talk to him. The idea—him invading her life even more, glimpsing how things were here—outraged her nearly to tears. Why did she have to see him ever again? But there Mr. Priddles was, every single day, at the front of class, smiling to himself as he cued up the music.

Later that week, the name Matilda Zylberberg boomed over the school speakers. Tooly leaped up from her desk. Even if she was in trouble again, she could at least waste some time slow-walking to the admin offices. When she arrived, someone awaited her.

"So sorry, darling."

Before Tooly could respond, the woman picked her up like a bundle and hugged her. "I *completely* forgot my things at home. You'll vouch for me, won't you? Or are you going to turn Mommy in to the authorities?"

Bewildered, she glanced at the woman, then at the receptionist, who responded with a smile. "You guys good to go?"

"Apologies for being such a ditz with the ID."

"No problemo. Just sign here, Mrs. Zylberberg."

"You're a gem," Sarah told the secretary, and led Tooly outside, pointing to the front gate.

Holding the girl's hand, she whispered, "I hate schools. They give me the creeps."

"Where are we going?" Tooly asked.

"Wherever you like, Matilda. Sorry I vanished—got *so* busy. But I've been aching to see you."

"I'm not allowed to leave."

"Is this a prison? Course you can go. What were you even doing that was so important?"

"The hypotenuse."

"Don't even know which subject that is!" She slipped on white Ray-Bans and offered her hand, bangles clinking. Uncertainly, Tooly took it. "I'm here to see if I like you," Sarah said. "But I have to say, I think I adore you already. I really do. Ready? Off we go!"

"I can't."

"You don't want to?"

"I . . ."

A tuk-tuk waited outside the gates, engine belching, frame shuddering.

"I'm not supposed to get in those. They're dangerous." Paul had always said that. "Aren't they?"

"Not if I'm here. Come on, you!" She tickled Tooly's arm, making the girl giggle, then drew her into the cab, arm around her shoulder, tugging her closer along the vinyl seat. Sarah said something to the driver, squeezed the nine-year-old around the middle again, kissed her cheek. "What fun!"

"But I . . ." Tooly began, her question drowned out as the vehicle tore into traffic.

"You know who I am," Sarah assured her. "You remember me."

They took a sharp turn, causing them to slide across the backseat, Sarah squashing Tooly, making them both laugh. The driver, Tooly noticed, had handlebars rather than a steering wheel—a tuk-tuk was just a motorcycle, it seemed, with a bench at the back and an awning above. Warm wind rushed at her face, row shops blurring past, bumpy roadway disappearing beneath, jolting them up and down.

"*Khao neow ma muang*?" Sarah told the driver. "There was a place along here—I saw it before. *Khao neow ma muang*?"

He looped around, pulled over at a food stall, pointing.

"You're a marvel," she told him, folding a twenty-baht note into his hand and hoisting Tooly onto the sidewalk in one airborne hop. "Now *this*," Sarah said, "is the most gorgeous thing in the world. Have you tried it?"

"I don't know what it is."

"I woke up wanting *khao neow ma muang* and thought, I hope Matilda hasn't tried this, so I can be the one to introduce her to it. It's heaven. Better than heaven, since heaven probably drags on forever, which must get so boring. This is much perfecter."

"Perfecter?"

"Much more perfecter. Here." She twirled around, facing the food stall, raised her eyebrows at the Thai vendor, who smiled back. "Two, please."

"This girl in my class," Tooly cautioned, "went to the hospital after eating cuttlefish on the street."

"Two times out of three, you don't die from street food. And this isn't cuttlefish." The vendor chopped a mango, scooped out sticky rice, drizzled it with coconut sauce, sprinkling toasted sesame seeds atop. "No need to worry about food poisoning—I'll probably eat all yours anyway."

The vendor handed the first serving down to Tooly, who held it, the heat of sticky rice warming the underside of the Styrofoam platter. "Mustn't be polite with me," Sarah said, rubbing Tooly's back encouragingly. "If I had *mine* first, I'd never wait for you."

Nevertheless, Tooly rested her plastic fork on the rice—Paul minded if she ate first. Finally, Sarah received hers and took a mouthful, eyes rolling to indicate euphoria. "*Much* better than heaven."

Tooly took a nibble: melting mango and coconut-scented sticky rice, slightly salted.

"You have to get the balance of mango to sticky rice right with each bite," Sarah counseled. "It's an art. Something my friend Humphrey taught me."

Tooly tasted a grain of the sweet rice. "You were outside my school bus that time."

"I was. Everywhere I go, I look for you. If I get lucky now and then, and you happen to be there, how nice!" Noticing Tooly struggling with a mango lump, Sarah jabbed it with her own fork. "Here."

Tooly bit it off.

"Listen, my favorite person"—to be addressed this way produced a surge in Tooly—"my favorite person, you have no idea how many people would love to meet you."

"Who would?"

"Everybody in the world who hasn't. You're just the best." She turned to the vendor, asking, "Isn't this the best girl you've seen in your life?"

The old woman clucked.

"It's a known fact you are," Sarah said. After only three more bites, she patted Tooly's hair, stroked her chewing cheeks, and announced that they must leave. "Terrible to do, but there's a party to prepare for."

"Okay," Tooly said, the food losing flavor. "Uhm, I don't know how to get back from here."

"You're not coming with? Abandoning me in deepest darkest Bangkok?" Sarah drew a long white cigarette from a packet of Kools in her purse, lit up, and exhaled a minty stream, then extended her slender arm into the roadway, causing two motorcycle taxis to screech to a halt. "I'll let you take the first one."

"I never went on a motorbike before," Tooly said.

"Poor thing, you look so worried!"

Her driver barked, "Where you go?"

Tooly didn't know how to direct him to her school, so stated her home address. Sarah paid Tooly's driver, hiked up her skirt, and climbed onto the other motorcycle. "I hate this part," she said. "Hate the going-away bit. Big kiss, my dear."

"I'm a bit scared."

"Don't be! Oh, Matilda, I had the most wonderful time. Did you?" Her motorcycle roared off, cutting through traffic, and was gone.

Tooly tentatively grasped the driver's orange bib, but he yanked her arms tight around his midriff and gunned the motorbike toward the gridlock, weaving through at speed, a terrifying, thrilling ride that ended with a sharp turn down her *soi* and a sudden halt, Tooly's momentum squashing her into his back.

Her legs wobbly, she took the elevator up, then dashed for her room, as if this escapade might have left a visible mark that Shelly could see. When Paul came home, she feared that the phone would ring, the school reporting her latest infamy. Instead, she and Paul ate in air-conditioned silence. He was getting up in the mornings again and going to work. Yet he hardly spoke, and they hadn't watched wrestling in days. After dinner, he retired to the computer in his bedroom, while she sat for hours on a deep leather armchair in the living room. She fell into a strange sleep there, then dragged herself to bed, still feeling the motion of the motorbike as she lay on her mattress.

The next evening, while Paul worked in his room, Tooly went downstairs, imagining that Sarah might still be out there. The building porter at the front gate saluted when she left, careless that this tiny girl strode into the night. Traffic grew louder as she neared Sukhumvit Road. An aproned maid passed, carrying a fish by the gills; it kicked, kicked. Plastic tables around a food stall stood vacant, an empty bottle of Singha on its side, rolling back and forth. Neon arrows pointed to the entrance of the King and I massage parlor, before which stood a trio of cheerless Japanese men, each on a different step, each smoking, one inhaling, then the second, then the third. In unison, they disappeared inside.

November arrived, and the heat remained implacable. When Tooly turned ten, she told nobody at school. Whenever possible, she sneaked out and wandered the neighborhood, glancing around for Sarah. But weeks had passed since their adventure. Every morning, she awoke longing for another.

It arrived.

"Come out and play," Sarah said through the window of the microbus.

At her stop, Tooly hurtled off the bus and raced back toward Sarah. Such an odd way of walking, the woman had: shifting speeds, hurrying as if taken by a gust, then spinning around and beaming at Tooly, kneeling to stroke the girl on the top of her head, hopping a step ahead, then striding normally again.

"Before I die," Sarah proclaimed as they ambled through Sukhumvit, "I will learn flamenco. Promise you'll keep me to that, Tooly."

"What's flaminging?"

"Flamenco? It's Argentinian dancing. Or is that the tango?" She thrust her arm forward, cocked her chin in demonstration. "Anyway, very moody and melodramatic. *You* would love it."

This casual assumption of Tooly's preferences—of how she was—thrilled the little girl.

"I know exactly what you're like," Sarah affirmed.

After a long pause, Tooly responded, "What are *you* like?"

"Me? Well, I like bread with strawberry jam and believe raspberry jam ruins everything. I think those who joke around with such matters are barbarians. And I'm right about everything. Except in the morning, when I'm wrong."

Tooly looked up to see if she was being teased. "I keep trying to think of something funny." She showed her empty hands.

"You are the most adorable thing. Say whatever you like around me."

"Where were you born, Sarah?"

"On a game park in Kenya."

"Did you see lions?"

"Thousands."

"Did you pat one?"

"Oh, yes."

"Did he bite you?"

"He licked my hand and smiled."

"Lions smile?"

"If you pat them nicely. Do you like animals?"

Tooly nodded enthusiastically.

"Know where we should go?" Sarah said. "That crazy market with the wild beasts. Shall we?"

"We shall!" Tooly said intrepidly, then: "Am I allowed?"

A tuk-tuk driver deposited them before Khlong Toey, at the fringe of the open-air bazaar, which reeked of panicked fowl. Sarah took Tooly's book bag so the girl could walk freely into the throng. On either side were tarps to keep sunlight off the produce: purple eggplants, green gourds, tamarind pods, cassava roots, taro. Vendors called across the market aisles, negotiating and laughing, while laborers in coolie hats dragged carts up and down. Tooly looked upward between adult bodies, and the sky dazzled her. Sarah shaded the girl's brow, pointing to a stack of warty vegetables. "Ugliest thing you've seen in your life. This is fun, isn't it," she said, clutching Tooly's arm. "Just you and me. Lead the way!"

Tooly pushed on, peeking into buckets filled with fried baby crabs, red chilies, oyster mushrooms, mouse-ear fungus. Under netting were live toads (eyeing her) beside flayed toads (pink-muscled, arms flung back). On a butcher block lay pig heads. In a metal basin, shiny fish flopped, two leaping over the edge as if in coordinated jailbreak, only to land pointlessly on the concrete floor. A fishmonger tossed them back into the squirming mass. The paving stones were specked with feathers of the live geese crammed into cages, necks bent to fit inside, the metal wires caked with droppings. Sarah must have read Tooly's expression. "Ready to leave?"

But seeking the exit only drove them deeper inside the market, each aisle offering a different wriggling horror. "That way?" Tooly suggested, and went ahead to prove herself brave. She paused at a bamboo cage of long-beaked birds. "Look!" she exclaimed. "Pied kingfishers!"

"What?"

"They hover over the water. I've seen them before. Their wings go five hundred times a minute, and they look like they're standing in the air. Then they see a fish and they go down into the water and bite it."

"They're beautiful," Sarah said, studying the overstuffed cage. "I'm tempted." She glanced down at Tooly. "Tempted to open it and free them."

"The owner's right there."

"Fuck him!"

Tooly had only heard children swear; it was astonishing to hear a grown-up trying it. "Won't they fly off?"

"I hope so. Now, listen; here's the plan. Don't run when I do it. We'll just walk slowly away, cool as can be. They'll never know it was us." She fiddled with the cage latch. The kingfishers flapped with anticipation. The door sprang open.

But the birds stayed inside.

"Why aren't they going?" Tooly asked in a whisper.

One ventured out, fluttering to the ground.

"Run!" Sarah shouted, snatching Tooly's hand, urging her on. "Quick! Quick!" They bolted, Tooly scrambling to keep up, suppressing wild nervous laughter as they barged into carts and flunkies. The netted toads watched them rush past.

By the road, Tooly grabbed the knot at the back of Sarah's cornflower-print dress. Like a horse reined, Sarah slowed from canter to trot to a clopping stop. They caught their breath, grinning at each other. Sarah wiped sweat from her forehead, then reached for Tooly's face, plucked off a fallen eyelash, rolled it on her fingertips. They watched it float to the sidewalk.

After the tuk-tuk ride back to Sukhumvit Road, Sarah gave an affectionate yank of the girl's long frizzy hair and returned her book bag. Goodbye was implicit. Tooly nearly followed her, but she hadn't been invited. Sarah blew a kiss and spun off down the road.

Tooly looked down her *soi*, at the end of which stood Gupta Mansions, where Paul would be waiting in high agitation because of her tardiness, with Shelly upset because dinner was cold. A wordless night, a thin sleep, another school day tomorrow. Tooly wished not to exist, to be erased, imprisoned as she was in this unpopular little junk of a girl, exhausted by the constancy of herself.

Bangles clinked, followed by the scratch of a lighter flint. Tooly spun around. Sarah stood there, eyebrows raised, blowing white smoke, a plume swaying left and right. "I'm stealing you."

"Are you allowed?"

"If people only did what was allowed, how dull."

"But," Tooly said, faltering, "I don't know who you are."

Sarah tucked Tooly's hair behind her ear. At this affectionate touch, the girl's face turned down.

"You know me, Tooly," Sarah said. "We've known each other forever."

# 1999

DUNCAN HAD BEEN LIVING at 115th Street for months before his parents visited. Naoko urged her husband to go, but Keith left Connecticut only grudgingly. Finally, she prevailed—it was this or invite their son's new girlfriend to Darien for the holidays. So he agreed to tolerate New York for one day, attending a midday Christmas concert at the Met, then scheduling a drop-in at Duncan's apartment to meet this female. At each metropolitan inconvenience Keith encountered— holiday shoppers, the impossibility of parking, the accent of a garage attendant—he turned irritably to his wife, as if she were to blame for the world.

In the week before their arrival, Duncan had considered tidying his room but opted for passive rebellion. His defiance dissolved when Naoko called from a phone booth outside Lincoln Center to say they were on their way. He spent the next twenty minutes stuffing soiled laundry under his mattress, wiping down the bathroom basin with paper towels, hiding dirty dishes in the cupboards.

"I can offer you white wine or . . ." Tooly said, hands clasped before her, looking from Naoko to Keith, then back at Naoko, who presented the more sympathetic countenance. "Actually, white wine is all we have. That okay?"

"Plus, we got three types of chips," Duncan added.

Keith, an unblinking lump of middle-aged Scottish clay, looked askance at the sofa, where his wife invited him to sit. "I only drink if I'm getting drunk," he said. "And I'm not getting drunk with my son."

"I've gotten drunk with him," Tooly said, "and I can recommend it."

Duncan gave an embarrassed cough.

"Diet soda," Keith ordered. "Can we get the TV going?" He did the honors, switching to *NBC Nightly News,* which was broadcasting a segment on New Year's security measures after the arrest of an Algerian caught with explosives at the border, possibly for a terrorist attack in Los Angeles.

"Wrong," Keith told the television, when the anchor spoke of the upcoming Year 2000 celebrations.

"What is?" Tooly asked, handing him a soda can.

"The Year 2000," he said. "If the counting starts at one A.D., you don't reach the millennium till 2001. Not like there was a Year Zero. How hard is that for people to understand?" He looked at the TV again, which now showed footage of Bill Clinton joshing with a foreign dignitary. "Can this guy just go?" Keith said, meaning the president.

Naoko's wandering gaze suggested that it wasn't the first time she'd heard such laments.

"It'll take industrial cleaners to get this guy's stench out of the Oval Office," Keith continued. "It's time to restore dignity to our country."

"I like hearing such patriotic American views delivered with a Scottish accent," Tooly said, offering a smile.

"Give me one iota of evidence changing anything I just said to you," he said, glaring at her.

Late that night, Tooly lay in Duncan's bed, thinking about his father, who, during a hundred hectoring minutes, had not once looked at his son. While Tooly knew it to be unfair, she couldn't help but like Duncan slightly less for having this man as his father.

Duncan hugged her back, sliding his legs up to spoon with her. She felt vaguely unsafe with anyone behind her like that when sleeping. "Flip!" she said jovially, as if he were an egg. Their positions reversed, she pulled herself against his back, warming it with her naked front.

"Your spoon was a travesty," she told the nape of his neck. "I had to act."

"You're a spoon fundamentalist."

"I support traditional spooning values. You have cheapened the office of the spoon and it's my job to restore honor and credibility to the spoon."

He twisted around, laughing. "Tooly?"

"Duncan?"

"I completely fucking love you."

She smiled and poked his cheek, then got out of bed and lay on the floor among dust balls, printer paper, socks under the bedframe. "It's boiling in here tonight."

"The super went away for the holidays and left the heat going so that no one complains."

His arm hung over the edge of the mattress, and she encircled his wrist with her thumb and forefinger, holding still for a minute. But, eventually, you must do things with things. She pulled his wrist closer and nipped the bumpy bone, causing him to yelp and laugh. Tooly stood, stretched, and put on yesterday's outfit, then went to the living-room window, peeking onto the fire escape for the pack of house cigarettes. None left, and Noeline had gone for the holidays.

She gazed down at the street. Seemed ages since her first night here, when—contemplating an icy walk home—she had preferred the warm bedcovers (and the warm man) in Duncan's room. She could've slipped those credit cards from his wallet then, and concluded it. Instead, she'd nested here, they mistaking her for one of them, she making the same error—until that pre-Christmas dinner, when Tooly observed anew the division between her and other people.

Venn was the only person who protected her. And she wanted to have something for him, to justify her time up here. Duncan was the obvious target, yet she couldn't bring herself to do that. The others? Emerson was her preference, yet gaining his confidence required stroking the man's ego, and she refused. Standing in the dark corridor, she noticed the light under Xavi's door. She rapped with one knuckle, as if her others weren't so sure. "Hey," she said, as he opened. "Want to walk the pig with me?"

They borrowed the animal and were off, footprints and hoofprints down the frosted sidewalk. Xavi was skittish about touching Ham, but she forced him to pat the creature, which seemed to cause the pig to fart, sending them into tears of laughter. Composure regained, they continued to the red-brick path across the Columbia campus, which was nearly deserted this close to the holidays—just the distant hollers of a few frat boys. Ham kept bumping into her leg, like a child jealous when the grown-ups chatted.

"I'm a detective," Xavi remarked.

"How's that?"

He named a street in Brooklyn—to her alarm, the street where she and Humphrey lived. Weeks earlier, Xavi explained, he had found a city map in the corridor by the front door, amid all the Chinese menus and America Online marketing disks. At first, he'd assumed it was garbage, because it was covered in pen lines. But he'd never owned a map of all five boroughs, so he'd kept it. Problem was that the lines made navigation nearly impossible. What *were* those? Delivery routes? There was a pinprick hole where ink had saturated and loosened the fibers of the page. Everything radiated out from that point, at the end of a small street in Brooklyn, just off the Gowanus Expressway.

He took her map from his inside pocket. So there it was: must've fallen from her pocket on that first visit, when she'd opened her coat and flopped atop Duncan on the floor. "Never seen it before in my life," she said.

Xavi grinned. "I'm a detective!" To celebrate, he took a cigarette from his velvet jacket and lit it grandly. He had a peculiar way of smoking, cheeks filling, as if not to inhale. He inquired about her place in Brooklyn, but she diverted the conversation to his studies, and how he was going to make the fortune that they all knew would one day be his. Pure finance was extremely lucrative, he explained, but it left him cold. Entrepreneurship was what appealed. A dot-com, maybe.

"Can I get a drag off that?" she asked.

"Only if you give me a million-dollar idea."

"I have a ten-cent idea," she responded, grabbing the cigarette.

He took out his PalmPilot, which he flipped open with a flourish, rapping the stylus pen on the screen, like a conductor's baton on the music stand. "Go."

"Well," she said, exhaling smoke. "What about a dishwasher-like product, but for the whole apartment, so you pour detergent into a hole in the floor, press a button, and leave for an hour, then return, and the house is clean."

"I like it," he said, smiling. "Very practical."

"I notice you're not writing that down. Oh, and I always think about how they should make it so that cars run on tracks and are controlled electronically, which would end accidents and traffic jams."

"This idea already exists. It's called a train."

"Spoilsport," she said. "What about the salt shaker?"

"What about it?"

"I hate salt shakers. I don't want a little heap of salt on my mashed potatoes," she said, paraphrasing Humphrey. "I want salt evenly over the whole area. A salt sprayer. Make it happen!"

"I'll do my best."

She took another drag, returning the cigarette. "What's your big idea?"

"You are not the only one who can be secretive."

"Oh, come on! I gave you solid gold. The salt sprayer! And the train—I just reinvented the train! Don't I get credit for that?"

"Okay, okay. My big idea," he said, "is Wildfire."

As they walked, Xavi delivered a version of the presentation he'd done in class. "The greatest impediment to online commerce is that the modern consumer is afraid to input bank details on a website. Both sides—sales point and client—want to do business. But they need a secure way to take the next step. That is where Wildfire comes in: a new form of money, for all transactions conducted on the information superhighway. You send a credit-card payment to Wildfire, mail a check or bank order, and in exchange you get tokens redeemable with cooperating businesses on the World Wide Web. Consumers get security and vendors get income. Furthermore, Wildfire tokens offer protection against instability in the world. You are safe from currency fluctuations, from government irresponsibility in monetary policy, from devaluations. Keeping money in the currency of the country where you happen to be born makes no sense in today's globalized world. We need a virtual currency for a virtual future: Wildfire."

"Xavi!"

"What?"

"That sounds like an actual idea."

"Yes, of course."

"How did you come up with that?"

"You like it?"

"I mean, I don't know anything. But it sounds insanely great."

He laughed shyly.

Tooly—calibrating her effect on him—considered commending him even more lavishly, or kissing his cheek, or saying they must go into business together. She inhaled the bracing air. "I always wanted a hand muff, like in those glamorous movies about the tsars," she said, then unglamorously lost her balance and snatched his arm to steady herself. She held it all the way to the corner of 115th Street. Outside the building, she handed him the leash and pushed away, skating down the frosty sidewalk in alternating black streaks. "Are you staying in the city through Christmas and New Year's?" she shouted.

"For part of it."

"I'm around, too," she said, skating back.

Tooly had no seasonal festivities at her place in Brooklyn. Humphrey boycotted public holidays, considering them rank conformism. But when she stopped in they did play Christmas Ping-Pong. Even that was ruined by the presence of Sarah, sulking because Tooly hadn't come for a shopping expedition on her twenty-first birthday. Worse still, Venn hadn't been in touch—never had he ignored her like this. She'd waited *weeks*. Her flight to Italy was in a few days, and she pressed Tooly to come along. When the invitation was rejected, Sarah stormed off into the night.

Humphrey looked up from his book and wiggled his eyebrows, which made Tooly laugh. He called her over to the couch and wondered if perhaps she *should* consider Sarah's offer, especially since there was a job there at that leather-goods store.

"I'm not going anyplace with the empress," Tooly responded with irritation. "And you just know there'd be no job waiting once I got there. There probably isn't even a leather-goods shop. Can you imagine Sarah running a store? You can't shoplift from yourself."

He ducked behind the book.

After a minute, Tooly prepared him a smashed-potato sandwich, an edible apology for having snapped.

"I have items," he muttered, as she delivered his food. "Items for discussing purposes."

"I'm sure. Let me guess," she said. "We should run away together?"

"If I tell you," he said, "then you get cross at me. You hate me, maybe."

"Whatever you have to say," she said, amused, "I think I can handle it."

He frowned, on the verge of speaking, wet lips flapping for a moment—then he curled forward and resumed his book, *The Unreality of Time* by J.M.E. McTaggart.

Tooly preferred that he keep reading. His "items" were only ever pretexts to keep her at the apartment, which saddened her, since she longed to be elsewhere.

Yet she couldn't entirely spurn Humphrey. Mostly, it was from pity. But another motive lurked, one she denied: she had no money to manage alone, and he'd always helped with small amounts. She had too much pride to ask Venn for cash, and, anyway, she saw him too irregularly. On occasion, Venn noticed her penury and slipped her a few banknotes. But she regretted those occasions, which only reinforced her uselessness. She could have taken a job, of course, and wouldn't have minded. But something was always afoot with Venn and she had to remain available—he could call at any minute and say, "I'm leaving tomorrow. Coming?"

THE DAY BEFORE New Year's Eve, the city awoke white. A blizzard hit overnight and sanitation trucks plowed the streets at dawn, driving snow into gritty ranges that rose from the gutters and sank to the cleared sidewalks. Tooly strolled through the West Village, stepping between two parked cars on Hudson Street, up an icy hillock whose peak collapsed underfoot. She stamped her snowy sneakers on the pavement, causing the automatic glass doors of a residential building to part. Right past the doorman she went, with such confidence that he merely returned to his horoscope. On the ninth floor, she found a low-lit hallway, doors all the way down. One was ajar, and she entered.

A man stood at the far end of the room, his back to her, gazing through floor-to-ceiling windows at the view of Manhattan.

"Excuse me," she said, hesitating in the doorway. "So sorry to bother you but—this might sound weird—but I actually grew up in this apartment. I happened to be walking by and was wondering, would it be insane if I asked maybe to peek inside? I'm getting a flood of memories even just standing here. Is that—"

"Very nice," Venn said. "You'll ask to use the toilet next."

"I'm too old for that line," she said, closing the door behind her. "Pity, I wouldn't mind walking into random apartments when I need a bathroom. Actually, yes—why don't I?"

The place was sumptuous, floorboards and walls brilliant white, a white orchid on the coffee table before a leather divan, a braided pachira tree in a pot. Tooly checked out the bookshelf, which contained only volumes about beads, buttons, and Bakelite jewelry.

She joined him at the windows. The panes were four times her height and as wide as the entire apartment, a crystal cityscape of West Village rooftops steaming, high-rises crammed in higgledy-piggledy.

"Who lives in this place?" she asked. His eyes looked so intently ahead that she followed his gaze, only for him to turn to her, a grin creasing his cheeks.

"Who lives here?" he repeated back.

"Yes, here. The place where we're both standing right now. The apartment that—I think I can confidently say—isn't yours."

"You mean this place, where you grew up?"

"Seriously, whose?"

"Just a friend, duck."

"Speaking of your ladyfriends, Sarah is still holding out hope of hearing from you. And Humph is going nuts dealing with her. Could you just see her before she leaves? Or at least phone her at the apartment? It's easy for you, hiding out here in luxury. But we have to deal with her."

"And the boy-lawyer?" he asked, meaning Duncan. "How's that?"

"I'm making friends with the whole place."

"Friends? Make them fall in love with you."

"I might have something for you from there."

He pointed a remote control at the shutters, which lowered with an automated whirr, wiping out the city. "We ready to go?" He often spoke of "we" like this, as if he and Tooly were akin, which flattered her, since she viewed her personality as so small and his as so large. He understood her character and spoke of it so convincingly. When she was little, and he praised her as brave or uncomplaining, she sought to become that way. Until, gradually, she adopted the traits he claimed to have seen from the start.

They set forth into the snow. Venn went most places by foot, and she had assumed this habit. He was as likely to walk for three hours as three minutes, and never informed her of their destination. They tracked north today, past Fourteenth Street, through Chelsea, east at Penn Station, along secondary streets uncleared except over subway grates or where muddy footsteps had preceded them. For blocks, he said nothing.

"So," she asked, to break the silence, "the owner of the white apartment? Anything special?"

"No, no."

"Don't you get the urge to stay with any of these women?"

"Absolutely not. You know me."

"I know you," she said. "But I don't get you. You seem to be cutting out more and more stuff these days."

"That's exactly what I'm doing. I try to distance myself from things."

"What for? I don't see what you gain from that."

"I achieve a peace in it, I suppose," he said. "It's about recognizing how little I need and sticking with that, as forces around (and in me) tempt me to set it aside. I try to get rid of everything unnecessary."

"Meaning what?"

"Everything possible. Even unnecessary thoughts," he explained. "Fear, for example. The only way I was able to deal with fear was to reconcile myself with death. And no longer fearing death makes it so much easier to live how you want, without the interference of conventions, so many of which are just ways of staving off death anyway."

"How so?"

"Things like family, kids. Some people have children expressly so they'll be looked after in old age. They want adulation guaranteed, even when they're no longer worthy of it. The love they give is only because they expect it in return. There's always that condition, and it's at the root of failed love, marriages, friendships."

"Not always a condition," she responded. "Isn't that the point with stuff like marriage and children? It's supposed to be unconditional."

" 'Supposed to be' is just a way of saying 'isn't.' The reality is that people marry and procreate because of pressure from friends, from family. But there's something vital lost the moment couples define themselves by an achievement anyone—good, bad, bright, or boring—achieves with the same simple act. For me, starting a family would be capitulation. Not least because it'd force me to have lunch with uninteresting people whose only point of reference is that our kids take the same dance class."

They walked on in silence. "I don't want kids, either," she said, looking at him.

"Why would you? Children are not remotely interesting till they grow up," he said. "Even then, few turn out to be."

"I was interesting, wasn't I?"

"But you weren't much of a child. Like I never was. We were hanging around in kids' bodies, waiting for time to rectify the mixup."

"Some children must be nice."

"How many did you like when you were one? I defy anyone to tell me that having them is meaningful," he said. "It's supposed to make you more loving and nurturing. But those are things I aim to be irrespective. People who must have a child to be kind are missing something in their emotional setup; they require someone's neediness to give their lives meaning. Life has enough meaning and beauty already. Discovering that is a proper pursuit. Not just making helpless little organisms. Or marrying whoever once turned you on. Bonds between people form in particular circumstance and times, and ought to end once those pass. But people are so frightened of being left alone that they collect all these malformed relationships. Accepting loneliness is everything."

"You're crazy," she said, laughing.

He chuckled. "I'm challenging my crazy self," he said. "Testing my limits and getting stronger in the process. Can I go without friendship, pleasures, warmth? Can I walk for twenty-four hours straight through the night? Can I challenge a tyrant? If yes, what have I achieved? An insight? A vanity? A change somewhere in me? To pursue my own life satisfies me in the way that parenthood must for mothers and fathers. Most of them would find my views offensive. But later they'll find themselves attracted to me."

Rounding the corner, they confronted a peculiar scene. At the entrance of a closed office building across the street, a bum stood, tottering over a sleeping bag, which he jostled with his foot before unzipping his filthy black jeans and, right there, urinating on it.

"I think there's someone in that sleeping bag," Tooly said. "He's pissing right on them."

"Stay here."

"Wait a second." But he was already crossing the street.

The bum—knuckles covered in blue tattoos, face inked, too—zipped his fly, cursed the sleeping bag and kicked it, provoking a howl from within. He grabbed the end of the nylon bag and dragged it, a body flailing within. Noticing Venn, the bum paused, glaring from under a scabby brow. "Guy's a faggot," he said, by way of explanation. "He's blocking my house." He hammer-fisted the sleeping bag, prompting another muffled wail.

Venn pointed down the street. "Go that way. Now."

"It's my motherfucking door, man."

A toothless face jutted from the sleeping bag, nose bleeding, greasy comb-over flopping in the wind. "Aren't you just Mr. Sunshine," he babbled. "I think we're in love now."

"See?" the bum told Venn. "Guy's a fag."

"Leave it."

"Tell the fag to leave."

"Now," Venn said. "Or I rip your ears off."

"What you say?"

Venn didn't repeat himself.

As the bum unleashed another kick at the sleeping bag, Venn rammed him against the building. The bum struck the wall with a thud and fell to the snowy pavement. Venn dropped atop, knee in his chest, pinning him, muscles straining as he pushed downward.

"Hurting me, asshole!" the bum hollered. "Can't fucking breathe!" After futile squirming and howling, he went limp. When Venn dragged him to his feet, the bum lunged for a head-butt. Venn caught him by the throat and eye socket, jutted a leg behind his, thrust forward his shoulder, knocking the man to the pavement, against which he bashed his face twice, before pulling him to his feet and frog-marching him a short distance away. "You're done."

Bleeding, the bum stumbled off, stopping at the corner to shout back curses.

Tooly knelt before the madman in the sleeping bag: a little person, sweet-faced, effeminate, and so damaged that he could have been thirty or seventy. "You okay?" she asked.

"Why," he answered, "why don't you go screw yourselves." He cackled and pulled his head back inside the urine-drenched sleeping bag.

"A lunatic," Venn said calmly, and turned to Tooly. "Ready?"

He resumed their walk as if nothing had happened. She hastened to match his pace, shaky but determined to exude nonchalance. "Look." She held up her hand. "I'm trembling and I didn't even do anything! You're completely calm."

"Does no good to get frightened in a situation like that."

"I don't get frightened because I think it's a good idea."

"Always best to keep your wits about you—a big man like that could have fallen and cracked his head, especially on a snowy day. Anyway, nobody walked past."

"You were watching for bystanders during all that?"

"Well, I can't count on you to be my lookout," he said cheerfully.

"Venn," she said, "did you tell that guy you'd rip his ear off? Please tell me I misheard that."

"I never said that." He paused. "I said 'ears,' plural—there's no point taking just one."

"How do you even think of a thing like that?"

He threw an arm around her, pulled her over, knuckled her ribs, earning a squeak.

To witness violence but be spared—to stand behind his shield—always left her giddy. It made her talk and talk. She boasted lavishly of all she'd gathered for him about the students. Venn listened intently—he'd always shared her curiosity about the lives of strangers. Indeed, he was the one who first stirred that interest in her.

"This Duncan likes you?"

"He does."

"He's in love with you, duck!" Venn said. "How could he not be! How could he not be."

"But wait—listen." She returned to Xavi, detailing his idea for the online currency. Venn knew all sorts of business guys. Could he make something of this?

"Are you saying take his idea?"

"No," she responded. "Would you want to?"

"Much rather get him involved. Could fit beautifully at the Brain Trust."

"That's what I thought."

"But there's the fee to join, plus the monthly rental," Venn reminded her. "The kid has that kind of cash?"

"He's on scholarships, I think, and gets help from friends."

"Plus, he's buddies with your boy-lawyer, who has funds."

"Don't know," she said, hoping to move this away from Duncan.

"Dear me. What are you doing up there?" he teased. "You don't know if the boy-lawyer has funds? I know already, and I never even met the guy! His father's an architect in Connecticut. His folks are covering his law school and lodgings comfortably. Is he getting student loans?"

"Not sure."

"Tooly, Tooly," Venn said affectionately.

"What?" she replied, amused.

"These are things you should know by now!" Delighted, he told her, "What would I do without you, duck? You're still the only person who makes me laugh."

"You'd be a wreck without me."

"Exactly right. I was saying before how I test myself by going without, right? Doing that shows me what I do need."

"Which is?"

"Just walks like this. Conversations like this. Humor like ours." He looked at her, earnest now. "I depend on you."

She nodded fast, heart racing. He walked on, and she kept in stride. "But Venn," she asked, "do you like this Wildfire idea?"

"I'd give your African friend a cubicle at the Brain Trust for nothing. Unfortunately, they're not mine to give. I only look after that place."

"For your venture-capitalist guy, right? Maybe he'd be interested."

"Mawky is looking for companies that are ready to launch—not looking to hand-hold, as he puts it. But if your friends are serious, if they can rustle up basic funding and get this moving, it might be interesting."

"You like the idea, then?"

"Listen, send me the African kid. We'll have a chat. Then if you and your friends raise enough for membership and a few months' rental, I'll find a place for you. And if you get that far I'll put you together with Mawky."

"Seriously?"

"I'll always help you, Tooly."

"But not if you're just being nice. Not as a favor. I want us to do a proper project together."

"My project with you, as far as I'm concerned, is our friendship."

"Who cares about your lousy friendship."

"I know, you want glory. Why not? You're in New York. Ambition is the municipal pastime. If you want, just keep tickling those boys uptown. It'll produce something."

"You think?"

"The lawyer's parents must be shelling out fifty thousand a year for NYU already. If their son loves you, they'd be open to funding your future."

"Don't know if going through Duncan is a good idea. The father is a massive lump of jerk."

"That part, duck, is up to you."

Alive to the tremors of her mood, he patted her cheek, which made her smile. "Tooly, neither of us is interested in stuff like this. You won't find anybody who cares less about money than me. How much do I need for a year of living well? How much do I spend? Nothing. Money is totally uninteresting. What you and me want is freedom from fools. The less cash, the more you have to deal in fools. Money is dull. But independence? *That* is interesting."

Her life among the students seemed so distant and frivolous when she was with Venn. Those kids had no clue—all their debates about the left and the right, as if ideology mattered anymore. Despite their dinner-table bravado, none of them would have stepped in to help that battered man back there, though all would have wanted to. But Venn intervened. He didn't act for praise; he cared nothing of what people thought. Nor did he fear spittle or punches, if suffering them was necessary in order to live as he intended.

They reached Times Square, where the glittering ball drop and the fireworks installations were in place, vendors hawking Year 2000 paraphernalia, tourists stumbling around in sensory overload. She and Venn passed unnoticed through the crowd. They could have chosen almost any of these strangers and spun them in knots within minutes. Venn and she had engineered many people in the past. It was intoxicating, the unholy control of another human. They never did so with cruel ends, however—engineering another's fate was not necessarily destructive. Often, Venn knew better than they what was best. After all, he had been engineering her for years.

AFTER HER ANZIO TRIP, Tooly phoned Duncan. She wanted to see Humphrey again and was coming back. Duncan was relieved—"Got worried you'd left me with this situation," he said—and insisted that she save on New York hotels by staying in their basement. She, in turn, insisted on helping out while there.

This proved timely because Bridget was about to start her new part-time job, which left a gap in the ferrying of Mac to his summer courses at the YMCA each morning. Thankfully, the triplets didn't require a driver to their day camp, enjoying transportation courtesy of various peer admirers, whose moms shuttled them everywhere. "Abi, Mads, and Chlo are the rockstars of third grade," Duncan explained. Mac enjoyed no such fan base. He had not even been invited to a birthday party in several years.

That first day, Tooly dropped him outside the Y and parked the family minivan at the train station, commencing her two-hour commute to south Brooklyn. She intended to get Humphrey reading again, out of that room, out of his torpor. He still had moments of clarity, according to Duncan.

"Hello," she said, closing the door after herself. "I came back."

"Okay," he replied from his armchair.

"Not pleased to see me?" She stood at his window, daylight silhouetting her. "I flew back over the ocean so we could spend a few days together and talk. I'd like to discuss some things with you, Humph. Okay? And we can go out, too—fresh air, walks, chess possibly. When you're ready, we'll talk."

"Don't know what you're saying." She found his hearing aid by the sink and helped him insert it. He stuffed his hands between his thighs, blinking toward the convex reflection in the switched-off television. "Is there coffee?"

"Let me make you a cup." She did so in the communal kitchen, returning with two mugs of Nescafé, his abundantly sugared. He raised the coffee, lips twitching to meet the mug.

She looked into her own cup, stared at the black liquid. Hearing him speak—Russian accent gone—incensed her anew. She mentioned her visit with Sarah. "You know who I'm talking about," she said. "Don't you?"

"Frankly," he responded, "I find your questions strange."

She left him for a few minutes to finish his drink and occupied herself by organizing his books by subject. Yelena had lined them up by size—tall with tall, short with short—creating peculiar neighbors: Plato's *Republic* beside *The Ultimate Food Processor Cookbook* beside *Selected Cautionary Verses* by Hilaire Belloc, each a long-lost acquaintance of Tooly's ("The Chief Defect of Henry King/Was chewing little bits of String").

Humphrey mumbled something.

"What?" she asked, arms laden with volumes.

"Relieved to see you again."

"What's that?" she said, stalling because the remark upset her.

"I'm relieved to see you."

"That's nice, Humphrey." She spoke louder than intended.

"I have a problem with my memory," he said. "It's uneven. Depends what cells are attacked. Blood doesn't flow in that direction. But I don't want to exaggerate the problem." His lips smacked together; he took a breath.

Her pocket rang. She took out the cellphone: Bridget calling, with an apology and a plea. Starting her new job was requiring nightmarish admin, and the tech guy still hadn't set up her laptop. As an exceptional favor, could Tooly pick up Mac this afternoon?

So, all the way back to Connecticut she went. Outside the main doors of the Y, the pudgy boy waited. She tapped the horn of the minivan, opened the passenger door. He failed to notice, so she parked and walked over. Mac recognized her only when she was three steps away. "Oh," he said shyly. "Hi."

"Were you waiting long?"

"Don't think so."

"Went well today?"

He nodded, and she handed him a banana, having bought two from a grocery store outside the Sheepshead Bay subway. Mac peeled his oddly, not like a blooming flower but removing a single strip all the way down, then finding nowhere to put it. He looked for a garbage can, as if one might materialize amid the parking spaces. In distraction, he dropped the rest of the banana on the tarmac, then crouched and resumed peeling, one strip at a time, right there on the ground. How odd, this boy. "Come on," she said gently. To spare his evident embarrassment, she kept walking toward the vehicle.

Mac hurried after, catching her hand, but only for a few strides. "Whoops—I'm not supposed to do that."

"Why not? You're allowed to with me."

When Bridget arrived home, she changed into civvies and debriefed Tooly on her first day at the law firm. While she chatted, the long-faced triplets yanked at their mother's jean pockets. "There's going to be a revolution," Bridget warned, and stepped away for a bit of blender-grinding and oven-checking, then returned to the conversation. Talk of the job shifted to her anxieties about Mac, who was being left behind at this new school, already his third. "But boys are always slow to get going. He seems smart to you, right?" she suggested. "Was he being good when you picked him up?"

"Absolutely fine." She recounted the banana anecdote, thinking it endearing.

But Bridget looked so disappointed.

The triplets scowled at Tooly, then at their mother, who detailed Mac's troubles and his diagnosis of TDD (temper dysregulation disorder with dysphoria), which his psychiatrist was managing with Seroquel, Azaleptin, and Lamictal, a cocktail that left the boy sluggish and dissociated and had doubled his weight—but otherwise seemed as if it might be working. Bridget was so connected to her son, tortured by anything that afflicted him, yet powerless to suffer it on his behalf. It didn't occur to her that it could be unwise to speak openly of one child's flaws before his siblings, who were likely to report it back, possibly with malice. At least Mac wasn't present, having disappeared downstairs to snoop at Tooly's things, which was fair game as far as she was concerned. She'd have done the same had a strange grown-up invaded her home.

When the tuna melt was served, Tooly excused herself, claiming to have eaten earlier. In truth, she just needed a break—wasn't accustomed to so many people at once. And she had resolved to intrude as little as possible during her stay, planning to skip their meals (only partly because eating with a YouTube soundtrack made her want to scream into her sleeve). But, as soon as dinner ended upstairs, Mac came down to the music room and watched her tune the ukulele. "Want to try?" she asked.

"I'm supposed to be doing piano," he said, pointing at the Yamaha keyboard in the corner.

"Oh, sorry—I'm in your way."

"You want to play with me?"

"I can't really sight-read music," she explained. "I just battle at this piece by Rossini. It's all I know."

"I mean play Xbox."

"What does that involve?" She found herself being pulled upstairs.

Still puzzling over game-controller buttons, Tooly was already riddled with bullets. Duncan appeared in the doorway, eating a microwaved burrito and checking his BlackBerry, still in suit and tie. "How's it hanging?" he asked, mouth full, flopping on the couch and turning the plasma screen to a news channel.

"We were playing!" Mac complained. Finding no recourse, the boy departed.

Duncan switched among CNN, Fox News, MSNBC, and CNBC,

appearing to scrutinize Tooly with faint irritation. "Do you work out?"

"I walk. Does that count?"

"I sit on the train. Does that count?" It seemed to: he had spread, especially in the sitting regions. "You notice many changes in your body from walking?"

"To be honest, Duncan, I make it a policy not to look below my neck. I try to keep all this area"—she indicated from collarbones down—"free of major injury, but I don't see any reason to actually look at it. Hey, it might be terrible to ask this, but you don't have a small drink I could steal, do you?"

"Wait here." He rose from the couch. He thumbed in a text. He looked at her. "Why did I just get up?"

"Drinks."

"What? Oh, right. Some old wine in the fridge, possibly? I could open something."

"Not just for me," she protested, her voice fading from lack of conviction. She did want a drink; this day had constricted her.

He returned from the kitchen with a bottle of Beck's for her, then lay on the floor, raised the volume on CNN, and checked both cellphones at once, each intermittently bleeping, as if the two devices were communicating with each other. "The girls just texted me that you play the ukulele. What's up with that?"

"That's thanks to you—you're the one who got me into music."

He pointed the remote at a couple of debating pundits. "The Bush crew were right on one count: people in this country *don't* live in the reality-based community."

Bridget appeared in the doorway. "I sense a state-of-the-Union rant," she warned Tooly. "Listening not advised." She asked her husband, "Are we going to have your decline-of-Western-civilization thing now, where you end up railing against call centers?"

"I'll try not to drag the call centers into it. But, parenthetically, call centers do mark the decline of Western civilization."

Tooly laughed.

"I'm not actually kidding."

Bridget looked at Tooly. "He's actually not."

"Explain," Tooly said.

" 'Explain' is the single most dangerous word to utter in front of my husband."

"Okay, here's my theory. So, like, in the past," he began, "when the American people acted like dumb-asses, it actually didn't matter. Because we were being led by smart-asses, right? But now we're basically run by lobbyists and pollsters, while Congress is a bunch of squabbling brats. So when the people act like dumb-asses today it matters. We had the war on terrorism, the war in Iraq, the war in Afghanistan. We're going broke buying these billion-dollar drones to chase a bunch of clowns through the Pakistani tribal areas. Meantime, every serious country is burning past us."

"You make it sound like a race," Tooly said.

"That's what it is. There's, like, one point two billion Chinese, and they want what we got. They become as rich as we are? Well, they just can't. We're at war already. You hear this stuff about hacking? I guarantee you, China has a zillion geniuses stapled to their desktops figuring out how to ram us. Look how they're hoarding our debt. We basically mortgaged this country to Beijing."

"I remember people saying doomsday stuff like this in the 1980s," Tooly noted. "How America was falling apart and Japan was going to run the world."

"Japan was a boutique. China is the whole shopping mall," he replied. "Our country was in charge of the world for a few seconds. So what did we do? Bitch-slapped Milosevic and Saddam, let global warming go out of control, and convinced the world that we're a bunch of whack-job crusaders. And went broke doing it. That's the story of our generation—the peak and the collapse, all in twenty years."

"I don't actually mind the U.S. not being in charge anymore," Bridget commented. "Not like we did such a great job with that whole superpower thing."

"You think that *we* suck at it?" Duncan responded. "Check out the competition. You want Russia and China running stuff? Russia is, like, the scariest place in the sort-of-free world. And the Chinese will sabotage every climate-change proposal till they've had their fair turn at fucking the planet."

"Language."

"But, Duncan, I don't get where you stand," Tooly said.

"He's an against-everyone guy," Bridget said.

"All politicians in this country are forms of Blagojevich," he said.

"Obama isn't," Bridget said, trying to wrestle the remote from him as he switched to Fox News.

"Obama's from Illinois," he said. "A politician cannot come from Illinois and be clean."

"Isn't that where Lincoln was from?"

"Yeah, and you saw what they did to him."

"Well, *I* think Obama is clean," Bridget said.

"His feet are clean from all that water you think he walks on," Duncan said. "Today's leaders aren't at the standards of the past. Nowhere near."

"Hmm," Tooly began hesitantly, wondering whether to speak her mind. "I don't know," she said. "Just, I always wonder if all this stuff about decline is false nostalgia—as if the old days were full of people opening doors for each other and memorizing poetry and playing the piano."

"That's exactly how I imagine the old days!" Duncan said, laughing.

"People in the old days were as rotten as people now, don't you think?" she continued. "They were probably *more* ignorant and violent. There were great people back then—I'm sure your grandparents were very nice, especially to you, their grandson. But people from the Greatest Generation also spent a fair bit of time abusing and enslaving each other. No?"

"You think this current period is so fantastic?" he retorted. "Everything is progress everywhere?"

"Not progress or decline. I just think most people probably have a few years at their peak, and attribute to that period all the hope and wholesomeness they had then. Once their moment has passed, everything seems in decline."

"You're saying I'm past my peak," he said, amused.

"That's exactly what she just said," Bridget affirmed, clapping.

"Except, except, except," Tooly interrupted, "you're actually even weirder, because you believe all the best stuff happened in a period you didn't even live in."

"Come on—you're way worse," he said. "At least I embrace the techy zeitgeist. You own a frickin' bookshop, my dear. Do you even have a computer there? Are you familiar with these newfangled machines?"

"As a matter of fact, I do have one. And now I've got that cellphone you lent me."

"You have a tablet yet?"

"I'm waiting till the stone ones come out, the ones that come with a chisel."

"My point exactly."

"No, you're right in a way," she acknowledged. "I don't feel involved in a lot of what's going on. But that's always been true for me." So much of her childhood had revolved around the lessons of the Soviet Empire and World War II that, once Tooly set out on her own, she'd needed a while to acclimatize to the present. It wasn't 9/11 that did it so much as the Iraq War; sometime around 2003, the twenty-first century seemed to detach from the twentieth. "And I'm still not sure which century I fit in. Maybe neither."

"That's such a cop-out. We're the same age, pretty much. You've been part of the same period I have. Secretly, you're a declinist like me. You just don't want to sound negative. Any period is *not* as good as any other, just like any place is not as good as any other."

"You could rank times and places?"

"Easily."

"Then you'd have to admit that this time and place are pretty good," she said. "No chance of war breaking out in Darien, Connecticut. You're well-off, educated, healthy. Your kids take filmmaking and modern dance at day camp. They'll live long and happy lives. So everything is in decline?"

He shook his head, annoyed—her summary failed to explain why everything was so irritating nowadays. "Missing the point," he said.

He was right to notice something missing. She had not stated her fundamental view: that, for Duncan, time and place, fortune and misfortune, had only a glancing impact. He was temperamentally condemned to embitterment and would revert to that condition regardless of circumstances, just as lottery winners, after the euphoria, ended up as morose or cheerful as they'd ever been. People did not see the world for what it was but for what they were.

All fell quiet, except the background chatter of a peppy news anchor: ". . . from the back of the bus—and the front of it, too!—with a story up close and personal, a no-holds-barred look at the success of Michele Bachmann's bus tour. Stick with us, for the last word in fair and . . ."

He turned off the television. "All these people should be put in jail," he said. "Not just any jail but some nightmare place where they get beaten around the clock."

"I'm putting the kids to bed," Bridget said.

Tooly excused herself, too. "I need a good sleep tonight."

Duncan remained, staring at the black screen. The rant had quenched nothing. He awoke his two phones, each bright and ready to behave, just as the outside world never would.

IN THE COMING days, Humphrey's mood varied—talkative one visit, distant the next. Overnight, he stumbled around his room, restless but afraid to venture outside, even to use the shared toilets. By morning, his late-night activities were evident in the piles of toppled books, bedcovers strewn with documents, food on the floor.

Yelena came early to ensure that no disasters had befallen him, made breakfast, washed him. Tooly took over around midday, occasionally crossing paths with the Russian woman's son, Garry, an engineering student who was trying to resolve Humphrey's problems with the television remote.

Once everyone else had gone, Tooly turned off the blaring TV and posed questions about his accent and about their past. But each query distressed Humphrey—he wanted to help, but failed to summon what she wanted. A few times, he snapped at her. At other times, he was endearing, such as when he offered her a bunch of cherries that Yelena had left.

"Grapes," Tooly corrected him. "Thank you. I'll have a few."

Whenever she succeeded in dipping into his memory, it was his childhood, not hers, that came out—climbing a statue, or milking a cow, or throwing an apricot pit and fearing he'd blinded a girl. They were reminiscences she already knew, but he insisted on recounting each to the end. Occasionally, an unfamiliar anecdote emerged, such as when he recalled, as a very little boy, lying atop his mother while she did read-throughs of plays and falling asleep to the flip of pages.

"She was involved in the theater? But you never say your parents' names, do you, Humph. Where did all this happen?"

"I lay there and heard pages turning."

"Does it feel," she asked, "when you're telling these stories, does it feel like it's you? Or does it feel like a different person back then?"

"I'm the same as I was," he said. "Only later."

After a minute, she asked, "Would you like a walk down to Emmons Avenue? We can go slowly. You set the pace."

But he never wanted to leave his room, just sat in his armchair, staring toward the window. Tooly settled on his bed, leafing through books, yet struggled to concentrate. When leaving for the day, she closed the door after herself and stood in the hallway, often for more than a minute. Felt abominable to leave. She arrived back in Connecticut later and later. The McGrorys stopped expecting her for dinner.

Besides Yelena and Tooly, he had no visitors. But phone calls came often, always from medical-bill collectors, badgering him over a small fortune owed for a hernia procedure several years earlier. Humphrey believed he had paid, so Tooly asked them to send an itemized bill. The invoice was four pages and incomprehensible. Nobody—least of all those demanding the money—could explain what anything was for, only that the bill *was* correct. Pool your family resources, they told her, and pay (including for inexplicable items, such as $12,184 for "Assorted"). The cost would have been less—though still unaffordable for Humphrey—had he been enrolled in Medicare. But nobody could find any document attesting to his identity, citizenship, even his right to be in this country. The medical-bill pestering made him refuse further checkups, including those he needed on his eyes, hearing, and memory. He kept pill bottles—for high blood pressure, cholesterol, memory acuity, glaucoma, a vitamin deficiency—under the cushion of his armchair and claimed he took his doses in her absence, though she disbelieved him.

This was proving to be a disaster. Venn would know what to do about it—he'd even know how to handle those bill collectors. "Do you remember *anything* about where he went?"

"Those lights," Humphrey responded. "What are those lights?"

She followed his sight line to the switched-off TV. "Nothing. A reflection."

"Is it time for dinner?"

"Look. Bright outside." She pointed out the window, then at the wall clock. "See, twelve-fifteen P.M."

"You take its word over mine?"

Two weeks passed, and her scheduled return to Wales neared. She had understood nothing here. The mystery of his accent remained, as did the puzzle of Venn's disappearance, and all the questions about her abduction. She tried not to think of her impending return, and would not have, had it not been for a call from Fogg. Mr. and Mrs. Minton—the academics who'd founded World's End Books and still owned the property—were raising her rent. Trouble in the stock market had halved their retirement savings; they couldn't afford to rent at a loss any longer. Nor could Tooly afford to pay more.

World's End Books would last perhaps three months. She could keep employing Fogg that long, but no more. He needed to find employment elsewhere. Perhaps this was better for him—the shop had been too cozy a niche. She freed him of any obligation to keep it going till her return. After all, it wasn't even certain when she'd be back.

"Wait, you're staying? I thought he wasn't telling you anything."

"He's not. But I can't leave right now," she said. "I'm sorry, Fogg. You'll have a great reference from me."

"Ah, well," he said, quiet a moment. "Shame, really."

He'd grown up in that shop. There was no other bookstore in the village. But he might apply for another kind of service job—at the minimarket, perhaps.

For two days, Tooly felt nauseated by all this. But she reminded herself that one mustn't get attached. Thereafter, if Fogg called with work questions she kept the conversations short. When he asked after Humphrey, she conveyed little, withdrawing her private life from public view again. His calls stopped. The bookshop—indeed, Caergenog itself—faded from reality. The McGrorys were delighted to learn that she was extending her stay. It spared them finding a new driver for Mac.

Among Humphrey's books, Tooly kept returning to her old copy of *Nicholas Nickleby*, the same bashed-up paperback she had when they first met. The smell of it recalled so powerfully Mr. Priddles's vile classroom, where she'd hidden in these pages.

"Can I read you a bit?" she asked Humphrey. "I know you don't like made-up stories, but this one is nice. You won't have to worry about your eyes. Just close them and listen. Okay?" Before he could refuse, she began:

There once lived, in a sequestered part of the county of Devonshire, one Mr. Godfrey Nickleby: a worthy gentleman, who, taking it into his head rather late in life that he must get married, and not being young enough or rich enough to aspire to the hand of a lady of fortune, had wedded an old flame out of mere attachment, who in her turn had taken him for the same reason. Thus two people who cannot afford to play cards for money, sometimes sit down to a quiet game for love.

"What do you think?" she asked.

Eyes closed, Humphrey nodded gravely. She went on, her attention only half on the text, the remainder contemplating her old friend. To her knowledge, he had achieved nothing to outlast his life—no off-spring, no legacy. Nor had he believed in anything more than this existence. No afterlife, in the religious sense of harp-strumming on clouds, nor in the secular sense of worldly accomplishment.

What he had done with eighty-odd years was absorb the cleverest minds to translate themselves into print; he'd played chess; he'd pondered. And why *not* just use life as one pleased? Why spend an existence tormented by alarm clocks? Or did his failure to produce anything amount to tragedy, a waste of the fact that his particular consciousness, among the infinite possible variations, had popped into being?

If he had achieved little, this resembled Tooly's own path to date. Her twenties had rushed by. Now her thirties were well upon her. She had the sense of never completing any stage, of failing to grab any single year and take hold. In teen years, people yearned to be liked; in their twenties, to be impressive; in their thirties, to be needed. But she had jumbled it, some phases too early, others not at all.

"I like that man," Humphrey interrupted as she read on. "What's his name?"

"That character? He's called Newman Noggs."

"You feel that you could see him! With the thing about his buttons."

Before much else could be learned of Mr. Noggs and his buttons, Humphrey was snoring. After an hour, she readied his macaroni-and-cheese dinner on the counter, sticking a sign on the microwave in giant capitals to explain again how it worked. She hesitated in the hallway. The night before, he had dropped his dinner and eaten only a few bites salvaged from the floor. She sighed to picture him on his knees, reaching shakily under the bed for a chunk of dusty chicken.

On her way out, Tooly gazed down the empty staircase. If Venn walked up these steps (she looked to where he'd stand, and she smiled, seeing him grin at her), he could explain everything. Not just the muddle of her past but the muddle of her present, too—what to do now, where, and with whom.

Tooly had no further commitments that evening. No children to drive, no one expecting her anywhere on earth. She walked to the Brighton Beach boardwalk as dusk fell, sat on a bench there; a blustery summer evening. Yelena's son, who had finally fixed Humphrey's TV remote, happened to be walking past, an Eastpack day bag slung over his shoulder. She wondered whether to say his name, and if it would carry through the wind.

He noticed her. "Yo," Garry said. "You're the daughter of that old man."

"So they say."

He asked what she was doing there, just sitting, as if this were an insufficient activity. "The Starbucks is open late, if you're looking for one."

She was not. He wouldn't believe there wasn't some object she required.

Relenting, she said, "I wouldn't hate a drink."

He contemplated this, then snapped his fingers badly. "You won't like this place—I can show you."

It was the sort of terrible suggestion that immediately won her over.

She realized as they approached the bar that Garry hadn't intended to deposit her at its door (in which case she planned to sneak off to the subway) but to join her. The sign promised: "Russian & American nightclub: Live music and dancing every night starting 9 P.M."

"We're early for the dancing," she said.

He opened the door. Eastern European pop music blared, the bartender chanting along. Garry ordered for them, switching impressively to his native Russian—"водка!"—voice deepening as he did so. A carafe of vodka arrived. He waved away Tooly's attempts to pay for her share.

"Are you supposed to sip each shot?" she asked. "Or down it in one gulp?"

He was inconclusive, so she tried both ways, alcohol seeping into her, pushing back the day.

Would Humphrey be sleeping still? Or plodding around, discovering her note on the microwave, unable to find his glasses. Strange to think of him, so near yet following his own story line, separate from hers.

No point badgering him with questions anymore, she decided. He had no answers for her. Time to erase this. All that matters is now. Nothing before. Stop thinking. Stop.

As Garry drank, his deep voice became less baritone, and he responded to her humor, his distracted blue eyes fastening on her now, looking downward, since he was a tall young man, lean and long-limbed.

"Do you have a patronymic?" she asked. "Like those characters in Russian novels."

"We also exist in real life, not only in Dostoyevsky books."

"I'm becoming aware of this. But is your proper name something like Vassily Petrovich?" she speculated. "I like the sound of that. Makes me feel like there'll be a droshky waiting outside."

"Only the el train."

He put his hand on her knee, then, with the next shot, moved it to her thigh, then her hip, then her shoulder. "Are you climbing?" she asked.

She enjoyed his kiss, though it was slightly odd, given that he was probably seven years younger than she. "You are a cougar," he declared.

"Am I? Not on purpose."

"Now what?"

"Now what what?"

"I still live at home," he informed her.

"Do you know that Chekhov story 'The Kiss,'" she went on, "where this unlucky officer mistakenly—"

"Not everything we Russians do comes out of Chekhov."

"Or Dostoyevsky."

"More Dostoyevsky, perhaps."

# 1988

A BEER BOTTLE SWEATED on the café-terrace table. Beside it sat an extra glass for Tooly, so the ten-year-old could taste alcohol for the first time. Her deck shoes skimmed the pavement as she swung her legs back and forth, the plastic chair edge impressing a sweaty line under her knees.

It was late, and she hadn't returned home. Her heart sank at the thought of Paul. But if she mentioned him Sarah might take her back. Tooly closed her eyes, clutching the strap of her book bag.

"No one will take that, I promise," Sarah said.

"Just, I'm famous for forgetting stuff."

"Are there valuables inside?"

Tooly, normally private about her bag, opened it for Sarah to see: ring binder, *Nicholas Nickleby*, gym shorts and T-shirt, specks of grit mysteriously accumulated, her sketchbook. "You want to see my drawings?"

"Are you a good artist?"

Tooly shook her head. She handed over the sketchbook, watching for Sarah's reaction, the woman's eyes smiling first, lips joining in.

"It's all noses," Sarah remarked.

"I can't draw a whole face."

"They're very nice noses."

"Can I see in yours, Sarah?"

"In my nose?"

Tooly laughed. "In your bag!"

Sarah opened its clasps, baring the scents and treasures of the adult female: a compact, tissues, lipstick, cigarette pack, disposable lighter, a pair of underwear and a toothbrush, sunglasses, tampon, nail polish, chewing gum.

"What's that little hammer for?"

"In case I get locked in somewhere and need to break a window."

"Sarah?"

"Hmm?"

"Is your bubble gum nice?"

"Want to try? Take anything you want," she said. "Are you liking that beer, by the way?"

"It's a bit sour. Not sour but . . . I heard once," she said, "that if you get drunk it's like being awake and asleep at the same time. Is that true?"

"It's lovely, being drunk." Sarah swigged from their beer, arm draped over her chair, cigarette tip grazing the sidewalk, legs extended, crossed at the ankles.

How odd that, a few hours earlier, Tooly had been in the school microbus, blocks from home, then swept off to Khlong Toey Market, now here. She took another frothy sip. "Can I ask a question?"

"They're the best thing to ask, my dear."

"You didn't like school when you were little, did you?"

"Hated it! Awful. Hardly went." She had spent far more time with her father, Ettore, an Italian immigrant who moved to Kenya after the war to open a game park for his wealthy compatriots. Lacking capital and land, he'd married someone with both, a well-off English girl. Ettore and Caroline—"Now, *they* knew how to make cocktails on a hot day," Sarah said—produced three daughters, of whom Sarah was the youngest and, to her father, the favorite. A handsome tanned man with a repository of bawdy jokes in six languages, he took Sarah everywhere, making her the official safari photographer at age eleven. Her sisters remained at the house, mastering domesticity and waiting until suitable gentlemen arrived to determine the course of their lives.

Ettore considered his eldest daughters unseriously, an attitude Sarah absorbed, exchanging wry glances with him at dinner. Most of his clients were men, but it was their wives whom he bedazzled. By adolescence, Sarah found herself gaining charms of her own, appraised by men now, which both appalled and addicted her.

"The English colonists hated our operation," she recalled. "Now and then, one of our clients insisted on a submachine gun, or used nail boards to hunt the elephants, which was considered terribly uncouth."

"Did you live in the jungle?"

"We lived in a house. A big house, full of junk. My mother collected pointless bits of furniture. We were in the middle of nowhere. Not ideal for young people. They'd hit a button at nine P.M. and everyone over the age of forty fell asleep."

"And how long have you lived in Bangkok?"

"I'm just visiting, Matilda. Only got here a few weeks ago."

"Are you leaving soon?"

"Don't know yet. Depends."

"Why did you come?"

She tucked Tooly's long frizzy hair behind her ears. "Because of you."

Confused but shy about asking more, Tooly sipped her glass of beer, looked at the street, turned back. "Where do you live, normally?"

"I don't live normally. I'm on vacation from now till forever. The world is too interesting to pick one place and stick to it. Don't you think? When you meet people like my sisters, who never move, who still live in the town where they were born—I'll never understand it. They're a different species. In life," she stated, "there are people who stay and people who go." She scrunched her empty pack of Kools, depositing it in Tooly's palm. "Wait here, my dear. Must replenish."

Tooly watched Sarah disappear into the café. *Were* there people who stay and others who go? If Tooly could choose, she wanted to be someone who went. A hand stroked her face from the other side. "Success," Sarah said, unwrapping the new pack, taking her seat.

"I'm feeling asleep and awake at the same time," Tooly said.

"Put your head down, if you like." Sarah laid her open hand on the tabletop, a pillow for the girl. Tooly released the book-bag strap and rested, closing her eyes.

She awoke sharply, frightened by the noise, the neon. Two more empty beer bottles sat on the table. "I have to go," Tooly said. "Is it late?"

"It's supposed to be late. Where we're going doesn't start till after dark."

"I was thinking about those kingfishers you let out of the cage."

"Lovely, wasn't it?" She kissed Tooly's hand. "So," she said, standing. "Ready?"

"Maybe I should go home."

"Do you *really* want to?"

Their tuk-tuk buzzed down the road, bouncing over each pothole. Car headlights streaked past. Taillights peeled off left and right before them, and faces on the sidewalk whooshed by. "That's the market where we were before," Tooly noted. They drove down a deserted *soi*, and the tuk-tuk stopped. A shadowed alley lay ahead.

"You won't get in trouble," Sarah said, rightly guessing Tooly's thoughts. "I'm looking after you. Okay?"

As they walked into the dark, a trio of young guys appeared. One approached Sarah, saying they were on vacation from West Germany and had heard about an underground bar around here. Without breaking stride, she claimed ignorance—but not without a flicker of a smile that dragged the three boy-men in her wake. She cupped her hand behind Tooly's head as they walked, telling the guys, "*This* is the person you should be talking to. She's the one in charge."

Grinning, they crouched beside Tooly and begged, "Come on, little girl. Please, please, show us!"

Tooly pressed her lips tightly together, breathed through her nose, hurrying alongside Sarah.

"Hey, I can hear music," one of the Germans said.

A disco beat pulsated in the distance. The buzz of conversation grew louder. They entered a concrete garden with high walls on either side, and behind it a house in near-ruins. Revelers stood outside, drinking from plastic cups, shouting to be heard.

Sarah pushed through the crowd, greeting acquaintances as she went, then stopped before the front door, waving to two huge bouncers.

"Is this music your fault?" she asked the one with the skinny leather tie.

"It's Venn who wants this sappy shit."

"You can't let Venn pick the music!"

The other bouncer shrugged. "He's the boss."

The crowd inside—mainly foreigners, but Thais among them—swayed, flirted, anticipated punch lines, stared glassy-eyed, fixed cleavage and looked down it, searched for toilets, lined up at the bar. Amid the mass of bodies was an aluminum stepladder against which drinkers propped themselves. An upright piano by the far wall served as a makeshift table, and a disk jockey with headphones bobbed before Technics turntables. Light from a twinkling disco ball sprinkled white dots and, every few seconds, a gust pushed through the crowd as the floor fan rotated, clothes rippling, cigarette ends glowing. Tooly held tight to Sarah's bangles, bumping into strangers' hips, elbows, behinds. At the turntables, Sarah greeted the deejay with a kiss to his cheek, then raised the needle off the record, prompting both jeers and cheers. She flipped through a crate of records. "Guess I should have found something *before* I did that," she remarked, amused by the discontent. "What do you want to hear, Matilda?"

Tooly knew nothing of music. Paul never listened to it, so her awareness revolved around what she had encountered at school: sheet music from band, where she played the ukulele, her specialty being

"Three Blind Mice"; plus the horrible pop cassettes Mr. Priddles put on.

"This one?" Tooly asked, pointing to the only familiar album cover.

"I adore you and will do nearly anything you ask," Sarah said. "But *Ghostbusters* is where I draw the line. Actually—fuck it. *Ghostbusters* it is."

The record crackled, loudspeakers hissed, and the first eerie notes kicked in. The crowd groaned, causing Tooly to look around in fear. But Sarah was greatly entertained and hurried her toward the bar, looking back as a mob converged on the deejay, who rapidly put on Def Leppard.

A long table served as the cash bar, buckling under all the sticky booze bottles. The bartender, a Uruguayan named Jaime, raised both arms in greeting. "*¡Hola, chica! ¿Qué tal?* You good?"

"*Muy* good," she answered, helping herself to a Singha. As Sarah and he chatted, Tooly considered the grown-ups everywhere. She had never been the sole child among this many adults. It was so muggy in here, and her shirt stuck to her, the book-bag strap cutting into her shoulder. She took Sarah's icy beer bottle in both hands, tilted it, froth spurting just as her lips arrived, liquid dribbling down her chin. "Sorry," she said, looking up.

"I'll check if he's there," Sarah was telling the bartender, and took Tooly by the hand, chasing her up the stairs, sending her into giggles. Tooly burst onto the upper floor into another boisterous crowd. Sarah peered out the windows up there—that is, four large holes in the second-story wall—scanning the back patio, where partygoers hung out before a wall fresco of a dolphin. "Nope," she muttered, turning on her heels, slapping away the fug of smoke. "Anyone seen Venn?"

They came upon a sixtyish man sitting alone at a card table, a vinyl chessboard laid out, his hand lingering over a knight, then pulling back. He scratched his sideburns, which were like strips of burned toast. A handwritten sign hung from his table, fluttering each time anyone passed. IF YOU WIN ME, it read, YOU WILL BE VERY STRONG

CHESSPLAYER. In a storage room behind him were piles of boxes, videotapes, fax machines, broken televisions.

"Humphrey!" Sarah said.

This man—the oldest person at that party by decades—continued to stare downward, his eyes hidden under a dark balcony of eyebrows. He wore a polyester dress shirt, tie yanked to the side, blue tennis shorts over a modest potbelly, laceless white sneakers.

"I can't find Venn," she said. "Where is he?"

Still the old man contemplated the chessboard.

Sarah touched his arm and Humphrey flinched, then—perceiving who it was—his face lit up, transforming with pleasure. "My dear darlink!" he said to Sarah in a strong Russian accent, plucking out earplugs made of balled-up toilet paper.

"Who's winning?" she asked. "You or you?"

"Yes, sure—you making fun of me."

"Meet my personal bodyguard." She parted Tooly's hair to bare her face.

"Hello, bodyguard. Nice to meeting." He took her hand, sandwiching it between his. "I can tell only from looking that you are intellectual. Large ears, high on head. When high up, this means ears holding heavy brain."

Doubtfully, Tooly asked, "Do ears hold up your brain?"

"Of course," he replied. "This why I have famous large ears. This means intellectual. One day, if you very lucky, you have big ears like me."

The prophecy was not entirely auspicious, for the old man's ears were not only large but prodigiously hairy. Nevertheless, she thanked him.

He released her hand and turned to Sarah. "*Nyet.* I do not see Venn. But I keep my eyes plucked."

"You'll keep your eyes peeled," Sarah corrected him.

"How I can peel my eyes? No, no—I am not doing this."

"What else do you have to tell me, Humph? Things good?"

"How are things? Just look," he lamented, indicating all the boxes behind him. "This is out of control. How I can live here? He just take over. I cannot allow. These items—you know where they come from? If authorities find, they say I am responsible. Is no good."

"You going to talk to him about it?"

"Talk? What is purpose? I leave."

"No! You're going? When, Humph?"

"Tomorrow, first thing."

"You couldn't *bear* to leave me," she teased. "Listen, if you see Venn, say I'm on the prowl, okay? And don't dare leave Bangkok without saying goodbye."

Humphrey nodded, inserted his earplugs, and returned to the chess problem, his features resuming their dour configuration.

"Well, then. Think I'll let you explore a bit," Sarah told Tooly, kneeling to kiss the girl's forehead. She turned toward the steps down. "Now, where *is* he?" Through the banisters, Tooly watched Sarah disappear into the crowd below.

Tooly was unsure even where to look now, where to place her hands, how to stand. She gripped her book bag and stared down the staircase in case Sarah sprang back up. After an incredibly long time (four minutes), Sarah had not returned, so Tooly went downstairs herself and stepped into the crowd, dodging gesticulating hands, lurching knees. She stood on her tiptoes, leaning one way and the other, but could not spot Sarah. She pushed ahead, catching snippets of speech as she went.

"Must say," a man remarked, sipping from a straw plunged into a coconut, "must say I find it more than a little galling, having been locked in bamboo by the Japs, to take orders from them now. We beat the fuckers, didn't we?"

"The ones I deal with are harmless enough," his friend replied. "Stupid, but harmless."

"They eat raw fish, God help us. Can't trust a race that fails to cook its food. And why do these Orientals persist with the chopstick? Has no one apprised them of the fork?"

"The Thais use a spoon and a fork," a younger man interposed.

"Because the Thais are a likable breed. They even provide their lasses for our delectation," he noted, slapping the behind of one of the bargirls among them; she gave a plastic smile. "What gets my goat," he continued, "is that we gave the Japs a bloody nose during the war, and what happens during the peace? They get rich off us! Selling us awful cars and cameras and who-knows-what-else. All these Orientals do is steal ideas. Not an original thought among them. Everything's made in Hong Kong, but what's invented there? Nothing!"

"To be fair, Jeremy, the Chinese did invent things."

"Name one."

"Well, paper."

"Nonsense. That was Gutenberg, wasn't it?"

"And gunpowder."

"The Germans did that, surely."

"I heard the Chinese actually invented the fork."

"What in heaven's name are you going on about, Giles? A man invents a fork, he hardly uses a chopstick, does he? Even the Chinaman cannot seriously claim that sticks are an improvement over the fork." He turned sharply, noticing Tooly listening. "Well, well. What are you doing there?"

She darted away, pushing past more bodies, popping out among a group of toughs practicing fight moves on one another. The leader, a stocky Filipino with a mullet, wraparound shades, and Muay Thai shorts, demonstrated punches. "Should be a straight line. Use your shoulder to block the jab, then load up on the counter. Catch him on the button and it's good night." His disciples nodded. One of them, tired of being ignored, dropped to the floor and did pushups, before collapsing and looking up to see who'd noticed.

Tooly continued, finding herself before the upright piano, its lid covered with empty plastic cups. A middle-aged man in a creased pin-striped suit, mole on the side of his nose, sat at the piano stool, right hand stuffed in the jacket pocket.

"Are you going to play?" Tooly asked.

The question stirred only half his face, the left rising in a smile, the right side limp. He offered his left hand, which she shook, unsure how to grip it, so squeezed his fingers lightly. "No one would hear my playing over this awful heavy-metal music," he said.

"I can hear."

He looked upon her, distracted and worried. His eyes welled up; he nodded. Then his left hand went flat on the keys as if calming a horse and—quite suddenly—it leaped, striking a chord, then another, his good arm jumping between treble and bass in a high-speed dialogue till he leaned back, eyes closed, and played so softly that she perceived nothing, only black-and-whites depressed and rising.

A Japanese man in dark suit, dark tie, dark glasses watched with much seriousness. "Vely difficur," he pronounced. "Vely difficur piece." Accompanying him was a Caucasian woman with bulging breasts. Tooly looked at these. The pianist interpreted her grimace as a response to his playing and nodded. "That's a melancholy part, isn't it."

The Japanese man and his escort departed for the bar, and the pianist gazed at Tooly. "You remind me of someone I loved very much," he said, and kissed her on the lips. Revolted, Tooly leaped back, spun around, and ran, banging into strangers, wiping off her mouth, the book bag swinging as she hurried, looking for some way to discharge this repulsive sensation.

A teenage girl stood there, plucking at her black T-shirt to hide her figure. "Hey," she said.

"Hi," Tooly answered.

"Want to check out the medicine cabinet with me?"

"Okay."

As they went, the teenager introduced herself as Reena and fussed over Tooly ("You're so cuuuuuuuuute!"), downing a shot of tequila along the way. Reena was from Cleveland, which she described as "the most suck-ass part of Planet Earth. Like when you drive to the airport in a normal city? How it looks out the window? With nothing there? Not even kidding—that's like the *whole* of where I'm from. Yeah, I know." She was sixteen, fast-talking and gum-chewing, with a faint bleached mustache. Everywhere they went, she showily asked strangers if they had any pills, and chatted to Tooly as if each familiar name in her own life were universally known. "Derrick is twenty-eight, but it's so weird—we practically have the same birthday." She talked about his kissing skills, how the food in Thailand made her gag, especially fried locusts, which Derrick ate to freak her out. All the while, Reena gave Tooly aggressive hugs, stroking her hair like a doll, issuing a stream-of-consciousness account of her drug-taking: ". . . shrooms with my dad at his place in Maine, and smoked coke once off the end of a Marlboro, and, like . . ." Up her right arm, she had drawn the logos of her favorite bands in blue ballpoint: Mötley Crüe, Voivod, W.A.S.P.

"Are you left-handed?" Tooly asked.

"Oh, my God, how did you know that? Do you like know me? From another life?"

"There was a left-handed boy at my old school who put answers on his right arm to cheat, and he was left-handed, so I thought—"

"You are *smart*. You are *so* smart. You are *smart*."

Her headbanger boyfriend, Derrick, appeared, taking the chewing gum from Reena's mouth and sticking it in his own, his horsey front teeth exposed. "Buy me a beer," he told her, not registering Tooly. The slogan on his T-shirt read, NO ONE LIKES ME & I DON'T CARE. "Hey, buy me a fucking beer."

"Buy it your fucking self," Reena answered, eyes alive.

Tooly slipped into the crowd and upstairs, hunting for Sarah. She was at a loss where to situate herself, so lingered by the card table where that old man, Humphrey, sat before the chessboard. His attention was now on a book, which he drew close to his nose, then thrust far away, then drew close again, so she imagined its print changing size as he read. He turned the page with force: a wisp of his hair leaped, then fell. She rested her bag on the floor and sat atop it. He noticed her, yet only adjusted the cover to block her from view: whichever direction she shifted, so did the book.

"Gurul," he said finally, plucking out his toilet-paper earplugs, wincing at the din. The word seemed to be a foreign language, so she pretended not to hear. "Gurul," he repeated. This time she understood. He was calling her: "Girl." He placed the book facedown on the card table, toppling a bishop and a king, which rolled off the table and bounced on the floor. "You think you can win me?"

"Win you at what?"

"What this looks like? Water ski?"

"Are you good?" she asked, edging closer.

"I am high-quality chess athlete. Top ten."

"Top ten in the world?"

"If not galaxy."

"What are the rules again?" she asked. "The horses do something, don't they?"

"Horses go jump."

"Uhm, is that a good book?"

He considered its cover splayed on the chessboard—Spinoza's *Ethics*—as if he'd forgotten what occupied him a minute earlier. "Average to good."

"What happens in it?"

"Some bits, you have ethics. Some bits, not so much ethics."

"I like what it's called," she said, putting her finger on the word "Spinoza." She looked back at the crowd. "Do you know all these people?"

He closed his heavy eyelids with disdain, opened them slowly. "These people? They are trivial beings. Not intellectuals. Almost zero of them. Imagine what Samuel Johnson or John Stuart Mill will say if they see situation like this!"

Since Tooly had met neither of those people, she struggled to imagine their reactions.

"But is good to meet fellow intellectual," he continued. "I celebrate occasion with small drink. Unfortunate, I am impossibility to move."

"Why?"

"Because I find myself in sitting position. Might I ask of you one glass tonic water, one glass wodka? This makes two glasses. Separate glasses. Not mix up. You can do? If you don't want, is okay."

She proceeded downstairs. Jaime was so busy that he barely noticed her seeking his attention. A Thai ladyboy, also waiting, smiled as Tooly nosed around the bottles. "Okay, sweetie pie?"

"I'm supposed to get tonic water and 'what-something.'"

"The tonic water is—I just saw it. Look, it's there."

Tooly went behind the bar and poured herself a plastic cup of tonic water, drawing a glance from Jaime, who nearly said something but was occupied.

"There's nothing called 'what-something,' honey," the ladyboy said. "You go check."

Tooly returned upstairs, and found Humphrey shifting chess pieces in animated debate with himself. He glimpsed her approaching; his eyes warmed. "I think you not come back."

"What was the second thing?"

"First thing, tonic water. Second thing, wodka."

"What is 'what-kuh'?"

"What is wodka? Is like water, but with consequences."

"Consequences?"

"I mean detrimental." He stressed the first syllable: DET-rimental. "For high-quality chess athlete, wodka is highly detrimental."

She held still, bewildered.

"Don't worry. Is okay. Sit." From the storage room behind him, he found a spare folding chair and set it up for her on the other side of the card table. She sat, but found herself too far, her arms unable to reach the chessboard. With mock grumbles, he dragged the chair (with her in it) until her chest touched the table. She tucked one leg under her backside, which raised her, her other leg dangling, shoe tip above the floor, sight line over a forest of chess pieces.

"What your name is?"

"Tooly."

He asked again. She repeated her answer.

He clapped his thigh, laughing uproariously. "Most ridiculous name I hear in entire life! I would not believe it, if I do not hear it with my own eyes!"

"What's your name?"

"Humphrey Ostropoler."

"That sounds like the name of an elephant," she said, though this made her think of the nail board used to hunt elephants, which made her think of Sarah, which made her worry, which reminded her of Paul.

"You think Humphrey Ostropoler sounds like name of Asian elephant," he asked, "or African elephant?"

"The one with big ears."

"All elephants have big ears. This is why they are elephants not mices. So," he said, setting up the pieces, "you think you can win me at chess?"

"Humphrey Ostropoler, did you see Sarah? I can't find her. I think I'm supposed to go home soon. I don't think I'm supposed to be here."

"Don't worry. You wait few minutes and she will find you. I keep eyes on you. Make sure nobody bother you. Is okay?"

She nodded, studying the pieces. "Where are you from, Humphrey Ostropoler?"

"From Soviet Union."

She looked up, knowing only terrifying things of that country. She'd never met anyone from there, a place she imagined surrounded by a tall curtain, behind which were wrinkled villains stroking nuclear bombs able to blow up the world nine times over. "Do you like it there?"

"Is no-good country. You must stand in line for buying cabbage."

"I don't like cabbage."

"Me also. So imagine, you in line two hours and this is what you get. No-good country. Now we play." With precision, he adjusted each piece to the center of its square. "I tell you, Miss Tooly, you are going to wish very much—*very much*—that you bring me not only one wodka, but maybe seven. Because, as top-quality chess athlete, I beat you left, right, and center. I not show mercy because you are small-sized person. Game of chess is not . . ." But he couldn't find words for what it wasn't, so resumed: "I am top-ten chess athlete and you are, I predict, maybe only top fifty. For this, Miss Tooly, I give you three cheating opportunities."

"How do you mean?"

"When you make mistake move, you can take it back. Three times you can. Also, because I am good-heart man, I tell you rules first."

At each of her turns, she took many minutes, wanting to pose a hundred questions yet remaining silent and stuck. She twisted her hair into two ropes, clutching them, sucking a loose strand.

"You eat own hair—I never see such sneak tactic like this! Not even Spassky-Fischer tactics." Nevertheless, he let her take her time and nodded sagely as she pondered her options, as if to confirm the wisdom of her cogitation.

"These pointy ones," she asked finally, "can they jump two squares?"

"Pointy ones go like this." He demonstrated. "For examples, this square here. I know you already think of this because it threatens bishop at K4. Or maybe you prefer castling to control center?"

After a respectful wait, she pushed a timid pawn.

"This move is detrimental. I take your queen again."

"Can I have a cheating opportunity?"

"Is cheating opportunity number nine."

She counted in her head. "Eight," she said, then chose another move, equally disastrous.

"You are swimming on thin ice."

She moved again.

"Now you are skating on hot water."

Two moves later, it was checkmate. He reached across the board, sandwiched her little hand between his. "Thank you, darlink. Even though I beat pants onto you, you are high-quality intellectual." He sent her off to fetch his wodka as a prize, writing the word in block-letter printing for her to show the barman, and providing a banknote, too. She declined this, explaining that everything at the bar was free.

At the top of the stairs, she hesitated, worried about leaving her book bag with someone from the Soviet Union. Might he look inside? Actually, *he* had a good nose to draw. She pushed through the drinks scrum and slipped behind the bar, ticking her stumpy fingernails on the bottles, stopping at Smirnoff. To the amusement of Jaime, who watched but didn't intervene, she raised it with both hands and poured it into a plastic cup, filling it nearly to the top.

"You paying for that?"

She shook her head.

"What is it with you and Sarah?"

"Did you see her?"

"I saw her when you got here. Then I saw her making out with Venn, but I . . . what?"

Tooly couldn't suppress her horror. "You saw her smooching?"

A tipsy woman shouted for Jaime's attention, and he turned to take the order, noticing too late that Tooly had again walked off without paying.

The plastic cup of vodka was too full to safely carry with one hand, so she held it with both, her mouth to the rim, the liquid burning her lips.

"Is good," Humphrey said, taking a sip. "Now I help you find her." He stood from behind the table, smoothed down his tie. "I sit for too long. My leg goes to bed."

"To sleep?"

"Thank you, small person. At rare time, I am making mistake in English-language speaking, so thanks for accurate fixation. Now we find Sarah. You follow. Stay near. There are trivial beings everywhere."

Once downstairs, they needed five minutes just to cross the room. Identifying anyone in that crowd was impossible for Tooly, whose height limited her to views of guts and butts. As for Humphrey, he had height but his vision was weak. So they agreed to get Tooly to a higher vantage point: the stepladder. A couple sat on its lower rungs but moved when Humphrey hoisted her up. She climbed the rest of the way, grasping each next rung. He stood at the bottom, keeping it steady, ready to catch her. "Is okay?"

"Yes. But hold it!" she said from the top.

Everyone looked so different up there: Jaime at the bar and the serpentine queue for service; the deejay was going bald; a clownish drunkard slow-danced with a poster of King Bhumibol. The Thais watched this scene, smoking faster. They revered their monarch, a man known for humility and for playing the jazz saxophone. He was considered the sole blameless public figure in a country of corruption and coups. When the drunkard tongue-kissed his poster, it was too much: a *katoey* rushed him and a brawl exploded, spreading fast. Bystanders shrieked. Tooly looked down at Humphrey.

From his vantage point, he saw nothing, only heard cries, clothes tearing, the smack of knuckles on flesh. "Come down!" he said. The crowd surged like rough seas. "Down, please!" He raised his arms to catch her, but the crush of people pushed him off balance and toppled the ladder.

The ceiling flew away from Tooly, bodies spinning closer, the floor rushing at her. Her shoulder struck concrete, her head whipped back. As legs trampled around her, she curled up, teeth chattering, thinking how much trouble she was in. A high heel trod on her hand; a shin clipped her in the mouth.

Then someone grabbed her, pulled her upward. She clung to his arm, as the man pushed away the crowd and called out orders, which cut through the frenzied din. Gradually, the panic eased—just a few late shouts and shoves. Even after the man had released her, Tooly clasped his sleeve.

"All right?" he asked, cupping his palm under her chin, thumb across her cheek to her earlobe. His voice and eyes had an odd effect on her, seeming to silence the music that thumped in the background.

She hesitated, unsure how to respond to this stranger, with wild brown hair and mountain-man beard, whiskers parting above his lips as he grinned at her. She looked away, then at him again, realizing only after two glances what was odd about his eyes: one was green, the other black. (That pupil was permanently dilated, she later learned, due to a fistfight in his teens.) "I'm Venn," he told her. Others sought his attention, called to him. The room still twitched from the spasm of violence. He paid no mind, dealing only with her. "You got a bit of a knock there."

The back of her head throbbed where it had struck the floor. "It's okay," she pretended.

"Good girl," he said. "Good girl. You smack your head and not a word. That's what I like to see."

Disheveled and fraught, Humphrey reached them. "You are hurt, little gurul?"

"I'm fine," she said, emboldened, glancing up at Venn.

"I am relief," Humphrey said. "Very relief to hear this."

"Do you know Sarah?" she asked Venn. "She invited me to this party, but I can't find her now."

"I know Sarah. And I know who you are, Matilda."

He summoned the two bouncers and ordered them to guard the little girl—what the hell had they been doing, letting her walk around on her own? They were far larger than Venn, yet both listened, heads down. They led her by the hand to the front door, sat her on the floor, and amused her with silly jokes, letting her light their cigarettes. After an hour, she fell asleep, the toasty smell of smoke mingling with a dream about calculators.

Upstairs, Venn found a group of backpacking former Israeli soldiers who were sharing a joint, and he deputized them to clear everyone off that floor so it could be used by the girl to sleep. As he carried Tooly up there, she stirred but kept her eyes closed. The delicious sensation of being placed on a soft bed—he slipped the book bag under her head as a pillow.

"I'm a bit worried," she said, sleepy eyes flickering. "I'm supposed to go home."

"Nothing to worry about," he assured her, kicking the last stragglers downstairs and leaving her there to rest. "Nothing to worry about."

And she wasn't worried anymore. She woke just once more that night, the house nearly silent by then, traffic distantly audible, dawn light rising pinkly through the holes in the wall.

# 2000

THE DINER WAS at the corner of Atlantic and Smith, in the shadow of the Brooklyn House of Detention, a high-rise jail whose grated windows concealed any sign of the torments within. In there, cuffs and toughs; out here, milkshakes and pancakes.

Tooly took a booth by the window and opened the plastic menu, watching the street, delivery trucks trundling past. Since New Year's Eve, the snow had melted away, as had the millennial panic. They'd said a computer glitch would humble the industrialized world come midnight December 31, 1999. But the Y2K problem proved no problem, notwithstanding the billions spent to avert it. Nor did terrorists blow up New Year's celebrations in Times Square. The only notable events of December 31, 1999, were the conclusion of an airline hijacking in India, its passengers exchanged for imprisoned militants, who took refuge with the Taliban rulers of Afghanistan; and the resignation of the Russian leader, President Boris Yeltsin, who'd overseen the replacement of Soviet Communism and now left his little-known prime minister, Vladimir Putin, in charge of the largest country in the world.

But more immediate to Tooly's concerns was Sarah. This was a goodbye lunch, after which Sarah was to depart for Italy, following weeks of unwelcome inhabitation. In typical fashion, Sarah had nagged about having a "girls meal out" before leaving, yet now appeared unlikely to turn up for it.

After an hour, the remains of a fried-egg sandwich sat on Tooly's plate. She raised her hand for the check. At which point Sarah walked in, yawning from one table to another as if to trumpet her entrance. She dropped her handbag on the banquette, shoved her suitcase under the booth table—she was heading to the airport straight from here. Rather than address Tooly, she turned to a group of hipsters in the next booth. "Don't have a cigarette for me, do you?"

One did, a short guy in a porkpie hat, who fumbled in his overalls pocket for a compressed pack of Parliaments, which he shook out before her, two smokes jutting. She took both, placing one in her lips, the other between his. "You have to keep me company now," she told him. Out on the sidewalk, she twirled away as smoke ribbons rose, pranced on the balls of her feet down the length of the diner window and back, chatting with the young man. Amazing how Sarah—still furious that Tooly had been avoiding her—now reversed the burden of impatience.

"What are we having?" she asked, sliding back into the booth. She took Tooly's hand, rubbed it.

"Are you doing that because you're freezing?"

"Hello!" Sarah said, waving to each member of the waitstaff, concluding with the head waiter. "We'll have two large, hot coffees." She behaved as if time began only once she entered a room, mindless of the dirty plate and half-drunk egg cream on the table. Tooly didn't want coffee. Nor did she want to disagree this early on. So she sipped hers, which was tepid, sour, too long in the carafe.

Sarah peppered her monologue with references to her rich boyfriend in Italy, Valter, as well as others involved in his leather shop. She had to keep an eye on certain characters, though it was never specified why. As with many of her tales, this one contained puddles of truth, but these accounted for little of her rainfall.

"Sarah?"

"Yes?"

But Tooly had only wanted to interrupt the flow. She had nothing to say, so sounded like a child who states an adult's name just to see if it works. She played with the metal milk jug, replaced it, invented a question. "Do I seem like the same person from when I was little?"

"Who else would you be? Anyway, who cares, my dearest darling thing. Memories are so boring. They're always wrong, and only cause trouble. Remembering is the most overrated thing. Forgetting is far superior. Anyway, your childhood is over now." She scanned for a busboy. "Got to work to keep your cup full in this place. Waiter!"

He replenished hers, black coffee slopping into the enamel saucer, dripping when she raised the cup to her lips. "Whole time I've been here, Venn hasn't bothered to call."

"I haven't heard from him, either," Tooly lied. "He's busy."

"Now that I'm not here with money to give him, he's nowhere to be found."

Tooly rolled her eyes. "You with money for him? Please. Get serious. He looks after you, and you know that."

"If that makes you feel better."

"Not feel better. It's true."

"I'm a liar now? Can't believe you just called me a liar."

"I didn't say that. I said—"

"It *is* what you said." Sarah slammed down her coffee cup, chewed nail polish off her pinkie. "You want me gone? Well, you can just . . . All right? Because . . ." A tear trundled down her face, cleaning a line through her makeup. "I'm the one who kept all this going. I could have snapped my fingers," she said, "and your world tour would've been over years ago. You want to think I'm awful? Fine. You've turned twenty-one now, so I can't stop you."

"What difference does it make that I turned twenty-one?"

"That's why I came back here."

"So we could go shopping on my birthday?"

"Not for that. Because, after twenty-one, everything changes for you. I've been trying to tell you. My only advice is make yourself indispensable to him."

"Sarah, I don't have the messy feelings you have about Venn. I am not you. Not everyone is you. Okay?"

"Pay attention. Otherwise, things are changing."

"Seriously. It's stuff like this that makes him avoid you. Stop acting up, okay?"

"Acting up? You are, my dear. Not me. *You* are the one who's humiliating yourself. You don't understand half of what's going on here. Don't think you're above me. Because you are the worst kind of manipulator. You can't even look me in the eyes. There we go, that's better. Oh—gone again."

"Because I don't want to look at you."

"What a disappointment. We all liked you, Tooly. What a disappointment."

"You're saying things just to be hurtful now."

"I," she said, pointing at Tooly, "I was here *before* you. Okay? And I get you *completely*. Each time you make out like you're all *nice* and *sweet*, remember in the back of your head: I *know* you. I know what you're like inside." Sarah spun around, sweetly asking the hipsters for another cigarette. The guy in the porkpie hat, who'd supplied her before, did so again, though he declined to keep her company. When outside, she beckoned to him through the window. He pretended not to notice; his two friends stifled laughter.

Tooly resolved never ever to see Sarah again. She submitted to a hug and a peck on the cheek, paid (Sarah claimed to have no American currency left besides cab fare for the airport), and speed-walked back to the apartment to escape the pollution of that woman.

When Tooly came home, Humphrey placed his finger on the page before him and issued a woebegone sigh, which was his way of communicating serenity, an impossible sentiment while Sarah had been in residence. He dragged the chess set from under the Ping-Pong table and set it up on the couch, laying out all the pieces, placing each at the precise center of its square. "When is last time you win me?" he asked Tooly.

"The last time we played."

"If I play tennis against monkey, he also wins sometimes, because I am very surprised he even holds racket." He scrutinized her a moment, perceiving that she longed to go, to be uptown with the students, not here with him. "Why I bother?" he said. "You do not even sit and read anymore. Trivial being—that is what you are now. Trivial being, like everyone." He shifted about on the couch, eyebrows bumping into each other like two butting caterpillars. He had to retract his charge. "Even to *say* you are trivial being, darlink, breaks my heart."

"I should go."

The muscles of his face stilled. His brown eyes clouded, gazing fondly upon her. He gave another sigh.

"What?"

"I am happy. This is all. Not happy you are going; I am sad you go away, of course. But I am happy you are here now." He smacked his lips together. "Remember, I am counter-revolutionary and nonconformist. Why I should care about time? Why I should care that later you are not at this place? We are together at same time and in same place for many hours, even if mostly it is in past. What difference? Those events are still there, even if I am not."

"What are you talking about, Humph?"

"Trivial beings think there is only present—that past is gone and future is coming. But past is like overseas: it still exists, even when you are not there anymore. Future time, too. It is there already."

"Well, I'm not there yet. But I do need to get moving."

"First, I have idea I must run over you."

"To run past me?"

"No, I run idea right at you, and you tell me what you think. Okay?"

"I'm all ears."

"I work up to it."

"Humph, I have to go!"

"Do you accept I jump from window?" he said. "Or you get angry with me?"

Humphrey had a long-standing fascination with suicide, alternately romanticizing and recoiling from the idea. It was the ultimate expression of will, he claimed, the mind overcoming the body. Yet the act was tragic, too, given how often suicide was due to the Moron Problem: that simpletons could and did harm intellectuals, that foolish ideas became crazes, that babble was mistaken for brilliance. The Moron Problem made Humphrey want to quit life. Yet this granted victory to the morons. It was a dialogue he had conducted with himself for decades—a debate rendered absurd by the impossibility that he would ever act on it.

"If you jump from here, Humph, you'd just break your leg. We're only one floor up."

"This is accurate statement." He knitted his hands over his belly. "You become like Venn now, always going somewhere. Why this is?"

"I have things to do. I know you like doing nothing, but don't make me watch. Can you accept that?"

During her reproach, he curled his head till his chin grazed his chest, as if it snowed on him.

She prepared to leave. Had no duty here—they had been company to each other over the years, but she refused to pity him. Pity was the opposite of friendship. Venn had said that, and she repeated it in her head, arming herself against Humphrey's hunched silence. She fastened her duffle-coat toggles, feigning indifference to him, until something changed, and the indifference felt real. There—perhaps you could turn off sympathy.


DUNCAN APOLOGIZED FOR failing to invite her to his family home for the Christmas holidays—this whole break, he'd felt like crap.

"I was fine," she said. Indeed, she'd have hated it there, a stranger among those who'd known one another forever. Plus, Duncan's remorse had worth—Venn always advised her to watch for others' guilt, which had many practical uses.

She took a sweater from his closet. "And Xavi," she asked, pushing her head through the neck hole, "where's he?"

"Back later. He said you guys held a couple of meetings about his business idea."

There had been four such meetings, including a New Year's Eve party of B-school types. "His online-currency idea is really smart, actually," she said. "Just needs funding."

Duncan crouched by the stereo, working on a welcome-back tape for her, writing its label in smeared rollerball ink: "Year 2000 Mix by D-Mac." She had still not played his previous mixtapes, since the radio-cassette player in her kitchen in Brooklyn turned out, on closer inspection, to be only a radio. His compilations remained forgotten in her coat pocket, the tapes jiggling in their cases at her every step around the city.

She watched Duncan working the CD player and double-cassette deck, his eyes sinking shut at a favorite chorus, hands swatting the air during a drum solo. Observing him, she came unstuck from the present moment, experiencing it as if viewed a time hence, as if all this were long past, and he at this age resided only in memory. The song exploded, stopped dead. He spun around to look at her. "Amazing, no?"

"Very amazing," she responded, noting how he sought her approval. She pressed a kiss to his lips, slid her hands up his long-sleeved T-shirt and over his warm chest. She was the person of chief consequence in his world, but he was not that person to her.

"I got totally into classic rock over Christmas," he said. "It was like high school: headphones on in my old room, listening to my parents' records." He double-clicked a track on Napster, playing it through the laptop speakers: "Free Bird" by Lynyrd Skynyrd. He smiled, but the irony was lost on Tooly, and he had to explain that this was a notoriously clichéd rock anthem.

She paid close attention, glancing sightlessly around the room, then shook her head. "Never heard it."

"How is that possible?"

The song went on, the singer wailing, *"Lord knows, I can't change/ Lord, help me, I can't chay-yay-yay-yay-yay-yay-yay-yay-ange!"* Abruptly, the tempo sped up, and Duncan did something unexpected. The meek law student leaped onto his bed and gave the most astonishing air-guitar performance she had ever seen: arpeggios along an invisible fingerboard, hard-strumming every downstroke, eyes scrunched, tongue out, head banging, licking an air pick for effect, stepping on invisible distortion pedals, bending a whammy bar, swinging imaginary rock-'n'-roll hair from his face. This act—in addition to being incredibly funny—was absolutely fucking perfect. She watched, trying not to close her eyes.

"What the hell, McGrory!" she shouted at the fade-out, he standing above her on the bed, breathless. "What the hell!" she repeated. "That was genius!"

He tried not to smile too proudly.

"I didn't even know you knew guitar."

"That doesn't," he said, breathing heavily, "actually count as *playing*."

"You could start an air band."

He hopped off the bed and, fired up by her praise, fetched Emerson's acoustic guitar from the living room to show what he could do with a real instrument, which amounted to power chords and the opening to "Smoke on the Water," all of which impressed her. She gave it a try but the frets were too wide for her small fingers.

"I used to play the ukulele in school," she said, giving a tuneless strum.

"You played well, I see."

"Music is not among my talents."

His bedroom door swung open. "Wildfire," Xavi called to her.

"I know. We need to talk." She left Duncan to finish her mixtape and went to discuss business in Xavi's room. After an hour, Duncan entered and handed her the cassette.

"Quit law school and join us," she told him. "We'll be rich beyond your wildest imaginings."

In coming days, her planning with Xavi took hours. Soon she was entering his room without a knock, hanging around late into the evening, long after there was no further work. Duncan gravitated to his friend's room, too, though he still sought permission to enter. His comments were invariably negative—valid concerns but unwelcome, and Tooly dreaded his appearances.

She consulted with Venn by phone, recounting her progress, which seemed rapid to her. He loved how she really believed in this project, though he noted that it still lacked funding—hardly a trivial oversight. However, they had identified a source.

"Really don't want to ask him," Duncan responded.

"You don't ask," she said. "You mention that there are these entrepreneurs starting a dot-com, and you actually know these guys. They don't want outsiders involved because it could be huge. But they asked if *you* wanted to get in. That's all true. You don't ask for a thing. Let Keith think he's come up with the idea."

"My father doesn't operate that way."

"If he gets involved and it takes off, he'll think of you differently forever."

"Differently how?"

"Not as a kid asking for money but as a friend."

Duncan said nothing for a minute. "I really, really do not want to beg my dad."

Instead, he spoke with his mother, asking what his folks might consider contributing to Wildfire. Xavi made progress, too, meeting at length with Venn about the business plan. Venn showed him the view from the roof of the Brain Trust and an empty cubicle with a handwritten note: "Reserved for Wildfire." Xavi filled out all the paperwork to join the cooperative—once the funds came in, they were set.

# 2011

SHE ATE DINNER alone in the basement suite, a window high in the wall providing grass-level views of the McGrorys' backyard. The summer grew hot and light lingered far into the evenings now. Children's bare feet rushed past and little faces peeped at her, squashed against the panes. She was part of their household now, tending to Humphrey by day, back to Connecticut by night. When she ventured upstairs, the family welcomed her. They counted on her steady mood, knowing that, no matter how grouchy they were, she was impossible to upset. Mac, in particular, glommed on to her—except if Duncan returned early from work, at which point the boy trailed behind his father like a faithful pooch.

But Duncan was a rare presence. He missed most family dinners, often returning after the kids were in bed and departing before they rose. When home, he was pursued by emails. His respite was what Bridget termed "anger hour," a nightly rant at the cable news channels. It was peculiar: he spewed such vitriol in that house, yet acted with notable kindness outside it. Accounts emerged from Bridget of his decency toward new hires at the firm, toward strangers, and to Humphrey in the months before Tooly arrived. Bridget once cited an entire chapter in her husband's life of which Tooly had known nothing, how he had nursed a sick friend till the person's death. When she inquired about this, Duncan changed the subject—he couldn't accept praise.

Then, by breakfast, he was gone. It was Bridget who poured the kids' cereal and orange juice. She was present, involved, interested.

Yet it was Duncan's absence that shaped the household. The triplets used obscenities because it made him chuckle. When they threw a dart at Mac and it stuck in his butt, Bridget had to clean the pinpoint wound with rubbing alcohol. "Not funny," she said. But Duncan had smirked, and the girls noticed.

Such dynamics caused tension between Duncan and Bridget, but the hostility abated when Tooly turned up. She had become the glue here, mending and maintaining, but exhausting herself in the process. She longed—longed!—for time on her own, snatching what minutes she could alone downstairs, indulging in ukulele practice to hold them back, until one or another McGrory couldn't resist leaning into the music room, asking what she was up to. Aside from Mac, the most regular visitor was Bridget, who relished having a grown-up friend on-site.

Each night, Tooly got into bed with a glass of red wine and an old newspaper, since she lacked the concentration for anything more involved. Throughout her waking hours, she was prodded by a sense of responsibility, assuaged only when need did present itself—Humphrey coughing, calling for water; Mac panicking about an imminent sporting humiliation—whereupon she could act. Afterward, her uneasy vigil continued, dissipating only in sleep. But going to bed tipsy produced a shallow slumber, interrupted by trips to pee.

At dawn, she awoke weary—couldn't sleep in as she had in younger years—and stayed under the covers, floating around Caergenog till the present gained focus. She glimpsed the wine bottle on the counter, not half drunk as intended but nearly empty. She had barely noticed the third and fourth glasses of the evening before. Tooly resolved to skip her nightcap that evening, and bought nothing on the way home. Then bedtime came again, and unease with it, leading her upstairs for a nip of something. She stood in the dark house, looking out the front window, full glass in hand.

Sipping before one of the McGrorys' laptops, she resumed her late-night hobby of peeping at the lives of those she'd known. Running through names from the past, she typed in "Jon Priddles"—still at

King Chulalongkorn International School, it turned out: chairman of the board of trustees now, after "a beloved career as principal," according to the school website. She found information on Gilbert Lerallu, too, the owner of that pig at 115th Street, now critically acclaimed (the man, not the pig) for an album of avant-garde harpsichord compositions. When she typed in Xavi's full name, "Xavier Karamage," nothing relevant came up.

Of those she'd known in New York, he'd seemed the most likely to flourish: smart, ambitious, charming. There was no trace of him. She had tried to ask Duncan, but whenever she mentioned those days he cut the conversation short. She never pressed the matter. So many aspects of that period troubled her, particularly how she'd behaved.

"SLEEP WELL?" SHE asked Humphrey, unloading a few ready-to-heat meals from shopping bags. Her attempts to pull him from torpor, to get him eating properly, reading again, to rouse his intellect—all this had fizzled.

The former Humphrey grew harder to retrieve. Insidiously, the present Humphrey snuffed out the previous one, which came to seem implausible. People manifested so many selves over a lifetime. Was only the latest valid?

"Let me open the curtains—gorgeous sun today."

He frowned at the white-and-black object she held. "What's that?"

She handed over her newspaper, and he pressed the front page to his nose, then extended it, struggling for focus. She fetched his glasses and perched herself on the arm of his chair.

"Who's this?" he asked, tapping the photo of a disgraced New York politician who had injudiciously distributed photos of his crotch. It was a bad summer for powerful men, she informed Humphrey, with the humiliation of Anthony Weiner, the arrest of Dominique Strauss-Kahn, the humbling of Rupert Murdoch, the ousting of Arab dictators.

He pointed at another photo. "She looks strange."

"That's a man."

They worked through the newspaper, not by the words but by the faces, making a game of guessing each expression. Abruptly, Humphrey stood, the paper falling off his lap and coming apart at his feet. "Look at the clouds," he said, tottering toward the window. He shuffled back to his armchair, sat heavily, interlaced his fingers across his chest.

"What are you thinking, Humph?"

At length, he responded. "I don't know what's happening in the world."

"I'll leave the paper here for you. You can go through it after I've gone."

The next day, that copy sat untouched. She had the latest edition with her. "I read this amazing article, Humph, about how thirty-five hours of new footage get uploaded to this website called YouTube every minute. Incredible, no?" But how absurd to speak of tech marvels to a man who'd never left the previous century. She attempted to explain: electronic pulses hurtled around the world, sending information, photographs, video everywhere. "Sorry, I'm explaining it badly. I'll show you sometime."

He grunted at her description of the present. "I feel apprehensive," he said. "What am I supposed to be worrying about?"

"About nothing. I'm taking care of things."

He looked away, unconvinced. "Can't find what I want."

"Well, you have a lot to remember, Humph. Your life has been going on since the 1920s."

"How old would you say I am?"

"You're eighty-three."

"Am I?" he replied, astounded. "That's almost indecent!"

"But you feel like you're only six."

"Seven," he corrected her.

"You felt six the other day."

"I'm more grown-up than a six-year-old."

She kissed his cheek.

"Gosh, I don't know you that well," he joked. "Can I make you a coffee?"

"Let me," she said, and leaped to her feet, elated at this glimpse of the old Humphrey. There were times when it *was* him again, burning through thick clouds.

"Tricky spelling your name," he remarked, when she returned from the communal kitchen. "How would you do that?"

"What, spell it?"

"Yes, all right." He took the mug, drizzling coffee down his trouser leg.

She gave her name letter by letter. "And you remember my nickname: Tooly."

"Well, I'm not going to argue over it. How long are you staying?"

A horrible realization struck her: he didn't recognize her. "I was thinking of when I was a little girl, and I met you," she said. "You explained chess, and you let me cheat. You were very sweet to me."

"Nonsense!"

"You were," she insisted. "I was there."

Within an hour, Tooly stood at the window of a motel room on Emmons Avenue, overlooking the parking lot. On the bed behind her, Garry smoked. Every few days, they rented a room for four hours, which was affordable if they split the cost. The place made for a sordid rendezvous, wallpaper peeling, mattress covered with plastic, porn on Channel 33. Yet the awfulness amused them, and they competed to find the most repellent feature. Today, the winning entry had been dead cockroaches in the shower stall.

Garry had a handsome face, eyes narrowing to slits when he laughed. He patted her bare stomach; a dull smack. "You are too thin."

To disprove this, she pinched a bit of fat, then gathered her underwear to cover her nakedness. She took a drag of his cigarette for the intimacy, the damp filter, and listened to his young-man chatter about the inevitability of his own success, described with knee-jiggling zeal. He had grown up in Novosibirsk, dreaming of a million bucks. "Today, I realize one million buys nothing."

They spoke as if conducting different conversations, she the older woman, he the younger man, both conscious of the gulf, which had such different meanings for each. Afterward, they sat in his banged-up Pontiac in the parking lot, and he unpacked a picnic, food taken from home, supposedly to keep him going while he studied at community college.

"Doesn't your mother notice when so much stuff goes missing?"

He chewed with his mouth open. "She thinks I have a big appetite." In passing, he mentioned an upcoming vacation in Russia with his fiancée.

"Oh," Tooly responded. "Didn't know you had one."

"I planned this trip for ages."

"I mean," she specified, "didn't know you had a fiancée."

From a fling like this, Tooly expected only human contact and distraction. Both could be found elsewhere. "Let's leave it at this," she said, when he dropped her at the Sheepshead Bay station. She always felt a little relieved at an excuse to break up—one less thing to carry around.

Tooly returned that night to find the McGrory siblings at war, videogames bleeping in the TV room, their mother chewing her fingernail in the glow of an iPad 2—"Hey, you," Bridget said, "come hang out"—and since Tooly was a guest she had to, though what she needed was the opposite of their eyes. Then hers opened and it was time to rise and begin again, Mac staring at her, awaiting his drive to another unhappy day.

He had begged his parents to enroll him in this moviemaking course at the Y, and so refused to admit how badly he fared. His classmates were older and from a different school—when he spoke, nobody heard. To tell Bridget how miserable her son was would betray his confidence. So Tooly attempted, during the morning drive, to inflate him for the puncturing day ahead. She asked his opinion on matters that concerned her, like what she should do if Humphrey got a bit better; and where she might live after she left here, given that her shop was closing. She could live anywhere in the world now. Tooly took his answers seriously, so he gave them seriously.

"Live here. You could have your own house, but close."

"Couldn't afford to live in Darien. Not by a long shot, I'm afraid. But tell me something," she said. "If *you* could go anywhere in the world, where would it be? Even just to visit."

He fiddled with the side mirror. The boy had a way of vanishing, not hearing questions—it was infuriating to teachers ("Needs improvement"), to other kids ("Earth to Mac?"), to his father ("Hey. Mac. Seriously now."). She observed him, wondering about the inside of his head, whether it was far away and empty, or near and full. He was humming, and she recognized the tune.

"That's 'The William Tell Overture.' I was practicing that on my ukulele."

He denied that he'd been listening in.

"Come in next time. I don't want you hiding in your own house."

"Wasn't hiding."

"Oh dear. Everything I say is wrong, Mac, my friend."

His chin pruned.

She hated to see him on the verge of tears, but turning away seemed worse. She gave a pull of his earlobe and had a rush of—what would she call it?—a wish to suffer harm in his place. "I'll look after you," she said. "What do you think of that?"

"Okay."

"Things improve when you grow up. You'll see," she said, turning in to the YMCA parking lot. "Some people hate getting older, but it'll suit you. There are people made to be children and people made to be adults. Since you spend most of life as a grown-up, it's better to have the good bits then. Don't you think?" Tooly had no idea if what she said was hogwash, so asserted it as confidently as possible. She reached across him and opened his door. "Spit on the ground for luck."

He did so, smiling to be naughty. "I'm going to go in there with a good attitude," he pledged, watching her. "Even if I'm the worst of everyone."

"Be open to everything, listen carefully to what they're saying. And if someone says something mean, don't let them see you're upset. Just let it pass through you."

He nodded vigorously.

"They'll worship you," she said. "They all should. And if they don't they're morons! Must run, Mac. You must, and I must."

Throughout her afternoon with Humphrey—another needy male, this one at the opposite end of his life—she dearly hoped all went well for Mac. What an ache: consequences where you are of no consequence.

That evening, Duncan dragged Tooly into the TV room for company and vented at MSNBC.

"Speaking of phonies," she said, to divert his rage, "I was stretching my legs at the Coney Island boardwalk the other day and saw that big roller coaster. Made me think of Emerson."

"Why did the Cyclone remind you of Emerson?"

"Wasn't he doing a doctorate on the hermeneutics of roller coasters or something?"

"How do you remember this stuff?"

She had searched for Emerson online, and found him on a list of competitors at a triathlon in Coeur d'Alene, described as a college professor. She still felt lousy at having lost her friendship with Noeline. But she'd never known the woman's last name, so had no way of finding her online. Tooly had had so few female friends; perhaps it was having been raised by men. But she had come to wish now for female companionship, for a best friend as others had. It seemed to be beyond her.

"Poor Noeline," she said. "That was one relationship that was going to end badly."

"Actually," Duncan said, "they're married now." He held up his iPhone, swiping through pictures of Emerson and Noeline with their three kids at a cookout in Idaho, where they both taught college. They'd had a personal tragedy a few years earlier, when a disgruntled janitor opened fire at their child's nursery school, wounding four people and killing one, their son. Duncan had heard through mutual acquaintances, and got back in touch.

"The kids in the photo?"

"Adopted. They ended up adopting after that."

Tooly required a minute to absorb this story, to mesh it with her scorn of Emerson, which seemed callous now. Duncan muted the television.

"And Xavi?" she ventured. "I always thought he'd do something amazing. But I've Googled him, and all I get is some middle-aged white guy with a mustache in Ireland."

"Definitely not Xavi."

"No, I figured. Did he go back to Uganda?"

Duncan sighed. "I realize you don't know any of this."

"Any of what?"

"Xavi died."

The summer after business school, Xavi had co-founded a digital-rights-management start-up. But when the project stalled he'd accepted an offer from Goldman Sachs. He was still dedicated to entrepreneurship, but planned to work his way up at Goldman first, then use contacts to go it alone. After health coverage for the new job kicked in, he visited a doctor about a few nagging problems—he'd had no insurance since B-school, so had delayed the checkup for ages. They found a tumor: testicular cancer.

His plan was to undergo radiation and chemo without telling anyone at the job. He worried how they'd perceive him if they knew—as an African, he already stood out. So he fitted the treatment around his work schedule, taking the chemo drip at dawn, using vacation days to undergo the first surgery. No one at Goldman found out for months. Incredibly, he became a star there. "This was during that weird post-9/11 haze in New York," Duncan noted. "A few friends that he told about the diagnosis didn't know how to respond—couldn't absorb more scary news. A bunch faded away, especially when he got sicker. A lot of people saying, 'Lance Armstrong got over it!' Which was not helpful."

Finally, Xavi collapsed at the office and awoke in a hospital. The cancer had metastasized to his lungs, liver, bones. There was no hiding the condition now. When further treatment failed, the oncologist stopped returning his calls. Xavi grew sullen, and came to irrationally suspect that living in the United States had somehow provoked this illness. Duncan recalled Xavi sitting for his umpteenth chemo infusion, watching a debate on CNN about the proposed invasion of Iraq. The military campaign was being promoted by men decades older than Xavi, people who aimed to shape the future, while he would never even know how the conflict came out. "Emerson and Noeline visited once, but it ended uncomfortably. They spent the whole time arguing with him about the case for war."

"Xavi was for invading?" Tooly guessed. "They were against?"

"The opposite. Emerson and Noeline thought it was a just war."

One day at the hospital, Duncan caught sight of a familiar figure: the old man he'd met three years earlier, after Tooly had disappeared and he and Xavi had gone looking for her using her map. Humphrey was there for a hernia operation. When he heard about Xavi, he insisted on wishing him well. Later, after healing from his procedure, Humphrey returned to the hospital with a chessboard, recalling that he and Xavi had played during their sole encounter. But chess wasn't conceivable—Xavi was in intensive care then. Humphrey kept trying, even going to the hospice. "He used to sit in the water garden, alone with his rolled-up chessboard. Made cups of Nescafé for everybody. He'd go home, come back the next day. That's partly why I helped your dad."

"You told me before that you met Humph while visiting 'someone' at the hospital. Why didn't you just say it was Xavi?"

"Because I don't talk about this normally. He asked me not to."

Xavi wanted nobody to learn of his decline, even his family in

Uganda. It was better, he decided, that they believe he had abandoned them for glories in America than learn of this. He wanted nothing posted online about his illness, no health updates emailed to business-school classmates or Goldman colleagues, no photos of his dwindling self, in order that he exist only in preceding memories. He made Duncan promise never to hold a memorial service, as if dying before success were a public disgrace. Xavi never did see the end of the Iraq War; he died at the peak of the pandemonium there, though he'd stopped caring, having receded from the world in stages: aware of just the hospice, then just his room, then his bed, then his body, then nothing.

THE REVELATION HAUNTED Tooly all night, and the following morning, too. For some reason, it made her want Mac nearby. So, for this one occasion, she combined her two obligations, him and Humphrey, taking the boy all the way to south Brooklyn and skipping his dreaded sports course at the Y (wrestling that day).

As they approached Humphrey's room, the hallway shuddered at music coming from the adjacent door. After introducing Mac to Humphrey, she excused herself to visit the neighbor. An acrid drug stench came from in there. The woman responded through her closed door. "What you want?"

"Just wondering," Tooly called back, "if you could turn it down a bit! My father next door doesn't hear well!"

"What?"

"It's impossible for him to hear!"

The music cut out. "Too loud for you?" the woman asked. Then she cranked it even louder.

This was awful timing, since Humphrey seemed to be relishing his new acquaintance, already showing Mac various books—it was the clearest Humphrey had been since her first day here. Indeed, it was he who shouted into her ear about getting ice cream.

"Let me go fetch some," Tooly said.

"I can." He hadn't left the building in weeks.

"We'll all go together."

So Humphrey and Mac plodded along Sheepshead Bay Road, she monitoring the old man's equilibrium, ready to lunge and catch him. He barely noticed her, engaged in a marvelous gab with the boy. It occurred to Tooly that each of these two was oblivious to the other's reputation, therefore took him seriously. Plus, Humphrey was wonderful with kids. And Mac, unaccustomed to such attention, sought to merit it, speaking in full sentences rather than swallowing his meaning halfway.

At the Baskin-Robbins, Humphrey bellied up to the display glass, peering blindly at the buckets of ice cream. "Can you see all right?" she whispered, but he waved her away, to discuss with Mac the relative merits of mint chocolate chip and pink bubblegum. The boy chose a single scoop, watching wide-eyed as Humphrey took the banana split.

"What about you?" Mac asked Tooly, which made her smile—he spoke as if he were treating.

"Very happy to watch."

So she was: Mac speed-licking to avoid drips falling on his hand; Humphrey with his long spoon, operating with much concentration, much spillage, and much exercise of puckery lips. Two little boys, she thought.

"Very cold on my teeth," Mac observed.

"Hmm," confirmed Humphrey, who had few teeth left. "I try not to bite down." He took pains to compose each bite, a process so fiddly that each took a tantalizing minute, his mouth opening thirty seconds early, theirs watering from suspense.

Humphrey insisted on paying—absolutely insisted! But he struggled with the indistinct green bills (she had slipped cash into his pocket before they left). He squinted at the pimpled cashier, at the bills, then handed them all over, saying, "Take it." The cashier proved honest—it always surprised Tooly that most people were.

The afternoon was a success and, upon their return, even the music next door had stopped. But, despite herself, Tooly felt slightly hurt:

around a stranger, Humphrey had pulled himself together and was lucid at times, even making little jokes.

Back in Darien, she deposited Mac before the Xbox and sneaked downstairs for a moment alone. But Bridget was there, standing by the closed washing machine. She inquired how their jaunt to Brooklyn had gone. Then—without transition—said how unhappy she was in her marriage.

"Duncan is an old friend," Tooly interrupted. "I'm not who you should discuss this with."

But Bridget couldn't be stopped. She and Duncan had no romantic life whatsoever, she said, and he was in denial about it. They'd become like bunkmates. Though, even bunkmates interacted. Her eyes filled with tears to hear aloud her piteous state. "And," she joked, with a plucky sniff, "he sleeps right in the middle of the mattress, so I'm all scrunched up at the edge!"

"What happens when you talk to him about it? Not about the mattress. Things in general, I mean."

"On the few occasions I tried, he changes topic. To his pissed-off politics. Or he goes into conference with his BlackBerry. Does this thing where he, like, angles himself in bed when he's reading his Kindle, so I literally cannot see his eyes, and he goes, 'Mmmmmm?' It's the present/absent."

"The present/absent?"

"Where someone's present but they're absent. Talking to you but looking at the screen."

"He's probably exhausted. He works insane amounts, Bridget."

"I know. I know. And I do totally love him still. But I feel like— what's the word?—like I'm withering. Already after having the kids, I turned into this ogre. It took me, like, four years to regain a familiar shape. And now I . . . Thing is, I have this feeling if I go full-time at the office—and they've asked me to—something bad will happen."

"Meaning?"

"Maybe I'll meet someone there," she said, looking up testingly. "I want to be in love with someone again. I *so* miss that feeling. Thinking of someone when they're not there—you know? Like you have with Garry."

Tooly almost corrected that fantasy, but it was best to end such confidences, which seemed to affect Bridget dangerously. "Nothing's happened at your office yet," Tooly said.

"Heavens, no. How could I even find time for an affair? I haven't even seen my hairdresser in two months."

"That's your answer—have an affair with the hairdresser."

"There's the dream. Free highlights."

Each went her separate way, though Bridget dashed back downstairs a few minutes later to reiterate, "Obviously, I'm never going to do anything."

Poor Duncan. Because, Tooly suspected, Bridget *was* going to stray. She hadn't sought an opinion; she'd sought to desensitize herself to what already captivated her. If Bridget were to wander, Mac would be crushed. His mother was the only family member who was devoted to him.

Bridget must have found time for her hairdresser after all, because she came home with a shorter cut, rather like Tooly's. When Duncan returned that evening, he asked Mac, "What do you think of Mom without hair?"

"Uhm . . ." The boy showed both palms, weighing like a scale. He gave a nervous snicker. Whenever Mac found himself in awkward situations, he gave this snicker, which was utterly unconvincing, thereby earning Tooly's sympathy. The ability to laugh when a joke was not funny had unexpected value; it produced a different life. She'd never had the skill, either. Still, Mac was an extremely considerate young man, and she made a mental note to mention this to Duncan. She was always looking for ways to praise the boy to his father. But it wasn't her job to mend that relationship. Would Mac even remember this when grown? What would he do when his father needed caring for? He'd dote on Duncan. There was no balance in relationships, much as people sought it.

In the McGrory household, there was symmetry at least in the basement confessional. For it was Duncan who later cornered Tooly by the washing machine and told her more than she wanted to know, an admission that had nothing to do with love. "He's not down here?" Duncan asked, entering the music room, where she sat practicing her ukulele.

She stilled the vibrating strings. "Mac? Not that I've seen."

"Grrr." Duncan stood there, hands on hips, shaking his head at the electric piano. Among the causes of household tensions was Mac's failure to practice. They paid for weekly keyboard lessons, yet, in Duncan's view, the kid didn't make the slightest effort.

"You don't practice anymore, either," she noted.

"I don't have time. He has time." Duncan picked off the floor her copy of *Nicholas Nickleby*, which she'd been dragging back and forth to Sheepshead Bay, rereading it on the lengthy train rides. "Thing weighs ten pounds," he exclaimed. "Stop messing around and buy an e-reader. Screens won, my friend."

"Are you at a loose end right now, so decided to come and provoke me?"

"Pretty much," he said. "It just gets me that he has this opportunity and doesn't use it. My old Yamaha is awesome. I got them to hook it up to the house network, too, so you can track every practice session. Which is why it's so dumb when he pretends to practice. I can see on the computer that he hasn't."

"What a pain you must be."

"I know," he said, looking at her. "Am I a total jerk here?"

"You're one of the good guys, as far as I'm concerned. You looked after Humph. You're letting me stay here for nothing."

"At the cost of making you chauffeur my kid."

"True. You're a horrible person after all."

"Actually, could I tell you something? Not for repeating. I'm serious. Not to anyone. Ever." Lowering his voice, he said that he should probably do more with his son, that Bridget pestered him to, that he ought to, and he knew it. "But . . ." He looked away. He exhaled. "Problem is . . ." He shook his head. "The thing is that I don't like him," Duncan blurted. "Just fundamentally do *not* like this person. Aargh! Makes me sick to say it out loud. But it's true. I *dis*like him. Not his fault, poor kid. I feel unbelievably shitty saying this. You can never repeat this. Ever. I mean that." He paced. "Have I shocked you?"

"I'm not shocked. You know me."

"Isn't his fault. Really not. I feel sorry for him. But whenever he's in the room," Duncan went on, gaining momentum, "I fundamentally do. Not. Like this person." He turned his back, flipped the pages of her novel. "Never occurred to me, when Bridget and I were trying to have kids, that you might not like your own child. It's the last taboo."

"The last taboo? Still reasonably taboo to be a cannibal or a necrophiliac."

"You're not getting my point."

"I am, Duncan. Just avoiding it a bit, I guess. I've never been in your position. But I don't find it that surprising. There are so few people on earth one really clicks with. I know it's supposed to be biological. But each kid has his own personality, which I suspect parents don't consider beforehand. They imagine a pet. Some of them do. Not saying you did. But it'd be amazing if one just blindly adored that person. I know that's what society says parents do. So, no, I don't find it shocking."

"You don't get it," he said. "When you have kids, you do automatically love them. It's biological."

"You're the one telling me that's not true."

"No—I do love him. Just don't think I like him."

"How old is he? Eight? Can you even make that statement yet?"

"You don't get it."

"If you keep telling me I don't get anything, it leaves me without much to say."

"Will you have kids?"

"You make such an attractive case for the reproductive plunge. I don't know, Duncan. Childhood is so exhausting."

"As a parent?"

"I mean as the child. Not sure it's fair to drop somebody else into life without giving them a choice in the matter."

"You'll find it's kind of tough to canvass the opinion of sperm."

"I prefer asking the eggs—they're more articulate. Anyway, aren't you the guy who's always bemoaning the future of humanity? Saying how the worst jerks always have millions of babies, meaning the world gets worse every generation?"

"Exactly why decent people need to have kids."

"What, a war of demographics?"

"Thing is, who knows what'll happen. Maybe the world improves by the time we're seventy and you'll regret not having had them. You'll have missed out forever, and they'll never get to exist. No need to canvass any sperm and eggs on that—everybody would rather have a life than not."

"I mean, yes, of course. I can list the things that make life worth living, now that I've been in it for a while. I can also think of what can make it pretty awful."

"Like?"

"One stroke of bad luck. Think of Xavi. (Can't stop thinking about him lately; feels hard to believe that happened.) And even simpler stuff can warp people, make life bitter."

"Such as?"

"Well, I don't know. Such as one's father not liking them."

"I never said I didn't like anybody."

In one regard, Duncan was wrong: Mac did come down to practice the keyboard—she heard him puttering around in the music room most days. That said, he never played for long. He pressed the keys, hummed to himself, hoping she'd appear. She poked her head in, said hello, asked if he'd like company.

Something bottomlessly sad about the young. Mac—awkward, doped, a loner already—couldn't be enjoying the shark tank of childhood. Her urge to guard him brought Paul to mind. For years, she had refused to discuss him, tried not even to think of him. Among the names she'd searched for online, his was never one. But, spending all this time with Mac, she contemplated Paul daily.

That night, she typed his name into one of the laptops. She found her father, only a few hours' drive away.

# 1988

SUNLIGHT AND A DISTANT WHOOSH of morning traffic came through the holes in the second-story wall. Someone approached up the stairs.

It was the old chessplayer of the night before, who trudged past her in a rumpled shirt and tie, tucked into sky-blue polyester shorts. He closed himself in the bathroom, faucet gushing, a pee stream audible. Minutes later, he emerged, having brushed his wiry gray-brown locks into submission, only to scratch his head, mussing the hair back into a peppery swirl. He set up his card table and his folding chair. Once seated, he raised a book—*The Conquest of Happiness* by Bertrand Russell—and began to read, dabbing fingers to his lips, flinging aside each page, pointing at the text as if in heated debate, and he not necessarily getting the better of it.

"Hi," she said.

"What do you have to say for yourself?" he asked, eyebrows scrunching together.

"I'm a bit—" She looked at her bare knees, then up at his book cover, blinking at the daylight coming through the holes in the wall. "A bit worried."

Humphrey held still a moment, then slammed the book onto the card table. He stood, walked a lap around the room, laceless tennis shoes clunking with each step. She braced herself, believing he was about to roar. Instead, he stopped, looking at the wall. "I also am concerned." He turned to face her. "There is something I can get for you? I can help in some way?"

"I don't know. I'm just—I woke up a bit worried. My neck hurts. I didn't go home yet. Do you know if Sarah is here? Did she come back?"

"Not sure," he said. "I . . ." He resumed pacing, working himself into a terrible state over his inability to help.

Oddly, his worry eased hers; she found herself wanting to make him feel better. "Can we play chess again?"

He paused—yes, this he could arrange. He helped her onto the folding chair, dragged it to the table, and prepared the board meticulously. Her chess strategy, if it could be flattered with such a term, was to sneak pieces up the board in hopes of snatching away Humphrey's queen without his noticing. But each piece only found itself taken. For two hours they played, the sole interruption coming when Tooly rubbed her whiplashed neck, sore from her fall off the ladder the night before.

"No cheating," he said, standing. "I go away for minute."

"Can I cheat when you get back?"

"Of course."

He disappeared into the storage room, returning with a neck brace, which he attempted to fit for her, though it was far too large. When this failed, he brought her aspirin. Applying utmost discretion, he inquired as to her weight, height, and age, jotting them on a pad to calculate how many milligrams were safe to prescribe. He produced a cup of water, a saucer bearing her half pill, plus a heap of sugar to nullify any bitterness. As the day progressed, this sugar remained her only nourishment. He displayed no signs of hunger himself, prompting her to say something finally.

"When do you eat breakfast, Humphrey?"

"I reject concept of meals. Why I must eat breakfast in morning? Then in midday, I must eat lunch? No, no—when it comes to eating, I am freethinker."

"You only eat free things?"

"I only eat when hungry. Any times of day. Yesterday, for example,

I eat at night one cereal bowl." (She pictured him consuming the bowl itself.) "Today, I have cheese sandwich."

"You had that already?"

"No, but later maybe." He returned to the chess position, belatedly looking up. "Wait—*you* are wanting cheese-sandwich activity?"

He hurried her into the kitchen, designating Tooly the assistant chef, her only duty being to approve while he fried a hunk of orange cheese. Once this had melted, he used two knives to scrape it from the blackened pan and laid it across a bed of Triscuit crackers.

She devoured it.

"Is nice?" he asked.

"Really nice."

"But something bother you," he guessed.

"Just, I'm going to be in trouble. I'm supposed to be at school," she said. "Are you leaving here soon? You told Sarah you had to go this morning. Will I be on my own now?"

"We see, we see. You don't concern about," he said. "You want Coca-Cola, darlink? I can provide." He fetched a plastic cup of it, which she glugged. "More chess activities?"

"Maybe not."

"You have reading items?"

She produced the novel from her book bag. He inspected it, approving of the author, Charles Dickens, although he expressed reservations about invented stories. "Myself, I read only facts. Art is tool of conformity," he declared. "Art pleasure is connect with complacency. To resist domination of economic factors, artist must produce negative, not affirmative, culture. Avant-garde, in particular. Work of art should make unhappy. It shows horrors of world. More grill cheese?"

She nodded.

As he fried another, she contemplated his bewildering remarks, and decided that he had been talking about the difference between happy endings and sad endings, this being her distinction between books written for children and those for adults. Tooly let it be known that she had read several books with unhappy endings. There was one, she recalled, "where the main girl and her brother drown at the end."

"Drown?"

"Both of them."

"Avant-garde," he said approvingly.

As the day passed, they read, seated on opposite sides of the card table, each interrupting to make points. When she grew hungry, they ate, regardless of the hour; if she felt thirsty, he poured warm Coke. A scandalous and thrilling thought came to her: school was going on right then, Mr. Priddles's class happening without her. Then her attention drifted to Paul, and all pleasure dissolved.

She put down her book and got permission to go downstairs into the back garden, where she inspected the dolphin mural. Humphrey found a paintbrush and a can of red paint in the storage room, and let her draw noses on the wall. "You are magnificent artist," he commented.

"Am I avant-garde?"

He smiled, and left her out there while he napped. (The bed upon which Tooly had slept was his—he'd given it up for her, dozing all night on the floor downstairs.) Alone, she explored the dilapidated house, out onto the front patio, past its walls, a few steps down the deserted lane. She ran back inside.

Later that day, delivery men arrived with crates of beer and bags of ice, followed by Venn, the man who had saved her life during that stampede the night before. He conferred with Humphrey and gave orders to Jaime, who counted out the float and explained to Tooly how his bar setup worked. Others came and went, some depositing packages in the storage room upstairs, a few taking parcels, everyone answering to Venn.

Amid all this, Tooly stood against the wall, her fingertips on the bricks behind her, motionless as a gecko. When Venn looked over, he winked, as if there were a second level beyond what went on around them, and his glance acknowledged her entry into that level, available to him and her alone. When she had nearly gathered the courage to address him in front of everyone, he spoke to her, anticipating her thoughts. "Not to worry," he told her. "Everything's fine."

"Just that, I don't know how to get to my house from here," she said.

"We'll wait for Sarah on that," he replied. "And I'm around. Nothing to fear, duck." His voice—its deepness, its surety—captivated her. He assigned her little tasks: tell So-and-So; tag along while I resolve this problem. He adorned nothing with "please" or "thank you," yet was kinder than those who did. Wherever he went, she hastened just ahead of his stride, lest he lose sight of her and be lured away, leaving her among large strangers.

Even when partygoers began arriving, all greeting Venn, he continued to keep an eye on her. If he spoke to a particularly intimidating dead-eyed thug, he called Tooly over, introducing her and conveying his protection. He even said, "Grab my arm, little duck, if you need anything." As the crowd thickened, grown-ups crushed her and trod on her feet, so she went upstairs and sat opposite Humphrey, who had his toilet-paper earplugs in again. They read together, trying to ignore the racket. When fatigue overcame her, Venn cleared everyone off the upper floor, deposited her on the bed, and left her to rest, though the music boomed downstairs. Drifting off, she worried that Humphrey would be gone by morning.

Instead, he was there, pouring her Coca-Cola. He was not leaving, he promised, until Sarah returned and took care of matters. In this way, they passed that first week together. Tooly noticed that he wore almost the same outfit every day. She had scarcely more variety herself, just the school clothing she'd arrived in, plus the gym clothes in her book bag. When Venn noticed her increasing scruffiness, he dispatched two young Thai women—mainstays at the parties—to buy her outfits from a night market. Phueng and Mai must have argued, because they returned with separate hauls, Phueng with girlie pink T-shirts emblazoned with logos of My Little Pony and Strawberry Shortcake, while Mai had outfits that miniaturized her own look: off-the-shoulder blouses, zebra-print leggings, slouch socks. Both had bought toiletries and good-naturedly scrubbed the girl clean in the bathtub. Tooly let them, but insisted on staying fully clothed, her new rolled-up jeans bleeding indigo down the plughole. Afterward, they employed a blow-dryer on her. The humidity caused her hair to spring outward with comical frizziness, making even Venn laugh—the first time she'd seen that lovely sight—and he pressed her staticky head when next he saw her.

Phueng and Mai were freelancers—not bargirls tied to a particular nightspot but hairdressers who supplemented their income with "tips" from foreign boyfriends, hoping one would eventually agree to marriage and make the income permanent. As the night went on, they found customers, and Tooly was left alone. She visited with Jaime, who taught her about his trade: how you poured heavily early in the evening, then tapered off as the night went on; and how you managed the drunks, whom he referred to as *los zombies*. When the party reached fever pitch, Jaime spoke less and pointed more: get me that, hand me this, run upstairs, more ice. "Look at this one," he said, of an approaching zombie, the woman's eyelashes out of sync.

"C'mon, kiddo," the woman snarled. "Pour it a little stronger, will ya."

The two bouncers were supposed to keep the peace, but it was usually Venn who broke up fights. When he intervened, the combatants soon submitted—at most throwing a late punch over his shoulder, which only earned a hard slap from Venn. Even men twice his size reddened and apologized. During such scenes, he flashed Tooly the quickest of winks to show her not to be afraid, that this wasn't real. All around were raised voices—including his own ferocious outbursts—while she, against a wall, glowed inside to know what was really happening. "I never lose control, duck," he'd explained. "I choose to get angry."

The roughest men adored Venn, and women were equally drawn to him, though many of his girlfriends derided the cult of Venn—rogues adopting his speech patterns and requesting the music he liked (schmaltzy seventies love songs). After a couple of weeks, they were even calling Tooly "duck," as Venn did, treating her like a bar mascot, patting her head with coarse paws, offering low fives. Sometimes they inquired if her dad was around, by which they meant Venn. Once, she mentioned the disgusting piano player who, on her first night there, had kissed her. A dozen of the hardest men on the premises gathered for details on the culprit. She later heard that he'd "been sorted out," and never saw him again. If anyone bothered her now, a wall of villains closed around her. This protection imbued her with an intoxicating power over grown-ups. But she avoided using it, since violence—even in her favor—made her whole body tremble.

From listening in, she learned that Humphrey rented this house, although the things in the storage room belonged to Venn's associates. These included a Bulgarian ex-wrestler who bleached one-dollar bills in the bathtub, using desktop publishing to reprint them as hundreds; Nigerians who smuggled brown packets in disassembled televisions; and a Brazilian who showed Tooly a plastic tube surgically implanted in his left arm that, when he flexed, sucked air through a hole in his fingertip, allowing him to "disappear" pretty stones from a jewelry shop in Bang Rak. Such characters increased Humphrey's wish to leave—if the police found this stuff, they'd blame him. But Venn was watching out. "Baksheesh for Bangkok's finest" was how he put it, meaning bottomless drinks, nightly entertainment, and weekly envelopes for the precinct commanders.

After days of taking up Humphrey's bed, Tooly obtained her own space, a camping tent in the storage room with a padlock on the inside for privacy. "You're staying a little longer than planned," Venn told her.

"Am I going to be in trouble?"

"Not a chance."

The thought of Venn standing up for her with Paul was frightening—even to think of the mismatch made her guilty.

Now that Tooly was stowed in the storage room, she took the opportunity to snoop around, finding designer watches, golf memberships for Panya Resort, fax machines, a stack of U.S. marriage certificates and blank Canadian passports, twenty-four-inch color TVs with the insides hollowed out, packets of expired pharmaceuticals (where Humphrey had found her aspirin), an industrial sewing machine, restaurant tables. Finding herself among these objects, it occurred to Tooly that she, too, was a stolen good.

Each morning, she unzipped her tent and peeked out.

"Conversation and debate?" Humphrey asked, handing her a glass of Coke. As she sipped, he opened his notepad, pen in hand, its tip aimed at the ceiling, and wrote, ITEM 1—MAKE LIST.

He immediately drew a thick line through this. "Done," he said, and tossed the pad on his unmade bed. "Important to be productive. Already, I achieve something. Good mornink." The pad—and, indeed, his productivity—made no further appearances for another day.

Sarah's absence, so scary at first, grew less troubling. Tooly's days assumed a pleasant routine. She raced around on the lower floor, leaping as she went, singing loudly and tunelessly—a long warbling note. The turning fan whirred slowly toward her, blowing her off balance. "What are you reading today, Humphrey?"

He responded at length, circumnavigating anything resembling an answer in order to hold her attention, tossing forth references, personal commentary, perplexing claims: that a man called Francis Bacon had experimented with the refrigeration of chicken in a snow drift, caught a cold, and died; that Thomas Hobbes was born prematurely when his mother heard that the Spanish Armada was sailing up the English Channel, thus condemning her son to a lifetime of poor digestion.

While speaking, Humphrey gesticulated wildly, as if skywriting the names of his idols. He was of the firm opinion that, had the Great Thinkers been around, had they stumbled across this house, they'd have become his personal friends. "Sir Isaac Newton and I, we are like two peas in a pond." Sadly, it was trivial beings who were in abundance; the Great Thinkers proved so hard to find.

"Who's your favorite writer, Humphrey?"

"Samuel Johnson, Yeats and Keats," he said, pronouncing the two last names to rhyme, "Kafka, Baudelaire, Baron Karl Wilhelm von Humboldt, Thomas Carlyle, Fichte, Demosthenes, Cicero, Rousseau, Aristotle, and Milton."

"If you had to pick *one*."

"That is who I pick."

"It's not one."

"Also," he added, as if the unmentioned might complain, "John Locke, Plutarch, Thomas Paine, John Stuart Mill."

Much as he enjoyed rambling, Humphrey liked nothing more than listening to her. He wasn't simply being polite—he thirsted for information and swallowed any she offered, even the plots of novels she'd read. She told him about the World Wrestling Federation, too, and the controversy over whether it was all fake, which intrigued him.

"Fabulous information you are giving," he said, stirring his coffee with a ballpoint pen and licking it, unaware that the heat had breached the ink cartridge, dyeing his lips blue. "You know who you are reminding me of?" he said, wiping his mouth and spreading ink across the back of his hand. "John Stuart Mill. He was child prodigy like you, always eating watermelon."

She sat cross-legged on the floor, half of a watermelon in her lap, digging into it with a wooden cooking spoon so ineffectual at chiseling that she gripped it with both hands, which meant the juice-slippery melon kept leaping from between her knees and bouncing across the floor.

With no sign of anyone retrieving Tooly, Humphrey soon took on her education, loading her down with reading material. Each time she returned to her tent, she found a fresh volume at its entrance.

"You have read Spengler yet, darlink?"

"What is Spankler?"

"You are ten years old, and you not read Oswald Spengler? How this is possible?" He placed a copy of *The Decline of the West* by the tent.

Humphrey had no friends at the parties, just a few trading partners. Their dealings were mostly in expired pharmaceuticals and medical prosthetics, such as a pair of flesh-colored plastic legs he was constantly trying to sell, each wearing a scuffed black dress shoe and a red sock. "How much I get for this?" he asked Tooly, placing one before her.

"Just one leg?"

"I give half price if you buy two."

"A hundred baht?" she guessed.

"Not even left shoe without sock do I sell for hundred baht! This is high-demand product."

Nevertheless, the legs sat around (stood around) for days before he found a buyer in a cuddly Cameroonian named Lovemore Ngubu, who planned to paint the legs brown and ship them to Yaoundé for sale at his uncle's electronics-repair shop. It was Lovemore who told Tooly that Humphrey had served time in jail.

"Not jail," Humphrey clarified, when she asked about this. "It was Gulag. That is like jail but made by Russians, so worse."

"What did you do?"

"Communists say I am social parasite, which is big exaggeration."

"What was it like in jail?"

At first, they kept him awake for days in complete isolation, he said. To stay sane, he tried to recall his life, framing recollected events as if they were photographs, looking at each in detail. Talking with prisoners in adjacent cells was forbidden, but he and a neighbor had a sewer pipe in common, so they communicated with a tapping code used in Russian prisons since tsarist times. It was at this point that Humphrey started playing chess seriously—different taps connoted different moves. The man in the next cell had been there for eight years, and each day paced back and forth, counting his steps to calculate the distance, mapping in imagination the walk back to his hometown, thousands of miles away on the other side of the Soviet Union.

"What happened to him?"

"They let him out, but his body is ruin; he dies. After this, they send me north for chopping wood."

"What was that like?"

"Hungry every day. They tell us when to eat—little soup with grains—and when to sleep. Very cold. Everybody dreaming of food all night. One prisoner, he is crazy, kills friend—they find him eating."

"Eating what?"

"Eating friend. They mix me with common criminals. This is where I become corrupted. Before, I am honest man," he said. "It is so cold up there all time. Even here and now, where it is so hot and sweating, I am cold in my bones. Yes, it was bad in Gulag. Another man, he puts ground glass in his eye just to get to hospital. Other politicals, they try hunger-strike."

"What's that?"

"You stop eating as protest. But only works in country where they care you are not eating. In Soviet Union, they stick tube in you with boiling soup, and this destroys stomach right away. There is saying in Gulag: 'Only first life sentence is hell. After that, everything gets better.' You want Coca-Cola?"

His resentment over those six years of detention had expanded into a generalized hostility toward his birth nation. If one mentioned anything to do with the Soviet Union, he remarked contemptuously, "Typical Russian! This is typical Russian way of behave." As for the language, he refused to speak it even when his countrymen approached him—a provocation that would have led to violence had Venn not intervened. Humphrey even spurned Russian in written form, saying that English was more beautiful than the ugly Cyrillic script. There were many people who had the misfortune of being born in the wrong place. He was one of them.

"How did you get out of Gulag, Humphrey?"

"I run away hundred miles. At Black Sea, I get boat to Turkey, through Greece, bottom of Sicily, into Portugal. I meet man at dock and say, 'Mister, where this ship is going?' He tells me, 'England.' I am thinking, Very nice—land of Samuel Johnson, Bertrand Russell, John Stuart Mill. I say, 'I can come? Is all right?' He says, 'Yes, why not.' Then, halfway into sea, someone asks, 'Why you are going to Africa?' I say, 'No, I go to England.' He says, 'We go to South Africa on this boat.' So, that is where I end. Years, I am stuck there. Why? Because trivial being tells me wrong boat. It is example of Moron Problem. If not for moron, I have different life, write many books, have nice fat wife and children. But no. This idiot"—Humphrey pronounced the word as if it contained only two syllables: EED-yot—"this idiot, he has been highly—how should I put to you?"

Remembering one of his favorite words, she said, "Detrimental?"

"Yes, highly detrimental. But there is important fact I learn: half your life is decide by morons," he explained. "Does not matter how brilliant you are. You can have intellect big as John Stuart Mill. Even *he* probably has many difficulty from idiots."

"I have difficulty from idiots," she told him. "My old school in Australia sent the wrong information to the place I go to now, and they're making me do a whole year over."

"Why they let this happen? It is like something from Soviet Union. Just because moron sent wrong papers?"

"I *told* them."

"This makes me fury. Quite fury. Why they do this to you? They do not realize you are high-quality intellectual?"

"I'm supposed to be in fifth grade."

"You should be in sixth! In seventh! Better, I put you in medical school. That is how intellectual you are."

"I hate trivial beings."

"I hate them also. But careful; it is trivial beings that run the world."

So went their days—talking, reading, commending each other's forbearance in a world bedeviled by the Moron Problem. Whenever it suited them, he cooked a meal. His specialty was anything potato-based: potato sandwiches, potato pie, and his favorite, smashed-potato pizza.

"What's your favorite food, Humphrey?"

"Me? I like all things eatful."

That was daytime. When night fell, all changed. Some evenings, Venn kept her near. Other times, he entertained associates, and she watched from a distance until he summoned her. "Little duck!" he said, scratching his thick beard, lines crinkling around his eyes. And she walked away from Humphrey as one might from a classroom friend when a fancier after-school companion arrives. She was ashamed of him, and he knew this, so let her go. Yet he watched from afar. When she was tired, it was he who asked Venn to banish the revelers upstairs, a trick that Humphrey, despite his pleas to the crowd, had no power to effect.

# 2000

A COUPLE OF DAYS PASSED before Tooly noticed that the students' apartment was less populated, and that the missing person was Noeline. She and Emerson had broken up. Without her there, he walked around shirtless, stroking his blond ringlets, and inserting his opinions everywhere. That is, he hadn't changed at all.

But Noeline had, as Tooly witnessed when they ran into each other on Broadway. She appeared jollier, slimmer, and was startlingly affectionate, insisting on a hug. Neither had eaten lunch, so Noeline proposed Chinese. Tooly loved the idea; it was exciting, a professor inviting her for a meal. Since she couldn't afford to dine out, Tooly pretended to have no appetite, but agreed to sit and watch. Noeline falsely attributed this abstention to dieting and insisted that Tooly was thin enough to eat whatever she wanted—who cared, anyway! She requested an extra plate and extra chopsticks, making the case that it wasn't a diet violation if you hadn't ordered it.

Noeline chose General Tso's chicken and white rice—not brown rice, which was the only kind she'd been allowed during her year with Emerson, who was a nutrition hard-liner. Tooly sampled the food, then laid down her chopsticks, took up her napkin, dabbed her lips, trying not to look famished.

"What's your opinion," Noeline inquired, "of thongs?"

"The sandals?"

"No, no. Thong underwear. The kind that goes up your butt."

"Don't think I have a strong opinion about it."

"Okay, can I just tell you something? The thong is why Emerson and I broke up."

"You found him wearing yours?"

"I wish. No, he wanted me to wear one, which—if you have any familiarity with my butt, there's just no cause to expose more of it. He called it 'a point of principle.'"

"Your butt, or the thong?"

"The one in the other."

"So did you?"

"It's a long-standing credo in my life that dental floss is not for covering one's nether regions."

"And this was an ongoing issue?"

"You have no idea. Once he fixates on something, you can't pry him off it. Anyway, why don't *men* have to wear a goddamn thong?"

"It wouldn't work," Tooly said. "They've got stuff to hold up."

"They wear boxer shorts, and those don't support anything."

"Maybe they need an underwire thong."

Noeline loved this and clapped her hands. "That's a totally disturbing image." As she continued her review of the Emerson relationship, squirmy details emerged, including sexual quirks and small cruelties. "When you see what looks like an ideal relationship from outside," Noeline remarked, "you don't realize how much crap is going on inside."

"Hmm."

"What's that mean?"

"Just that your relationship didn't seem all that ideal to me. You guys argued a lot."

"How do you know that?"

"Thin walls."

"Well, that's kind of embarrassing."

"And he was rude to you, I thought." Tooly took a sip of water. "Are you offended if I say this stuff? Is it better that I keep my mouth shut?"

"The more awful things you say about him, the better. Badmouthing this jerk is my favorite sport right now. But wait—you didn't like Emerson?"

"Noeline, I don't think *anybody* likes him. There's a saying: 'Every cockroach looks beautiful to its mother.' But when Emerson calls his mom she lets the answering machine get it."

"That is fantastic!"

"I can keep going?"

"Yes, please!"

"He's arrogant. He's pushy. Constantly showing off. What is it with taking his shirt off all the time? Yes, we know he works out. Congratulations, you have abs. But it's winter in New York, not July in Malibu. And I don't doubt that he knows a lot, but it's—"

"He doesn't know one-tenth of what he claims," Noeline interrupted. "He thinks he'll do what I did and go from postgrad straight to teaching at Columbia. Dream on."

"Really?"

"They like us to make our bones on the mean streets of rural academia. I got insanely lucky."

"You were good, probably."

"Lucky. Anyhoo, back to insulting the loser. I just used the guy for his body. I'm joking. Whatever. I'm pretty cynical about relationships. And I blame my parents. Even though they live on different continents, they keep up this amazing relationship. They've allowed each other to pursue separate careers. And they love each other still. So they've ruined me. Because that is not the rule. Most guys cannot deal with a smart woman. Male-female relationships are basically incompatible with mutual dignity. But society mounts all this pressure on heteros to mate for life or be outcasts."

"How does society do that?"

"Like, consider the romantic comedy. That whole genre is intended to guilt us into breeding. Women are made to look lonely and pathetic if they ever dare be independent. 'Fear not, loser girl—here's dimple-cheeked Hugh Grant, who will save you with his mumbly bullshit!' It's social engineering to make us make babies."

"Did Emerson want babies?"

"I could never procreate with a guy as stupid as him. Okay," Noeline said, smile rising. "I'm going to tell you something. But don't pass this on to anyone."

"I don't know anyone."

"Seriously, it could bounce back on me. Get this: I basically wrote half his doctoral thesis. Not even kidding. You have no idea what shit he had in there before I looked at it."

"What's his subject again? Something about roller coasters?"

" 'The Sign, the Signified, and the Cyclone: Lacan Goes to the Fairground.' "

"What does that even mean?"

"Who knows. But fine, I worked with it. And then *he* goes and fucking breaks up with *me*! Like, what is up with that?" She took a big mouthful of food, talking and chewing together: "Good to vent . . . My friends all hated him, so now they're, like, I told you so . . . . Anyway. Duncan? How's stuff with him?"

"Fine."

"You in love?"

"Me? Gosh, I don't know that I have that emotion. I like people," Tooly said. "But there's not a separate emotion involving stardust and harps. Nobody's convinced me such a thing exists. What exists, I think, is liking to a greater or lesser degree. But this idea of a magical separate thing is sort of a swindle—like you were saying about romantic comedies."

"I never said I didn't fall in love. I do constantly. That's my problem. You must not have met the right person."

"I don't think there are 'right people,' " Tooly said. "Just variations on types."

"How did you get so cynical at such a young age?"

The answer, which Tooly failed to give, was that these views were not necessarily hers. They belonged to Venn, and he was the most convincing person she knew. "It's complicated."

"Is this the part where you get all mysterious and clam up?"

"Probably, yes."

The camaraderie cooled. "I don't really fall in love, so I'm not with Duncan, no," she said, trying to make reiteration sound like disclosure. "I do *like* Duncan. He's a nice guy. And I feel sad for him."

"Ouch."

"Not in a bad way."

"No, no—most men want to be pitied," Noeline said sarcastically. "Actually, maybe they do. Holy shit! Maybe that's the key to everything!"

"I don't pity him. I'm just saying I don't get sentimental about people."

"Isn't sentimental what you're supposed to get about people? If you don't, what's the point of going out with Duncan at all?"

"There are rational reasons."

"What's the rationale of sleeping with Duncan McGrory, whom you sort of pity?"

"Well, we're working on a business project. Me, him, and Xavi. This Wildfire online-currency thing."

"That's not serious, is it? I thought that was just you guys messing around."

"It's getting serious."

"And that's your reason for dating Duncan? I completely don't believe you."

"I have this friend," Tooly said, "who is like an extreme version of me, in terms of not being sentimental about stuff. He's purely rational—yet also decent to people who deserve it, and tough with those who don't. Doesn't care about rules, or how you're supposed to act. He behaves how he thinks. That's how I try to be."

"You're in love with this guy?"

"No, no, no—he pretty much raised me."

"Aha! So, *this* is the guy you live with in some batcave outside Gotham."

"I live with someone else, actually," Tooly said.

"Your parents?"

"My parents aren't in the picture."

"You're an orphan?"

"I didn't say that."

"So mysterious! But I'm getting somewhere. You're using Duncan, and you're in love with a mysterious superhero. Only kidding! Hey, should we get more tea? You have to come to my place sometime—I have all sorts of awesome herbal teas. Are you into drinking tea and bad-mouthing guys sometime? We have to do that."

"Name the date."

"Tooly, why don't you apply here to college? You totally should."

"I can't go to college. I was a disaster at school."

"What were your grades like?"

"I got C's."

"I don't believe that."

"I'm glad you have this misconception about the size of my brain. If I could open up my skull, you'd find a little peanut in there. I never even graduated from high school."

"Bullshit."

"I only went till I was ten."

"What? How is that even legal?"

"My life to date hasn't been entirely legal."

"Divulge. Right now."

Tooly shook her head, laughed downward.

"I'll pry it out of you, young lady!" Noeline said. "How the hell do you talk like you do if you dropped out at ten? You're, like, the only person I know who says words like 'scoundrel' in conversation and makes it sound normal. My students—kids who can, like, reel off SAT words—*never* say things like 'scoundrel.'"

"I read a lot, I guess. Lots of words that I say, I've only seen in print—I'm probably mispronouncing half the stuff."

"I noticed. But all college is, Tooly, is reading. It's reading lists, plus professors checking that you read the reading lists. Well, that's not entirely all. But a lot of it. You've never been to my place on West End Avenue, right? You have to come over."

"Can I see your books?"

"That is my favorite question ever. Tea and books?" She clinked Tooly's cup. "Then, afterward, I can see your place, right?" she teased. "Somehow, I don't think that's happening—I don't get to visit the batcave, do I. How about you introduce me to your mystery man?"

"Wouldn't be a good idea."

"I'd fall in love with him?"

"Very possibly."

"I *have* to meet him, then. And you guys live together, right?"

"No."

"Just testing. But you grew up in that apartment on a Hundred and fifteenth, which was how you came to meet Duncan, right?"

"I lived there for a few years when I was a kid, yeah."

"That composer dude with the pig downstairs, Gilbert—I was talking to him one time, and he's been there thirty years. He's the last remaining rent-control resident from before Columbia bought the building. I mentioned how I knew this girl—meaning you—who lived in the building as a kid. I calculated that it must've been in the eighties. He said that's impossible; the whole building was single-room-occupancy back then. No kids allowed. You weren't allowed to sleep more than one person per room."

"That's weird."

"More than weird," Noeline said, smiling. "Come on—I just confessed to, like, forging a thesis or whatever. That's the end of my career, if anyone knew."

So Tooly confided part of the truth: that she had never lived in that apartment; that she was fascinated with seeing inside strangers' homes, so she had a hobby of talking her way in. Originally, her house visits were conducted with that guy, the aforementioned male friend, who occasionally needed to look around someone's home. "Way easier for a little girl to get in than a grown man."

"But sorry—*why* were you guys doing this?"

"It's interesting meeting complete strangers, seeing what their apartments are like. Haven't you ever wished you could just peek into someone's place?" Tooly said. "And people are different at home. You can figure out stuff."

"What stuff? Which things to burglarize?"

"We never did that. I never did that."

"So why, then?"

"Opportunities come from knowing people."

"Is that why you hang around at Emerson's place? Opportunities?"

"Maybe."

"Wow. You are cold. Well, if you end up burglarizing their place, please take Emerson's tofu. It's the object that means most to him in the world."

Tooly laughed.

A week later, they bumped into each other again. Noeline stepped from the bathroom at 115th Street in pajamas, sheepishly bypassed Tooly in the corridor, and hastened into Emerson's bedroom.

# 2011

SHE TOOK HIM.

Mac was scheduled that morning for floor hockey, a sport at which he demonstrated absolute ineptitude and corresponding dread. Tooly clicked him under the passenger-side safety belt, tossed a bag of their belongings on the backseat of the minivan, and drove right past the Y, taking the turnoff for interstate south. He looked at her. "Is this the right way?"

"No."

"Oh, good. Today was quarterfinals." He stared out the window, incurious about the change of plans. Mac tracked their mileage through Westchester, checking the odometer against the highway signs. After a silent patch, he said, "Trees don't count as being alive because they don't have heads." He returned to his open window, warm air fluttering his belt strap, the late-July sun intensified through the windscreen.

"Don't you want to know where we're going?" she asked.

He shrugged. They drove that whole morning, playing car games and listening to the radio. She inquired about his moviemaking class, and he explained his Flip videocamera, with the combination of patience and inexactitude that young children exhibit when informing their elders about the present day. He fell asleep for a couple of hours, miles rushing beneath them, past Philadelphia and Wilmington, southwest around Baltimore, before they turned off for Lodge Haven, Maryland.

That name had always felt privately hers, the place of birth listed on every form and passport of her life. But she remembered nothing of the place, just a Washington, D.C., suburb that she'd left as an infant and never seen since. She woke Mac gently, houses sliding past, a neighborhood of long lawns, basement romper rooms, college stickers on car windows.

"It's okay that I kidnapped you?" she asked him.

"It's okay."

"We can travel around and I can show you all sorts of things. No piano lessons required, and no Seroquel."

He looked down, ashamed of his medications. "I like my piano lessons."

"In that case, we'll find a piano teacher and kidnap him, too."

"Where are we right now?"

"We're going for lunch with my father."

"With the banana split?"

"No, not him. My real father," she said, scanning the street for the address.

At a distance, she spotted him kneeling on the lawn outside his home, pruning a flower bed beneath the bay windows, his back to her, trowel in hand, a long strand of white hair on his balding head flapping back and forth in the wind, like an arm waving Mayday. She lowered her window. Paul turned, smoothing the hair across his head, raising the trowel in greeting. "That you there?" he asked, shading his eyes with gardening gloves, his arms sun-freckled, polo shirt tucked into khakis. "Park in the driveway, or on the street. Nobody tows here."

An urge to stamp on the pedal and zoom away came over Tooly. She pulled to the curb, cut the engine, and reached over to Mac. "Shake my hand for luck."

"Why?"

"Just an old habit."

But he wouldn't, so she unclicked his seatbelt. "Hungry for lunch?"

As they crossed the road, she watched Paul's thin mouth, which wavered rather than spoke, as if the lips were engaged in a dispute over how to greet her. "So," he said, "you found the place."

During all these years apart, Paul had existed for Tooly as a character in her story, one who had left the stage. Now he stood before her, a little man around sixty, awaiting a response. Custom suggested she inform him that the drive was easy, the traffic sparse, his flower bed lovely. Instead, she said, "It's such a pleasure for me to see you again," and touched his forearm, whose slenderness discomposed her, a warm, brittle limb. He was so much smaller than he ought to have been. His arm tensed at her touch.

Paul ushered them inside his home, where he ran a consultancy of which he was the sole employee, working on contract for U.S. government departments like Homeland Security, Defense, and State to produce white papers on risks to the telecom grid: How easy would it be for foreign nation-states to hack in? Could we have a Stuxnet here? What effect would a disaster like the tsunami in Japan have on systems at American nuclear plants?

In the front room, framed prints of sparrows and owls hovered on the wall. The bay window overlooked a mowed front lawn, bird feeder hanging from the oak tree. He assigned Tooly and Mac seats and inquired about refreshments—milk or ginger ale?—then went to prepare lunch.

"Can I help with anything?" she called to him.

"No, you can't. You can wait there."

Mac remained seated but Tooly stood, tensely browsing his books. These volumes were the scenery of her childhood. On the first page of each, he had written his full name, including middle initial, proclaiming that this book, on his shelf, in his front room, did indeed belong to him. Flipping through *The Complete Birder*, she discovered his pencil notations in the margins, marks too faint to read but for a single comment, "Interesting warbler," followed by the impress of an exclamation point that he had erased.

It was clear without asking that he'd been alone all these years—

his solitude evident in the television squared to a seat at the far end of the couch, a line of HB pencils on the coffee table sharpened to pricking points and awaiting bird books in urgent need of his name. Within the folds of the curtain, a telescope crouched, its capped nose turned down as if too timid to peep outside. His binoculars rested on a high shelf, which she could reach these days, and did, sliding them from their satin-lined case and trying them at the window, finding neither birds nor planets, only a garage across the road, the wavering sky lined with power cables.

"Lunch is served."

She torqued around, caught playing without permission. He waved away her apologies and led them into the kitchen. From a deep serving bowl, Paul ladled coconut-cream soup, with tiny eggplants bobbing, sweet basil, Kaffir lime leaves, lemongrass. Every course was Thai—tom yum soup, red curry with rice, sliced green mango—in bittersweet tribute to the last point of their acquaintance.

"I left out the hot peppers," he assured Mac, "not knowing how you took it. Some young people don't appreciate spice. Some old people don't, either."

"Nice?" Tooly asked Mac.

He nodded fast, swallowing.

"I thought of you recently," Paul told her. "The wrestler 'Macho Man' Randy Savage died."

"Do you always think of me when you hear about wrestlers?"

"Yes, actually."

"Me, too," she said. "Did you actually enjoy that stuff? Or was it just to be nice to me?"

"I found it relaxing," he answered, preparing himself a spoonful, his rimless glasses steamed from the soup. He removed them and, with much deliberation, wiped each lens with a corner of the tablecloth, blind eyes blinking, pink dents on either side of his nose where the spectacle pads had pressed.

The sight of this—for reasons that escaped her—made Tooly too sad to speak. She tried to eat, but swallowing was impossible.

For a minute, the only sound was the boy's slurps. Each time he made this noise, she looked to Paul, expecting irritation, finding none.

"You used to avoid foreign food," she told him.

"I've come around," Paul said. "Only, not the very spicy stuff." He'd taken cooking classes in Thailand, he informed her.

"I'm impressed." She would never have imagined him taking a course. "I'd love to do something like that. I'm crazy for classes."

"You used to hate them in school."

"Maybe that's why I like them now."

After the soup, he asked, "And can you still count a minute?"

She smiled, not having thought of this childhood trick in nearly a quarter century. "When I was little," she explained to Mac, "I could guess exactly how long a minute lasted by counting in my head. Shall we test me after lunch?"

But Paul unstrapped his watch right then and dangled it before the boy. Mac stared, nonplussed at the antiquity of calculator functions. "It's this button," Paul explained, and Mac pushed it, liquid-crystal numerals cycling onscreen.

Tooly scrunched her eyes, counting silently to sixty. "Now?"

"Thirty-seven seconds," Mac informed her.

"Terrible!" she said.

The boy gave it a try. Long after what seemed a minute to Tooly, he raised his finger.

"Fifty-five seconds," Paul reported. "Very good."

Paul had remained in Thailand for eight years after her departure—by far his longest overseas residence. Without Tooly around, he no longer needed to keep moving. He had married, and his wife lived here with him. "You remember Shelly, don't you?"

"Our housekeeper?"

"Well, not in a long time." Shelly had stepped out to the Costco in Beltsville to give them time alone, and to supply herself for the yearly trip to her home province, Nong Khai, where she and Paul owned a house. "Year by year, I'm phasing out my work. She wants us to retire there. Within five years, I won't have to be here at all."

He asked about Tooly's bookshop, her life on the Welsh-English border, her travels, all of which she had mentioned in their phone call. While she answered, he folded his napkin, placed the spoon and fork perpendicular to each other, rotated them like clock hands, leaned back in his chair, crossed his legs one way, then the other.

"I've been waiting," he interrupted, drawing his chair up to the table. "I've been waiting to hear from you. It was years. I thought I wouldn't." He went quiet, tried to finish, voice rising in pitch but strangled in his throat. He forced a laugh, unthinkingly tapping the boy's arm.

"Ow, get off!"

"Excuse me. Sorry," Paul said, hand raised. "Pardon me."

Mac—unaware of the distress emanating from the man—asked when they were having dessert. There was none. Could he get down and play on his phone? He could. The boy departed for the front room, where he lay on the floor, swiping at a game onscreen, indifferent to their conversation in the kitchen.

"I always wanted to explain myself to you," Paul continued. "Always wanted to. I had a duty—thought I had a duty—regarding what I did. I wanted to explain that, but planned to wait till you were grown. Then I never heard from you. I wasn't going to interfere. Didn't want to disturb your life."

Tooly could have claimed that she'd been prevented from contacting him, but that was untrue. She hadn't wanted to. They had been a team once, she as vital to him as he to her. Yet she had abandoned him. Knowingly, she'd done so.

"I felt it was not in your interest that you stayed with your mother," he explained. "That was why I acted. That's why I took you. It wasn't selfishness. I hope you realize that."

"I know."

"She'd just go absent, days at a time. Stop me if you don't want to hear this." Since Tooly didn't object, he continued. "She could only fix her attention on the thing in front of her and nothing else. And we weren't it. You were so undersized when you were little—is it possible that was caused by your mother neglecting you? I had a duty, I thought. Not only as your father but as a human person. Which is why I acted. But only with good intentions."

From adolescence, Paul had been a joiner of clubs and teams—not by preference but against it, plunging himself into uncomfortable social situations in the hope of converting himself into a different person, one more affable and easygoing. But his nature resisted experience: he remained frustratingly the same. By college, he'd submitted to introversion, taking a degree in computer science, which led to a job in D.C. at Ritcomm. After a few years, they appointed him to run an overseas project, a ten-week contract with the Kenyan government. It proved a disaster. The independence leader, President Jomo Kenyatta, was dying, and members of his inner circle were contesting power and enriching themselves from state programs. When Paul refused to cooperate, officials shunned him. He petitioned Ritcomm to return stateside, but this risked voiding the contract. They told him to sit it out.

With nothing to do, he booked a countryside tour, lured by the promise of birds. Also, he hoped for cooler locales, since heat aggravated his respiratory problems. But the tour guide drove homicidally, and constantly sought to divert Paul to bordellos and shady jewel merchants. Part of the tour had been touted as a two-night "bird safari," yet turned out to be nothing of the sort. Paul found himself at a ramshackle former hunting lodge run by a louche Italian and his miserable English wife, both serious drinkers. Big-game hunters used to stay out there, but the independent Kenyan government had banned blood sports. A few lodges had transformed themselves into nature parks; others offered illegal hunts. When Paul refused such an expedition, the Italian owner lost interest, telling him to wander the grounds and look skyward—that was the bird safari. But traipsing through the bush seemed madness, with savage creatures out there, so Paul remained in his room, feeling aggrieved. The daughter of the lodge owners turned up, offering to show him the few birds found on the premises, several in cages. Previously, her job had been to photograph guests with their kills. She asked him about America, gazed too directly at him.

He returned to Nairobi and resumed his nonexistent job. To his surprise, the young woman from the lodge appeared at his hotel with a tale of woe: her ex-boyfriend had tried to shoot himself, and all the white settlers in the area falsely blamed her and made life insufferable. She had nowhere to stay in the capital, so Paul booked her a room at the hotel—on a different floor, however, to avoid any suggestion of impropriety. She knocked on his door late that night, inviting him to the bar for a thank-you drink. He ordered a glass of milk, listening as she recounted her life, a series of injustices and misfortunes, it seemed. Well after closing time, they continued their conversation on a lobby sofa—it was she who spoke—before breaking apart at around 2 A.M. and taking the elevator to their separate floors. At dawn, there was a knock at his door. She stood there. Only because Paul was half asleep did he have the courage to do what followed.

For the first time, he understood the accounts of sane citizens hurtling toward disaster because of romantic passion. He'd thought lovers were showing off when they made their ardor public. But his need for her proximity overwhelmed reason. It was a need too expansive for his insides, requiring outward acts. They had "relations" (Paul put the matter delicately, even decades later), which he'd always thought a fearsome milestone, but which she offered with intoxicating ease. There was—despite his lifelong expectations to the contrary—a little territory available to him. Not just the confines of himself but in her, too, and a place they might have together. Before his departure, Sarah was pregnant. They flew to the United States, and he bought a home for his new family.

"Where?"

"You're in it."

But, soon after arriving, Sarah recanted the plan to marry, a shock to Paul. After all, she was pregnant—he hadn't imagined that a woman might willingly *not* marry under such circumstances. But she seemed to find him intolerable, even repugnant. She came to blame

Paul for everything, be it the immigration official at whom she'd cursed or the obnoxious shop detective who'd accused her of shoplifting. When Paul noted that the U.S. surgeon general had deemed smoking noxious during pregnancy, Sarah reached for her lighter. Just as impulsively, she broke down and apologized, appearing so disconsolate that her underlying decency was plain to him, and she was redeemed. Their daughter, Matilda, arrived. The situation only worsened. Once, Sarah left the girl in her bath seat and spun on the tub faucet, then went to make phone calls. She'd only turned on the hot tap. The infant howled and howled, and Paul ran upstairs, finding his tiny daughter's feet submerged in scalding water. "Thank God it was a weekend and I was there. You can imagine what it made me wonder about days when I was away at the office. For years, you had those burn scars on your feet."

"Was that why you always made me wear socks around the house?"

"Maybe, yes."

The day he saved her in the tub, Paul went down to the basement and paced. He loathed Sarah with an intensity that exceeded his former desire for her. The easiest option was to move out, have nothing to do with her. But he had duties to this small person, who hadn't chosen to be included in his mistake. So he resolved to live an unhappy life, to allow Sarah her manipulations, her relations with other men, and whatever else she was up to. He'd work and ignore the rest. This was to be his life.

However, Paul's acquiescence only riled Sarah. She grew more provocative, seeking to spike him into rage—and he had a temper, if pushed. During one such quarrel, she threatened to take their child back to Kenya, or maybe farther, and live as she pleased, and never see him again. He believed her. Yet Sarah seemed not even to care for Tooly, playing with her for just a few minutes before losing interest or berating the infant—only to then cuddle her, leaving their daughter stupefied. Daydreaming of escape, Paul recalled that road trip in Kenya. How far from the world he'd felt. You could disappear overseas, especially in poor countries. It was like leaving the present.

Ritcomm won a major government contract to modernize communications at smaller U.S. diplomatic outposts. It was 1981, and the State Department was connecting even the most far-flung tentacles of the United States to Washington, or at least to a regional mainframe with access to the visa lookout system. This meant using local phone lines. But hooking into an overseas grid—generally operated by a state telecom company—incurred security risks. You couldn't allow foreign nationals to do the installation; it would take just one Soviet infiltrator. But the U.S. government lacked suitable specialists to do the work. So it contracted Ritcomm. The company itself struggled for staffers willing to take the work, which meant a rootless existence, only a few months at each consulate.

Paul volunteered. As an installer, he'd have a generic maintenance account to log on to the mainframes, which allowed him to read the bad-guy list. Not only could he vanish overseas; he'd have access to the very system that would flag his name to U.S. officials when Sarah reported him. He prepped their disappearance by apologizing to Sarah for being so boring, promising to take her on an expensive vacation—or, if she preferred, she could go alone with Tooly. Yes, Sarah answered with alacrity, that's what she wanted. He agreed, on condition that she obtain an American passport in their daughter's name. Tooly could have traveled on her mother's passport but it was Kenyan, he noted, which might mean delays and complications. Better to secure their daughter a U.S. passport, which could subsequently help Sarah herself obtain citizenship. Paul filled out the application. Sarah signed everything.

"Then," he said, "I took you."

Life abroad had been hard. Foreign locales exacerbated his allergies and his asthma. The food made him sick. And fear of capture kept him in constant anxiety, especially at border crossings. He had access to the American watch lists but not to foreign ones, so each international flight was a cause for fear. Had Sarah reported him to any other nation? Might they detain him on arrival? If so, what would happen to Tooly?

Paul persuaded Ritcomm to base him for a full year in each foreign hub. The company agreed, because he was such a useful employee: never wanted to come back, neither for home leave nor permanently. (Indeed, he refused to return to America at all, leery of heightened security stateside. His responsibility to guard Tooly prevented him even from traveling back to California when his adoptive father was dying—an omission that wrenched Paul still.) A full year in each city, he figured, allowed Tooly to attend a full grade. But the plan stumbled in Australia, since schools there worked on a different calendar, which later led to dispute over which grade she was rightly in. He couldn't risk arguing the case—he sought to be forgotten the moment he left any room. He avoided teachers and parents, remained distant with colleagues. Once again, Paul commented, he'd thrust himself into a situation that he could not manage.

"But you did manage, amazingly well," she said.

"I found it tough." Partly, it was the risk of discovery—that she'd say something imprudent. He came to rely on his own daughter. She was his sole companion. "But never a moan from you. You settled in wherever we were. New kids, new friends, never complaining."

"You didn't complain, either—and never one mean word about my mother. I remember you saying she couldn't be around, and we kept things private in our family. But nothing nasty ever. You were protecting me." She watched his hand, wanting to touch it, but couldn't somehow. "You were brave to do this, you know."

"Brave? I lived in constant dread." Then his worst fear was realized: she failed to come home. Something had happened, but what recourse did he have? The Thai police? They were notoriously corrupt. She'd never mentioned any friends in Bangkok; he didn't know where to start looking. Her school called the next day, asking where she was. He claimed Tooly was at home, ill. He was in a panic. Couldn't report her absence to the embassy—or should he? What if some bad person had her? What if she'd run away, or had an accident? Then Sarah got in touch.

"How did she even know we were in Bangkok?"

"That trick you had of counting out a minute?"

"What about it?"

"You remember a guy named Bob Burdett, from the U.S. Embassy? You might not recall this, but he was over for dinner once. You came out of your room and showed how you could make your eyes vibrate and did your one-minute trick."

"He was getting violent with you. I came out to try to help."

Bob Burdett—a wannabe spy always trying to impress the station chief by finding "subversives"—had invited himself for dinner because he hadn't liked the look of Paul. During the meal, Bob Burdett tried to provoke his host into saying something anti-American. Toward the end of the evening, a small girl stepped from a bedroom. How odd to conceal her like that. And no mother in evidence. Bob Burdett checked with contacts at other U.S. embassies Paul had passed through, and heard versions of the same story: a systems specialist, barely remembered, no wife or daughter anyone knew of. Further burrowing turned up the name of a Kenyan national, Sarah Pastore, who had entered the United States with Paul several years earlier. A contact in military intelligence located her, still in the United States, though with an expired visa. She'd been arrested for shoplifting and awaited deportation. Bob Burdett reached her, posing as a State Department official. What was her relationship to a man named Paul Zylberberg? Had he ever voiced any socialist tendencies? Was she aware of a little girl? If the child was Sarah's, why was she not there in Bangkok? Had she filed a missing-persons report? Didn't she want her daughter back?

Soon thereafter, Sarah arrived in Bangkok.

"I was in a bad state after you went. I hoped you were fine, but there was nothing I could do. Legally speaking, I'd kidnapped you. I had no rights. Sarah needed only turn me in. We came to an arrangement, but I had no right to expect you'd contact me," he concluded. "You were angry at what I'd done. You had every reason to be."

"I wasn't. And I'm not."

"You found a good school in the end? With friends you liked?"

Her childhood after Bangkok would have appalled him—never another day in a classroom, tramps for babysitters. She gave a sanitized summary, inventing an adolescence that was varied and carefree. As she rolled out this fantasy, she recalled the truth and found herself sorrowful, though unsure why.

Paul had always worried, he said, about whether the money for Tooly was sufficient. Sarah demanded that four thousand dollars be paid monthly in exchange for never reporting what he'd done. "I'd have sent child support anyway—all I could possibly afford. I often sent more than what was expected. She really didn't need to threaten me. And I'm sorry, Tooly, about cutting it off when you turned twenty-one. I was hurt that you never contacted me. Suppose I hoped you might write or something. Which was unfair."

Her insides tightened, yet she could say nothing—needed Paul to think all had been fine. But she'd known *nothing* of any payments, let alone a cutoff at age twenty-one. She had turned that age in New York, in 1999. Sarah had shown up then, just before her birthday, promising to tell her something. What?

"Sorry to be going on about this," Paul said. "I'm sure you and your mother are close. As you should be. I really had no right trying to raise a little girl. Never was good with children."

"You were good with me." She looked directly at him, needing to impress this upon him. "And, Paul, you're happy in your life now," she said, to reassure herself as much as to inquire.

"Shelly's been a godsend. Didn't think I had space in my life for someone, but she's been, yes, a godsend." But they'd become friends only after Tooly left, he added decorously.

"Just think, if I'd been there, that would never have happened."

"Well . . ." Paul didn't welcome hypothesizing—he'd settled on a past, knew which elements hurt him, which provided comfort, and wasn't prepared to reconsider.

He inquired about this young fellow, Mac, whom she had arrived with.

"No, he's not mine. I stole him."

Paul looked up pointedly. "That's a joke."

"It better be—it is," she said. "Actually, we should be going. Long trip back to his house." She stood. "Look—I want us to meet up again. Can we?"

He rose as if unprepared, as if he hadn't considered this outcome. "I'll get bottles of water for your drive," he said hastily. "You need to stay hydrated on the road."

As he fetched them, Tooly stared hard at the floor, trying to compose herself.

He returned with a gift he'd been keeping for years: her old sketchbook of noses. "And this photo—thought it'd give you a kick. Us on the plane to Thailand. Remember that Australian girl, the teenager sitting beside me who took our picture? The one who kept smoking the whole time?"

It was a Polaroid, showing more of the overhead bins than of its subjects: Paul in the middle seat, earnest, young, fatigued; Tooly by the window, far more smiley than she'd believed herself to be then. "I'm always available for you," he said, as they hesitated by the front door. "Always have been; always will be." He extended his hand.

"You used to wake me every morning with a handshake," she said, talking fast in order not to cry.

"Did I?" he said, self-conscious now, lowering his hand.

But she took it, holding it between both of hers. "Can I just say something quickly?" she asked. "I felt—actually, still feel—so terrible about everything that happened, about what I did. I left you there alone."

"You were a little girl, Tooly."

"That doesn't matter," she said. "I was still me."

Seated in the minivan with Mac, she took a moment to calm herself. A sedan was parked down the street, she noticed, a middle-aged Asian woman in the driver's seat, waiting for her to leave. Tooly started the engine, pulled out, and watched in her rearview mirror as Shelly exited the car and returned to her home.

As Tooly negotiated the unfamiliar streets of Lodge Haven, she wondered what it was like to live in a suburb like this, to have been *from* here. She switched on the car radio, using an NPR interview to orient herself again in the present:

*Host*: Uhm, before we get to why you think this is a result of climate change, which is I think what you're saying, what are some of the records that this month's heat wave has set so far? And I'll say we're recording this on Friday, July 22, so—

"This trip is boring," Mac said. "It's taking forever."

"Sorry," she responded. "I was selfish to take you with me. I wanted company, and thought you might enjoy it."

She reminded Mac that he had agreed to say a quick hello by phone to Humphrey, which would be so welcome, particularly since she'd been unable to make her daily visit there.

Mac said the old man "smelled gross," at which Tooly fell quiet and drove.

The sun was low when they arrived. She had phoned Bridget to say she'd taken Mac out, claiming it was just to look at birds. Tooly asked Mac to stick to that account, and infiltrated his belongings and medications back upstairs. She overheard him in the TV room, talking to Duncan.

"I'm doing an email right now, Mac."

"We went to Maryland."

"Good for you guys."

It wasn't for her to intrude on this family, or to alter anyone's life. I'm not made to be a mother, she thought. Anyway, not to Duncan's child.

THE NEXT DAY, Humphrey looked around upon waking, anxious, then soothed by the sound of her voice. She helped him stand and led him down the hallway to the communal toilets. Yelena had been unable to come that morning, so Tooly sponged him down in the shower stall, dried him. "You'll feel better after a shave."

"Everything keeps going on so long."

She stood him before the mirror and lathered his cheeks with hand soap, which made him sniff shyly.

"Well, you've been around for a while, Humph. You're eighty-three now."

He turned to her, jaw soapy. "Am I? It's almost indecent."

"Hold still, my dear Humphrey." She ran the safety razor gently down his jaw, then helped him brush his remaining teeth, a white bubble of Colgate on his lower lip. Another resident walked in, spat in the toilet, then pissed with the stall door open.

She led Humphrey back to his bedroom, helped him into fresh clothing, brushed his hair. "Done."

Once returned to his armchair, he glanced around quizzically.

"Nice and comfy?" she asked.

"I was on a ship," he said, "and we wore black armbands the whole way."

"You've told me this story before."

"Had to hold mine because my arm wasn't thick enough," he continued. "They were made for a man's arm."

"Where were you going, Humph? Where was the ship going?"

"Then they sewed my armband smaller, so it fit me."

"I remember you telling me that." She wondered if all this rummaging through his past interfered with a merciful process of forgetting. These retold snippets of his childhood returned with diminishing pleasure, it seemed. "Know where I took Mac? To see my father. He told me all sorts of stuff about how Sarah used to be. Said he used to send her money for me."

"Who did?"

"My father, Paul, sent Sarah money."

"Oh, yes," he said. "I think that might be right."

"You remember this?" she said. "But wait—Sarah was always borrowing off *me*. What the hell was she spending it on?"

"I was on this ship, a liner," Humphrey continued, "and I had to wear a black armband."

"Humphrey? What was she doing with all that money?"

"But the armband was too big on me."

"I know this story."

"What happened was . . ." His was cable-car conversation: you could get on or you could get off, but you couldn't divert it from its track. Didn't really matter who was listening, she or a stranger. Except that Tooly was the last person who listened to him at all.

He fell silent, pensive. "There are things," he said, as if preparing her for a shock, "that people claim happened to me, and it's completely blank. I think I'm getting away with it for now. But if people start noticing—I don't want people looking after me. That's undignified. I need you to tell me if you see I can't manage anymore. Do you understand what I mean?"

"I understand." She sat on the edge of his bed, watched him, wondering how direct to be. "Humph, I will be honest with you."

"All right," he said rigidly.

"You asked me to say if I thought you couldn't manage anymore. I think that's the case now."

"Most ridiculous thing I ever heard!"

They sat in silence.

"When I get to that stage," he continued, "I'll jump out a window. But I'm not at that stage. So you can damn well shut up about it."

She didn't recall his ever having spoken to her so aggressively. Such words were not shocking in themselves, but from his mouth they wounded her. "Sorry," she said.

He shifted in his armchair, pressing the TV remote, unable to produce any effect.

"Can I help you, Humph?"

"No, you cannot. Television's broken."

The push of a single button would have lit it up as he wanted. Yet she couldn't think of a tactful way to take it from him. He closed his eyes, clearly not sleeping, hands twitching with rage.

Since her arrival in New York, his condition had only worsened. It was as if he'd been clinging on, and her presence had allowed him to release.

"It's okay, Humph. I'm making sure everything's all right."

He spoke again of his exhaustion with being alive, of his desire to be gone already. She struggled for a response—she might have felt the same in his position, into the ninth decade of life, blind and deaf and trapped in this miserable room. "Dear Humph, I know it's rotten, this situation you're in. It is. But you'll be free from it soon."

"I'm impatient," he said. "I want to be done."

She took his hand, but it remained limp in hers.

"You're here now," he said, "and I'm afraid of you going away, me being alone again."

"There are other people. There's Yelena."

"But you are Tooly Zylberberg."

"I am," she said, smiling sadly.

"The favorite person of my life."

Her eyes welled up. "I'm not going away," she promised, fighting to maintain a steady voice. "I'll stay as long as you need me."

"When my father died," he said, "his breathing went very slow."

"Do you remember that, Humph? Where was it?"

He recalled looking out a window at a big tree. And imagining himself seen from space, a miniature dot of a human being, there at the southern tip of the African continent.

"This was in South Africa, was it? Can you tell me more about your life there?"

"At my age, you can either have time or you can have dignity."

"How do you mean?"

"If you're not careful, it gets too late to do anything about it, and . . ." He gazed at the convex reflection in the switched-off TV, then around the room. "I don't want you staying. It's horrible here— that awful bitch next door with her loud music and those little boys of hers that she treats so horribly. I can't bear it. I don't think I should have to keep going forever. It's enough now. I've had an interesting time. I've seen many things. I had friends. Not many. I've had friends. Not many."

"Have you been lonely in your life, Humphrey?"

"The people who liked me are all in books. I would've loved to meet a woman who took an interest, but it didn't happen. When you and me kept each other company, I wasn't lonely then. We were friends."

"We were; we are."

"I'm glad I didn't stop my life earlier. I wouldn't have known Tooly Zylberberg."

"And I wouldn't have known you," she said. "Think how different I would've been. I wouldn't have read John Stuart Mill!"

"Yes, yes," he said. "My old friend."

"Who knows how I'd have ended up without you."

"I didn't let that happen."

"I know you didn't, Humph. Thank you."

"Don't thank me, please. Don't thank me," he said. "I can't bear it if you thank me. Please, don't thank me." He leaned forward, rested his hand atop hers, head bowed, and she saw the crown of his rumpled gray hair.

She exhaled, very slowly.

"I'd like to make you coffee," he said.

"Let me."

"Would you?" he responded, as if amazed at such generosity. "Thank you, do. Thank you, do." He brought her hand to his mouth and kissed it, dry lips grazing her fingernails.

She walked fast to the communal bathrooms, hugging herself to stifle her distress. She splashed water on her face. He had been forced to use these toilets, these filthy shower stalls, for years. She returned with his mug. This time he drank not in big drafts but slowly, sipping like a connoisseur, like one who wants to pay attention.

As she patted his veiny old hand, it occurred to her that not only would he soon not exist but that, when she no longer existed, no trace of this man would remain anywhere. It would be as if Humphrey, now pulsing before her, had never been. Within a generation or two, not even your photo was identifiable: just a person, at some forgotten event, in old-fashioned clothes, the distractions and appetites of that day lost, an image framed halfway down a stairwell, or stuck in a drawer, or saved in digital code. Once you; in time, a stranger to all.

Upon leaving the building, she dialed Fogg, needing to be transported from this time and this place. As the call clicked through the circuits—in that instant of hissing quiet—she anticipated his buoyant voice. Yet by the first ring, regret gripped her. She had to tell him definitively.

It was the first time they'd spoken in weeks, and Fogg had much to recount. "Where do I even start? We've had drama of the highest order here in Caergenog: police are investigating criminal damage to two pushed-over fence posts on Dyfed Lane."

She smiled. "I miss being there."

"Yes, yes—what torment," he said, "you living it up there in New York City."

"Did you talk to any bookstores in Hay yet?" she asked. "I told you—sparkling reference from me, whenever you want."

"That's settled then, is it? You're not coming back?"

She shook her head, said nothing. "I have to stop your wages soon. I'm so sorry, Fogg. World's End is yours for a penny, if you want it. All stock included. You'd still have to cover the rent. And utilities. Probably, I should pay you to take the place. Would if I could."

That evening, she lay in bed, remembering Xavi—lately, she kept thinking of him. She went upstairs to help herself to a drink, and awoke one of the McGrorys' laptops. She typed in his name: Xavier Karamage. As ever, the only result was a middle-aged white businessman with a red mustache, the director of a company at the International Financial Services Centre in Dublin.

She called the number. There was no answer—it would be dawn on the other side of the Atlantic. So she waited. At 4:12 A.M. Connecticut time, she tried again. A receptionist picked up. It was good luck, the woman remarked, since the company staffed the office only one day a week. Tooly asked if Mr. Karamage was present. He was not. Further questioning indicated that he didn't often appear—indeed, the receptionist had yet to meet him, despite having worked there for two years.

"The name is so unusual," Tooly said. "African, right?"

"No, no. American, I think. But, sorry, what can I help you with?"

Tooly asked for a number where Mr. Karamage might be reached, but the receptionist wasn't disclosing it. Tooly could leave a message, and Mr. Karamage would reply at his leisure. The problem was, Tooly explained, she'd been ordered by her boss to send a birthday present to Mr. Karamage. The courier required a phone number to take the delivery. And the gift had to get there on time, or her boss would murder her.

"Sorry. Can't give out his number."

The receptionist suggested that Tooly send the gift to the office. Though, of course, it was hard to say when he'd receive it, since he hadn't been there in two years. After much coaxing, the receptionist gave a long sigh, then put Tooly on hold, returning finally with a mailing address in rural Ireland. She was not giving out any phone numbers, but Tooly could try sending the gift there.

Tooly stayed awake for another hour until Duncan arose. She asked if he might arrange for Yelena to do more hours with Humphrey that week, and if Bridget could make alternative arrangements for Mac. She apologized profusely, but there was a crisis at the shop—she had to fly back immediately.

But it wasn't to Wales that she flew.

# 1988

TOOLY KNELT ON A CHAIR at the sink and turned on the taps, organizing dirty plates and cutlery. Steam rose and sweat trickled down her brow as she gazed into the swirling dishwater. Briefly, the name of this city was lost to her. What was outside this house? She dropped a knife into the water, its surface sliced with a plop, tossing up a grape of liquid that peaked, flopped back within itself, the suds sliding closed. How strange, she thought, that there were people doing other things right at this moment in different places. Everyone she'd ever known was alive somewhere, thinking different things.

"Can I have coffee again today?" she asked Humphrey when he entered. In her early days here, Coca-Cola had been her morning refreshment, but she had copied him lately, drinking instant coffee with cream and lots of sugar, establishing a way of taking it that was uniquely hers. Nothing felt quite so grown-up as having ways particular to oneself.

During her time in this house, she had discovered not only coffee but extraordinary books, too. Much of what Humphrey lent bemused her: blocks of text, abstractions about "will" and "reason" and "negative potentialities"; or grim histories about the NKVD and the Nazis. She did her best to read a few pages—just enough to pose questions. Today, he was explaining politics in Russia.

"There is long tradition," he began. "First, we must have bald leader. After, hairy leader. Bald, then hairy. Tsar Alexander II, he is bald. Then, Nicholas II. He got hair. Next comes Lvov. Bald like cucumber.

Then Kerensky. Lots of hair. Lenin is very bald. Who must come next? Stalin."

"He was hairy?"

"This is reason he wins leadership battle. Trotsky also has fool head of hair, so it is close race. But Stalin has more. Also, he is more idiot. So he wins. After hairy Stalin, they need bald. They look around Politburo and see Khrushchev—perfect! Then Brezhnev, also fool head of hair. Then Andropov: bald. Chernenko: hair. Gorbachev: bald."

"With the stain on his head?"

"Yes, but you don't make fun of. It's not nice."

"I wasn't making fun of," she said. "Humphrey?"

"Yes, darlink."

"You know more than anyone I ever met."

He shied away from this, as if tickled under the chin. "When I was little boy like you—"

"I'm not a little boy."

"Little girl."

"You weren't a little girl."

"Tooly, stop. I am trying to instruct in historical materialism. When I was little boy like you, we have horse at bottom of garden and get fresh milk every morning."

"You milked a horse?"

"No, no, no. We milk cow. Also, there is orchard for eating fruit. Once, I throw middle bit of apricot—what this is called?"

"The pit?"

"I throw pit in eye of girl by mistake. I am very frightened that she is blind and I go to prison."

"You did go to prison."

"Not for apricot pit. Because of Communist Party idiots."

"I thought you liked Communists."

"I hate them, and capitalists, too. All reactionaries."

"Who do you like?"

"I am Marxist, but non-practicing," he explained. "This is only sociable theory in life. Communism does not work, because people are selfish. But, personal speaking, I cannot see capitalism working, either. That's exploitation and greed and selfishness."

"Humphrey?"

"Yes, darlink?"

"Where do you keep all your books?" Fresh volumes materialized constantly, yet he had no shelves anywhere.

Humphrey stood abruptly, and she feared having offended him. He marched to the storage room, edging past her tent, pushing aside fake designer clothing, medical equipment, expired pharmaceuticals, barging toward a free-standing closet crammed against the back wall. He yanked at the jammed door. On the third pull, it burst apart in an explosion of hardcovers and paperbacks.

"Are you okay?" she asked, stepping through the mess to help him.

"Books," he said, "are like mushrooms. They grow when you are not looking. Books increase by rule of compound interest: one interest leads to another interest, and this compounds into third. Next, you have so much interest there is no space in closet."

"At my house, we put clothes in the closets."

He sneered at this misapplication of furniture. "But where you keep literature?"

She went downstairs to prepare herself a smashed-potato sandwich. Returning, she found him flipping through a number of recently liberated editions, and she picked up one herself, her sandwich crumbs cascading onto the pages.

"Intellectuals never eat and read at same time," he told her. "It is against law."

"I've seen *you* doing it."

"Yes, because I make this law."

"If you make that law, can I make the opposite law?"

"Sure. Then we go to court."

"What happens then?"

"Depends on judge."

"Who's the judge?"

"I am judge."

"Can I make it against the law that you're the judge?"

"I veto your law."

"What do you mean, 'veto'?"

"Veto is like if you make big sandwich—careful and nice you make it—and I come over and eat sandwich. No question asked. This is how veto works."

She offered him a bite.

"No, no—is okay, darlink," he said. "You eat, and I teach you Western civilization."

"Can I veto?"

"I do not advise." He cleared his throat. "All Western civilization begins with—"

Footsteps came up the stairs. "You nut," Venn said, smiling.

"Hello," Tooly said brightly, standing.

"I've talked to Sarah," he said. "She's meeting with your dad right now." Venn glanced above her at Humphrey. Tooly turned and found Humphrey returning the look. It was the first time she had noticed such a communication between them—an exchange at an altitude that excluded her. Had they done this before? Had they done it always?

To draw their attention back to her height, she said, "I washed all the dishes."

But the men had matters to discuss and went downstairs. She remained on the upper floor, sliding along the walls, playing at being stuck to them, then jumped into her tent and browsed Humphrey's books.

That evening, Venn looked in on her. "How old are you, twelve?"

"Ten," she answered, delighted at his mistake.

"You want to work with me?"

She nodded.

"Okay. So the people coming and going here—your job is to start paying attention, hear what they say. Who they're friends with, who they don't like, any other details. We'll discuss it later. You're somebody, little duck, who notices everything, just like I notice everything. Almost nobody else does. People have got no idea who's walking behind them on the street, no idea where anybody's hands are, no idea where anybody's head is. But we pay attention. Which is tiring. But that's how we are." He cupped his hand against the side of her face and left her to think.

She attempted a little reconnaissance at the party that night, although he had left before they had a chance to discuss it. She took refuge in her tent, trying to read a book on Western civilization, but stared emptily at the page, sifting through observations she planned to make to Venn. Tooly heard her name only on its third utterance. She scrambled from her sleeping bag, undid the padlock on the tent zipper, and raised it, the orange nylon parting on a woman's midriff, then a face.

"Darling dumpling," Sarah said, reaching to stroke Tooly's cheek with the back of her hand. "May I come for a visit?"

Tooly shifted to make space, and Sarah lay down with a puff of deep fatigue, hugging Tooly from behind, stroking her hair.

"You were away for ages."

"Don't scold me," Sarah said. "I've been looking after your future."

"Sorry."

"And now," Sarah resumed, "you're free. From now on—from this second—you can invent yourself. Make up anything you want, Matilda. Be someone who laughs at jokes or someone who never smiles. Someone who sleeps all day or who's up at dawn. You can be a liar. You can be honest. Be a kind person or a horrid one. Whatever you like, my lovely. But you must be brave to live like we do, to know there's nobody else in the world but us. We're a team. Better than a normal family, where you *have* to stick together. With us, it's because we *want* to. In a normal family, everything needs explanations and apologies, and you end up shackled to people you have nothing more in common with than any name in the phone book." Sarah fumbled about in her handbag. "Where are my cigarettes?" She sparked her lighter, took a drag, exhaled through the flap, her shoulders bare in an open-backed blouse, the naked curl of her spine. After a few minutes, she flicked the butt out, zipped the tent, closing them snugly inside. They lay there, drifting off to sleep, mindless of the noise of the party downstairs, her perfume mingling with tobacco scent.

Hours later, Tooly stirred. Sarah had stepped out. The girl looked between the tent flaps, peering into darkness. The festivities had ended, the music silenced, the chatter gone. Only two voices remained—Venn and Sarah, arguing downstairs.

"She doesn't have her passport with her. How would you propose taking her anywhere without a passport? And the father's not giving it up."

"I could put her on my Kenyan passport."

"It'd take months."

"Have one of your friends make us a fake."

"You don't actually want this girl, Sarah."

"Why do you say cruel things like that?"

"Don't pretend to be so sensitive now. You're the one who ditched her these past weeks, and vanished to wherever you went."

"Didn't vanish. I just couldn't handle it, okay? Don't say things to hurt me. Please?" she said. "Look, if he doesn't give me that passport, I'll turn him in."

"If he's locked up, you get nothing."

"Can't you go to his place and just take it?"

"No."

Shortly afterward, Sarah raised the tent flap, whispering, "Will you have breakfast with me tomorrow morning?"

"Are you staying, Sarah?"

"Wherever you are is where I am. From now on."

The next morning, Sarah was gone. Only Humphrey remained in the house. "Humph," Tooly asked him, "did you ever play in your school band?"

"I was world-class violin genius. But jealous rival hits me in knees with trombone. Did I tell you this story?"

"Why would a jealous rival hit you in the knees? You don't play a violin with your knees."

"You ever try playing violin *without* knees?"

"I only played the ukulele."

She sat, right there on the floor, sudden sadness deflating her. "Humphrey?" she said. "Humphrey Ostropoler?"

"Yes, my friend?"

"I just like saying your name."

"You can say it."

"I know things about birds."

"Tell me."

"Birds used to be dinosaurs."

"I cannot believe. It is lie."

"It's true. They're the only dinosaurs left. Or, they came from dinosaurs or something. Do you know how birds fly?"

"Flapping of wings."

"I mean how they can fly and we can't."

"Also flapping of wings."

"They have hollow bones, so it makes them light. And there's this thing called lift, which I've heard about a million times. Let me remember. Okay, so, lift . . ." She drummed her lower lip. "Okay, so what happens is birds have curved wings. And the wind, when it goes past, blows faster over the top bit. Wait, I'm getting this wrong. Okay, what happens is the air pushes up on the bottom of the wing and makes them go up."

Chin in hand, he nodded in fascination. "Please, continue."

She found herself feigning expertise, trying to field his queries, Humphrey addressing her as if she were the absolute authority on matters avian.

"You open up whole new world for me," he proclaimed, leading her to the backyard, where he stood, hands in the pockets of his shorts, gazing in wonderment at the sky. "Up there is such life going on! I never think of this before."

A distant jet appeared, gliding slowly across the blue. Passengers were looking out through the portholes, down at this city, at the roof of this house, unaware of these two staring back. The people up there were thinking of destinations, of faces awaiting them at the airport, of faces they'd just left, just as she had on so many flights, before turning from her window to Paul, his face in a bird book.

Instead of a bird, a raindrop landed, then more, plump ones splatting against her face. Humphrey went back inside, calling her to follow. She resisted, tongue out to catch drops. When she joined him, her hair dripped a trail through the house. Humphrey had a towel ready for her. "What is your address?" he asked.

"My old one? It was Gupta Mansions in Sukhumvit."

He took her hand, fetched her book bag from the tent, walked her to the front door. "Come," he said. "Time to go."

# 2000

EMERSON OPENED the living-room window to shout at Tooly, who sat on the fire escape. "Put that cigarette out when I'm talking to you," he said. "The smoke is blowing inside, you dick."

"You're the one who opened the window."

"Excuse me, do you pay rent here? Put that out and get inside."

She was not in the habit of obeying Emerson, so finished at her leisure, and even contemplated climbing down the fire escape to the sidewalk, going back into the building, and entering the apartment by the front door, just to defy his command. But it was freezing, so she climbed in.

Presumably, his complaint pertained to a recycling infraction. Or did he have a suspect in the plunder of his peach Snapple? She stood before him, struggling to take seriously the remonstrations of a shirtless man in flip-flops. Until she grasped the subject.

"Wait, wait, wait. What?" she said, to delay matters. "What are you even talking about?"

But she knew. This had come from Noeline.

"You never grew up in this apartment at all," he said. "You're trying to rip off Duncan. He's been talking about getting his parents to invest in your little scam. You're a fraud, and I'm telling him. You're lucky I don't call the cops."

"This is crazy. Can I talk to Noeline, please?"

"So you admit it!"

"I didn't admit anything. I'd just like to speak with her."

"Are you telling Duncan," he demanded, "or am I?"

Tooly had assumed that indiscretions on both sides during that lunch had canceled each other out. If anything, it was Noeline who'd made the most damning statements.

"Can you ask her to come in here, please?" Tooly said. "I'd like to talk to her alone."

He marched off. After a minute, Noeline entered the kitchen, avoiding Tooly's gaze.

"Your boyfriend just threatened to call the cops on me."

"You lied to Duncan, to Xavi, to me. You've been living here for weeks without paying, eating their food. You falsely represented yourself."

"Are you serious? What if I told him a few of *your* comments? How you wrote half his thesis?"

"I find it sick that you're trying to harm my relationship with Emerson. I actually love him, an emotion you don't have, according to what you told me. If you're suggesting—if you're even considering claiming—that I helped him inappropriately, I will *aggressively* deny that. If I said anything that was exaggerated—and I don't recall doing so—it's because my relationship was in a difficult position, and I was upset. If you want to take advantage of that, then you're way more sick than I thought."

"I'm not telling anyone what you said, Noeline. I'm not a snitch. I'm just saying that I thought we were—"

"A snitch? What is this, jailhouse lingo? The stuff you told me wasn't blurted out in a state of distress. You were totally calm—just another day for you. You don't have an ounce of feeling for any of us. Willing to mess with Duncan's family for some scam you've got going with this older boyfriend of yours."

Tooly shook her head. These accusations were an offense to her self-perception, and she retaliated with an offense of her own: "Just—go screw yourself, okay?"

"Duncan is an 'opportunity' for you, right? This hobby of slithering into people's homes for 'opportunities'? It's parasitic, okay? We're telling Duncan if you don't."

"What I said isn't what you're making it out to be. I really, really like Duncan. I'm friends with Xavi and, I thought, friends with you. I don't know Emerson that well, but if you think he's great now, maybe there's more to him."

"What's that supposed to mean, that I 'think he's great *now*'? See, this is why you need to leave."

"I was never going to tell anyone what you said."

"What, exactly, did I supposedly say?"

"You remember what. But who cares?"

"Just leave. You know? Just say goodbye to Duncan, if you have to, then leave. You're here to mess with people. For some of us, this is our actual life."

Emerson appeared again. "Is she telling Duncan, or do I get to?"

"Since when are you concerned with Duncan's welfare?"

"Hey," he shot back, "I don't appreciate some high-school dropout like you questioning my intelligence behind my back."

Tooly looked at Noeline, who looked away.

"This is a moral issue," he continued. "Possibly even criminal."

"What are you talking about? What crime?"

"Entry by false trespassing," he improvised, making his way out. "I'll be raising this with Duncan in the next twenty-four hours unless you do. You'd better start thinking up excuses."

Tooly looked at Noeline, and her anger drained away. "You're one of the most interesting people I've met in this city. One of the most interesting in years. I don't know what I did to make you mad. And I'm not trying to change your opinion. I'm just—I don't know—just so sorry this is happening."

Blushing, Noeline rushed into the bathroom, slammed the door after herself, and turned on the faucet, which ran for several minutes.

Tooly looked down the corridor toward the bedroom where Duncan was studying. But she found herself knocking on Xavi's door. "Emerson has gone nuts," she said. "I need your help."

"What now?"

"Seriously. He's lost it. Can we strategize?"

"Wrecking Emerson's plans is my favorite pastime. What's he up to, that stupid man?"

She gave a summary of Noeline's accusations.

"Well," he responded, unconcerned, "there's no swindle. Wildfire is my idea, you've offered good suggestions, and the project is progressing. I don't care what Emerson says. Don't care where you came from or how you ended up here."

"Thank you, Xavi. Thanks. Really."

He told her about incorporating the company, which he'd researched, and that it looked possible that Duncan's father might contribute money for them to set up at the Brain Trust. "But, before that, I do want to check something with you. Something I've been wondering for a few weeks now," he said. "No, wait. I'm embarrassed." He shook his head, raising his hand to hide the smile.

"Come on. Tell me."

"I just was wondering. I just wanted to know," he said, looking directly at her, "just want to know before we go any further. If I walked over to you right now and kissed you, would you be okay with that? We wouldn't have to do more if you didn't want," he said. "Or we could."

Tooly—who lacked much of a figure, who eschewed sexy outfits, who crossed her legs in a manly way because it was more comfortable—believed that any guy who expressed sexual hunger for her was either unselective or a compulsive womanizer. Perhaps Xavi was the broad-minded type, and didn't care if a lover had already hopped into bed with his best friend. But Duncan would mind—he'd mind painfully—and he was next door.

She needed Xavi, though. He'd advocate on her behalf, puncture Emerson's claims when they came. If she spurned him, she risked losing that support. If it was just a question of allowing her body to be used, she didn't care—she had indulged a few men over the years, when it had been useful to learn more about them. She had just let it happen, and joked about it afterward with Venn. This would be no different. Plus, Xavi was handsome. Though far less attractive now than he'd ever seemed.

"Right this second?" she said.

He smirked. "I just want to know if we *could*. After you answer me, we do whatever we want, or maybe nothing."

"Okay, then."

"Okay what? What does that mean?"

"Okay means yes."

"Okay," he said, nodding, looking at his dress shoes. "What a disappointment."

"What is?"

"You know," he said. "You know."

"I was only joking, Xavi."

"You were not."

"I was."

"I noticed all this little flirting you've been doing with me for a while now," he said. "But you must understand: Duncan is my brother."

"Wait, wait," she said. "You misunderstood. We'll keep things businesslike now. Seriously."

"No more business between me and you."

"Come on."

Xavi shook his head. "It's okay," he said, meaning no.

"I didn't even . . ." It wasn't worth finishing the sentence. She left, stood there in the corridor, looking at the front door.

Gathering her courage, she entered Duncan's room. "Hey."

"Hey."

"Will you come outside with me? I need to take Ham for a walk."

"Got tons more work. Is later okay?"

"Can it be now, Duncan?"

"You just called me 'Duncan' instead of 'horrendous blob.' You've got me worried," he kidded.

"I'm sorry to interrupt your work. You know I normally never do. Just need to talk."

"Wildfire stuff?"

"Something else. Would you mind?"

Duncan—pleased to be needed, an emotion she so rarely exhibited toward him—closed his textbook. He wanted someone to rely on him; it was what he sought most. In a way, she had, taking refuge in his bedroom, finding status at his side and food in his refrigerator, making his place a home of her own in Manhattan. And, by mistake, she had grown so fond of this boy.

She tugged Ham's leash to hurry him outside, wanting to escape the building, as if Emerson might leap out and ruin everything.

"What," she asked, to establish an easy tone before the tense explanations to follow, "what would you do if you could do absolutely anything with your life?"

"You always ask me that."

"I do not."

"Well, versions of that question."

"Because you never answer to my satisfaction."

"How about you tell me what you *think* I should do," he suggested, "and then I'll say for you."

"If it was up to me, I'd say you should be involved in music. That's what you love most."

"Music? Never."

"What, then? And I want a proper answer, not this I-don't-really-know-but-law-school-isn't-so-bad stuff."

He pondered. "Okay, here's my honest answer: architecture. That's what I always wanted to do, what I thought I'd do."

"Then you should. Why can't you?"

"I'm twenty-four. Too late in the game."

Before Duncan could guess at her ideal future, she interrupted to inform him that Emerson was making all sorts of claims about her as a result of things she'd said to Noeline. Tooly readied herself for the obvious next question: If those two are twisting your words, what *did* you say?

But he sought no details. She handed him the leash. They walked in silence through Riverside Park. "Don't really know what you'd want to do, if you could do anything," he said belatedly, the pig yanking him around the other side of a tree trunk.

"Will I do well?"

"At what?"

"In my life."

"You could. Why not."

"I never thought so either."

He looked at her, studied her. "Tooly," he said, "I don't care what you said or didn't say to Noeline. I don't care about their opinions. I'm not listening, even if they try to tell me something."

She looked down. To lose ascendancy in this relationship made her want to hide till he left. But what was so terrible? Did she consider Duncan so beneath her that to be vulnerable before him was intolerable? After all, wasn't vulnerability the point of a love affair?

But she lacked the courage to tolerate it. She reminded herself that she and Duncan owed each other no debt; that it was kinder to conclude this now than to keep implying, as she often had in small, subtle ways that he wasn't quite for her, that his choices—law, for example—were somehow less meritorious than her chosen lifestyle, which consisted of avoiding choice altogether.

Removing herself from this relationship, as in mind she was trying to do, provided a sharper view of its elements, including a suspicion she'd long harbored that, while Duncan had love for her, was intrigued by her, amused by her, cared deeply for her, he lacked the sexual passion that fused two strangers. He found her body of interest, but little more, and she hadn't wished to know this before. As they strolled, she almost told Duncan her explanation for why this was, to ease his mind by articulating what might have been a dreadful secret for him: that he was in love with someone else and seemed to have been for many years, someone whom he had followed from high school to college, whom he had joined back in New York under the pretext of attending law school, allowing them to share quarters again—a best friend residing in the next room, who, Tooly felt certain, had no idea of Duncan's attachment, nor would ever have accepted it. She wondered if Duncan himself did. She suspected that, had she dared cite this now, he'd be furious, and their final moment of companionship would be ugly. She put her mittens onto his icy hands, though he protested. At the corner of 115th Street, when he turned toward his building, expecting her to follow, she kissed him at length. "Be sweet to the pig," she joked, winking at him, and continued alone, hastening as she went, pinching herself in punishment at such sentimentality.

A FEW FEMALE customers looked up, tracking Venn toward the purple sofa, off which he plucked a crushed newspaper. The furniture in the café was elementary-school chic: primary colors, hard plastic, initials scratched into wood. Tooly stood before the counter, perusing a jar of oversized cookies. "Plain coffee?" she called to him, her question unintentionally broadcast to the hushed room, consisting largely of lone customers flipping through ring binders. As the barman fiddled with a faulty multidisc CD player, Tooly opened one of the ubiquitous binders herself, expecting a drinks list but finding dating profiles. This Upper West Side hangout, which she and Venn had entered at random, seemed to be a matchmaking café.

To demonstrate that her relations with Venn were not of this nature, she sat on an armchair opposite him rather than sharing the sofa—although calculated distance probably resembled a first date even more. As he scanned the newspaper, she leaned forward to read the back page, a story about the presumptive Democratic nominee, Vice President Al Gore, on a visit to Texas, talking up the inexperience of his opponent for the White House, Governor George W. Bush.

She informed Venn that Wildfire had come to nothing.

"Ah, well," he responded, folding the newspaper. He appeared amused, as if he'd wagered on this outcome and, although it was unfavorable, enjoyed having been right.

"Does this put you in a bad position now?" she asked.

"How would it?"

"Well, I told you to reserve space at the Brain Trust. That guy you're overseeing it for, is he going to expect rent and joining fees now?"

"Which guy?"

"The guy who owns the place. I forget his name. That venture-capital guy."

"You mean my friend Mawky Di Scugliano? Who got shot as a kid when gunmen tried to rob his folks' Italian restaurant?"

"Yeah, him."

"Dear Tooly, I've never met such a person." He had no idea who owned the property where the Brain Trust was based. That school bus in the center of the office space, he'd heard, had been left there by a dim-witted fashionista who'd set up an atelier there two years earlier and ended up in rehab. The floor had been empty since. Until, without permission, Venn sent in cleaners, had technicians hook into existing phone and power cables in the building, moved in desks, hired a bum off the Bowery to operate the freight elevator, and started renting out those cheap cubicles. "I never spent much time there in case someone turned up who actually did own the place!" he said. "I suspect it belongs to the Buddhist temple downstairs, but the monks never complained. Vow of silence: priceless." He laughed. "Thing about the Brain Trust is that it sort of worked. Those kids were having a great time coming up with stuff. Ridiculous ideas, of course, but one might hit the jackpot. There's nothing to say that ideas must be good to succeed. Somebody could make a fortune yet because of the Brain Trust."

"So, wait—there is no cooperative?"

"I hardly even know what a cooperative is. And if there was a cooperative it'd be ridiculous. It'd mean the most inventive kids would have to split their proceeds with the duds. How is that fair? This way, it's all spoils to the victor."

"So those guys there were essentially paying you thousands of bucks to turn up each day in an abandoned office space?"

"And paying in cash, Tooly. In cash."

"Can't be safe for you to keep that place open."

"I agree."

"Could we go somewhere else now, Venn? I want to leave this city. Not telling Sarah this time. Maybe not telling anybody," she said, too cowardly to specify Humphrey.

"I agree," he said. "I think it's time."

"Yes!" She leaped from her seat with excitement. "Yes!" She sat, beaming. "I want to plan a whole project together, start to finish. We could pull off something amazing. Don't you think?"

"I'm certain of it."

"You pretend that it's everyone for themselves," she said, "but I owe you tons. I know all that you've done for me. I know you better than anyone."

"You do," he said. "We're the same, me and you." He took out a cellphone and rose from the sofa, then knelt before her and tied the laces of her Converse sneakers, one shoe to the other.

"What are you doing?" she asked, smiling.

He cupped his hand against the side of her face. "You're the softest person on the planet, Tooly. You couldn't kill a wasp if it stung you on the nose. Even then, I see you shooing it out the window."

"I can be horrible and dishonest if I put my mind to it."

"If only!" he said. "Don't let anyone take my newspaper. There's something I need to show you in it. I've got a surprise for you. I'm tempted to say a great surprise, but I'll call it an interesting one." Venn raised his finger, indicating that she must remain quiet, and he stepped from the café onto Amsterdam Avenue. He opened his flip phone, dialed a number, and sauntered down the sidewalk, passing from view.

All sounds were louder suddenly: a rock CD playing, the smack of the snare, the repetitions of the singer. The café was filling up now, and not just with lonely hearts.

"Some guy was in our lab today. Don't know what he was, a resident or something. And the professor was, like, 'You don't knock, you don't stay.'"

"He's like that."

"I'm really surprised at the level of detail in this class."

"The teaching quality this year is so superior to the first year."

"I know!"

At another table:

"He interviews a lot of people for the school."

"He's such a dad."

"He is a dad."

"The funny thing? The woman who wrote that book is a friend of the Heckers."

"Hey, when are you going to the shower Saturday?"

"I think I'm going to go on Saturday."

And another:

"Finally, after months of anxiety I called her, bless her heart. She's in Detroit. So I call her last night to see what happened. She said she'll find out tomorrow."

"Wasn't she up for a job?"

"Lots of jobs."

Tooly could never have conversations like these. The only place in the world where she fit was beside Venn. She watched the window, sitting upright each time a man entered her field of vision. She smirked, looking at her laced-up shoes, realizing how much like those nervous daters she must have seemed, glancing up whenever the door opened. He never did come back.

# 2011

MAKEUP APPLICATION WAS NOT Tooly's strength. Summoning her art-class skills, she underscored each eye "gesturally," as her instructor might have said, then blinked at the blurred image of herself reflected in the rearview mirror, peering through two black smudges. "Oh, this is ridiculous," she said, and dangled a bead of spittle into a tissue to dab both eyes clean. A certain muss of the hair seemed stylish, while another was vaguely like a teenage boy. Did she look "severe"? Who had said that about her?

She drove from Cork Airport in her rental car, across South Tipperary, east past Clonmel, following signs for Waterford, toward the destination, Beenblossom Lodge, which she'd pinpointed on an online map. In the middle of a two-lane country road, she stopped the Nissan Micra, left clicker blinking. She was jittery to think that "Xavier Karamage" could be minutes away. She'd made this trip to Ireland without invitation or announcement. Would he be there? She turned down a private driveway.

Expecting the house to appear, she drove at walking pace. But the driveway continued for more than half a mile through woodland, offering strobe views between tree trunks of an emerald field containing a pond with a small island. Finally, she arrived at a gravel clearing bordered by rhododendrons. Beenblossom Lodge was a Georgian manor, ivy over the sash windows, pert chimneys at each end of the slate roof, a four-columned portico flanked by Regency urns overflowing with pansies. She pulled in beside a black Range Rover and a pink Mini, and turned off the engine. She sat a moment, looking at the front door.

If she was wrong about what this house contained, her trip would have been a colossal waste, and nothing would be clearer. But if she was right? She remained in place, the back of her bare knees sticky on the vinyl seat.

She knocked at the front door. Waited.

Knocked again.

A flame-haired young woman in jeans and riding boots answered, blue dress shirt undone two buttons too far down her freckled chest, presumably the result of breastfeeding, given the shiny-lipped infant at her hip. "Hullo!" the woman said cheerfully, scratching her red mane with the aerial of a cordless phone.

"Sorry to bother you," Tooly said. "I was looking for Xavier Kara-mage. Is this right?"

"Yes, of course," she said cheerily, in the cut-glass accent of the English upper classes, then told the telephone, "Mummy? Visitor. Yes, yes. Love to all." She hung up and addressed Tooly—"Please, do come in"—then led the way down a long entrance hall, pine floorboards mottled from dried mud, orphaned shoes among children's toys, a radiator piled with mail, a pewter vase containing an unhinged shot-gun, field-hockey stick, fencing épée, hedge clippers, a deflated foot-ball. "My appalling husband is out putting an end to innocent lives," she said, toe-pecking a baby rattle, which skittered down the hall. She turned through a doorway, jiggling the baby on her hip, voice trailing off: "Can't even say when the horrible man will be back."

Tooly followed, passing a door to a somber library, then a bur-gundy dining room, down five steps into a rustic kitchen with wood-beam ceilings, a vast open hearth, and a cottage window overlooking parkland.

"You know, I don't even know who you are," the woman exclaimed, sitting on a long bench in the kitchen, placing the baby on the table before her. Popping a grape into her mouth, she offered the bowl to

Tooly. "So busy with the christening, I'm not even thinking straight. Please, take one. Take a bunch. Take them all, if you like."

They exchanged names, Tooly describing herself as an old friend of Xavier's, saying she'd been passing through the area.

"Well, I'm relieved we didn't know you were coming," Harriet said. "Was going to have to get quite cross with the brute. He has a habit of keeping guests waiting. And so, Tooly, ought I to know who you are? Sorry, that sounded rude. Of course I should." She scratched her hair, said, "Far too little sleep."

"You expect him back soon?"

"Yes, yes. As soon as he's finished his murders." She gathered that this required explanation. "Ferrets," she added. "I'm not fussed myself—leave them alone, don't you think? But my ghastly husband unearthed a nest of them in an abandoned warren and has been on the verge of pumping car exhaust down there for days. Far as I'm concerned, ferrets are sweet. It's like having foxes dashing about the garden. He's of another mind. Probably right—they are considered pests. Still."

The infant gaped at Tooly, who looked back, eyebrows raised. Harriet considered the two considering each other. "Babies stare like that. I am sorry."

"I don't mind. Don't often get the chance to just stare at another person. Long as he doesn't mind if—"

"She."

"Long as she doesn't mind me staring back."

But the baby lost interest in grown-up noises, and her abrupt inattention stifled them.

Harriet said, "An angel passes."

"What?"

"It's that thing French people say when a conversation goes quiet. Speaking of angels, *c'est le diable qui s'approche.* Hello, darling." She stood to greet her husband.

His four dogs scampered through the scullery, each different in size and color, from an ankle-nipping Scottie to a hip-high Old English sheepdog, with a Jack Russell and a bull terrier in between, each sniffing, leaping, barking, racing through the house. "Not on the furniture, boys!" she cried. "Nor you," she told her husband as he kicked off his rubber boots by the washing machine.

He leaned over and kissed his wife. A gentleman farmer, he appeared, in waxed Barbour coat and tweed cap, which he tossed onto the table. Harriet placed the hat on the baby's head, swallowing the infant up to her wobbly neck, prompting a terrified *Waaaaaa!* "Oh, you silly!" Harriet responded, removing the cap. Seeing its mother again, the child burbled, and Harriet swooped in to smooch her cheek. "Only one angel here! Isn't there, darling!" The baby chortled.

Harriet insisted—and her husband seconded it, brushing aside Tooly's objections—that she stay overnight in the guesthouse, just the other side of the stable yards. He fetched her shoulder bag from the Micra, led her past a dozen stalls, three horses harrumphing in there, toward her lodgings around back.

"I knew," she said. "I *knew* this was going to be you."

They walked for a minute, neither speaking, she closing her eyes for a few seconds, electrified and tranquillized at his proximity. "This place is amazing," she said. "How much land do you have here?"

"If I told you in acres," Venn asked, "would that mean something to you?"

"Probably not."

"In that case, about a hundred and forty acres."

"Is that half the size of Texas?"

"Not quite. But respectable for South Tipperary." He opened the door to the guesthouse, slid her bag in.

"You don't seem surprised that I just turned up."

"I'm never surprised, duck, never surprised."

"You don't mind that I came, do you?"

"Tooly, Tooly, Tooly," he said, putting his arm around her. "A bit late to ask that."

They reentered the main house via the scullery and found Harriet tapping at her iPad, the baby mesmerized by the screen.

"I'm going to show our young friend the property," he informed his wife, not yet having informed Tooly.

"Wonderful," Harriet said, raising the baby to her husband. "Kiss."

To Tooly's surprise, he dutifully did so, stooping to the baby's pudgy cheek.

Overnight rain had softened the turf beyond the stable yards, and she and Venn squelched toward the trees, the four dogs hurrying along. All this sploshing rendered their outing distinctly ridiculous—she started laughing, looked over, found him grinning back. Onward they went, mud thickening on her shoes. "So," she observed, "you are the proud owner of a bog. Congratulations. And where the hell are you taking me?"

They reached an open-topped wartime jeep, which he used for zipping around the grounds. To the yapping mutts, he said, "Those of you that are coming, get in now." All four leaped in, followed by Tooly.

Venn gunned the jeep down the dirt road, kicking up mud, the dogs thrusting their muzzles into the wind. With his elbow, he guided the wheel, noting sights as they went: where Harriet went riding, where they held hunts, the apiary down the hill. He wore no seatbelt, so neither did Tooly, gripping the door handle, wind chapping her face. Venn pulled up at a score of cedar-box hives misted with bee clouds. He cut the engine, its growl replaced by the buzz of the insects. He hopped out and inspected a honeycomb frame swarming with bees.

"Shouldn't you wear protective garb?" Tooly called over, she and the dogs remaining a safe distance behind. "Don't they bite?"

He returned, held up his hand, lumpy from stings, and revved the engine.

"You idiot," she said.

Off they went, the vehicle rattling on rutted cattle guards, his arm shuddering as he made a sweeping motion over the windscreen to indicate the land before them. "It's all her people's," Venn said. "They're Anglo-Irish. The family goes way back." During the Irish War of Independence, he explained, her ancestors handed over the manor against their will, when nationalists held a match to the place. Long after, the Beenblossoms had made annual pilgrimages to visit the family graveyard—Harriet used to come with her grandparents. Then, two years ago, Venn earned their undying gratitude when he restored the estate to Beenblossom ownership, persuading the existing owners, who'd been ruined in the property crash, to accept a risibly low bid.

"The recession has been terrible in Ireland, hasn't it," Tooly said.

"Only as bad as most places," he replied. "The same old story: unregulated property market, wild mortgages, the obvious crash." Conifers brushed past the jeep on either side. "Supposedly, it was the history of poverty in Ireland that made them lose their minds." He paused, reflecting. "Actually, history was to blame for a lot of this crash. Certainly what's destroying Europe."

"How do you mean?"

"Well, trying to staple all these different countries together," he said. "This whole European Union idea, getting sworn enemies invested together so they'd stop slitting each other's throats—and with the Germans to finance it all out of war guilt. Only now the Germans are asked to pay the debts of Greece, Spain, Italy, and every other country that stuck its hands in the public pocket. What they're really saying is 'How historical do you feel?' They're asking, 'Will you still pay for what your grandparents did seventy years ago?'" He turned off-road, driving through high grass, and parked before a wired-off pasture occupied by foraging chickens. "History is the issue," he continued. "People, it turns out, aren't a product of their own time. They're a product of the time before theirs." Keys swinging in the ignition, he hopped from the jeep, splatting into mud. "Need a hand?"

"If Europe is such a mess, why are you in it?" she said, stepping out.

"I came *because* things were a mess. I used to think you needed to go where places were flourishing. But you have to follow chaos. That's where the dynamism is. As the poet said, 'In Italy, for thirty years under the Borgias, they had warfare, terror, murder, and bloodshed, but they produced Michelangelo, Leonardo da Vinci, and the Renaissance. In Switzerland, they had brotherly love, they had five hundred years of democracy and peace, and what did that produce? The cuckoo clock!' "

"Which poet said that?"

"I've done well in Ireland," he continued. "But I'll be out of here soon."

"Where to?"

"Why? Do you want to warn them?" He pinched her arm fondly. "There's opportunity wherever there's distress, little duck. Obviously, I'd prefer that no place fell into ruin and no one suffered. But success requires failure, sadly. Success is relative: you make a billion while everyone else makes a billion and one, then you just got poorer. Individuals don't rise together. That's a great lie of our time, like this myth of meritocracy: 'Work hard enough and you will make it! Just want it enough!' Everyone *does* want it enough. But only a few can win and nearly all will lose. People can't accept this, so they convince themselves that, secretly, privately, in their own terms, they're not failures. But, ah well," he concluded, smiling, "the individual ego, like the national ego, is wonderfully impervious to fact."

He led Tooly into an aluminum shed, its corrugated walls lined by nest boxes with hens peeking out, each of which he checked in turn.

"I'm annoyed that you're not more shocked I found you," she said. "Aren't you a *little* bit impressed?"

"The name gave me away," he guessed. He had been gathering names, and other information about people, for years. At the Brain Trust, for example, each applicant for membership had filled out detailed forms with personal data that they would never have disclosed in other settings but that they surrendered unthinkingly on an official-looking form. Long after the demise of the Brain Trust, several former applicants had the same strange experience, a growing sense that their lives were haunted: strange charges on their iTunes accounts; a failure to receive mail; businesses calling them about products they'd never bought. It was as if a double operated under their names. Xavi had visited the Brain Trust once on Tooly's recommendation, had met with Venn, and he'd filled out those forms. When he died, his identity became all the more valuable—no Xavier Karamage to interfere with the actions of "Xavier Karamage."

"But that photo online, the guy with a red mustache?" Tooly asked.

"Who knows," Venn answered. "Just a picture sucked from cyberspace by the computer geek who set up that website. My whole company, as I'm sure you realize, is somewhat of a shell operation."

"Your receptionist hasn't even met you."

"She gave out this address? Can't say I'm too impressed with that."

"Not her fault. It was my cunning that pried it from her!"

"Of course it was."

"How long have you been here, Venn?" she asked, with an unexpected surge of emotion. "I've been wondering for *ages* what happened to you. Thought you were going to be in touch. Where were you?"

"Where? There aren't places anymore, duck," he responded. "No locations now, just individuals. You didn't hear? Everyone's their own nation, with their own blog. Because everybody has something important to say; everybody's putting out press releases on what they ate for breakfast. It's the era of self-importance. Everyone's their own world. Doesn't matter where people are. Or where I was."

"Nicely dodged," she said. "And, for the record, this isn't supposed to be 'the age of self-importance.' Everyone's busy fighting for causes on social media, aren't they? The whole Occupy Wall Street movement."

"Clowns of no consequence," he retorted, taking a brown egg from a hutch, turning it over appraisingly. "Long after their tents are gone, Wall Street will still occupy. Not the other way around. Was there ever any doubt?"

"The protests in Greece and France and Italy?"

"Those aren't for a social cause. They're riots for self-interest. It's Greek statisticians and Italian taxi drivers and French bureaucrats all saying, 'How dare anyone threaten our entitlements?,' while their countrymen starve. You have to admire the gumption."

"The Arab Spring stuff isn't all self-interest," she countered. "And they're doing it through social-media stuff."

"The Arabs rebelled because of Facebook? They rebelled because they're *not* on Facebook. Because they're *not* installed in their hardware like the West is. Don't imagine that digital code topples generals. It's analog human beings. Not tweets and viral videos. That's just the sideshow of our times."

"You've become another declinist," she said. "Everywhere I go! I was with this old friend in Connecticut—you remember that law student, Duncan? All he talks about now is doom and collapse. But there were way worse times than this. People used to suffer famines in Ireland, right? You can't imagine that today."

"I agree with you," Venn said. "The West isn't collapsing. Empires don't crumble like they used to. Westerners are just in a bad mood. Suddenly, they don't have their way, and they won't stand for it. A bunch of spoilt children. (Then again, the difference between spoilt brats and successful adults is never that large, is it.) But anyone who frets about the fall of empires is missing the point. You have no West or East now. Like the poet said, 'No such things as societies anymore, just individual people.'"

"Who's this poet you keep quoting?"

"There is no poet," he confessed. "They're just lines I pick up. When I go, 'The poet said,' people lean in close and listen. Which makes me laugh. Especially since nobody listens to actual poets anymore."

"But you, at least, are not predicting the end of the world."

"Definitely not. Things are changing, but I don't mind that. Look at what everyone's so upset about: pollution and corporate greed and obesity. It's all just forms of gluttony. Even this global-warming farce. Horrific. It is. But inevitable, too. Nobody can stop it now. All that happens if you quit consuming is someone else eats your lunch." He smiled. "Remember all that nonsense about globalization—how the world was a village, how free-market democracy was going to unite the world? There are only individual operators, some pretending to belong to a group, others so naïve that they really believe a group exists.

"And your lawyer friend," Venn continued, "for all his moaning, is he really acting like life is under threat? Or is he just sitting there, grumbling on his blog? Underneath it all, people trust in progress. Scientists will cure their lifestyle diseases; the Internet will fix their love lives; technology will solve the oil crisis. Because technology is progress, and progress goes on forever. But progress played a trick. It presented the ultimate gluttony of all: those double clicks that turned everyone into rodents pressing buttons for the next sugar pellet. People who used to deride the losers for watching ten hours of TV a day won't hesitate to click a mouse for longer. 'Did she answer my email yet?' That's the new obesity. And nobody admits it even happened," he said. "The sci-fi movies got it wrong. No robots marched in to enslave humanity. What happened was far more ingenious: the servants became masters by their perfect affability. No microchip was implanted in any human head. People just handed over their brains. The real clash of civilizations wasn't between Islam and the West, or China and America. It was between what people had been and what they've become."

"You make it sound nightmarish."

"Not really." He tossed the egg, caught it. "Just like it's always been. A huge majority of fools; a tiny minority that runs the show."

"If that's what you think, why aren't you worried?"

"Because I'm not part of any of this. I just watch."

"Me, too."

He shook his head. "You joined in. As you should, duck, as you should. It's exhausting standing outside forever. I've been working at it my whole life. You can't blame yourself for having been swallowed by your times. They eat nearly everyone."

"Except you're not outside society anymore," she said. "You've got a family. The very fact that you married and had a kid is amazing to me, given what you always used to say about cutting ties."

He sidearmed the egg at her. All she could do was dodge. But instead of exploding on the wall it bounced off intact, rolled along the chicken-wire flooring, stopping at the toe of his rubber boot. Niftily, he kicked it up into the air, caught it, peeled the shell. "I always keep boiled ones in my pocket," he said, biting down. "Care to try?"

She nodded uncertainly.

He underarmed a second to her, and she snatched it from the air. It burst in her hand, raw egg dripping. He laughed, threw his arm around her, cleaning her off with a linen handkerchief, and continued with their tour of the grounds.

As they drove through the estate, Tooly told him about Humphrey, how they were back in touch and how she'd been caring for him. "It's bizarre," she said. "But he doesn't even sound Russian anymore."

"Why would he?"

"Well," she responded, even more confused now. "Because he is one."

Venn did a three-point turn, heading back toward the house. "That man is as Russian as we are." Humphrey had indeed been born in one of those places in Central Europe they'd erased, Venn said, but he left as a small boy and was raised in safety in South Africa. He'd trained as a pharmacist there, owned a couple of shops, looked after his father, never married. When his father died, Humphrey went traveling. But the world proved a lonelier destination than predicted: all these people and none approached his café table. Even the waiters found him a bore. So he'd concocted a fresh self, the Russian exile, mimicking how his father spoke. People caught him out early on, so he kept moving cities, refining the act. "He wanted to stop for years, but was petrified you'd be upset with him! He got stuck, the old fool."

"I guess he gave it up after I left." She had further questions about the old man's life, and Venn answered them all, reveling in the comical biography of Humphrey Ostropoler. She smiled at the account—

Venn expected that response, and she obliged. But to do so stung; she felt protective of the absent Humphrey, his private life bared despite decades of secrecy.

Abruptly, Venn pulled up at the edge of a field. "This is where you get out." He sent her squelching back to the house and reversed away to complete his farmerly chores.

When Tooly stepped inside, Harriet was in the kitchen, watching tennis on her iPad. "Can I get you anything? Glass of wine?"

"Please. Thanks."

Tooly took a large sip, and considered Harriet, who seemed kindly disposed toward her, not because she was Tooly per se but because Harriet was favorable to all human beings (and ferrets), and Tooly fit one of these categories. People had to be demonstrably evil to constitute rotters for Harriet—until then, they were jolly nice. Whenever Tooly encountered that mind-set, she was baffled. Surely experience eroded faith in human beings. Then again, some people trusted and thrived because of it. She watched Harriet with the baby in her arms, a scene of contentment that Tooly couldn't conceive of inhabiting, and it was hard to insist that she was the wiser.

Venn cooked goose for dinner, a bird taken from their own stock. As they ate, Tooly found her mind drifting. "I keep thinking about what you told me before. That stuff about Humph."

"Let's not bore Harriet with talk of old friends," he interrupted— evidently, she wasn't supposed to introduce their past into his present.

Chastened, Tooly sipped her wine. "You two have lived here a while?" she asked, since Venn had evaded the question earlier.

"*Do* we even live here?" Harriet asked Venn. "Technically, I suppose. But we seem always to be elsewhere, don't we, darling. Disgraceful to say, but we're here largely because of taxes. The Irish, mysteriously, charge hardly any of them."

"That'll change," he said.

"Yes, with the market things and so on. Turns out it's frighteningly easy to become an Irish resident, or to claim you're one. My husband is an absolute master at that sort of wheeze, aren't you. We still spend a fair bit of time in London. And I love Tokyo. My parents have a place in Scotland, where the whole Beenblossom clan descends like some sort of pestilence this time of year. Which is why we're hiding out here. All right," she said, rising and handing the baby to Venn. "You cooked, darling, so I clean up. Those are the rules. Begone, both of you. Reminisce boringly—I insist."

Venn and Tooly retired to the library. He placed his daughter on the carpet, where the infant practiced crawling, flopping intermittently onto her belly, gaze fixed on her father. The four dogs slept, each in a different corner of the room. From an antique-globe bar, he extracted a Cognac decanter and two snifters. Books lined the walls, each volume identically bound in Bordeaux leather, silver letters imprinted on the spine, gold paint on the page edges. Classics, poetry, essays. They didn't have the smell of reading books; they were furniture. She knelt beside the baby, who looked glassily around. "I'd like a one-piece outfit like yours. Most convenient," she told the child, then turned to Venn. "Shouldn't she be sleeping now?"

"Lots of life left for that. Everything is too interesting to sleep if you've not been alive a year."

The child goggled open-mouthed at her father, oblivious of anything else in the room.

"You're surprisingly credible as the family man, Venn," she remarked. "I'd be a disaster as a mother—I couldn't trust myself to look after a brood. Don't even know how to hold one of these properly." She leaned over to try, then thought better of it, took another sip of Cognac, finding herself more uncomfortable with each remark. "Mind if I help myself to another drop?"

"You drink fast these days."

She poured, but refrained from sipping for a minute. She sat on the oxblood sofa, he on its twin opposite, a glass coffee table between them, stacked with *Country Life* magazines. "I saw my parents recently," she said. (How peculiar to use that phrase, "my parents," in reference to Paul and Sarah.) She recounted what Paul had said about sending money to Sarah for years, and that Humphrey had remembered this, too. But what had Sarah spent it on?

"Well," he answered. "On me."

"What?"

"The woman, you may recall, was a bit stuck on me. The only way she figured to keep her hooks in was monthly funding," he said. "Your father made those payments directly into Sarah's account, but she refused to just wire it nicely along. Insisted on handing it over in person—her way of clinging on. Meant I had to tell her every place I moved. And when she turned up I put on a good show—just enough rejection to keep her interested."

Tooly paused, trying to absorb this. But something didn't fit. "You took me everywhere you went. Why didn't you guys just plant me somewhere, then? The checks were coming in anyway."

"Plant you where? If you started sobbing in a corner somewhere, then sooner or later someone telephones Daddy. Better to make you merry and compliant. And there was Humph to keep you busy."

"Was he earning off me, too?"

"No, no. Humph was an unpaid volunteer. I told you, a sad and lonely man. And everything was fine until you went and turned twenty-one, at which point your father rudely stopped paying. Though the whole thing was a bit tired by then. Humph was terrified," he recalled, laughing, "that I might take you with me once the money stopped, that I'd do something awful with you. You remember how I tied your shoelaces that day?"

"Of course."

"Couldn't have you running after me and making a scene on the Upper West Side, could I."

"I know you're trying to get a reaction from me."

"Well, of course. What else do people talk for?"

"You weren't just keeping me sweet. I was your friend."

"You were my salary. And, since you had to be around, I put you to use. Now and then, you came in handy. Though never nearly as handy as you thought."

"But you weren't living off me," she insisted. "You had all that other work."

"Such as?"

"I don't know. Like in Barcelona, you were helping that guy with his factory. Those Romanian gangsters were hassling him, and you fixed it. Right?"

"What an imagination!"

"You told me that."

"Like I said, what an imagination. My Barcelona businessman was just another citizen, a little excitable, a little greedy. If he wanted to believe I was a one-man Mafia, who was I to disappoint him?"

"But I saw you dealing with tons of scary guys."

"I met a few over the years. That's not to say I was mixed up with them. Thugs are not famously strong in the forward-planning department—why would I tie my fate to sediment like them? Maybe certain souls have mistaken me for a magician, the man who'll get around the rules, fix the competition, grant them all the power they never deserved. And maybe some gave me funds in the fantasy. All that ever produced, little duck, was a timely reason for me to find my next town."

"But I thought . . . Venn, I waited *years* to do something with you."

"What were we going to do together? Your dot-com with those hapless college kids?"

"You're the one who encouraged me to figure out something with them. Wasn't that the point, for me to find us opportunities?"

"I sent you into people's houses, Tooly, like one sends a child to collect pretty shells on the beach: to get the kid out of your hair. You weren't about to come back with anything useful. Actually, you probably should've stuck with the lawyer. You'd be comfortable now."

"I needed to hook up with someone to get anywhere in life? I'm that useless, you think?"

"Well, how would you say you're faring now?"

"I know you're just giving me a hard time, Venn. But I want you to know that I paid attention to what you said. All that stuff. About managing without other people. I'm that way now. We really are similar."

"Couldn't be more different. I only said that because it kept you in love with me."

"Come on—this coldhearted thing isn't convincing me."

"Really? What am I doing wrong?" he asked, winking.

"What you're doing wrong is that I remember. I remember how you spent your own money to fly me and Humph along whenever you moved. How you paid for whatever apartment we were in. You weren't living off me. You completely took care of me. For years."

"That was Humph. I never paid for one of your flights, your food, your rent. You only assumed it was me, and I saw no need to say otherwise."

"Why would he do that?"

"To make himself necessary. Otherwise, babysitting was a job anyone could've done."

"But after New York," she protested, "you kept supporting me."

"How? I haven't seen you in years."

"My passport," she answered, meaning the bank card he'd secreted there, and the account that had served as her safety net for years, and with which she'd bought World's End.

"Never touched your passport—Humph thought I'd spirit you away from him if I had it. Which was crazy. I could've sold you, I guess. But how much was I seriously going to get?"

"I know it was you who set up that card, Venn."

"Just tell me what I did," he said, "and I'll be happy to take credit."

Harriet entered the library. "Oh, darling, you are useless!" she told her husband, picking the infant off the carpet. "You just left her asleep on the floor—I should call social services."

"She was so adorable. I couldn't move her."

"Actually," Tooly said, standing, "you know what? We were just calculating that I won't make it back in time if I leave tomorrow morning. I'm sorry, Harriet, but I should get going."

"Sure," she said indifferently, and carried the baby upstairs.

Tooly collected her shoulder bag from the guesthouse and walked around Beenblossom Lodge. Venn stood in wait, leaned against his black Range Rover.

"You really affected my life," she said. "Everything I chose to do, how I am now. I think you changed me more than anyone I ever met."

"Did I?"

"Why do you think I was in love with you?"

"You obviously were."

"How come you never tried anything?"

"I'm not an animal," he said. "I'm not someone who just launches himself at any girl on the premises. Anyway, you're ugly, aren't you."

"You're just being cruel now."

"If you don't want to know, don't ask the question. Think of it this way: if you'd been attractive, I'd have had you and got bored (fast in your case, I'm guessing), and you'd never have lasted."

"I won't hassle you again."

"Thank goodness for that. Wouldn't want you going the same way as the ferrets." He embraced her, locking his arms around her lower back, inhaling to expand his chest and compress hers, his knuckles cracking as he squeezed the air out of her. "An absolute pleasure," he said, kissing her forehead. "Don't ever fucking do this again."

Her high beams swept across dark tree trunks, burst out into the roadway. She drove toward Cork, gripping the wheel, then turned into a closed Morris Oil to calm down. But she had to escape this place, so drove onward, tire treads kicking up pebbles.

In a hotel room outside the airport, she sat naked on the bed, running her fingers over her ribs, his grip there, that kiss on her brow. It was as if she had brushed aside a lock of hair and found an eye, a throbbing eye, a hideous growth blinking at her, repulsive yet her own, fed by her own blood. This is how he seemed, incorporated into her yet monstrous. The shower wouldn't cleanse her. She left her muddy clothing in the hotel bathroom, abandoning her entire outfit there, and arrived for her flight hours early, just to be among strangers at the terminal.

SATELLITE IMAGES SHOWED the swirling eye of Hurricane Irene inching up the Eastern Seaboard. The authorities warned of flooding, a shutdown of mass transit servicing New York City, a state of emergency across the region. "It's going to be up to individuals to get out of their own areas," Mayor Bloomberg announced on television, ordering the evacuation of high-risk zones, including where Humphrey lived in Sheepshead Bay.

He was asleep when she opened the door to his room. Someone—Humphrey couldn't recall who—had run tape in X's across each windowpane to stop the glass from shattering during the storm. The rest of the room seemed to have been visited by a hurricane already: books everywhere, dirty clothing strewn about, used cups and plates on the floor. Yelena had left town, stuffing Humphrey's bar fridge with ready-to-eat meals before departing. He had helped himself to a few, but thrown out none of the refuse, nor washed himself or shaved in a few days. Tooly spent two hours restoring order, helped him to the bathroom, cleaned him, returned him to his armchair. Mentioning Venn hardly stirred Humphrey, while references to the coming hurricane puzzled him.

As he slept that afternoon, she went through his documents. She discarded junk mail, then organized his bills by date. It didn't take long to find the bank statements. As she put them in order, she found payments in each of the cities she had passed through during the preceding decade, including one final transaction from a few years earlier, the transfer of the remaining balance to the Mintons in Caergenog. "You," she said when he awoke, "were the one helping me. My magic bank account."

He frowned—waking was always hard for him. Forty minutes later, the statements still lay in his lap.

"Why did you give me all that?" she asked. "It was all you had left, wasn't it. And I was so stupid with it. As far as I'm concerned, the shop belongs to you. It's not worth much. But I'll sell it, or try to. Whatever I get is yours. And we can move you somewhere decent. Okay?"

"You went lots of places," he said, gazing down at the bank statements.

"Did you read those to know where I was?"

"I thought of you doing things."

"And I thought of you, Humph. Often, I did."

"I wasn't doing anything worth thinking about."

She took his hand.

"You have a bookshop!" he declared. "You really are my dream girl! I imagine you there, ringing up all the sales."

"We don't make many, I'm afraid."

"You," he said, "are the favorite thing I did in my life. Even if I didn't make you."

"Don't say things like that." She blinked. "Look, you have to come see the shop. Wouldn't that be nice? Let me describe it for you." She gave her best portrait of the village, the former pub that contained World's End, the first editions, the snug at the back, and her lone employee. "You'd enjoy Fogg; you two would get on so well. I can imagine you having debates for hours on end."

Humphrey gave a short nod, by which he communicated that this trip would remain only a fancy. "I'm in the same place as my favorite person I knew. For nearly all of existence, before and after now— nearly all of it—I don't get to be with you. But now I am. I even helped you a bit in your life."

"You helped me so much."

"I don't remember everything that happened in my life," he said, frowning. "Parts, I do."

Ever since her first visit to Sheepshead Bay, he'd been beset by these fragments—his past flickering, repetitive but incomplete. She'd been able to help only by replaying anecdotes he had previously recounted. But now she did know his story. "Venn explained all about your life," she said. "Shall I tell you?"

"All right," he said, looking blindly past her. As Humphrey listened, he squinted at the X's on the window. Tooly *had* seen him exert himself before—when Mac visited, for example. "Do your best," she urged him. "Tell me if this sounds right."

She went on, watching him, his eyes closed tightly with concentration. At times, he specified that he just couldn't recall this bit, or interrupted with small corrections. At other points, he added details she'd never known. Mostly, he paid attention.

His mother, Tooly began, was born at the turn of the century into a middle-class Jewish family from Pressburg, then part of the Austro-Hungarian Empire. The family spoke many languages, but their first tongue was German. As a young girl, she had aspired to a creative life, to act and paint. And by her late teens she frequented artistic circles, where she fell for an aspiring actor, a Russian Jew who had left Leningrad to make a name for himself in the West. But his career was hampered by stage fright, worsened by his thick accent. He decided to write and direct instead, but the fragile confidence that had undermined his performances foiled his offstage career, too. He was an endearing nebbish, though, so she married him, telling her parents only after the union was legal.

Her husband proved inept at earning and, increasingly dispirited, he drifted into radical leftist politics. To support them, she took work as a seamstress, producing costumes for local productions, while auditioning for parts herself. When she became pregnant with their first child, her father—a doctor—exhorted them to cease these theatrical pursuits; her husband must start contributing. He took work at a jewelry shop, whose customers he privately referred to as "bourgeois stone collectors." The workers of the world would rise against capitalist modes of production, he informed his wife, since history was inevitable. Exploitation and greed could not be the fate of the species.

Their first child, a daughter, was born with a kidney ailment. Three years later, they bore a boy whom they did not call Humphrey Ostropoler, but who decades later adopted that name. The family, in the grip of revolutionary ardor, became communal farmers. Doing so at the start of the Depression was not an inspired plan. Scenes from those years remained with Humphrey: the milk cow at the bottom of the garden; the orchard where he and his sister had stolen apricots when starving; how he threw a pit that struck her in the eye.

Humphrey grew, but his sister remained stunted. At age five, he was the taller, though she was the elder by three years. Doctors drove syringes into her, dosed her with powders, cut her apart. When she writhed in bed, her mother stood on one side, her father on the other, Humphrey holding her feet. "Help me," she whispered. "Please, help me." They placed iced facecloths on her forehead, which at least gave them a sense of doing something.

His sister died at age eleven. She had feared being forgotten, but the opposite proved true. Humphrey gained a doubleness of experience, incapable of fitting through the narrow doors beyond which others lived, being two people now. He still refused to say her name. But, his whole life, he saw his sister in any little girl, and wondered what she'd have become, had she lasted the nearly unimaginable seventy-five years since her disappearance.

Humphrey's father gave up ideology after his daughter's death. He resumed work at the jewelry store, no longer moaning about the clients. His wife, by contrast, adopted his former political fervor and intended to act on it. Reports circulated about arable land in the Soviet Union, available to committed foreigners. Her husband had left the USSR as a young man, and resisted returning. She pressed him daily, citing the tumult in Austria, where Dollfuss turned the nation into a Fascist state, and in Germany, where Hitler had taken power.

Nazis in both countries agitated for unification, which would put the Reich at their doorstep. It was time to go East.

From impatience, she decided to travel ahead and, if all went well, they would join her. Humphrey's father read her letters aloud. The boy shared his mother's enthusiasm for the cause and viewed his father unforgivingly. They should have gone—his father spoke fluent Russian, and could have helped. The Communist bureaucrats disbelieved her story, and held her at the border. Finally, Humphrey's father packed up their belongings. But the train took them in the wrong direction, north to Rotterdam. He informed Humphrey that his mother had died. They took a ship for South Africa, wearing black armbands on board, their grieving restricted to the time at sea.

His father polished diamonds in Johannesburg, and they lived in an adequate house in Orange Grove. Humphrey attended local schools, and was young enough to learn the language rapidly, his foreign accent gone by adolescence. Soon he and his father spoke only English together. At school, there was a map on which the history teacher stuck thumbtacks to mark the latest battles in the European war. South Africa was almost a straight line south from the fighting. It was up there in Europe that Humphrey ought to have been. He had—and not for the last time—the sense that his life unfolded in the wrong place.

The war ended, and he graduated from secondary school, after which he studied to become a pharmacist, a choice determined by early exposure to medicaments during his sister's illness. Potions, when rightly dispensed, alleviated suffering. As for doctoring, he never considered that, retaining a distaste for his punitive maternal grandfather, who exercised that profession. Or had done so. Neither he nor any of her family had been in touch since Humphrey and his father arrived in Johannesburg.

Jewish agencies issued lists of those murdered in Europe, and Humphrey glanced down the rolls, looking for someone whose name was the same as his, as if a doppelgänger had conducted his proper life, and death, up there. Lists of survivors arrived, too. One woman shared his sister's name; another shared his mother's. He wrote to the authorities overseeing the displaced-persons camp, identifying himself, inquiring into the story of this woman with his mother's name. Weeks later, he received an answer: she had survived three years in various Nazi camps but weeks after liberation had committed suicide with laudanum.

Humphrey and a fellow student opened a pharmacy. After a few years, they had three stores. Humphrey bought two apartments, both in the same building, one for himself and the other for his father, whom he lodged a floor above, meaning that he could attend to the man by listening to his footsteps. They spent lots of time together, since Humphrey had a limited social life. The rules of romance perplexed him: the more you liked someone, the less they liked you; the less you liked them, they more they liked you. How could it ever work? By his thirties, he pretended to be jaded, kibitzing with the pharmacy assistants and playing the curmudgeon, which endeared him to women in a thoroughly nonsexual way. It was preferable to being shunned.

He considered moving with his father to England, which for him represented the height of civilization. South Africa had never suited them: heat and exploitation and complacency. But his father resisted another move. Finally, the man in the apartment above was too frail, forgot names, locked himself out. Humphrey tended to his father as long as possible, then admitted him to the Jewish care home. To erase the present, Humphrey disappeared into books. He contemplated death, ran through the imagined stages of his own suicide, toying with laudanum in the pharmacy after hours.

When his father died, Humphrey was in his forties. Just as his mother had once done, he yearned for a world of bohemian intellectuals. He lingered at cafés in Hillbrow frequented by the university students. But he was two decades older than those kids. He studied chess as an excuse to interact with them, and treated them to coffee so they'd stay in his company. Embarrassed to be just a pharmacist, he said—and it wasn't a lie—that he'd come from Europe. To exoticize himself further, he adopted an accent. Rumors circulated that he was from the Soviet Union, because the false accent was, unintentionally, that of his Russian-speaking father, who had never shed his Old World syntax, constantly bungling idioms: "I wouldn't believe it if I didn't hear it with my own eyes!" and "Never count your eggs before they cooked!" However, someone recognized Humphrey from the pharmacy and, to humiliate him, turned up with a modern-languages student who addressed him in Russian. Humphrey sold both apartments, plus his share in the pharmacies, then figured out how to get his savings out of the country, and set out to find the intellectuals.

His first stop was London. He didn't fit in, lacking the education and social sense. He experimented with playing the Soviet dissident again, but was caught out and moved countries, refining the impersonation over time. He had ample savings, and didn't spend much anyway. By the 1980s, he was in Asia, passing through Thailand, where he rented a house—he often took overly large lodgings, in hopes of attracting company. He met a young Canadian, a charmer with a thick beard who welcomed a place to stay, then invited others to join him. Soon Venn was using the house as he pleased, while Humphrey was confined behind his chessboard, toilet-paper earplugs to block out the pounding music below.

"Which is when I met you," she concluded.

Throughout much of this account, Humphrey had listened, his eyelids clenched shut, squeezing from his synapses the weak pulses of recall. But, by the end, he had faded.

"I'm not going anywhere," she told him. "It's you and me again. But I'm finding a place out here in Sheepshead now. Don't have tons of money, so I'm hoping there's something in this building. Wouldn't it be nice if I was on the same floor? Or maybe I could get a room on the floor below you, so I can hear when you're walking around!"

He mumbled a few words—the spasms of a spent brain. Without further warning, he was asleep, deeply so, forehead still furrowed from the preceding effort.

By nightfall, she helped him onto his mattress and cleared a patch of space for herself on the floor, lying parallel to his bed. She gazed up, able to make out his shape under the covers, hearing his slow breaths, and she reached her hand over his wrist, which quivered at each heartbeat. When people have children, she thought, they don't think of them as adults, don't think of them as old or lonely. They think of having a baby, not having an old man. Tooly was glad that Mac had met Humphrey. Maybe someday the boy would be the last person in the world to remember him.

After sixteen hours of impenetrable sleep, Humphrey was slow to wake the following morning. She smiled, informing him of the remarkable duration of his slumber. Tooly expected to encounter the man who had exerted himself the day before, but such a person had retracted. She sought to summon anew the details of his life, but he betrayed no interest.

Nevertheless, for the first time since her arrival Humphrey was peaceful. He could not see or hear properly, and remained doubtful about the time of day. But he knew who she was, and was uncommonly affectionate, holding her hand as she sat beside him. He kept saying this was the perfect life.

"What do you want to eat this weekend?" she asked. "I want us to have a blowout. Something we can't afford. The shops will be shut when the storm arrives, so I have to pick up stuff beforehand." She emptied out her wallet: less than forty dollars. "Champagne? Actually, probably can't afford that. But a bottle of wine? Or vodka? You used to like vodka tonic. I can make you cocktails, Humph, and we can make toasts about things. What do you think?"

He loved the idea of a celebration, but wanted no alcohol—didn't want to dull anything now. Tooly abstained in solidarity, stepping into the liquor store, then out again with nothing. She prepared him a smashed-potato sandwich, not because it was the lunch hour but because it gave him pleasure. And who cared about time? That was mere conformism!

"Is it all right?" she asked, watching him take a bite.

"Oh, God."

"What?"

"Oh, my God!"

"Is it terrible?"

"It's delicious!" he shouted, turning wide-eyed to face her, though unable to orient to her.

"I'm so happy to hear that, Humph."

"I *love* smashed-potato sandwiches!" he cried. "How did you *know*?"

"Because I know you."

"But how did you know?" He looked blindly beyond her. "How did you know?" Without waiting for an answer, he took another bite. "Delicious!"

After only one further mouthful, he fell asleep again, sandwich still gripped. He grunted when she tried to ease it from him.

Hurricane Irene was supposed to devastate New York City but had diminished into gales and heavy rain by the time it hit that Sunday morning. She went out to witness the wild weather, which always stirred her. Despite the evacuation order, the neighborhood wasn't empty. There was even a café open. Two young Russian women served, conversing in their language with four male customers, all brazenly nonchalant in their defiance of public-safety warnings.

Tooly asked what damage there had been around here. They spoke of a few fallen trees and toppled power lines, and said the bay had overflowed. But nothing too serious. She bought a black tea and sat at the window, gazing at the empty intersection. A grocery store across the way was boarded up. The barbershop had its shutters down. A traffic light swung in the wind, changing colors without any vehicles to respond. Seemed almost unreal: the pelting rain, the chattering Russians behind her, Humphrey just around the corner, Duncan in Connecticut perhaps peering out the window at the storm, Venn in Ireland with wife and baby. Maybe Fogg was at World's End, listening to the radio, dusting the stock. All these places at once.

With nearly her last dollar, she bought a croissant for Humphrey. When she returned, saying his name softly in case he slept, he remained still, because his heart had stopped.

## 1988: The End

HUMPHREY BECKONED HER to follow him out of the house. She reached for his hand, but it rose, resting on her head. "Your hair is wet from rain," he said, as they walked down the alley. "Warm now, also."

"Because of the sun," Tooly explained, touching the hot crown of her head, sandwiching his fingers there and holding them for the entire walk to the main road.

The traffic—buses and tuk-tuks and motorcycles, fumes tickling her nose—overloaded her senses after weeks inside that house. He hailed a taxi and helped her into the backseat, flopping in after her and giving her address. Odd to hear him say "Gupta Mansions," as if a character from this version of Tooly had wandered into the previous version. She watched him looking out the car window, his old eyes following each vehicle they passed, focus dragged along with it, then the next.

The taxi stopped at her street. "Very soon," Humphrey said, opening the door on her side, speaking differently than he had, more seriously, "very soon you will grow up. Being small is hard bit of life. But you are nearly done with it. When you are grown, Tooly, you can be boss till the end. You are someone who must be boss of your life, not pushed around. So be careful."

"I'll be careful of trivial beings," she suggested, to please him.

He smiled sadly. "Yes. Of trivial beings."

"And the Moron Problem."

"This also."

She stepped from the taxi, watching him, unsure what was happening. "Are you going?"

"Good luck for your life," he answered through the window.

The driver turned the cab around. Humphrey's head was visible in the rear window as the taxi drove away.

She stood beside a pothole, looking into it, then stepped over and continued down the *soi*, past the fruit stall, past the tailor pumping his foot-pedal sewing machine, past the construction workers in bandannas.

It was Shelly who answered the door. She backed away to let Tooly in, bowed, hastened to her quarters. Paul was still away at work. Tooly found her bedroom tended and tidy, bed made, sheets tight. The apartment was air-conditioner cold, its thrumming units rippling the curtains. On the desk, her schoolbooks were lined up. She opened her book bag, looking for *Nicholas Nickleby*, but had left it behind. She took out her sketchbook of noses instead, yet couldn't bring herself to draw more than a line, so left it on the desk. She jumped onto the bed, landing on her knees, mattress jiggling—her first proper bedding after weeks in the tent. She let herself fall flat on her face and lay still, her mouth dampening a patch of bedspread.

At the sound of Paul arriving home, she awoke with fright but did not move for several seconds. Finally, heart racing, she walked into the living room.

"Tooly." He gaped at her, absently putting down his briefcase. "Tooly."

She held still.

Paul reached out, and she extended her hand to shake his. He'd only meant to touch her arm.

"Did Sarah bring you?"

Tooly shook her head.

"Are you okay? You look so thin. Are you hungry?"

As they ate, he asked if she wanted to stay with him and that she could—he'd figure it out somehow. They could leave right now, move again. Did she want that? But these questions were too direct coming from Paul—she expected him to be otherwise, so didn't know how to answer.

All fell quiet, like their meals of old. Just the tremors of his desire to speak. So strange after days of free discussion with Humphrey and everyone there, after all she'd done—drinking coffee each morning! cheating at chess! debating one of the Great Thinkers!

She asked to get down from the table, and went to her room. She hadn't had a door for so long, and was unsure whether to use it now, if it would be rude. From the other room, he cleared his throat, as if to call her back. She knew where he'd be: seated stiffly on a chair, work folder in his lap, willing her to join him.

However, she found him otherwise than imagined. He lay on the couch, arm draped over his eyes. She stood beside him, looking at his shielded face. He reached over to draw his daughter nearer. But she turned, spiraling away.

On her balcony, Tooly gazed down at the lit swimming pool in the courtyard, a pane of blue glass. The shacks on the other side of the wall were dark. Lights from distant skyscrapers dotted the night.

She slipped out, ran down the stairs, passed under the jacaranda trees, beyond the saluting porter, up toward Sukhumvit Road, into the first tuk-tuk.

The destination she gave was Khlong Toey Market—she and Sarah had passed it that first night. Upon arrival, she handed the driver all her money, the tips from helping tend bar. She was on her own in a swirl of strangers, and looked for the alley. She tried one, but it was wrong. She walked up the next. All grew darker as she went. She closed her eyes, the better to listen for music and crowd noise. She heard only traffic, far behind her now. Tooly turned a blind corner. And there it was: the house. She crossed the concrete patio and tried the front door, which opened immediately.

All three of them stood there, their conversation interrupted. The way they regarded her—Venn smiling slowly, Sarah reaching for her cigarettes, Humphrey compressing his lips—it seemed that the discussion might have been about Tooly herself.

"I figured you'd make it back, little duck."

"Thank God, thank God, thank God—thought I'd lost you," Sarah said, though she was looking at Venn.

"Look what I got," Tooly said, taking out her passport.

Venn lifted it from her hand, flipped through, and handed it to Sarah, from whom Humphrey grabbed the document. He appeared uneasy about the girl's return, lips parting as if to object, though he had no power to dissuade anybody. He had tried. But people didn't listen to him.

"See," Sarah told Venn, eyes wide. "She *wants* to come with."

"You're being unrealistic."

"It'll arrive in my account every month; he promised. It'll come to me and I'll share it with you. I don't mind."

"Who's looking after her?"

"I will," Sarah said.

"Me, you, and her going around together?"

"We'll be company for you," Sarah told Venn. "You can do what you like. With whoever you like. I'm not trying to make some claim on you. You won't get sick of me. I promise."

Humphrey addressed Tooly: "They're not staying here. You know that? They'll be going some other place. You might not like it. I won't be there. There won't be school, probably. It might not be safe."

Tooly nodded her assent.

He appealed to Sarah and Venn: "You can't take her."

"How much are we talking about?" Venn asked Sarah. "And monthly, right?"

Humphrey shook his head unhappily. "Look, look."

"What?"

"If you do this," he said, "I come."

Venn smirked. "What do you have to do with anything?"

"I keep eye on her."

"Sorry, but I don't travel like that," Venn said.

"We don't need to all go together," Sarah argued. "Just tell me where you're headed. I'll get there on my own. Me and Tooly will join you."

"And Humph comes along and babysits whenever you wander off?" Venn said.

"I'm not wandering off. It'll be a decent amount, Venn. It's yours as far as I'm concerned."

"Do what you like, Sarah. You, too, Humph. Makes no difference to me." Venn winked at Tooly, who grinned back.

Sarah lit a shaky cigarette, blew a smoke cloud, and patted her thigh to call the girl nearer, hugging her tightly, kissing her cheek so hard that Tooly's neck bent from the pressure. "What have you done?" Sarah whispered. "What have you done to your poor, poor father?"

# 2000: The Middle

AFTER WAITING AT THE CAFÉ nearly an hour, Tooly acknowledged that Venn was not returning. She walked once around the block, knowing it to be fruitless, then proceeded north. At 115th Street, she stood across from Duncan's building, uncertain if she wished to be spotted. She studied the building's façade, the vertiginous fire escape, and distinguished windows at whose other sides she'd stood, the rickety iron balcony where she'd sat, her legs curled beneath her, sharing a damp filtered cigarette, wondering if the bolts in the brickwork would hold.

She walked through Morningside Park, past a guy rolling a joint, his lizardy tongue sliding across the cigarette paper as he watched her. Through East Harlem, she continued, skirting the concrete projects, past adolescents in camouflage and skewed NY baseball caps, stuffing junk food and catcalling. She kept going for hours, crossing the footbridge to Randall's Island, on to Queens, wending her way south to Brooklyn, reaching her street after midnight, traffic grumbling along the Gowanus Expressway. She entered the building, climbed to their floor, put her key in the front door, but didn't turn it. She listened to the sound inside: a page crinkling as it turned.

"Tooly?" Humphrey asked through the closed door, then opened it. "Hello, darlink. You are asleep?"

"What do you mean?" she said, puzzled. "I'm standing up."

"Certain animals sleep standing."

"I'm not one of them."

He made for his customary seat at the end of the couch, expecting conversation. But Tooly continued into her bedroom.

Awakening the next morning, she remained under the covers, wishing to escape herself in sleep. She reached for her watch on the floor, opened one eye to read it, daylight streaming around the edges of her bent blinds. A few minutes after noon.

In the shower, she pressed her forehead against the tiles, water whispering down her back, skin goosebumped. A strand of her hair remained stuck to the wall, a black S on the white tile. She wanted nothing for breakfast, took only a few gulps of water from the faucet. She microwaved yesterday's coffee, hands shivering from caffeine and fatigue, which angered her obscurely. She abandoned her mug in the sink.

"He went," Humphrey said, meaning Venn. "This is better."

"We're meeting up."

"Where?"

"Haven't decided," she said. To avoid his gaze, she looked into her cupped hands.

So much of what Tooly thought, said, her mannerisms, attitudes, and humor, had come from Venn. There was no meaning to "Tooly" without him inside it. The two were akin: living among others but estranged from everyone, recognizing the pretense, forsaking a place of their own for the right, as Venn put it, "to relieve citizens of their transitory property." He and she had no interest in riches, only in remaining free of the fools who reigned, and always would.

"We have items and activities to discuss," Humphrey said.

"I'm not interested," she said. "Not interested in hearing your conversations with the Great Thinkers. Just because you own books by smart people doesn't make you smart. All you do is sit there. You're wasting time."

"I know that."

"You are," she said, repeating the charges not from conviction but in distress at her own cruelty. "All you've done is sit there, looking at what other people did. You don't do anything; you never did anything in your life. I know you had a hard time a long time ago in Russia. I'm sorry. But I—"

"This is our last conversation. Can it be nice? Please? We were friends, and now you are sick of me. But everything you say I will think about many times after. And you are right. You are right. But you are going now."

"Where am I going? I have nowhere to go."

"You're leaving."

"Why?"

"Because," he said, "I like you to go." He went into her room, returning with her passport, which he placed on the Ping-Pong table.

She clasped her hands to hide their tremors at what she'd said, what was happening. This was what Venn had spoken of: cutting out the unnecessary, managing alone. She opened the passport, and a bank card fell into her hand. "That's not mine," she said.

"There's money on it. You take it."

"I'm not taking your money," she said, unable to look at him.

"No? Well, it's not money from me. Since when I have money? It is from Venn. He leaves it for you. He says, 'Tell Tooly that PIN number is her birthday, month and day.' That is what he says."

She closed her hand over the card.

"He tells me he is leaving today," Humphrey continued. "He says you should go, too. You must get on train and go somewhere very interesting, do something you always want to do."

"It's *not* our last conversation." She pinched the bridge of her nose, leaned forward, eyes stinging, clutching the couch upholstery until her arm went weak.

He sat beside her. She took the book from his lap—essays by John Stuart Mill—turned it over, looked at him. "Don't look sad, Humph. Please. I can't bear it."

"Sad? That is lie—it is complete and utter fabric."

"Fabrication," she said, sniffing, smiling.

He fetched his Ping-Pong paddle. "Game before you are going?"

She shook her head, but made two mugs of instant coffee.

He tasted his. "Where's sugar?"

"I put in two heaping tablespoons already."

"Must be more heaping."

"Humph," she said, "we're always going to have lots of conversations. Okay?"

He smiled. "But, Tooly, I'm not really alive—I am already with my friends," he said, pointing to his books. "I died already and I'm only watching now. You can go on with this twenty-first century. I am staying in number twenty. It is nicer for me." The concerns of his century—inspiring millions, swindling them, murdering them—had once amounted to everything, then expired, as the species repeated itself in different generations, in different bodies, uniquely animated in each person, yet united by one fear: that upon their own deletion the world went extinct, too. The times to which he had peripherally belonged—a world war, the ideological battles thereafter—had ended, but his physical powers had not exhausted themselves, nor had the organism stopped. "I know what twentieth century has for breakfast," he said. "It is too much work getting to know new century."

"We'll let everyone else test number twenty-one," she suggested. "What do you think? If it looks nice, we'll join them."

"Is good idea." He rose as if to give an after-dinner speech, then sat back down and patted her hand. "You so sweet, darlink. I go get fresh air." He spent twenty minutes locating his coat and roll-up chess set in case he wanted to study positions, plus a few dollars in loose change. All this he narrated loudly. Farewell unstated, he closed the front door after himself. Even then, he muttered on the landing for a minute before clomping downstairs, the building door squeaking open, crashing shut after him.

Ten minutes later, Tooly left, as he had intended her to do. Reaching the end of their street, she checked the contents of her shoulder bag, ensuring that everything was there: clothing, passport, bank card. "Oh, well," she said, pressing a knuckle into her breastbone, pushing as hard as she could, as if to cave in her chest. "Oh, well."

Her train left Penn Station, passing the smokestacks of New Jersey, factories with windows smashed, rusty bridges, residential streets, houses whose insides she filled with blaring televisions, pregnant silences, uproarious laughter, sex, showers, cigars, chatter. She had no location of her own and none in prospect—less in common with those home-dwellers than with the sinister types lurking at each station the train pulled into, its brakes squealing to a halt, air vents gusting, a bag of chips crinkling behind her. "Last call for . . ." Trenton and Philadelphia, through Chester, Pennsylvania, Wilmington, onward.

## 2011: *The Beginning*

THE PASSENGERS EXPLORED their trays of foil-covered treasure, but she turned down her meal, irking the airline steward, who kept telling her that it was free. She looked out the window, smelling rubbery eggs, watery sausages. Flying reminded Tooly of her father. Whenever they'd had a bank of three seats to themselves, they left an empty one between them, she at the window, nose pressed to the glass, Paul on the aisle, looking around for a stewardess to request another ginger ale for his daughter.

There were no empty seats on this flight from New York to London. The passengers were crammed in, bulging over the armrests onto each other. She read a copy of *The New York Times,* whose front page contained a report that neutrinos may have broken the speed of light:

> Even this small deviation would open up the possibility of time travel and play havoc with longstanding notions of cause and effect. Einstein himself—the author of modern physics, whose theory of relativity established the speed of light as the ultimate limit—said that if you could send a message faster than light, "You could send a telegram to the past."

The purported discovery was shaky, the article continued, but the idea was wondrous. How Humphrey would have loved pondering it! And how odd that events went on regardless, leaving behind those who should have witnessed them.

It seemed inconceivable that he existed nowhere. Even when they'd been apart for years, she'd heard his commentary each time she ate a potato or looked at a Ping-Pong table. The proxy Humphrey inside her continued talking even now that the original had gone from existence. He most definitely *was*, therefore it was jarring—almost impossible—to know that he was not.

Humphrey had talked once about block time, an idea of the philosopher J.M.E. McTaggart, who in 1908 had posited that human perception deceives us: time only feels like a forward-moving flow because of the limits of our minds, whereas time actually exists, as does space, with everything in existence simultaneously, even if one is not there anymore. The events of twenty years earlier still exist, just as another country and its inhabitants exist even once you leave it. Block time was like turning backward in a novel, as Tooly had done in childhood, finding dear characters preserved, quipping and contriving as ever. Block time offered comfort to secular minds, for those who had no heaven in which to save vanished friends. Nevertheless, to Tooly there was something untrue about the theory; a slight comfort, but not true.

She returned to the article, recalling a conversation during which she (in an H. G. Wells phase) had lamented to Humphrey that people always talked of building a time machine to go back and see great moments of history, whereas she'd want to go forward and see what the world looked like then. He had been appalled: to see two hundred and fifty years hence would be devastating. "Maybe in two hundred and fifty years," he cautioned, "nobody plays Ping-Pong." His world would be extinct, even if humanity continued. Extinction, as he meant it, took place yearly, in increments small enough to tolerate, harder as they accumulated. To leap so many extinctions at once would be too painful. That conversation had been twelve years earlier, in a world already long extinct.

From Heathrow, she took the Tube to central London, then two trains onward to Wales, and a cab from the local station. She had the driver drop her at the top of Roberts Road, so she could stroll through the village.

Bag over her shoulder, she tapped on the window of World's End and entered, the bell above the door tinkling. She had doubted that the shop would be open anymore. But Fogg remained there on his stool. "Oh, hello," he said. "Are you back, then?"

Each sought the appropriate register to address the other. Before, it had been owner to employee, then during her absence—after phone calls and his assistance in her search—they'd become friends, only for her to drop all contact for weeks. Now they settled midway.

She explained her plan: to transfer formal ownership of the shop to him, then be on her way. If he didn't want World's End—and she'd understand—she would need to sell the stock, pay any outstanding bills, formally close the company, and lock up within a fortnight. These travels had decimated her savings. She'd be eating empty sandwiches for a while now.

That night, Tooly looked out the attic windows at the rain and the muddy pastures, sheep mewling in the darkness. Lying on her own mattress once again, she slept for eleven hours, utterly tranquil (a tweeting bird, sounds of distant construction, long stretches of oblivion between). Waking, she inhaled the smell of the rafters up here, which until her return she'd never realized had a scent. Her only unease was a hovering sense of responsibility—that she ought to be looking after someone. But there was no one anymore, just herself, which seemed so frivolous.

After opening the shop, she made an early sale.

"Find all you wanted, Mr. Thomas?"

"No, thank you."

"Can I help you find something else?"

"No, thank you."

"See you again, Mr. Thomas."

"Well, best be off now."

Fogg arrived with their shared newspaper, but without his customary cappuccino. He'd grown jaded about the quality of coffee at the Monna Lisa Café, he told her, so Tooly brewed tea for them both. He accepted his with thanks, flapping open the newspaper, front page devoted to rebellions around the world that summer. "Must be said," he remarked, "that everyone should live through at least one revolution."

It was such a wonderful Fogg comment—declaiming on global affairs as the two of them sipped tea inside a bankrupt rural bookshop. Yes, bring on the revolution!

"Why are you smiling?" he asked.

"Just the idea of a revolt here in Caergenog. Who would we overthrow? The fiendish village council with their dastardly plan to mend the overturned fence posts on Dyfed Lane?"

"Yes, yes, I know—you think I'm beyond stupid."

"I was smiling because I liked what you said," she protested. "Don't say that—that's an awful thing to say."

Among Fogg's charms was that nothing wounded him for long. "To be brutally honest," he resumed, pursing his lips importantly, "I'm not even sure I'd know *how* to start a revolution."

She suppressed her smile, lest he misread it once again. And perhaps she *had* inadvertently belittled him in the past. Why had she? That's just how she was. But damn how she was! She didn't accept that how one was is how one must remain. Consistency in character was a form of tragedy.

She resolved to blunt her flintier side, not to assume that she understood people entirely, and to accept that to be surprised or disappointed or even betrayed was not a catastrophe. It could be a revelation to learn that you were wrong, as she had been about Fogg, a notion he confirmed with what he said next.

"I have something to show you."

She walked around the servery to see what he indicated on the computer screen. It was a database of some sort.

"What is that?"

"It's that," he answered, pointing to each aisle of the shop in turn. "Took me millions of hours, and still not done."

While she was away, he had occupied himself compiling a catalog of the entire stock and posting it online, then publicizing it on various bibliophile blogs. A notable American antiquarian had emailed for prices, expressing particular interest in the vintage cookery volumes and animal books that Tooly had amassed. For walk-in customers, Fogg would have settled on a pittance for most of these editions. But, shrewdly, he had consulted competing prices online, and adjusted accordingly. By the next afternoon, he'd made his first Internet sales, almost eight hundred dollars from a single email. The dealer, delighted with his purchases, gave a favorable write-up of World's End Books on his blog, followed by a rave on Twitter that encouraged his followers to check out the shop's wares. Now, Fogg explained, a good deal of each workday was spent handling overseas orders, responding to emails, going back and forth to the post office.

"Fogg," she exclaimed, "this is incredible!"

"Actually earning a bit of money."

"This means the shop is even more yours now."

He raised counterarguments, but her attention kept drifting to the window. How she had ached for a proper hike while away—she must go for a scramble right this instant. "Sorry," she interrupted, "but it's going to rain later. Would it be okay if I dashed out for a walk? I'll be back, and we'll continue this. I promise."

"Or I could come along."

"What about the shop? Then again," she remarked, "how much walk-in business are we really going to lose."

When he caught up with her at the ridge summit, Fogg was breathless, raising his hand. "Completely out of puff."

Previously, Tooly would have marched ahead. But she waited till he was ready. When he apologized for his slow pace, she reduced hers. "Nice to have a calm wander for a change," she said. "No point running ourselves ragged."

"Look!" He pointed out a hare darting through the gorse.

They watched, and when Fogg turned to her, aglow with pleasure at his sighting, she hopped over to hug him.

"Physical harassment," he joked, blushing.

By the time the weather had changed, they were in the little old

Fiat, trundling back to Caergenog. And by the time she'd parked opposite the shop they had reached agreement: although Fogg refused to
take full possession of the shop, he might take half. That is, he'd accept nothing officially, but she would proceed on the assumption that
each owned fifty percent of World's End and that any profits (even to
*mention* such a possibility was extraordinary) would be split. "That's
non-negotiable," she insisted. "Really, you should have it all. With my
business acumen, this place would've been bankrupt ages ago."

Later that week, Duncan phoned. After Humphrey's death, he had
encouraged Tooly to return home and pledged to take care of the
paperwork. He called now to update her on the disposal of Humphrey's possessions, having traveled down to Sheepshead Bay and
glanced through everything, finding only garbage, junk mail, tons of
old pill containers.

"Humph was a pharmacist once," she explained. "He liked to keep
all sorts of cures around to help people. When you throw away the
drugs, I think you're supposed to pull off the labels so they don't get
misused on the street."

"They were pretty much empty already."

"No," she corrected him, "did you check under the cushion of his
armchair? There was a bunch of heart medication there. I saw it recently."

"I checked there. Just empty bottles."

When could Humphrey have taken all those? Tooly had gone out
that morning. He knew well the effect of those drugs.

"So, in theory," Duncan continued, "you'd get anything."

"What? Sorry, I was thinking of something else."

"Just saying how Humphrey left no will. But if there's anything left
in his estate you'll get it as his daughter."

She wasn't sure how best to explain, after all this time, that Humphrey was no relative of hers. "Sounds like there's nothing of value
anyhow."

"That's pretty fair to say. Given the outstanding bills for that surgery he had," Duncan said, "we'll move toward declaring him insol-

vent upon death. I'm going to Sheepshead this weekend to oversee the removal of his junk."

She hated that strangers would rummage through Humphrey's belongings, then toss it all away. "Should I come back and deal with this?"

"Seriously, it's fine."

"If there are fees, you have to bill me."

"Don't worry."

"Duncan," she said.

"It's fine."

He couldn't accept gratitude, so changed the subject to talk of the winter break. His kids were still grumbling about not having gone anywhere that past summer. Unseriously, he and Tooly chatted about the family coming to visit Wales the following year. She offered free lodgings at World's End—he'd been so generous to her, and the inn rooms would accommodate them all for as long as they liked. But his family was a closed circle again, she an outsider, one whose lifestyle had initially looked like novelty to the McGrorys, briefly like inspiration, and finally like subtle criticism. Sometimes it was best to leave the past where it lay.

During this period, Tooly kept her grief over Humphrey to herself. She contemplated him when opening books, speculated about his opinion, imagining how it would have been to show him around the shop, which really was his. She kept busy, working with Fogg to complete the database, dealing with online sales, which were not quite as rampant as he'd suggested but kept them afloat.

Toward the end of Humphrey's life, he had abstained from alcohol, wanting clarity of mind, and Tooly had stopped in solidarity, no matter how she had craved a drink. Since then, she'd ceased the solitary tipples of old, abolishing her nighttime habit of vanishing into glasses of red wine, that nightly amnesia starting around 8 P.M. Anyway, she was collaborating so much with Fogg now that her evenings were no longer solitary. She reserved time to practice her ukulele (oddly, she'd gotten slightly *better* by not playing these past weeks). Even as she strummed, her new cellphone often trilled beside her in the attic, with a text from Fogg posing a catalog query. She thumbed in half a response, then gave up and went downstairs to answer him. For breaks, they closed the shop, took afternoon hikes past the priory, up into the Black Mountains.

When they returned from one such ramble, there was a delivery truck idling before the shop, hazard lights blinking. The driver unloaded six boxes. An invoice was thrust at her; the van zoomed off. Duncan had sent these. She peeled off the packing tape and the cardboard flaps popped apart. Inside: volume after volume, crammed in, and the smell of Humphrey's room.

His books were cheap editions, mostly—dust jackets missing, bindings torn, pages unglued and falling out. Many were too worthless even to consign to the Honesty Barrel. She sorted them, pausing here and there, losing herself for hours in familiar copies—there was the edition of *Nicholas Nickleby* that Paul had bought for her a quarter century before, that she had read in secret at King Chulalongkorn International School, had lugged to that house party in Bangkok, left behind with Humphrey, and from which she'd read to him in Sheepshead Bay. So strange that this had taken place weeks before—seemed at once like a single day and many years ago.

She organized the worthiest volumes on three low shelves against the right wall of the shop, with a sign identifying the new section: HUMPHREY'S BOOKS. There were about a hundred—that's all it amounted to in the end—and they were all for sale, including his prized blue volume of essays by John Stuart Mill. Inside each cover, she wrote his name, picturing a stranger years later opening the book, reading "Humphrey Ostropoler," and wondering who had possessed that name, and why he'd surrendered this edition. People kept their books, she thought, not because they were likely to read them again but because these objects contained the past—the texture of being oneself at a particular place, at a particular time, each volume a piece of one's intellect, whether the work itself had been loved or despised or had induced a snooze on page forty. People might be trapped inside

their own heads, but they spent their lives pushing out from that locked room. It was why people produced children, why they cared about land, why nothing felt equal to one's own bed after a long trip.

For days, customers failed to notice Humphrey's Books. Then, a sniffly-nosed Jaguar driver crouched before them, gathering on the cat-scented carpet a pile of volumes to buy, including that edition of John Stuart Mill essays. To avoid the sight, Tooly made a trip to the post office.

Along with business parcels, she brought two padded envelopes, one containing *Palm Groves and Humming Birds: An Artist's Fortnight in Brazil*, a copiously illustrated 1924 rarity with maroon pigskin binding, gilt title lettering, and marbled end papers that she mailed to Paul. The other envelope was for Sarah, containing a work on coin collecting and a coffee-table photo book of Kenyan landscapes. She addressed it to the seaside apartment in Anzio on the assumption that this was where Sarah might be, now that the weather had turned cold.

When Tooly returned to World's End, the customer had gone, along with several of Humphrey's books, leaving the remainders leaning at glum angles. She crouched before them, stricken with regret, and shifted the leftovers to hide the gaps.

"You said I could sell those," Fogg reminded her.

"No, yes, I know. I'm trying not to be stupid about it."

He tapped the sales ledger with his pencil. She glanced up, then returned to reordering the section. He yammered on with uncommon noisiness about—well, she didn't know what—and kept tapping his pencil on the ledger. "I'm trying to get you to come over and look," he said.

She obliged, reading the sales entries, including those for a dozen of Humphrey's volumes.

"Yes, I know."

From under the counter, he produced them all. "I'm the one who bought them. Out from under his runny nose."

She thanked Fogg, but returned them all to the Humphrey's Books section.

"I'll just have to buy them again," he warned her. "Could get dear after a time."

"Okay," she relented. "I'll keep these ones. Thank you."

Sarah never did respond to her package. But Paul did, with a touching note, thanking her for the visit that past summer and for the beautiful volume, which would be ideal for the flight he was about to take, heading off for two months with Shelly to their house in Nong Khai. He wrote of his efforts to cultivate dwarf banana trees there, saying he longed to show off his renovations but could convince no one to trek out there. Tooly was welcome to visit—and even to bring somebody. He'd be honored to meet any companion of hers.

"Fogg," she said, "would you accompany me through the jungles of Thailand?"

"You being honest?"

"No, not really."

He departed to alphabetize Asian History for a few minutes, then returned. "You know what I am?" he said. "I'm . . ." He wandered into the reference section.

"What are you, Fogg?"

"Thesaurus."

"You're a thesaurus?"

"The word begins with an *h*. Where's the thesaurus?"

"Hungry?"

"No, why do you ask?"

"You said you begin with an *h*. Did we sell it?"

"Sell what?"

"The thesaurus. Are you hypnotized?"

"How do you mean? Oh, another *h*-word. No, no."

"Are you heroic? Or happy? Or hangry?"

"Not any of them," he replied. "What's 'hangry'?"

"When you're hungry and angry at the same time."

"I've been that. Many a time." He snapped his fingers impatiently, unable to recollect the word.

"What's it to do with?"

He went outside, door tinkling. Through the window, she observed him dipping into the Honesty Barrel, his arm disappearing in there. She half expected it to emerge drenched and clutching a trout. Instead, he returned with a battered Roget's thesaurus and stood flipping its pages. "There," he said, suddenly hesitant, splaying the book, thumb under the word. "That one."

"That's not an *h*-word. It begins with *b*."

"Right you are." Not having received the desired response, he closed the book over his thumb and went back outside to the Honesty Barrel.

It was a cool autumn day, feathery clouds and a sun too timid to warm the village yet. Roberts Road was empty, as if there were nobody but Fogg in the village of Caergenog, in the nation of Wales, in all the British Isles—none but him there, feeling like an ass. He cursed himself for trying to sound clever with her. If only the earth would open up and swallow him. A forbidden thought entered his mind, a sexual one about her, and his knees weakened. Can't think things like that at the Honesty Barrel! He imagined making her a meal using a cookbook, not the tatty old ones in Recipes & Eating but a posh volume bought brand-new in Cardiff, with photos of how food never really looked. He fantasized about the two of them in a proper town, poor but happy. His invalid brother had decent help now, and his mother had met someone—it wasn't mad for him to consider leaving here, at least for a spell. He was younger than Tooly, but could make the case that it was better for an older woman to be with a younger man since women lived longer, and if they went with older men they risked becoming nurses, as his grandmother had done for thirty years, poor devil. He daydreamed of a city, where things happened, where they'd attend meetings—he'd never been to a proper meeting. Everything was under way in the world, right at that moment!

He brushed off a ladybug, which had climbed from the barrel up his arm, and he dithered to avoid returning, removing his thumb finally from the thesaurus, from under that word beginning with *b:* "besotted." He'd meant it as a joke, or to be taken as a joke, anyway, or to be taken not altogether as a joke.

In his pocket, the mobile phone beeped and wriggled. They'd said on the radio that the entirety of human knowledge was available on these handsets, that smartphones had outsmarted their owners. But, for now, he was in control, and the nagging gadget had to wait. He took only a glance at the little screen, enough to see that the text came from Tooly. He pocketed the phone and finished tidying up the Honesty Barrel. Soon he'd read her message and he would know. But not yet. That present had not arrived yet. This one lingered.

# Acknowledgments

FIRST OF ALL, to Alessandra Rizzo, my companion through everything. Also to my marvelous parents, Clare and Jack, and my dear friend Ian Martin. This book is not about my sister Emily, but her life infused mine when I wrote the novel. My affectionate gratitude to her, whose friendship, wise suggestions, exquisite cooking, wild energy, and wonderful madness are unforgettable; as long as I have my memory, she will be there.

Many thanks also to my elder sister, Carla, and my brother, Gideon, and their respective families: Joël, Talia, and Laura; Olivia, Tasha, Joe, Nat, and Adam. And to Alice and Greg, who offered such invaluable support to my parents. My particular gratitude also to those who helped Emily, including Kris Beardsley, Bessie Alyeshmerni, Emily Spencer, and Wendy Chun-Hoon, along with many more in Washington and beyond.

In researching and writing this novel, I encountered generosity and assistance around the world. In Bangkok, from the Mader family: Ian, Eunie, Emily, and Mia. Also, Dolores Nicholson and Denis Gray. In New York, Irena Stern, Esteban Illades, Neha Tara Mehta, and Vandana Sebastian at Columbia; plus, Ned Berke of Sheepshead Bites. In Italy, my affectionate wishes to Aldo and Margherita Rizzo, and Benedetta. My thanks also to Rosaria Guglielmi for so kindly allowing me to start this novel in Anzio; also to Chicca and Valerio, and Alberto for his photographic help. In London, Mareike Schomerus and Jonathan Silverman. In Canada, Brian Malt. Farther afield, Judy Baltensperger, Laura Gritz, Dominic Perella, and Kevin Sprager. My special thanks also to Christopher and Katy, superlative guides in Connecticut and now dear friends.

As ever, many thanks to my agent, Susan Golomb, as well as Soumeya Bendimerad and Krista Ingebretson at the Susan Golomb Literary Agency. Also, to Natasha Fairweather of United Agents in London. At the Dial Press, I am indebted to Susan Kamil for all her efforts on the page and numerous acts of kindness beyond it; great thanks also to Noah Eaker. At Random House of Canada, Kristin Cochrane and Brad Martin. At Sceptre, Suzie Dooré and all her marvelous colleagues there. Warmest appreciation also to my international publishers and editors.

Finally, an affectionate thanks to all my favorite bookshops—in Vancouver, London, Hay-on-Wye, Rome, Paris, New York, Portland, Caergenog (if only it existed), and elsewhere—where I found haven and company.

## About the Author

TOM RACHMAN was born in London in 1974 and raised in Vancouver. He attended the University of Toronto and Columbia Journalism School, then worked as a journalist for the Associated Press in New York and Rome, and the *International Herald Tribune* in Paris. His first novel, *The Imperfectionists*, was an international bestseller, translated into twenty-five languages. He lives in London.

tomrachman.com

## About the Type

This book was set in Garamond, a typeface originally designed by the Parisian type cutter Claude Garamond (c. 1500–61). This version of Garamond was modeled on a 1592 specimen sheet from the Egenolff-Berner foundry, which was produced from types assumed to have been brought to Frankfurt by the punch cutter Jacques Sabon (c. 1520–80).

Claude Garamond's distinguished romans and italics first appeared in *Opera Ciceronis* in 1543–44. The Garamond types are clear, open, and elegant.